Angels Unaware

a&b

Angels Unaware

MIKE RIPLEY

First published in Great Britain in 2008 by
Allison & Busby Limited
13 Charlotte Mews
London W1T 4EJ
www.allisonandbusby.com

Copyright © 2008 by MIKE RIPLEY

The moral right of the author has been asserted.

A CIP catalogue record for this book is available from
the British Library.

10 9 8 7 6 5 4 3 2 1

13-ISBN 978-0-7490-8083-9

Typeset in 11/16 pt Sabon by
Terry Shannon

MIKE RIPLEY is the author of fourteen previous novels in the 'Angel' series, which have twice won the Crime Writers' Last Laugh Award for comedy. He was a scriptwriter on the BBC's *Lovejoy* series and, for ten years, the crime fiction critic of the *Daily Telegraph*. Since 2000, he has reviewed for the *Birmingham Post* and has established a crime fiction gossip column, 'Getting Away With Murder', on the Internet at *www.shotsmag.co.uk*. In 2008 he became a tutor in crime fiction and creative writing for Cambridge University's Institute of Continuing Education and was a consultant on the BBC2 series *Murder Most Famous*.

After twenty years of working in London within the brewing industry, he retreated to his adopted East Anglia and became an archaeologist, thus becoming one of the few crime writers who really did find dead bodies on a regular basis.

At the age of fifty, he suffered a stroke and wrote about his recovery in *Surviving A Stroke*. He served on the government's Stroke Strategy Steering Group and works to promote the Blood Pressure Association.

AVAILABLE FROM
ALLISON & BUSBY
In the Angel series
Angel in the House · *Angel's Share* ·
Angels Unaware

ALSO BY MIKE RIPLEY
In the Angel series
Just Another Angel · *Angel Touch* · *Angel Hunt* ·
Angels in Arms · *Angel City* · *Angel Confidential* ·
Family of Angels · *That Angel Look* · *Bootlegged Angel* ·
Lights, Camera, Angel! · *Angel Underground* ·
Angel on the Inside

Other titles
Double Take · *Boudica and the Lost Roman* ·
The Legend of Hereward

Anthologies
(Edited with Maxim Jakubowski)
Fresh Blood · *Fresh Blood 2* · *Fresh Blood 3*

Non-Fiction
Surviving A Stroke

In memory of
Michael Dibdin and Rodney Wingfield,
who went on ahead during the writing of this book.
But especially for Alyson and Beth,
who were there at the start, twenty years ago.

*Do not forget to entertain strangers, for by so doing,
some people have entertained angels unaware.*

Letter to the Hebrews, 13:2

"The gentleman vanishes; never, never to reappear."

Arthur Conan Doyle
(whilst writing *The Final Problem*)

PROLOGUE

I'd never actually done an official risk assessment on how best to act when looking down the muzzle of a loaded gun being waved six inches under your nose. To be honest, I had never done a risk assessment on anything, which probably explained a lot about how my life had panned out so far.

All I knew was I shouldn't have been in the position to worry about things like risk assessments, let alone loaded guns. Being a private detective sounds a lot more exciting than it actually is.

For a start, private eyes don't do murder cases, despite what you read or see in the movies, as the police tend to feel rather territorial about murder investigations. Perhaps it's the overtime.

Your average confidential enquiry agent would much rather be sitting in a white van with a directional microphone or a camera with a lens long enough to find the *Beagle* lander on Mars, waiting patiently to get the dirties on a cheating husband or wife playing away from home (surprisingly, a growing part of the business). Or they would sit quite contentedly at a computer screen going through electoral rolls to find missing family members or debt-defaulters – often the same people. Best of all, though, they're happiest when they can sell a client an electronic domestic security system complete with CCTV, so that they can sleep soundly in their terraced house in Balham surrounded by enough bells and whistles to wake the dead, or at least the neighbours, when the alarms get triggered accidentally by a pigeon landing on the window sill.

But they should stay well clear of murder investigations, and usually do. For a start, they don't have the forensics available to the police, the manpower (the cops have branches everywhere) or, to be honest, the respect. Face it, in England if you tell someone you're a private detective, they simply can't contain a smirk, a giggle and an inevitable 'Yeah, right.' Tell them you work for an all-female detective agency and there isn't a dry seat in the house.

Which is why I've stopped telling people. If pushed, I'll say I sell home and business security systems (I don't, but I know a man who does) but to more casual acquaintances I'll usually say I'm a fashion photographer, as I can blag my way through a conversation about fashion (which is dead easy with men as it invariably revolves around female underwear) even though I know precious little about photography beyond the point-and-click technique.

Not that I should have been worrying about stuff like that; not in the predicament I found myself in now.

It just wasn't fair. I wasn't even supposed to be working, let alone facing down an armed murderer who had already killed three times; and traces of the blood and hair of their latest victim were smeared on the wall of the flat in Stuart Street.

My flat, my own personal bolt-hole; but I shouldn't have been there.

I should have been miles away in the bosom of my new family, putting my feet up on paternity leave, for I had just become a father.

That was something else I should have done a risk assessment on.

CHAPTER ONE

I was in The Gun on Brushfield Street, having the first drink of the day.

There was a time when that could have meant the first drink of the day or the last drink of the day before, and the specific time in question would have been a few minutes either side of 6 a.m. That was in the days when The Gun, sitting dead across from Spitalfields wholesale fruit and veg market, kept what were politely called 'market hours' which meant that the pub opened when the market traders wanted it to, i.e. when they knocked off work about 5 a.m., which was good news for the rest of us who were still thirsty but had no homes to go to and, let's face it, at that time of a winter's morning, no one was going to ask if you really were a Spitalfields trader, even if you staggered in wearing a tuxedo. In fact, I actually knew wholesale greengrocers from Woolwich who had regularly turned up for work at 3 a.m., when the trucks arrived, wearing tuxedos because they'd been up West in a casino the evening before and it wasn't worth going home to dress down.

Of course, the market's long gone now. Today it's a shiny piazza of coffee shops, pâtisseries, jewellers, sandwich bars and, for bizarre reasons which escape me, several very up-market bicycle repair shops. What Billingsgate was to fresh fish and Smithfield is to meat, Spitalfields was to fresh fruit and vegetables, but now it's been 'developed' or 'regenerated' as the government likes to call it, so that you can buy a hundred different pre-prepared sandwiches on fifty different types of partially baked frozen bread products and a thousand different mocha-choco-freezo-latte-malty drinks which may or may not contain actual coffee. And what is the government spending our hard-earned taxes (well yours anyway) on? Telling everybody to eat five portions of *fruit and vegetables* a day.

Just don't get me started.

Yet The Gun had survived, amazingly. There had been rumours that it was going to be redeveloped itself; in other words demolished, probably to make way for another Starbucks. Well, you can't have too many can you?

But The Gun was still there and still had the signs outside advertising 'Truman, Hanbury & Buxton', a brewery company long since engulfed and devoured in the name of progress and a name which would mean nothing to the majority of Londoners these days even though it was once nationally known. When *Punch* magazine ran a famous cartoon in about 1900 of a top hat-and-tailed drunk lying in the gutter giving a statement to a passing police constable on his beat with the caption 'I've been attacked by three men, officer – Truman, Hanbury and Buxton', everybody had got the joke. Nowadays, kids doing media studies would see that cartoon and ask what a police constable was and why the dude on the floor hadn't kept a tighter grip on his mobile.

Inside, The Gun had gone more open-plan than I remembered, with tables laid with cutlery in the faint hope that customers might want a snack with their beer and cigarettes. There seemed to have been no takers for the day's special offer of 'vegetable pizza' and everyone seemed to be smoking, making the most of their last few months of freedom before the tobacco police finally got around to enforcing their ban on doing it in public places with the light on, as they already had in Scotland and Ireland. There was a pool table which looked fairly new and the old legendary jukebox, where the records hadn't been changed since the Sixties, had gone but otherwise it was still recognisable as The Gun; only the hours it opened had changed.

Ironically, since the market had gone and licensing law reform had allowed pubs to open all day, there was little call for the market licence which had enabled The Gun to start the daily party at around 4 a.m. Thus, as the marketing men would say, it had lost its USP – unique selling point.

The barmaids were younger and more attractive than I remembered, both tall with blonde hair cropped short, almost boyish, and dressed in identical black tops and trousers. They were polite and extremely efficient and smiled a lot at the customers as if genuinely pleased to see them. They were, of course, Polish.

It was time to impress my client.

'Dwa piwa, prosze,' I said, pointing a finger towards the Adnams pump.

Tall Blonde In Black No 1 did the universal hand gesture, palms facing down one above the other in front of her chest, then increasing the distance between them: *large or small?*

Two half-pints, keep 'em small, I semaphored back and when she handed them over she smiled a stunning smile, and the smile got brighter when I said '*Dziękuję*' to thank her. I was so taken with that smile I never even checked my change.

'I'm impressed,' said my client.

'With the pub? You suggested it, I haven't been here in years.' I feigned innocence and handed him his beer.

'No, that you speak Polish.'

'I don't really,' I admitted, 'but these days it helps to know one or two key phrases, especially in pubs and hotels. It's only polite.'

'Key phrases such as?'

'Oh the usual, please, thank you and *Nie zrobiłem nic złego* and also *Czy jestem zaaresztowany?* – "I haven't done anything wrong" and "Am I under arrest?"'

By now Tall Blondes in Black No 1 and No 2 were listening in with a twinkle in their eyes.

'Do they really come in useful when chatting up the bar staff?'

'You'd be surprised. Anyway, why have you dragged me kicking and screaming to this den of iniquity? It's not one of your usual haunts, is it?'

'I never knew this place existed and my office is only two minutes walk away. I was told it was one of your hang-outs.'

'By whom?'

'Salome.'

'Oh.'

I had first met Terry Patterson, years ago, through Salome Asmoyah who had been a neighbour of mine at the time and the object of thinly disguised lust, at least on my part. Tall, dark, sultry, absolutely gorgeous, intelligent and with a highly paid career ahead of her, Salome had only one minor flaw which otherwise would have qualified her as The Perfect Woman. He was called Frank and she'd foolishly fallen in love with and married him long before I moved in to the flat below at Number 9 Stuart Street in beautiful downtown Hackney.

Salome had worked as a broker with high-class firm Prior, Keen, Baldwin, which had been quite a force in the City at one time but I'd heard that it had been taken over by some overseas interests, the Bank of Tierra del Fuego or something like that, who had imposed massive redundancies. I hadn't thought much about it at the time, as I knew that Salome had moved on by then, and I hadn't given Prior, Keen, Baldwin a minute's lost sleep since.

When I'd known them, Terry Patterson had been their Head of Security Systems and he had reluctantly employed me for a couple of weeks to help sort out a small internal matter of suspected insider trading. Being black, which was rare in the City then, and being female (even rarer), Salome was automatically the prime suspect for the persistent leaking of financial information and market tips, and her own firm seemed to be quite happy to let her take the rap. Hardly surprising, really, as by far the majority of her fellow brokers and markets analysts were white, male, public school Lombards (Lots Of Money But Are Right Dickheads).

Knowing absolutely nothing about insider trading or the marginally more honest dealings of the City, but being white, male and not giving a shit who I offended, I was the perfect choice to ride to Salome's rescue. Which I duly did. And even though it all ended in a rather ugly way, Salome was left free and clear, and I did all right out of it as Patterson was pretty decent about letting me hang on to a Prior, Keen, Baldwin Amex card for a month after the job was done and dusted.

'So how is the gorgeous Salome?' I asked, secretly quite pleased that she'd remembered me.

'Still bloody gorgeous, dammit,' said Patterson, 'with two kids and a big house in Surrey now, and still married to that big bruiser, Frank.'

'Never could work out what she saw in him,' I muttered, though my heart wasn't really in it as Frank had never done anything to me.

'About 200K a year as a corporate lawyer, devoted father and provider of big houses in Surrey.'

'Shallow. That was her trouble, she was always shallow.'

'She speaks very highly of you,' said Patterson.

That didn't make me feel any better. Being 'spoken highly of' was akin to being 'just good friends' or 'always remaining fond of each other' in the divisional rankings of red-blooded male/female relationships. What really peeved me was that Frank and Salome had moved upwards and onwards from Hackney, where we'd been housemates, and not once in the intervening years had she got in touch – well, not unless you count the birthday cards, the bottle of vintage bourbon every Christmas and the case of champagne when she'd heard that Amy and I had got married. Other than that, not a peep, and now I found she'd been chatting away to Terry Patterson about me. Typical woman.

'How come she's speaking to you about me at all?'

'Your name came up in conversation—'

'I hate it when that happens.'

'—at a party at work. That's at my new job of course, not the old PKB set-up. They got taken over and downsized.'

'I read about that in the *Financial Times*,' I lied. 'You still in security systems?'

'No way. I'm with the parent company now, German investment bank and all their security systems are computer programs. I wouldn't have a clue where to start, so I moved across into Human Resources.'

It must have shown on my face that I wasn't following him, though the truth of it was I wasn't really interested in him.

'I know what you're thinking,' he said rashly, 'but it wasn't a Muppet shuffle.'

'A *what?*'

'A sideways promotion – a Muppet shuffle, where they can't afford to ditch you so they sideline you – it wasn't one of them, it's a real job. It's just it's...'

'In Human Resources,' I finished for him and he nodded, sighed and sipped his beer. 'Don't beat yourself up; it's a dirty job but somebody's got to do it.'

'Do they? You know, I'm not too sure about that.'

I couldn't quite believe it. He was less than halfway down a small glass of beer and he was getting morose, and even seemed to be looking to me for approval. Most worrying of all was how he had failed to notice how totally disinterested in him and his career path I was.

When I had known him before, albeit briefly, he had been a thickset wedge of a man who wore suits Robert Mitchum could have acted in and who wanted answers to his questions quick, without worrying too much about how much it cost as his expense account was both long and broad. Nowadays, he was a couple of stones lighter, which was probably good for his health but made him look somehow wasted, as if his weight loss had been a result of appetite-suppressing drugs or extreme stress and cigarettes. Most of his hair had gone too, so he had shaved what was left close to his skull, making his head look disproportionately big. I suspected he was missing the City high life of the previous decade, but then so too was the City. There was a time when one of his business lunches would have started in a wine bar with a dozen oysters and a bottle of champagne at about 11.30 a.m. and then moved on to some Michelin-starred chop house. Now, he was relegated to meeting me in a backstreet pub sipping half of bitter and weighing up the possibility of a toasted cheese sandwich.

'I can't say Human Resources is exactly riveting, it's mostly ticking boxes or inventing boxes for other people to tick. That and making sure everything is inclusive and nobody feels *ex*cluded, God forbid. It's all about sticking to the rules and if there aren't any rules, then inventing some. Oh, and enforcing a no smoking policy and trying to make sure the bank doesn't leave a carbon footprint.'

Patterson stared into the remains of his beer, but made no move to buy another round.

'Well, that's enough about me, we should talk about you.'

At last I took an interest.

'What about me?'

'I hear you're in the detective business with a firm called Rudgard & Blugden,' he said quietly, like he was sharing a secret.

'Well, yeah. That's because you rang their office and asked for me.'

'Yes I did. Salome mentioned it in passing and so, when in need of a detective agency, I thought of you. After all, we did sort of crack a case together when I was in systems security.'

'Sort of is right. I just blundered about a bit.' I didn't point out that his role had been to basically pay the bills whilst making sure he didn't get his pin-stripe dirty. 'With R & B Confidential Investigations it's a proper job and we don't do City or financial fraud as a rule.'

'It's not a financial fraud, at least not as far as I know; it's a missing persons case. You do them, right?'

'Yes, we do them. We could probably give you testimonials as to how good we are, except that most of the people we find have gone missing deliberately and don't actually appreciate being found.'

'That's it,' he said enthusiastically. 'That's exactly the sort of thing I'm after.'

'You'd better explain. Perhaps over another drink?' I showed him my empty glass which matched the one in his hand.

'No, I can't. I have to work this afternoon and if you are out of the office for more than an hour at lunchtime, the bank has the right to breathalyse you.'

'Bloody hell, you poor sod. Who brought in *that* nugget of industrial diplomacy?'

'The Human Resources department,' he sighed.

'Somehow I just knew you were going to say that. I've got to watch it myself anyway as I'm driving, so what say we have a tonic water and a ham sandwich, if they can run to that.'

'Yeah, that'd be good,' said Patterson, but made no move to attract one of the hovering barmaids.

'Are you not putting this on expenses? I thought you invited me to lunch?'

'Well, I was going to,' he said, shuffling his feet, 'but when I rang your office yesterday they said you were on leave, so I never cleared anything with accounts. When you rang this morning and said you could see me, I didn't have time to get the request countersigned.'

'You work for a bank, right?'

'Yes.'

'That has billions of pounds or dollars?'

'Euros actually, and trillions is probably nearer the mark.'

'And you have to requisition your entertainment expenses and have them approved *in advance*?'

''Fraid so.'

'Bugger me, it's not like the old days is it?'

'You can say that a-fucking-gain,' he said with feeling.

I reached for my wallet and desperately tried to remember if I knew the Polish for *Can I have a receipt?*

I shouldn't have been listening to Terry Patterson. I shouldn't have been in the pub. I shouldn't have been pretending to be working. I should have been at home, on paternity leave, looking after my newly born child, comforting and tending to the every whim of my wife, who was now out of hospital and settling into our new house in the country and her new role as a mother. For mothers are the very essence of life, and all are fine and noble creatures worthy of worship in temples specially dedicated to them. At the very least they deserve to be pampered, protected and honoured.

Except mine, that is.

She's as mad as a badger.

Basically, she had never got over the Sixties, and personally, I think Fleetwood Mac have a lot to answer for, but it is far too late to apportion blame or seek compensation. Suffice it to say, my mother was tie-dyeing her shirts, 'crafting' her own Christmas cards and making picture frames out of seashells glued onto rectangles of cardboard way beyond the age when such activities are thought cute or even endearing (about 8). As the wife of a fairly prominent husband, such things were tolerated, even smiled upon by middle-class friends, but when she and my father got divorced, she saw it as a chance to finally discover the true hippy inside her. She didn't go the whole hog and move into a tepee in the hills of North Wales, but she did decamp to a small riverside village called Romanhoe on the north-east coast of Essex (although she insisted it was in Suffolk because that sounded classier) which was already home to a few genuine Sixties throwbacks who had gone there as students and never grown up. They had formed themselves into an informal artists' colony which required no previous artistic experience, or shred of talent, to join; the only membership qualifications appeared to be the ability to roll a cigarette with one hand and the knack of drinking all night in one of the local pubs without ever having to buy a round. My mother had fitted in quite snugly.

She adopted the name 'Bethany' and tried her hand at painting – almost exclusively watercolours of the Romanhoe waterfront, and when those didn't sell (because everyone else in the village was painting the same scene much more professionally), she tried sculpture, quilting, pottery, scrimshaw and even installation art using scrap metal and a welding torch, although the local fire brigade took a dim view of that one.

But she was happy, or at least I think she was. She certainly cheered up no end when she finally got a computer with Internet access and discovered that she could sell virtually everything she had daubed, kilned, stitched, whittled onto driftwood or welded, to those millions of art lovers out there on eBay.

She dressed as she thought an artist should and wouldn't have looked out of place in one of those black-and-white British films of the early Sixties with *Beat* or *Bongo* in the title. Even if her wardrobe nowadays came from Oxfam rather than Country Casuals, she took great pride in her scruffy bohemian look, actually claiming that it was highly fashionable and nowadays known as *boho chic*. I'd never had the nerve to tell her that the line between boho (bourgeois bohemian) chic and 'bag lady' was wafer-thin and I was pretty confident she'd broken through a while back.

But she was happy enough out there on the muddy Essex coast and, as I lived in London, I was happy she was out on the muddy Essex coast.

Not even the news of my father getting a life peerage from a grateful Labour government for reasons which escape me now (and probably the government too) tempted her out of her artistic commune. In fact, the only time I heard her mention it was when she told a Saturday night saloon bar crowd that *she* had been offered a peerage at the same time and could have been a peeress in her own right as the government were doing a 'bogof' (buy-one-get-one-free) offer that week. It got her a laugh and several free drinks.

Even when my father had a stroke whilst on his way to Romanhoe to see her, she made no attempt to visit him in hospital or offer to help with his rehabilitation. Mind you, that could have had something to do with the fact that he was dating, with a serious risk of remarriage, the model Kim McIntosh, some thirty years (and the rest) younger than him and who was still referred to in the tabloids as 'nineteen-year-old topless stunner Kim', even though she was no longer nineteen and didn't go topless any more – at least not for money.

But that's fairly typical for my parents; they always were dead selfish.

There was I, having to go through the three most traumatic experiences a man can: moving house with a pregnant wife, becoming a father *and* holding down a job where they expected – almost demanded – that I go in every day. And what support did I get from my family? My father has a stroke and my mother goes into a major sulk and expands her eBay business to offer personalised voodoo dolls.

At least she was holed up on the Essex coast, a safe distance, or so I thought, from the house Amy and I had bought (well, Amy mostly) in the tiny hamlet of Toft End outside Cambridge, which was about 70 miles as the broomstick flew from Romanhoe, and Mommy Dearest no longer owned a car. She maintained it was part of her green credentials to forgo the internal combustion engine, but I knew it was because she'd lost her driving licence on more than one occasion.

What I had totally misjudged – which just goes to show you can't trust mothers – was her reaction to becoming a *grand*mother for the first time. I was convinced she would go into total denial and in all probability turn homicidal. That was why I had sent my father to break the news just as soon as he'd recovered enough from his stroke to walk. I'd fixed him up with a driver/bodyguard and a car to do the job, as I'm not totally heartless, but I did ensure I was several counties away when he broke the news to her.

Not only did she not go ballistic, as I had expected, she

blindsided me by going all…maternal. I arrived back at our new house in Toft End to discover she had 'come to help' and had brought a suitcase. That was two weeks before Amy went into labour, and she was still living with us.

That's why I was back at work, or at least pretending to work.

It got me out of the house.

'As I said,' Patterson was saying, 'when I rang your office yesterday, they told me you were on leave – paternity leave – so I just left a message, not really thinking you'd get in touch as you probably had enough on your plate.'

'I check my messages every day,' I told him, 'and yours seemed worth following up, for old times' sake.'

'So everything went well with the birth…?' he fished.

'Absolutely fine, mother and child doing very well.'

I could have said *both* mothers were doing well but it wasn't really any concern of his. I decided to stick to my Rule of Life Number 41: a problem shared is two people laughing behind your back.

'So what's your problem?' I asked him. 'You said something about a missing person.'

'It's a bit complicated,' he started, looking wolfishly over my shoulder where someone, I could smell, was lighting up a cigarette. 'The bank I work for, Kredit Schwaben AG, has a number of investments…'

I held up a hand.

'Hold it. I told you we didn't do financial scams.'

'It's not a scam, well I don't think it is, not on the bank at any rate, though it's costing us money.'

'What is?'

'The disruption to the schedule.'

'What schedule?'

'The filming schedule. The bank is financing a film – well, a TV film really. It's supposed to be a showcase Anglo-German co-production and is a hot favourite to win the big drama awards. Naturally, it's being made over here with a British cast and crew.'

'Why naturally?'

'Have you ever *seen* German television?'

'*Das Boot* was damned good, so was *Heimat*.'

'Fair enough, but a German TV programme which doesn't mention the war?'

'You got me there,' I admitted.

Patterson took a sip of beer and sneaked a look at his watch. These German investment banks probably had a regulation that a lunch hour should not exceed 3,599 seconds unless you'd applied for an extension in writing. In triplicate.

'Anyway, KSAG are funding the making of a pilot episode and would obviously have a big interest if it goes to a series and gets broadcast and sold abroad.'

'KSAG?'

'That's the name of the bank,' he said patiently. 'Kredit Schwaben, AG.'

I knew that, I'd just forgotten. I had a lot on my mind.

'What does the "AG" stand for?' I asked, though I knew well enough.

'It's just the German for "PLC" at the end of a company name. The Americans would say "Inc." for "Incorporated".'

I put on my best blank face, just to wind him up.

'You know,' he said with a flicker of irritation, 'like Marks & Spencer PLC.'

'So it actually stands for *Aktiengesellschaft*?'

'Well, yes…I suppose so.'

He furrowed his brow at me, puzzled. I didn't care. I was regretting coming to the meeting already, and I think Patterson was too.

'Location filming was due to start this week but we've had to postpone. That's costing KSA…the bank…money, with no return or end product for its investment, and it doesn't like that.'

'I can follow that, but like I keep saying, Rudgard & Blugden Confidential Investigations tend not to do corporate finance cases.'

'But *you* have some experience of the film-making business,' he said, pointing his glass at me. 'Salome said she'd seen your name in the credits of a film.'

That rocked me back on my heels for a nanosecond. It was true enough that I had been involved with a fairly naff B-movie filmed at Pinewood a while back. It had been called *Daybreak* and had been about a group of beautiful, young and trendy New Yorkers who, when not holding down attractive jobs in publishing and advertising, went about their secret lives as vampires with politeness, hardly any violence and bags of style. The more discerning critics had called it '*Friends With Fangs*'. Others had opted for 'toothless', 'bloodless', 'unfunny and unscary' and (my favourite) 'no bloody good'. It had been made mostly in England because they got the studios cheap and the government offered lots of tax breaks and it was a time, possibly the last time, when the dollar was strong against the pound.

I had indeed appeared in the credits, right at the end, listed as one of the stunt drivers even though I never appeared on an inch of film. The credit had been a personal 'thank you' from the production company for sorting out a few minor problems for them, although I was officially employed as a chauffeur-cum-baby-sitter for the film's star, Ross Pirie. (I wonder where he is now?) The job had been, as usual, Amy's idea, as she had got in on the act by designing some of the clothes worn by the cast. I wasn't sure it had done her career any good, but it certainly hadn't done it any harm.

But what really knocked me back was the fact that Salome had seen the film and noted my name tucked away right at the end and usually only shown by the time the vast majority of moviegoers were not only out of the cinema, but out of the car park or on the night bus home. Then it occurred to me that she must have seen it on DVD: God knows it had gone there fast enough. Still, she had seen it and noticed me.

I couldn't let the beautiful Salome down now. I had to at least listen to what Terry Patterson was saying and pretend to be interested.

'That was a few years back,' I said modestly, 'before I worked for R & B Investigations, and I was only really involved with the crew and things like transportation. It wasn't as if I was the on-screen talent or anything.'

Now, admittedly, I might not have been so modest had Patterson not been there and I had been telling the story of my role in the making of *Daybreak* to, say, the two barmaids, as one of the few markets where the film had done decent business was, funnily enough, Poland.

'I'm not asking you to *star* in it, for Christ's sake! I just want you to find a writer.'

'A writer?' I said with a big grin. 'Go out and buy one. You're a bank, you've got money and I think they come pretty cheap.'

'No, I want you to find a writer who's gone missing. The writer on the pilot film has gone missing and the director is cutting up rough about it, saying he can't carry on without him.'

'How long since this writer went walkabout?'

'Just over a month ago.'

'Bloody hell, didn't anyone miss him until now?'

'Nobody's *seen* him for a month, but then nobody had to. It was only when questions came up about changes needed to the shooting script and we couldn't find him, that's when the director threw a hissy fit and delayed the shoot.'

'So where do I come in?'

'Do you still drive that de-licensed cab?'

That threw me slightly as well. When I had known Patterson first time round, I had indeed owned a black cab, the sort you see on postcards and calendars and souvenir T-shirts and which is as good an international logo or trademark for London as Big Ben or Tower Bridge. I still did drive a London black cab, though it wasn't the same one as when I'd known Patterson back then. That one had been called Armstrong and he'd come to a fierce and fiery, but totally noble, end in a field in Suffolk. I had replaced him with Armstrong II, a black Austin Fairway, which in the design stakes was three or four models out of date, but there were still enough of them around on the streets of London to make another one as good as invisible. At least I hoped so, as I had parked on double yellow lines further down Brushfield Street. (When did you ever see a black cab with a parking ticket?)

'Yes, I still use a black cab for jobs in town.'

'Bloody brilliant way not to get noticed,' Patterson gushed. 'Must come in very handy in your line of work.'

'Sometimes it does. Depends on the particular job.' Austin Fairways might be able to turn on a ten pence piece but they weren't exactly the vehicle of choice for a high speed chase, and if you were following somebody during rush hour you might be better off on a bicycle. 'What sort of work were you thinking of?'

Patterson put on his serious-but-concerned face, the one he probably used at interviews.

'I want you to go to a funeral tomorrow, down near Catford, and observe things from a safe distance, maybe take a few photographs.'

'Excuse me? Take a few happy snaps at a funeral? What's my cover if anyone spots me? Do I wave a press pass from *Psychic News* or something?'

'I meant discreetly. You've got a phone haven't you?'

I must have looked particularly thick to him.

'A mobile phone,' he said slowly so I could lip read just in case I was having trouble understanding him. 'They can take pictures these days.'

'I knew that,' I snapped, and I did. I just didn't know how to work one. How did you load the film for instance? 'But won't it be a bit rude to be using a mobile as the last rites are being said? I mean, if you want me to be really inconspicuous, I could download 'Mission Impossible' as a ringtone and then chuck the phone on top of the coffin and shout "It's for you!".'

'The funeral's at Honor Oak crematorium and surely no one's going to turn a hair at a black cab outside the gates. They'll just assume someone's ordered it. In fact, you could use that.'

His eyes sparkled to prove he really had just thought of the idea.

'Use what?'

'If anyone questions you, you can say you were ordered by Benjamin Nicholson. See what reaction you get.'

'Why should I get a reaction? Is he the guy they're burying?'

'It's a cremation, not a burial and, no, it's not his, he's the writer that's gone missing.'

'And you think he's going to turn up at this funeral? Is that it?'

'Well, yes. It's his mother's funeral. I mean, you wouldn't want to miss your mother's funeral would you?'

I bit my tongue.

The most unlikely people will feed you the good lines and, quite honestly, it's just too easy sometimes.

CHAPTER TWO

There was nothing to keep me in London if Terry Patterson wasn't up for an expense account lunch. Even if he'd offered I probably would have passed as I hate eating next to someone looking at their watch every few seconds. So, I rescued Armstrong II and cut across to Old Street to pick up the A10 north through Stoke Newington, getting to the M25 well before rush hour, thus managing to prove that modern London traffic did occasionally, just occasionally, move faster than the 8 mph averaged by horse-drawn cabs in the days of Jack the Ripper.

From there, it was clockwise round the M25 until I hung a left on to the M11 and I could give Armstrong his head all the way to Cambridge, though that wasn't saying much these days. He'd always been built for comfort, not for speed, and he was way past his prime now. In fact, he had 190,000 miles (genuine) on the clock when I bought him in the days back when I was footloose and fancy-free, living in Hackney with a psychopath of a cat called Springsteen and earning the occasional crust playing trumpet when jazz was fashionably *un*fashionable on the live music scene (for which read: pubs that still had a singing and dancing licence left over from the Second World War).

Then, jazz had started to get respectable again, and even popular. What was worse, it got *harder*. That's why I couldn't listen to some of the modern horn players, even when they did the old standards – they were just too bloody good. So I'd moved on to the salsa scene briefly. It was easier to play, there was just as much booze involved and the women in the audience tended to be younger and fitter than at jazz nights (or "nites" as they always put on the chalk boards outside the pubs).

But all that was before I had met Amy – in a pub as it happens – when she was an unknown, recently graduated design student trying to break into the rag trade with a few good ideas, some contacts in sweatshops in the East End around Brick Lane, and an utterly ruthless streak when it came to succeeding in business, coupled with an almost spotless record in keeping her past (and present) life hidden from the tabloid or 'red top' newspapers. That had been no mean achievement as a leading *fashionista* who had sold out her best designs to High Street retail chains, pocketed the cash and dropped out of the catwalk spotlight.

As for me, I now had a wife, a baby, a semi-invalid father, a rampaging mother, a job and a daily commute to and from a new house in that back-of-beyond they call the countryside where it's spookily quiet during the day and really, really dark at night. I was still getting used to country ways and, whilst it might have been quiet during the day, it certainly wasn't during the night. I mean, I've heard foxes shagging in Hackney – that's not unusual. There are probably more foxes living out of dustbins in London nowadays than there are in the rest of England put together. But out in the sticks, when they mate, they don't half go for it and by the noise they make you would have thought they'd sold tickets. The last time I'd heard noises like that I was on tour with some roadies from a heavy metal band and they *had* sold tickets.

I reached my turning just south-west of Cambridge and indicated left to pull off the motorway. Black cabs are a common enough sight on the M25 and not unknown on the M11, but where I was heading, to the little hamlet of Toft End, they still caused the locals to stop and stare – but there again, they probably did that when they heard aircraft engines. Who was it said that you should never go on holiday to any country where the people always look up at aeroplanes?

I was probably being unfair on the locals. I hadn't actually met many of them yet – not that there were many to meet. The population of Toft End was probably less than that of Dalston Lane, Hackney. Much less if you included extended families. I had a theory that they wouldn't show themselves until they'd finished building a giant wicker man statue out of corn stubble, but Amy had said I was being unfair and a 'typical townie'. I had asked her if I should take up morris dancing so I could blend in better and she'd snorted in disgust and pointed out that morris men only wore all those bells so they could annoy blind people as well.

No doubt there are GPS systems which can tell you to the inch the exact dead centre of Toft End, but for my money it has probably got to be a ghastly red-brick Thirties pub called The New Rosemary Branch built in a style made famous by a regional brewery, known as Greene King Gothic. Once I reach the pub I know I'm almost home, for the house Amy and I left London for is down at the end of a lane just beyond The New

Rosemary Branch and is actually called The Old Rosemary Branch.

It's a very narrow sunken lane and totally unsuited to an Austin Fairway being driven one way whilst a Tesco online delivery van ('You shop, we drop') is coming the other way. There was clearly no room for the two vehicles to pass each other and the situation was a classic stand-off. There was no point in playing chicken with the van, not that I had any doubts about the strength of Armstrong II's bodywork and engine block if it came to a head-on collision, but I didn't want to damage him as he was mine. The van driver, when it came to the crunch, was driving a van the company owned, and it was therefore expendable.

I flashed my headlights at the van, conceding the right of way and put the Fairway into reverse, edging my way back up the lane until I could tuck into the side and give Mr Tesco enough space to get by. As he drew level, the driver lowered his window and I dropped mine so we could chat, professional to professional, as he automatically assumed I was a genuine cab driver.

'Are they opening another pub down there, mate?' he said, pronouncing mate as 'moit' just to prove he was a local man.

'What, the house at the end?' I answered him, somewhat thrown by the question. 'It used to be a pub but it was de-licensed when they built the one up there.'

I jerked a thumb over my shoulder back towards The New Rosemary Branch.

'I reckon they're starting up in business again. I've never delivered so much gin in one drop-off before.'

Oh dear. My mother was making herself at home.

* * *

The Old Rosemary Branch was a tall, thin, three-storey white house with a domed tile roof, fairly typical of the area in the seventeenth century or whenever it had been built. It had been a pub up until 1933, when the licence had been transferred to The New Rosemary Branch, which had been strategically placed near the new, improved Cambridge road so it could cash in on the growing car and coach traffic. They had probably done good business during WWII, when the whole area was basically a huge aerodrome for American bomber squadrons, but then newer and bigger roads re-routed the traffic away from Toft End completely.

I wasn't sure how The New Rosemary Branch managed to stay in business now, for there were many nights when I seemed to have been the day's only customer. When my mother arrived and began to settle in, though, I seriously considered buying shares in the place. Amy's strict no smoking policy meant she couldn't light up in The Old Rosemary Branch, so she would tramp down the lane to The New Rosemary Branch to give them the benefit of her passive smoke, not to mention her charming saloon bar wit and her well-rehearsed opinion on just about every subject under the sun.

Needless to say, after less than a month she was barred for life.

Now she had discovered a method of stocking up on booze by going online and having it delivered to the door, it was only a matter of time before she would start proceedings to resurrect the licence of The Old Rosemary Branch.

Amy's Freelander was parked outside the house as I pulled in to the tiny drive off the lane. My mother was resting her butt against the offside headlight, her legs crossed at the ankles, her arms crossed under her bosom, but loosely enough to allow her right hand to move sufficiently to raise a cigarette to and from her lips. She wore faded blue jeans flecked with white paint and a billowing blue artist's smock, which for some reason carried an advertisement for Adnams beer and was also splattered with paint stains. I suspected mother actually bought them like that from Artists R Us or somewhere just for the look, for, as far as I knew, the last time she wielded a paintbrush in anger, it was to redecorate the kitchen of her cottage in Romanhoe after a chip-pan fire.

She tossed her head in a move she'd probably practised since puberty so that her mane of red hair settled away from her face, and blew smoke in my direction before she spoke.

'Where did you skive off to, Fitzroy? You should be here, looking after your wife and child.'

'I thought you'd taken on that job, Mummy Dearest,' I said kissing the cheek she offered and getting a nicotine rush from the smell of her hair. 'But we really don't want to look on you as cheap labour. It was always our intention to hire a nanny or an au pair.'

I don't know why I said 'cheap labour'; having my mother stay with us was turning out to be anything but cheap. God knows what she was spending of Amy's various accounts in Cambridge, or on the Internet, or what the next phone bill would be, but I'd already had to fork out cash well over the odds for unpaid minicab fares (which she just *had* to take ever since she'd 'mislaid' her driving licence – mislaid it in Swansea, that is). Quite by chance, though, I seemed to have struck a chord.

'Roy, darling,' she said, making the hairs on the back of my neck bristle so much I could hear them. It was always a bad sign if my mother called me 'Roy'. 'Can I ask a delicate question?'

'Go ahead, but I'm pretty sure the baby's mine,' I said, keeping my face deadpan.

She showed me the bored and slightly disgusted expression which all women practise secretly in front of their bedroom mirrors for years, but which comes naturally once they are mothers.

'Not that,' she said patiently.

'What then?'

I tensed myself. She was going to ask something excruciatingly embarrassing about her and my father, or, even worse, my father and his new girlfriend Kim McIntosh. I frantically tried to remember if I had promised my father not to tell anyone about his private medical prescription for Cialis, which was supposed to work better than Viagra for men with chronic high blood pressure. So much better in fact that the French had nicknamed it the 'Le Week-End' pill.

'It's about Amy.'

'What have you done to Amy?' I said, rather sharply.

With her arms still folded and still holding a cigarette, she managed to dig an elbow into my chest.

'I haven't done anything *to* Amy, but I might have upset her.'

'How?'

I was genuinely interested. Women who upset Amy generally end up dead and buried at a crossroads at midnight, or at least reduced to shopping at Brantano.

My mother dropped her head, allowed a well-trained segment of red curls to fall across her face and gave me the up-from-under look which only women can and which I'd seen a million times before, but was always difficult to resist.

'R-o-y...' she started slowly in a voice which summoned up images of fingers running through chest hair or TV commercials for caramel-filled Easter eggs and which was really disturbing coming from your mother '...is Amy...rich...or at least well off? I mean, I know you've never had five beans to grow a beanstalk from and this job you've got, well, it's not really real is it?'

'Oh it is, mother, believe you me. There's an office they expect me to go into *every day*; I have to keep receipts for any expenses; write reports on client meetings, at which I have to be polite to clients even though most of them are paranoid hysterics who deserve a good slapping; I have to maintain confidentiality at all times; do risk assessments on...er...risks; I'm told my performance has to go through an annual evaluation, whatever that is; *and* they're totally in the Dark Ages when it comes to lunch hours.'

'You mean they only give you an hour? You poor thing.' Mother gave me one of her patented 'looks'. I think it was No 6: Sympathy and Support. It wasn't to be trusted and was probably dangerous. 'But I'm glad to see you're finally pulling your weight and paying your way now you've got responsibilities.'

'Excuse me? Do my ears deceive me? Is this the "You're embarking on the voyage of life" lecture I should have had when I was a spotty youth? Let me remind you, Mummy Dearest, you forgot to give that lecture and if you had, then you probably wouldn't have mentioned that I was embarking on the *Titanic*.'

'Don't be churlish, Fitzroy, your father and I agreed – and

it was one of the few things we ever did agree on – that our children would stand on their own two feet as soon as possible. It's a harsh world and the sooner you learnt to cope, the better. We taught you self-reliance and resourcefulness. You should be grateful to us.'

'There you go, mother, always full of surprises. All this time I thought us kids had just been a nuisance, but it seems it was all part of a sustained programme of tough love.'

'If you want to call it that,' she said, rolling her eyes.

'I could think of other things to call it.'

'Oh, get real, Fitzroy. You came out all right didn't you? Look around you: nice house, beautiful wife, healthy child and you've even found somebody to employ you. I reckon your father and I did a pretty good job on you.'

I shook my head at what I was hearing.

'Tell me, Mother, what's it like to always be right like you?'

She shrugged her shoulders.

'Well, there's no peer pressure.'

Damn, she was good.

Inside the house, in the larger of the two living rooms (what had been the lounge bar – as opposed to the smaller, public bar – when the house had been a pub), I found Amy dressed in a vest and tracksuit bottoms working up a sweat on the Thighmaster or Stairmaster, or whatever it was called, which she had bought on eBay. It was a piece of kit she had got at a bargain price – probably because the previous owner had expired suddenly – as the opening shot in her campaign to 'get her figure back' after leaving the maternity hospital. I had told her she had nothing to worry about on that score, and she'd replied that I should visit either an optician or a psychiatrist.

So then I had proposed she join a gym and that there was bound to be a good one in Cambridge. That time, I got the look which suggested she hadn't ever realised until then that I obviously had special educational needs and pointed out that she couldn't possibly be seen in a gym in her present state. She had to get fit *first*.

I picked my way carefully across the floor, which littered with wrapping paper, open boxes, baby clothes and brightly coloured toys. It looked like the aftermath of an explosion in Hamleys. Even now the postman was delivering presents and 'Congratulations on your new arrival' cards by the sackload, almost all from friends and contacts of Amy's in the fashion business – hence most of the clothes were from Prada and we had enough Scottish cashmere bootees and mittens from Bora to fit out a family of baby octopi.

Treading carefully so as not to crush anything, I got to within three feet of Amy and started to reach for her. Her legs were pumping away on the up-and-down paddles as if she were running up a hill which kept shying away from her, the back of her vest was damp with a line of sweat down her spine and her hair, tied back in a scrunchy, was flicking between her shoulder blades as if keeping time. She was plugged in to her iPod and I could hear the distorted crackle of what could have been Green Day or maybe The Kooks, her latest favourite. I just knew her tongue would be protruding from between her lips in concentration.

'Don't touch the boobs!' she yelled without turning around, but she powered-down the treadmill and pulled out her earpieces. 'I'm waiting for that baby to wake up and demand a feeding, and the sooner the better. I'm feeling ultra-sensitive and can't stand the idea of being pawed at.'

'I wasn't going to grab you,' I lied, 'I was only going to say hello and ask how your day had been. Any problems with the baby?'

'Not the one upstairs asleep, but the one having a fag out in the garden is driving me up the bloody wall.'

I had to stand up for myself. She was, after all, talking about my mother.

'It was you who invited her to stay, darling, not me. I told you that creatures like Mommy Dearest always have to be invited across a threshold, otherwise their powers don't work, but once you invite them in, they're buggers to get rid of.'

'I didn't think she'd stay this long,' Amy pouted.

'I did warn you, and you should have let me tell her to leave.'

'You suggested getting her drunk and leaving her in that wheat field down the lane when the combine harvesters were working. You said you could pass it off as a bizarre gardening accident.'

'I'm sure she would have come round in time and taken the hint,' I said in my defence. 'Anyway, what's she done to rattle your cage today?'

Amy put a hand up to the side of my face.

'My cage doesn't seem to take much rattling these days, I must still be over-hormoned or something. I suppose she's doing her best.'

'I've never seen her do anywhere near her best. I've never seen her *try*.'

'Don't be mean. I'm just a bit stressed.' She wrinkled her nose suspiciously. 'Have you been smoking, you bastard?'

'No, honest, I haven't. I had to meet a guy in a pub and people there were smoking.'

'So, you've been drinking, then?'

'Hardly at all. It was business.'

I knew I was on shaky ground here. Amy had given up smoking and alcohol as soon as she suspected she was pregnant, neither of which she missed at all in comparison to giving up running her own business. Her decision to breastfeed the baby meant that the alcohol ban was extended indefinitely, as was her return to work – not that she'd told me of any plans on that score one way or the other, but I could tell she was feeling withdrawal symptoms.

'So, you've decided to go back to work, then?' she said accusingly, even though I had spent two hours pleading my case yesterday evening.

'I told you, I went to meet this guy Terry Patterson. I knew him from way back when. In fact, I worked for him once.' I caught the flash in Amy's eyes. 'It was perfectly above board and legit, and now he's got a respectable job with a German investment bank. He rang Rudgard & Blugden and asked for me personally, that's why Laura passed on the message. It was only polite to go and see what he wanted, for old times' sake. It's not as if I've been out on the lash or anything. I naturally expected an expense-account lunch but I ended up with a half of bitter and a curly ham sandwich. I'm starving actually, what's for dinner?'

'I doubt there's anything to eat. You see, I let your mother do the shopping online,' admitted Amy, though her expression made it clear that it had all been my fault.

'I met the truck driver in the lane,' I sighed. 'Did she order anything apart from gin?'

'A couple of gallons of tonic water and a catering-size tub of lemon slices.'

'Figures.'

'Oh, and about a ton of tortilla chips, crisps, pretzels, roasted peanuts and salted cashews in case your father came visiting. She said he loved salty snacks with his pre-dinner drink.'

'I'm sure they'll do wonders for his high blood pressure,' I said dryly, watching Amy's eyes widen, 'but I don't think he's got any plans to visit while she's here.'

'I can't say I blame him. You should have called in to see him and Kim whilst you were up in town.'

'You're right, I should. I'll try and do it tomorrow.'

Amy kicked some Harrods gift wrapping aside with her toes and for a moment I thought she was trying to locate a weapon under the debris strewn across the floor. But it was a towel she was looking for, the one she wrapped around her neck when exercising. She spotted it, picked it up and began to dab her chest before locking eye contact.

'So you *have* gone back to work, then.'

'Not properly. It's not like I'll be going into the office every day.'

'You never did that when you were *supposed* to be at work.'

That was a cheap shot, even if it was true.

'Look, it's just a one-off surveillance job which will take half a day.'

'And no one else in the agency can possibly do it?'

'I was asked for specifically and, anyway, it involves driving.'

Rudgard & Blugden Confidential Investigations' unique selling point had been that it was an all-female private detective agency up until the time Amy had bought a fair chunk of it from one of the founders, Stella Rudgard, and insisted they employ me. So now there were four female operatives and little old me, and I realised fairly early on that I was quite a valuable asset as, amazingly in the twenty-first century, I was the only employee who could actually drive. For most of the work R & B took on, this wasn't a problem as the bulk of it was within London and anything done further afield was usually subcontracted out to a local agency on a reciprocal arrangement, or a specialist supplier of, say, burglar alarms or CCTV gear.

'I must have a word with Veronica about that,' Amy said, more or less to herself. 'She really ought to incentivise Laura and Lorna into getting their driving licences.'

'*Incentivise*?'

'It's a word isn't it?'

'If you say so,' I said quickly.

'She could offer them a new set of pay-grade pathways if they took driving lessons and then re-evaluations once they'd passed their tests. Hold out the prospect of jumping several points on the pay scale at their annual review.'

'We have a pay scale?'

'Yes, I really must have a word with Veronica about staff training. You never know, we might be eligible for a grant or an Investment In People award.'

'Veronica's quite keen on training already,' I offered. 'She's got everybody studying for their European computer driving licences.'

Actually, that wasn't strictly true. Veronica had told me that I ought to do the ECDL course as everyone else in the firm was already capable of using the office computers. When I had protested that I was perfectly able to Google-whack anything on the Internet, that I was the undisputed high score office champion at pinball and that my iTunes list was longer than anybody else's, she'd got quite snotty with me and said that there were things called spreadsheets and databases which I really needed to know how to use if I was to pull my weight.

'Not to mention that we all have to have a working knowledge of the Health & Safety Act and be able to do risk assessments on each of our assignments,' I added. 'Veronica's well into all that.'

'Good,' said Amy, 'I knew I could trust her with senior management.'

Amy hadn't really had much choice. Stella Rudgard, the founding brains behind R & B Investigations, had even less aptitude for management systems and office protocols than I did. In fact Stella had a T-shirt which bore the legend: *I was working really, really hard and then I got distracted by something sparkly* which she wore with pride. Amy's opportunity to buy into the agency had come when Stella had jumped feet-first into a lightning romance with a young gentleman who came with a double-barrelled name and a healthy bank balance. Or, at least, it had been healthy when their romance had started. Now they were married and their honeymoon in the Caribbean had so far lasted over a year. Consequently, Stella's only active contribution to the firm these days was to have her name on the invoices and on the plastic sign at the entrance to our modest offices in Shepherd's Bush Green.

'Yeah, Veronica keeps the place running smoothly,' I said, 'and naturally she wants me to take my full entitlement to paternity leave.'

'Does Veronica have any idea how much paternity leave
you are entitled to?

Have you any idea yourself?'

'About six months?' I suggested.

'I think you'll find it's nearer two weeks, but I'm not sure.
You could always use a Tiger Tool.'

'A *what*?'

'Tailored Interactive Guidance on Employment Rights:
Tiger. It's a self-assessment program on the Net. It's what you
do nowadays; now there are no civil servants anymore. The
government makes up all these rules and then puts a toolkit
online to explain things.'

'What if you haven't got a computer?'

'Oh, I don't think that's allowed is it? Anyhow, I'm pretty
sure you'll have exceeded your allowance by now. Strange,
isn't it, that the office hasn't been chasing, wanting to know
why you're not at work?'

'You could have said something.'

'I might have needed you here.'

'What do you mean "might have"? I help with the baby and
running errands and stuff, don't I?'

'Not as much as you think you do, but you are invaluable
in one respect, in that while you're around I probably won't
actually kill your mother.'

I put my hand on her shoulders.

'Even if I'm back at work, you know I'd always alibi you.
I'm there for you.'

'That's a comfort,' she said, batting my hands away. 'Don't
press on me. If that baby doesn't wake up very hungry, I might
just explode.'

I kept my distance.

'Has Mommy Dearest been getting on your—' I realised I was staring at Amy's bosom again and stopped myself just in time '—nerves? I mean, more than usual?'

'I'm sure she means well...'

'She doesn't usually.'

'And it was good to have someone fussing over me when I was in hospital, I suppose.'

I had to admit, that had been where my mother had scored. Because of her age (over 30), Amy wasn't allowed to have her first birth at home as she had originally wanted, so when push came to shove (so to speak), it was a 4 a.m. dash to the maternity unit in Cambridge in the Freelander (she'd refused point blank to go in Armstrong), and to hell with the speed cameras.

That bit went fine, the birth went smoothly: mother and child in perfect health. Even my mother went all soppy at the sight of her first grandchild and insisted that she stay at Amy's bedside while I went home to email just about everyone in Amy's address books with the news and the one digital picture (of many) she'd allowed me to use, given that her hair was such a mess.

By the time I got back to the maternity unit, photographs were a hot topic. I had forgotten, with so much else on my mind, that Amy May the fashion diva was still a newsworthy property in certain quarters, even though she'd been keeping out of the limelight ever since she became pregnant. One of the nurses or midwives must have recognised her and let the word out. About half a dozen photographers, some of them stringers for cheap imitations of things like *Hello!* and some of them rank amateurs just chancing their arm, had started to gather at the maternity unit.

They hadn't bothered me, of course, as they had no idea who I was, but when it came to Amy and child taking their leave of the place, she'd said she really didn't fancy running the gauntlet of lenses, especially as none of them had actually asked her permission. I had agreed to drive the Freelander up as close to the entrance as possible and Mother had said, quite casually, that she would 'distract' the lurking paparazzi – though I, wisely as it turned out, never thought to ask how.

Where she got those two bedpans from I didn't like to ask; and if that really was urine in them, I didn't know, but the unsuspecting camera jockeys certainly thought it was. None of them suspected the small, red-haired 60-year-old lady in a smart red trouser suit (she'd made an effort for her grandchild) of being a homicidal maniac, or of being able to move so fast carrying two obviously full bedpans. To be fair, they did most of the damage themselves, tripping over each other to protect their cameras and avoid first a golden shower and then a clout with a metal bedpan, though I saw Mother aim a couple of kicks as well. And she did it all in total silence, which made it even more frightening.

In the confusion, I had no problem getting Amy and baby into the back seat of the Freelander, and I even left the front passenger door open for Mother to jump in as I pulled away.

We had owed her one for that, but from the tone of Amy's voice, mother's credit was running out.

'Doesn't she realise she's outstayed her welcome?' I asked Amy.

'Of course she does, she's not stupid!' she snapped at me.

'She can't possibly enjoy hanging around here doing nothing but watching daytime TV and drinking gin.'

'This is my mother we're talking about, right? Sounds like her idea of heaven.'

'Oh come on, you cannot be serious. Beth's an intelligent and independent woman, used to being the centre of attention in that village where she lives. It might be a small pond, but she's a big fish there. Over here, she's out of her element. She can't boss me around, I think she knows that.'

'Like you said, she's not stupid.'

'She must be missing her friends and, let's face it, the role of doting grandmother doesn't exactly come easy to her.'

'Neither did the role of mother.'

'Save it until I make you have therapy. Have you ever considered that she wants to go back to Romanhoe but something's preventing her?'

'No,' I said honestly and immediately realised it was the wrong answer. 'What on earth could prevent my mother from going back to her own little arts and crafts space colony, if she set her mind to it?'

'I have no idea, but I think you'd better find out.'

'She hasn't asked you for money, has she?'

'No, why should she? She buys her gin and fags on our grocery account and she doesn't go out. Why would she need cash? She hasn't tried to tap you, has she?'

'As if. She knows better than that. I just wondered if she could be keeping out of the way of the bailiffs. It wouldn't be the first time.'

'You should take her out somewhere; get her to tell you why she won't go home.'

'I doubt if she'll tell me anything,' I said, 'but I know

somebody who could take her out and show her a good time
and worm a few confidences out of her.'

Amy eyed me suspiciously.

'And who would that be?'

I couldn't resist.

'The name's Bond, Jane Bond.'

CHAPTER THREE

Amy insisted I should wear a black tie if I was going to a funeral. When I admitted I didn't have one, she said no problem I could borrow one of hers. I had no idea she owned six (not counting bow ties) and couldn't ever remember having seen her wear one. Still, you can never have too many accessories, can you? When I asked her when and where she ever wore them, she explained that it was useful at certain presentations or board meetings for her to adopt the androgynous look. I would, she said, be amazed at the effect she had on middle-aged businessmen when she turned up wearing a dark pinstripe, double-breasted suit, crisp white shirt and black tie and, of course, four-inch high black stilettos.

I said I would not be at all amazed.

I didn't tell her I had not actually been invited to the funeral and my brief was to hang around the vicinity pretending to be a taxi driver, and to try and grab some photographs of the real mourners. There again, I did know real cabbies of the old school who always kept a jacket and black tie in the boot of their cabs in case of emergencies, so I decided to go prepared. I chose a thin bootlace tie, but Amy vetoed that one on the grounds that it made me look like a Mississippi river boat gambler. She also scuppered my second choice, which was a wide 'kipper' tie made of black felt that looked like moleskin. Amy said that one only worked in conjunction with a push-up bra and would just make me look like a sad geek with a taste for Seventies retro chic. Roger Moore, she told me, had worn one just like it in *Live and Let Die*.

That reminded me that I had to ring Mrs Bond and ask her for yet another favour.

Jane Bond was the first 'local' we had befriended since moving out to the country. Since my mother had joined us, she was also the last.

Jane worked for the rather snobbish Cambridge estate agent firm which had sold us The Old Rosemary Branch and she had even brought us a bottle of champagne, still unopened, when we had moved in. If she wasn't yet sixty, she was probably not far short, though she certainly didn't look it. After thirty years as a well-behaved upper middle-class country housewife, she had come out of an acrimonious divorce with a wardrobe which Amy defined as 'excellent' (meaning it was well designed, expensive and didn't date) and the custody of an Aston Martin DB7 in British racing green, which I described as 'cool' (meaning it was well-designed, expensive and didn't date). She had failed, however, to stop her former husband from secreting most of his cash, so she had found herself honest, if menial, employment as a secretary to a boss with half her intelligence and nothing like as flash a car.

I had done Mrs Bond a sort of favour when we had been

looking to buy The Old Rosemary Branch in helping to get rid
of one of the junior partners in the estate agents she worked
for. Not that he had been a major league villain or anything,
just a bully and a bit of a pain in the arse really, and once he
was out of the picture, Jane had promised me a go in that
really rather super Aston Martin she owned. I had already
used up that favour; not for myself, but by getting her to agree
to drive my father out to Romanhoe to see my mother so he
could break the news that she was about to become a
grandmother. (Well, I sure as hell didn't dare do it.)

Theoretically, Jane and I were then all square but my
mother had insisted on accompanying her back to Cambridge
and descending on us, never, I feared, to leave. Consequently,
to my mind, that put Mrs Bond's account in the red again, so
she owed me one more favour. Or at least that was the moral
high ground I was standing on when I phoned her.

Fortunately she saw it my way, although there was a lot of
sighing involved before she agreed to take my mother out
around a couple of bars in Cambridge where my mother
wasn't known and Jane wouldn't be recognised. She
promised to find out if anything was bothering Mommy
Dearest and let us know when she sent us a bill for her cab
fares. I had just assumed she would be driving her beautiful
Aston Martin, which would also have given her an excuse
not to drink, as there was no way she could match my
mother's intake, but she said she would leave 'the green
beast' at home as she didn't fancy having to hose-down the
upholstery in the morning.

She may not have been looking forward to the evening, but
at least she was going into it with her eyes wide open.

* * *

'Are you going into this with your eyes open?' Veronica asked haughtily.

'Of course I am. How can I spy on the people there if I don't have my eyes open?'

'We don't call it "spying". What you'll be doing is "observing",' she said in a tone which made me wonder if there was such a word as 'matronising'. There ought to be.

I knew it had been a mistake to call in at the office; or rather, my mistake had not been in visiting our Shepherd's Bush Green nerve centre but being spotted by Veronica while I was hanging around waiting for Laura to make me a coffee, and then find me a camera and show me how to work it.

Once she had eyeballed me and demanded to know what I was up to, I told her I had popped in to open a case file on the computer as I knew Veronica was a stickler for paperwork, even if it was electronic these days. Each Rudgard & Blugden case file got a unique number which acted as a password on the office intranet, so that anyone who took a message, did a piece of research, made a report or found relevant documentation could enter it into the file if the DCFO (Dedicated Case File Operative) wasn't around – although Veronica did expect the DCFO to add a daily (and she really did mean *every* day) summary of progress.

Having intranet access to all the current files meant she could keep an eye on what everyone was doing and estimate the number of 'person hours' each case clocked up, which was a crucial part of the billing process.

I didn't know, or care, enough about computers to be sure but it felt as if Veronica were sitting in her office like a fat spider at the centre of its web, watching her screen and reading my case file entry even as I typed it. I knew that Lorna (the dark side of the Thompson Twins) was always checking up on my record-keeping, or 'data input' as she insisted on calling it. But then again she was the sort of electronic anorak who talked about 'keystroking' rather than typing.

The first thing to go on a case file was always the name of the client, just like in a police murder enquiry using the HOLMES 2 computer programme, the first name to be entered (and thereafter referred to as 'Nominal One') was always the name of the victim.

Veronica, I was sure, would be pleased and suitably impressed to see that our new client was the Director of Human Resources of the Kredit Schwaben AG bank with its address in Bishopsgate, which I was copying from one of Terry Patterson's expensive-looking business cards. Then, the template on my screen asked for a 'summary of client's objectives and outcomes', as it always did, and, as always, I was tempted to put in 'peace in the Middle East and an end to global warming', even though I knew Veronica had absolutely no sense of humour. So I opted for the quiet life and gave her a summary of what I thought were the client's objectives, namely to find a certain Benjamin (known as Benji) Nicholson who had been missing for over a month now.

Under the heading 'Client's Responsibility/Relationship', I paraphrased what Patterson had told me and noted that Benji Nicholson was a self-employed writer working with a production company called Oradea Films on the making of a film (or films) aimed at German television and backed by the aforementioned London-based German investment bank.

I assumed that by mentioning (twice) that our client was a dirty great bank and should therefore be good for the invoice we would eventually submit, the computer would be happy just to let me get on with the job, but, no, it wanted to know: *Initial proposed actions and likely outcomes.*

I knew from bitter experience that it never paid to let machinery see that you're angry or in a hurry, so I took a deep breath and typed in that my 'initial proposed action' was to attend the funeral of the late Mrs Clara Maria Nicholson at Honor Oak crematorium and that one likely, if remote, outcome was that her missing son Benji just might turn up to show his respects.

At the bottom of my case file template I added: *Fat chance, but it gets me out of the office*, then clicked SAVE.

I got Laura to lend me her mobile phone, an embarrassingly pink Motorola that could have easily fitted into a packet of King Size with room for half the cigarettes, after showing me how to take digital pictures on it. That seemed easy enough, hardly rocket science. Button on the left and the phone took photographs, button on the right and it shot about fifteen seconds worth of digital video. Look at the screen and what you see is what you get.

Laura didn't seem half as impressed with my new-found skill as I was and quickly got tired of me taking test shots of her. Nor was she impressed with my suggestion that I put our ad hoc training session down on my personnel file as another 'competency' or skill which Veronica could take into account at my annual staff appraisal. In fact she snorted in derision at the idea and muttered 'What do you mean *another*?' under her breath.

I was beginning to appreciate just how taxing Veronica's senior management responsibilities must be. You just couldn't get the staff these days.

Honor Oak Park is in that part of south-east London, the de-militarised zone between Dulwich and Lewisham, which is almost completely overlooked by anyone who doesn't live south of the river and might as well be abroad to most non-Londoners. I put this down to the fact that the tubes don't run there, which may be due to geology or some Victorian superstition about digging tunnels east of Brixton.

On the ubiquitous London Underground maps, the whole Honor Oak Park/Brockley/Catford area in the bottom right corner is usually covered up by the key which explains which lines are which colour. This doesn't help confused visitors searching in vain for underground stations at Catford, New Cross or Blackheath. They never think to ask (and nobody volunteers the information) about the *overground* railway network which links the south-east London badlands rather than an underground which never got built.

I can't say I knew the area well. Even though I'm not a licensed London cab driver, who has done The Knowledge, I do drive a black cab, and with that fact comes the responsibility of maintaining the legend that no black cab likes to travel south of the river, or certainly not further than Waterloo Station or the Oval if there's a Test Match on. I'm not sure how the legend arose, but in my student days I did attend a lecture by a mad archaeologist who claimed that the original Roman settlement of Londinium established itself as an enclave on the north bank of the Thames and decided to

stay there. Despite being a pretty unruly, Dodge City sort of a
town full of crooked merchants and shady lawyers where life
was cheap but sex was a fair price (some things never change),
that north-of-the-river outpost of Imperial Rome was still
thought reasonably civilised compared to the native British
shanty town which grew up on the south bank. And even
when the Romans built a bridge to join the two muddy shores,
you couldn't get a chariot or a torch-bearer to take you south
of the river for love nor money.

I did, however, know something about Honor Oak. I knew,
for instance, that when you emerged from Honor Oak Park
station (where there's no one to check your ticket outside of
the rush hour), the unwary traveller is greeted with signs
directing them to One Tree Hill, which must be a
disappointment to anyone expecting to step into the American
teen-drama of the same name. There isn't a basketball court,
or a perfectly toothed heart-throb in sight. There isn't even a
pub in sight, come to think of it.

This One Tree Hill is just that. A hill where there was
probably once a tree. To be fair, from space the satellite
pictures would show a reasonable amount of green space in
this part of London. There's even a golf course strategically
surrounded by three cemeteries: Nunhead, Camberwell Old
and Camberwell New; and Peckham Rye Common, where
they hadn't buried anyone for years – at least not officially.

Honor Oak crematorium was situated in the middle of
Camberwell New Cemetery. That I knew from my A-Z and I
had mapped a route (having long ago decided that SatNav in
cars was for wimps) which took me to the Brockley Way side
entrance and in plenty of time to have a snoop around and get
the lie of the land. I had even thought of grabbing a bite of

lunch somewhere before I had to do some serious detective work, but that went by the board when I found that Brockley Way went from nowhere to nowhere. The road ended at an old bridge going over the railway line from New Cross to Honor Oak Park, or more specifically at a sign saying 'Road Closed' without any attempt at an explanation.

I did a three-point turn in Armstrong, so at least I was facing roughly the right way if I had to make a quick exit. To my left was the cemetery with an access road to the crematorium. To my right was a concrete community centre which seemed deserted and blocks of low-rise, white concrete flats. Apart from the occasional St George's Cross flag with the word ENGLAND hanging out of bedroom windows, they too seemed devoid of all signs of life. If any of Britain's bright young film directors were looking to make yet another urban Zombie film, then their location scouts need look no further. Which reminded me of a conversation I'd once overheard on the top deck of a 159 bus going down Oxford Street, when one serious-looking student had said to his fellow anorak: 'Well, actually, it wasn't the worst Nazi Zombie movie I've ever seen.'

I had somehow resisted the urge to yell *'Then what was?'* because there are times when you just shouldn't ever get involved and, anyway, life's too short as it is.

There didn't seem to be anywhere I could get something to eat unless the crematorium chapel had a vending machine, which I thought was unlikely. Rather than sit in Armstrong and listen to my stomach rumble, I decided to scope out the place. Patterson had told me that the funeral was scheduled for 1.30 p.m. so I had well over half an hour to find a good spot from which to observe the comings and goings, though with funerals there tend to be more comings than goings, as every funeral cortège usually leaves with one less passenger than they arrived with.

I took Amy's black tie out of my jacket pocket and put it on using the rear-view mirror, then climbed out and made sure all the windows and doors were locked. I wasn't worried about Armstrong getting a parking ticket here, I just wanted to make sure he was still there when I got back.

The side road up to the crematorium wound through a plantation of thick-leaved bushes which provided a doubly effective screen, hiding the crematorium buildings from sight whilst blocking out the noise of passing traffic. The building itself was a dark red brick affair with a circular driveway approach so the official cars and hearses could pull up close to the main doors. Towards the side, there was an archway and porch and more doors, though these were propped open by rusty iron doorstops about nine inches high shaped, of all things, like cats sitting upright with their tails flicked around their front paws.

Under the archway there was a noticeboard on the wall with a single sheet of paper drawing-pinned to it, giving the running order for the afternoon's services. The name Clara Maria Nicholson was first on the list, with the time 1.30 p.m. and there were two more funerals slated for later on. I presumed somebody had wandered by earlier to pin the sheet up, but for now the place seemed deserted. But it wasn't totally devoid of life, as, from the entrance to the archway, I was being observed quite intently.

At first I thought someone had moved one of the iron doorstops just to unnerve me, but no, the big tabby cat was real enough. If anything, he was bigger that his iron statue representations, although just as inscrutable, and he had placed himself strategically in the middle of the archway with the sun at his back. When he saw me looking at him, he put his head on one side and stared right back, as if telling me that he was only following orders and that it was more than his job was worth to leave the place unguarded, especially with people like me on the prowl.

I was trying to think of some sarcastic put-down – which is the only thing that works with cats unless you have half a smoked salmon or some slices of roast pheasant about your person – when he uncoiled and walked like a gunfighter through the open door to my left.

I decided to follow him. After all, he seemed to be the official Graveyard Cat and knew what he was doing.

He lead me into a small, shadowy ante-room, which I worked out was tacked on to the side of the main chapel, where there was a variety of non-matching chairs dotted around the walls and the air was ripe with the smell of old lilies, rising damp and lemon disinfectant. All the chairs had a fine down of cat hair on them, and on the floor in one corner was an enamel bowl with two compartments; one containing water, the other some dried cat food.

The cat yowled at me until I sat down on one of the chairs and then promptly jumped onto my lap, turned around twice tickling my nose with the end of his tail, and then settled in a heap. Considering he was on the cat equivalent of a bread-and-water diet, he weighed a ton and I was sure my legs would fall asleep fairly soon after he did. But cats are never *really* asleep in the presence of strangers, especially when their heads are quite close to an empty, rumbling stomach, which I could tell was annoying him by the way his claws flexed.

Out of respect for those claws I was careful not to make any sudden movements and concentrated on staying awake myself. It was not easy, as I couldn't remember the last undisturbed night's sleep I'd had thanks to Amy getting up to feed the baby and working on the principle that if she wasn't sleeping, nobody was. But I had to admire the cat's choice of siesta spot, for even though we were in the middle of south-east London, with a railway line only about a hundred feet away, this cool little ante-room was so peaceful, you could hear a cat breathe. I suppose that, given it was in the middle of a graveyard, you didn't get much aggravation from noisy neighbours.

I didn't hear the cars arrive until they were crunching gravel outside the entrance to the chapel, and then doors were opening and slamming and there was a hum of indistinct voices, and all before I could prod the resting tabby on my knee into consciousness.

If anyone had come into the ante-room, I would have pretended to have been imprisoned there by the cat. I doubted that anyone would ask what I was doing there. After all, it was a public place, I was respectfully wearing a black tie, I was not causing a nuisance and I was obviously good with cats; therefore I was above suspicion. But nobody did come into the ante-room – why should they? They had come to bury Caesar, or at least Caesar's mum; or rather cremate her. They had booked an entire chapel. If they wanted to praise Caesar, or Caesar's mum, they wouldn't come in here for quiet contemplation. So I decided to go outside and join them, making a mental note not to mention Caesar out loud.

I levered the tabby cat off my lap and onto the chair next to me. He wasn't happy about it – there was no human cushion to rest on – and he howled at me just to make sure I understood that. I ignored him, because I can be tough like that sometimes, and walked out into the sunlit afternoon.

There was a hearse and two sleek limos outside on the gravel; all black and all Mercedes. Impressively, all the vehicles had old-style number plates (the cops call them registration marks these days) containing the same three-letter combination: MIB. Now that was worth a hat-tip, an entire funeral convoy registered as Men In Black, which of course is what they were in their black suits and ties and white shirts, most of them wearing sunglasses just to make sure they looked cool.

About a dozen people, all smartly dressed, milled around as the Men In Black carried the coffin into the chapel. More people started to arrive, walking down the driveway I had come down. I didn't know what the etiquette was when it came to making a quick exit from a funeral before it actually starts without being noticed. If I suddenly slapped my forehead and yelled 'Right time, wrong place!' and ran for it, someone was bound to notice and I was supposed to be a detective, observing discreetly.

So the best thing to do, I decided, was just to blend in quietly with my hands clasped in front of me and adopt an air of dignified silence in the hope that nobody noticed I was covered in light grey cat hairs.

Another Mercedes with an MIB plate approached and pulled up right in front of me, almost as if they were from the undertakers' security service and they'd discovered I was an interloper. But when the rear door opened, so near to me I could have held it open, the first thing to get out was a pair of black high-heeled shoes filled with slim, black-stockinged legs. Above the legs was a smart black two-piece suit filled by a smart young blonde girl of about nineteen. She wore a high-necked white top under the suit jacket and set if off with a single string of fat fake pearls. Her hair was swept back and held in a short pony-tail by what looked like a black bow tie.

I tried not to stare.

No one else got out of the car and the girl looked around her, nodding as she made eye contact with people she knew. Me she ignored.

For once I was grateful to be ignored. It was as if I had blended into the background completely and simply didn't register on her radar. She was going to sweep regally by me without a single *ping* on her screen.

Or she would have done if it hadn't been for the fact that Laura's phone decided to go off at that precise moment.

The ringtone was a loud and rather tinny download of the Arctic Monkeys' 'I Bet You Look Good on the Dancefloor' and suddenly I was being noticed, by everybody. Probably even the Graveyard Cat was somewhere behind me shaking his head in reproach.

The young blonde didn't break her stride, but she did switch direction and took two steps towards me until she was up close and personal and that damned ringtone seemed to be louder than ever.

But the blonde could shout even louder, and right into my face.

'If you're not waiting for a kidney, that is fucking rude!'

Then she punched me square on the nose.

*   *   *

She did it so quickly, then stomped off towards the chapel, that I honestly don't think any of the other mourners shuffling into the chapel realised what had happened. If we had been outside a nightclub arguing over a minicab, or in the car park of Sainsbury's claiming ownership of the last trolley, spectators might have been justified in expecting a fight to break out. But at a funeral? And if you're not expecting a public punch-up, nine times out of ten you can't believe what you've just seen and walk on by.

I wasn't sure I could believe it had happened: even for me it was rare to be punched by a woman I hadn't actually been introduced to. Yet there was fresh blood dripping from my nose, my eyes were watering, I was definitely swaying slightly on my heels, the tabby cat was probably laughing at me behind my back, and that damned phone was still telling me that I probably looked good on the dancefloor.

I put a tissue to my nose to staunch the trickle of blood and snot (I always carry plenty of tissues now there's a baby in the house) and fumbled out Laura's phone with my left hand.

'What?' I shouted at it, though it probably came out as 'Dot?'

'Darling, is that any way to talk to your mother?' said a refined female voice in my ear.

'In my family it sure as hell is,' I said instinctively.

'Who is this? And what are you doing with my daughter's mobile? Are you some sort of street criminal?'

I was tempted to say I was the one being mugged, both physically and mentally, but I judged I was in enough trouble.

'Oh hello, Mrs...? You must be Laura's mum.'

'Well, I more or less just told you that. They can trace stolen phones now, you know; very quickly indeed.'

Any second now she was going to tell me she was very close friends with a chief constable somewhere.

'Look, Mrs...? I'm sorry, I don't know your name.'

'It's the same as Laura's.'

That wasn't exactly helpful in my condition. I couldn't remember if I'd ever found out Laura's surname.

'I'm sure it is,' I said gently, 'and if you ring Laura at her office, she'll tell you that she's been very kind and allowed me to borrow her phone for a particular job I'm doing for her.'

'So you work for Laura do you?'

'Yes,' I said, partly because it was easier than arguing with the woman and partly because some of the mourners were hanging around the chapel door and giving me the evils rather than going on in.

'Well then, tell me who Laura's boss is,' the woman demanded.

'You mean Veronica Blugden?'

'No, not her line manager, the big boss; the new owner of the company.'

'You mean that marvellous fashion designer, Amy May?' I said carefully, in case it was a trick question.

'I suppose you must work for the agency, because that's not common knowledge.'

'I told you I did. I'm out on a job right now, which is why I have to go. So you'll have to excuse me. Ring the office and I'm sure Laura will vouch for me.'

'Sheridan.'

'Excuse me?'

'Sheridan. My name's Sheridan, and so is Laura's.'

Good grief; hadn't the woman got daytime TV to watch or something?

'Of course it is. Just tell Laura you talked with Angel.'

'You're Angel?'

'Yes.'

'Oh,' she paused. 'I've heard of you.'

That did it.

'Look, Mrs Sheridan, it's been ever so nice chatting but I really must hang up on you, I have a funeral to catch.'

So did a minicab full of soberly dressed late arrivals, who had seen the small blonde lady zap me with a straight jab as they had been coming down the driveway. As the minicab scrunched to a halt nearby, two middle-aged women emerged, each with one hand holding down a wide-brimmed black hat as if it was a steel helmet and they were about to run into a war zone.

'Why was Phoebe giving you a slap, then?' the first one asked accusingly, right in my face. Her accent told me she wasn't from very far away.

'Phoebe?' I said dozily, still not quite recovered from shock, violence to the nasal passages and the phone call from Mrs Sheridan.

'It's her mother they're burning today,' said the woman.

The other woman looked at her askance.

'Burying, Charlene, not burning.'

'But they're burning her first, ain't they?' said Charlene with native 'sarf London' logic.

Behind them, a big burly man in a dark suit tight enough to show that he either had very impressive upper arm muscles or that he had stuffed a leg of pork up each jacket sleeve, was paying off the minicab. He wore sunglasses and looked hard. He was, of course, totally bald and I'd bet good money he had a Union Jack tattoo somewhere.

As I didn't want to find out where, I decided to 'fess up.

'My fault entirely, I deserved that slapping,' I said, trying not to dribble blood and snot. 'Forgot to turn my mobile off and the bloody thing rang. I didn't mean no disrespect, it was just bloody thoughtless. If she hadn't slapped me, I'd have slapped myself. You're supposed to show a bit of dignity at a funeral, aren't you.'

I looked down in disgust at the phone, still in my hand.

'Bloody thing,' I said, then threw it into the nearest bush.

The woman known as Charlene was studying my face, but not showing any particular emotion herself. Then she said 'Come on, Jan' to her friend and they marched off towards the chapel.

Halfway there, she turned to the big ox of a man who was following on after paying off the minicab.

'Cyril, make sure your phone is switched off,' she shouted. 'If that thing rings during the service, I'll stuff it up your arse.'

As they disappeared into the chapel, I swung round to face the overweight tabby cat who was licking a paw, feigning disinterest.

'You didn't happen to notice where it landed, did you?' I asked him, but he pretended not to hear.

I found Laura's phone easily enough, without any help from the cat, and it looked as if it would still work, though I wasn't going to turn it on to find out. While I was rummaging around in the underbrush, I reviewed my position: mentally doing what Veronica would call a 'risk assessment'. She seemed quite keen on them, though I had never really seen the point. I mean, if there was really a clear and present risk of actual danger, then it was too late to be filling out useless forms. If you were going into a situation where you might be at risk and had the time to consider this carefully, then any sensible person would say 'That sounds bloody dangerous' and not do it.

My little brush with 'Phoebe' meant several things. Firstly, if it was her mother's funeral, then she must be Phoebe Nicholson and sister to the missing Benji Nicholson. (There was nothing to this detective business really.) Secondly, because she had distracted me, I hadn't had a chance to look at the other guests paying their respects and any daft idea about using the phone to take pictures was definitely out now, unless I fancied taking on an angry mob. But the arrival of Charlene, her mate Jan and the big bugger called Cyril by minicab did give me an idea.

I wasn't sure how long funeral services lasted, but I could hear muffled hymn singing coming from the chapel, so, fortunately, I didn't have time to do a proper risk assessment.

Having done their job, the undertakers' cars had all gone and I was alone in the afternoon sunshine. Even the Graveyard Cat had got bored and wandered off in search of other amusing examples of human behaviour.

I nipped back through the archway and into the toilets beyond the ante-room. There I splashed water onto my face, then soaked a paper towel and held it over my nose. It wasn't broken and the bleeding had stopped, but it still hurt every time I blinked and I made a mental note not to sneeze ever again.

In the mirror above the hand basin I checked for spots of blood, though most seemed to have been caught by Amy's black tie, as I didn't think it would look good to be seen running out of a graveyard with blood around my lower face.

There were a few cars parked on the driveway out of the cemetery, tucked tightly into the bushes so. the funeral cars could get through, but, as I'd seen some guests arrive by minicab, I was banking on the fact that there would not be enough cars to take everyone away; there never are at funerals but people don't like to make a fuss. I knew there would be a wake or some offering of what used to be called 'funeral meats' afterwards – Terry Patterson had said as much – though I didn't know where, because I hadn't being paying enough attention. Still, I now had a plan.

Emerging onto Brockley Way, I was relieved to see Armstrong II was still where I had parked, with all four wheels intact. I drove him into the cemetery down the driveway, parking on the gravel circle directly opposite the doors of the chapel. Then I checked my nose for leaks in the rear-view mirror, straightened Amy's black tie, got out and leant casually against the bonnet.

I've often found that the best way to observe people unobtrusively is to stand right in front of them, so they think they're observing you. It's a rule of life which ought to be in the private detective's handbook, should there be such a thing.

The petite blonde called Phoebe, the one who'd hit me, came out first, on the arm of a priest. They were flanked by a platoon of women, all dressed in black of course, offering words of comfort and handkerchiefs in equal proportions. Men in suits followed on, until the whole funeral party were gathered and spread out on the steps of the chapel as if waiting for a group photograph. But that was ridiculous; the very idea of anyone taking photographs at a funeral.

From inside came the faint strains of a Robbie Williams

song – something about loving angels instead – which I knew was the funeral anthem of choice in south London. It could have been worse: in Hackney they still play Celine Dion and that dirge from *Titanic*.

They milled around commiserating with one another and there was a lot of cheek-kissing and hand-clutching, no doubt some of it sincere. A fair proportion of the congregation lit cigarettes, probably on the assumption that the one place there wouldn't be a No Smoking sign was a crematorium.

It was a good five minutes before anyone noticed me, and it was the slightly brassy woman, Charlene, who did. I watched her point me out to her friend Jan and then to the big bloke, Cyril. When they looked at me I just smiled and gave them a slight nod. Eventually, whatever Chinese whisper they had going reached Phoebe Nicholson and she walked over to me, with Cyril, on Charlene's command, following a pace behind her.

When she got to within punching range I took the initiative and stood up straight.

'Miss Nicholson?'

'Yes,' she said, frowning and keeping her eyes on me, though I noticed her fists were clenched at her side.

'I'm sorry about my stupid phone ringing, I really am. I should have told you why I was here.'

She tilted her head slightly, indicating that I should go on.

'A Mr Patterson sent me to be of any service I could.'

'Who's this Patterson? Never heard of him,' she said and just behind her I'm sure Cyril actually growled.

'He's actually in the City, said he knew your family and hired me to come here and offer my services, if I could be of help in any way.' I did a half-turn and indicated that I was stood next to a black London taxi. 'On the transport front, that is. It's all on his account.'

'Do you know The Boot and Flogger in Southwark?' she said without batting an eyelid.

'That's Redcross Way, isn't it?' I said, and it seemed to convince her that I really was a cab driver.

'That's right. We're having the wake there, and there are bound to be people who need a lift.' I could see her thinking. 'And then some might need taking home I suppose. How long did you say you were at my disposal?'

I didn't think I had, but I liked her style.

'As long as it takes,' I said, which seemed to please her.

My only problem now was whether anyone would remember me in The Boot and Flogger.

Surely not.

Not after all these years.

CHAPTER FOUR

'Well, if it isn't young Mr Angel! Fancy seeing you after all these years.'

'Hello, Irene.'

I should have known. If there was one drinking den in London where they *would* remember you after seven, seventeen or twenty-seven years, it would be The Boot and Flogger. It might not be London's oldest wine bar, though Charles Dickens and Wilkie Collins would still recognise the ornate private dining booths and maybe even some of the sawdust on the floorboards. It is certainly not the poshest or even the best known, but it is famous for operating on the only remaining 'Free Vintner' basis under an Elizabethan charter of 1567 which granted members of the Guild of Vintners the right to sell wine without the need of an excise licence. Not that this particular arcane twist to the licensing law had anything more to do with them remembering me than did the name of the place, which often raises a snigger, though in fact, a boot and flogger is a basic machine for putting the corks in bottles of wine.

'Long time, no see.'

'You can't possibly remember me after all these years,' I said with a feeling of dread.

'I've been working here twenty-seven years come September,' said Irene, 'and I never forget a regular, even when they stop being regular. You used to come in with Peter the Printer and sit in that booth there. You always had the house claret and then a jug of port afterwards.'

It was having loyal waitresses like Irene which made The Boot and Flogger a unique, and dangerous, watering hole: women who took pride in their work and had memories like elephants.

'Got me bang to rights, Irene, but I haven't seen Peter for ages,' I admitted, hoping that my being recognised hadn't been noticed by the funeral party now filing into the bar.

'You won't have, unless you're a prison visitor,' Irene confided, lowering her voice. 'He had his collar felt for running off packs of pornographic playing cards he'd downloaded from the Internet and the Judge gave him five years.'

'They must have been pretty naughty playing cards.'

'They were, but there was also some stuff about not paying VAT for twenty years.'

'I didn't know him that well,' I said automatically.

'The printworks got sold off to some East Europeans – there's bloody hundreds of them round here now. They print their own magazines in Hungarian or Bulgarian or similar. Still, they keep themselves to themselves and they work hard, you've got to give them that. At least you can get a plumber round here now; there was a time you had to call one in from Bromley or Croydon.'

'That must be a comfort,' I agreed.

'You with the funeral party?'

There was no point denying it. If Irene wanted to know; Irene would find out.

'Sort of. I'm helping out with transport; I can't say I'm a friend of the family or anything.'

'Oh, she was a lovely woman. Nobody had a bad word to say about her,' Irene sighed, raising a tray of drinks from the bar.

'Did you know her well?' I asked.

'No, hardly at all, but you have to say things like that, don't you? The son and daughter used to come in here, though.'

Irene swivelled away into the throng of mourners with her tray of drinks. Like all funeral-goers, once out of the cemetery, the urge to talk – to anyone about anything, and loudly – was overwhelming.

The five I had given a lift to in Armstrong, after Phoebe Nicholson took up my generous offer, had started yapping as soon as they'd squeezed themselves in and slammed the doors shut. Not having the ethics of a professional London cabby and having a vested interest in intruding on private grief, I naturally slid open the partition glass so I could hear what was being said in the back.

The passengers nominated for the free cab ride included the mouthy Charlene, though fortunately not the supersized Cyril. He would never have fitted in Armstrong among those five women, no matter how well he knew them. If he had somehow squeezed in, he would have known them all a lot better by the time we got to The Boot and Flogger.

I didn't recognise any of the four women with Charlene, but then I hadn't paid too much attention as the mourners had arrived, being distracted by cats, mobile phones and bleeding noses. Fortunately for me, Charlene took it upon herself to interrogate them all mercilessly, and I soon learnt that they were all neighbours of the late Clara Maria Nicholson, who had indeed been a lovely woman who kept herself pretty much to herself since her husband had 'passed', and that must have been – what? – ten years ago. Was it really ten years?

You had to admit that Phoebe had done a marvellous job looking after her, though, didn't you? (I found myself nodding silently in agreement at this.) And she must have done it alone, because there didn't seem to be much of a family network to help, did there? (Where would we be without families, I mused to myself.) There was no family at the funeral, was there? Just friends and neighbours. Everything had fallen on poor Phoebe's shoulders, hadn't it? And the biggest disgrace of all was that her good-for-nothing brother hadn't shown his face, had he?

I wondered if Terry Patterson would accept a report (or Veronica would accept a case file update) to the effect that Benji Nicholson had not been present at his mother's funeral because the Rudgard & Blugden operative in the field had heard it from the back of a cab?

Doubtful.

I decided I ought to ask a few questions. That was, after all, what detectives were supposed to do. I was in the right place – a family gathering – and at the right time – a funeral wake where people naturally talk and gossip. If only I could think of the right question to ask the right person, I'd be set.

I caught Irene on her second circuit with the canapés and manoeuvred her up against the dark wood frame of one of the private dining boxes. After all, I hadn't had any lunch.

She seemed perfectly happy to stand there holding the tray as I wolfed down the coin-sized pieces of pastry onto which had been stuck a curl of smoked salmon or a roundel of beef with some gelatinous fixative. I remembered when The Boot and Flogger's entire menu was simply a thick slice of rare beef, ham off the bone, turkey or tongue, big enough to cover a plate. With that, you got a bowl of boiled new potatoes covered with parsley and butter. If you were a wimp, you could have a side order of salad or even vegetables if you asked politely enough.

'Seems a good turn-out,' I said to Irene, as it was the sort of thing you said at a wake.

Irene scanned the crowd with her eyes, checking for gaps in the canapé supply chain. Fortunately, she was happy enough to stay where she was and allow me to stuff my face.

'This lot would turn out for the opening of an envelope,' said Irene, and not exactly in a whisper, though with over forty people crowded near the bar, all chatting away, I don't think anyone took offence.

'You know the family?' I asked, selecting a circular pastry stuffed with pâté and topped with an olive.

'These ain't family,' breathed Irene scornfully, 'they're neighbours at best; at worst they've just walked in off the street for the free food and champagne.'

'There's champagne?' I said automatically, before remembering I was the self-designated driver.

'It's not proper champagne, just some cheap sparkling stuff from Eastern Europe. Phoebe asked us to get it in special.'

'Well, Phoebe's family, isn't she? And didn't you say she had a brother?'

Irene scoped the room again as if making sure.

'Phoebe's the only one. I recognise everybody else and they're all friends and neighbours. Maria's husband died years ago, before she moved here. She brought up those two kids on her own in a flat on the Peabody Estate round on Southwark Street; took on three or four cleaning jobs to pay the rent. She used to clean here, as a matter of fact. Packed it in when her health started to go a few years back. Phoebe stepped up good as gold, came back and bought her old mum a little house just off the Marshalsea Road, round the corner, and made sure she had plenty of home help. A whole string of 'em, Maria had, right up to the day she died. All nice girls, an' I reckon it was Phoebe paid for them all.'

'Phoebe came back, you said. Where from?'

'Dunno. Somewhere up north.'

'And the brother, Benji?' I tried between mouthfuls.

'Maria's son? Waste of space, him. He went up north too, but he never came back. Didn't lift a finger to help his poor old mum, and I'm not surprised he hasn't dared to show his face here today.'

Noticing her tray was now empty of canapés, Irene flashed me a quick look of reproach and turned to go to the kitchen for reinforcements. I began to scope the room for another waitress, but Irene had turned back to me.

'Maria's boy wasn't called Benji,' she said, nodding to herself in confirmation. 'His name was Ian, and I don't think he was your sort in any shape or form.'

I had no idea what she meant by that, but you don't argue with the lady carrying the food in a place like The Boot and Flogger.

* * *

I watched Phoebe Nicholson work the room, making sure she spoke to all the guests, shaking hands, receiving tentative kisses on each cheek and returning them with politeness but not enthusiasm, nodding her head and showing a thin smile in all the right places. She was methodical about it all, almost as if she'd allowed every mourner a set amount of time and when that was up, she was on to the next.

It took her about forty minutes to cover the entire party, which may by that time have included a couple of Boot and Flogger regulars who had dropped in for a swift fortifier before the commute home from London Bridge. Then she looked around the room to make sure she hadn't ignored anyone important, and when she was satisfied, went and stood by the bar which ran the length of the room. She signalled to one of the barmaids, who promptly filled a champagne flute with something sparkling and placed the bottle on the bar in front of her.

She seemed content to be on her own; perhaps she was vulnerable and in need of personal space in order to reflect on the day's sad business. I decided to join her.

'Do you think you'll be needing me any more?' I asked her.

'Who are you? Oh yes, the cab driver. Why are you here again?'

'The ladies I drove from Honor Oak, they insisted I should come in rather than sit outside in Arm...the cab. I hope that was all right.'

It wasn't strictly true; I'd just followed them in.

'No, not that,' she said, taking a sip of her wine. 'I meant why are you here at all? Today, at my mother's funeral?'

'It's like I said, I was sent here by Terry Patterson of KSAG to see if I could help out.'

'I've never heard of this Mr Patterson or his bank,' she said, raising her glass to drink and squinting at me over the rim.

'I'm sorry, I assumed he was a friend of the family. He said he worked with your brother in something called Oradea Films.'

'I haven't seen Ian for over a year,' she said quickly, her eyes flashing.

'From what I can gather, Terry Patterson hasn't seen him for a while either, and I think he's rather worried about that.'

She kept her face blank.

'Ian is a worry to everyone who knows him. He was a worry to our mother, but she's spared that now.'

She plucked at a blonde hair which had fallen on to the lapel of her black suit jacket and let it float to the floor, watching its descent to the sawdust with studied fascination.

She had a child-like face which, without make-up, would have been challenged for proof of age by most pub bouncers, but her hands showed she was nearer thirty than thirteen. The backs of the hands are always the dead giveaway with women, as one of the great philosophers once observed; or perhaps it was Agatha Christie.

I wondered what that face would look like if it ever smiled, but perhaps her mother's funeral wasn't the best place to start telling jokes.

'Your brother didn't come to the funeral?' I asked, pretending to be slow on the uptake – an act which Amy said I was extremely good at.

'No, he didn't. I don't even know if he knows our mother has passed.'

'That's sad,' I said, but in fact she didn't look sad, or any sadder than the average person at a funeral. In fact she put her glass down on the bar and poured herself another sparkling wine from one of the open bottles. The brand of wine seemed to be something called Romantine, which was a new one on me, though she made no move to offer me one; or say anything to me.

'Do you not keep in touch with your brother?' I tried.

'Is there any law which says I have to?'

'No, none at all,' I agreed. I had to; after all, I'd successfully avoided my brother – and my sister – for more than a year. Families can be terribly overrated.

'Then why are you so interested in my brother Ian, Mr Angel?'

'I'm not, but I think Terry Patterson of KSAG is worried because he hasn't seen him for a while.'

'I have told you already, I don't know this Terry Patterson person. Now, if you'll excuse me, I must see to my guests. There is no reason for you to stay; your taxi will not be required. Most of them can walk home from here.'

She placed her empty glass on the bar and for a moment I thought she was going to offer to shake hands, but instead she turned on her heels and headed into the nearest group of mourners.

Irene was serving another tray of canapés way across the bar where I couldn't catch her eye or wave goodbye, so I just headed for the doorway.

I know different people react to the loss of a loved one – even a mother – in different ways, but Phoebe Nicholson had shown remarkable self-control all afternoon. I judged she was a lady who liked being in control and I had noticed that, while she didn't wear a ring on her wedding finger, she did wear several including one thin silver one on each thumb. That was always a sign of a latent control-freakery.

Interestingly, although she had maintained she hadn't heard of Terry Patterson, she hadn't asked what KSAG meant, even though I'd mentioned it twice.

I had walked almost as far as Armstrong before I realised she had called me 'Mr Angel', though I couldn't remember telling her my name.

I crossed the river over Blackfriars Bridge and headed west through Westminster just as the rush hour traffic began to get into battle formation. I wanted to get back to the office in Shepherd's Bush Green before close of play, so I could give Laura her mobile phone back. The poor girl had been without it for nearly six hours. She was probably showing withdrawal symptoms by now.

It would also give me the opportunity to ring Terry Patterson and tell him I'd got precisely nowhere. The person he called Benji, but everybody else seemed to call Ian, simply hadn't showed. I'd got a bloody nose and the cold shoulder from a quite attractive blonde, and that was about it. Case closed. The invoice is in the post.

Laura was of course sulking, so I presumed her mother had rung her. She grabbed her phone from me and immediately checked for messages and missed calls, of which there seemed to have been dozens whilst I'd had it switched off.

I was just relieved the damn thing was still working.

It was left to Lorna, the other half of the Thompson Twins as I called them, to ask me how it had gone that afternoon.

Now, Lorna wouldn't normally give me the time of day, and I could only assume that she had picked up from Laura, or

Laura's mother, that I might not exactly have gone unnoticed at the Nicholson funeral.

'Everything went well,' I told her, 'or as well as a funeral can go.'

'So you got a result then?'

'Only a negative one. I did not acquire the target, because the target did not turn up to his own mother's funeral.'

'What sort of person does that?' she asked scornfully.

'People are sometimes funny about mothers,' I said, trying not to give too much away. 'But I reckon it's proof positive that Ian Nicholson is definitely missing in action somewhere.'

'I thought the client knew that. That's why they hired us, isn't it?'

'Yes it was, but now we can confirm it. We tell the client what he already knew and we send him a bill. Because he's paid for it, he knows the information is kosher, and he gets a warm glow from knowing his suspicions were right all along. That's just good business practice, isn't it?'

She gave me the evils with her eyes. I decided there wasn't much point in asking if she'd put the kettle on for a cup of tea.

'But is it ethical?' she asked.

'Are frogs waterproof? I'll bet you the client will be happy when I report back, which I'm going to do right now, so I can knock off early and go home to be in the bosom of my family. Stick around; listen and learn.'

I plonked myself down at my desk and grabbed the phone. I had punched in no more than two of Terry Patterson's numbers when Lorna said, as if it had just occurred to her:

'Would this Ian Nicholson you mentioned be the same as Benji Nicholson, or are we talking two different people?'

For a second I assumed she'd been snooping into my case

file on the office computer system, but then I remembered that Lorna never volunteered help in any way, shape or form unless it was to her advantage. Some people are dead selfish that way.

'After some intensive field work, I have ascertained that they are one and the same person,' I said pompously. 'Why do you ask?'

'Because this afternoon we had a request for assistance in tracing a missing person called Benji Nicholson.' she said, keeping her face Botox-straight.

'From whom?'

'From one of our associate agencies.'

'Where?'

'In the north.'

She was making me work for this.

'North of the Arctic Circle, or just England?'

She pouted at my sarcasm, which was at least some sort of a human reaction.

'Huddersfield, actually.'

'You mean Ossie Oesterlein, don't you?'

'Yes.'

I stopped punching buttons and put the phone down.

'Oh, crap.'

Most private detective agencies in England operate locally, almost as cottage industries. When an enquiry drifts out beyond their natural territory and can't be answered by an Internet search, then, in order to minimise on travel and overnight accommodation, the system of the 'associate agent' comes into play.

Calling them 'associate agencies' or 'regional partnerships' is actually only management-speak for an extended network of favours and trade-offs which the anthropologists are bound to have a word for.

Basically, if a client wants something or someone checked out in, say, Wales, and we can't be arsed to actually go there, then we contact our associate in Cardiff and essentially subcontract a day's work to them. They don't bill the client or us, rather they wait until they have a client who wants something checking out in London and then they ask us to do the work on a reciprocal agreement.

These 'reciprocals' were based on the number of operative hours worked per job and, just on missing person cases or false address checks (very popular these days) centred on Greater London, Rudgard & Blugden had built up a fair amount of credit with some of our country cousin associates. Veronica was always worried that our provincial partners would take advantage of us, with them not having to worry about London overheads, and kept a close eye on the number of 'person hours' they clocked up, threatening to send them actual invoices after it reached a certain limit. She was right in one sense, in that by far the majority of this balance of private eye trade came towards London rather than out into the sticks. But, as I said, that was a small price to pay if it meant not having to actually *go* to Wales.

Or 'the north'.

We never had to venture there as we had a man there: Ossie Oesterlein, our Friend in the North, otherwise known as 'Double-O' or sometimes 'Double-O-Seven', where the seven stood for his IQ score, according to Lorna, who rarely had a good word for anyone (whereas Laura thought he was a sweetie).

Ossie ran a one-man enquiry agency which was supposed to be the best in Huddersfield. It could be he was the only private detective in Huddersfield for all I knew, though I did rather admire the fact that his office was above a pub, showing his native Yorkshire sensibility for getting his priorities right. I also admired the courage he showed by always referring to R & B Investigations as an *all-girl* agency. Perhaps one day I'd give him a few tips in political correctness and sexual diplomacy, but only when I was sure he could stand the shock of discovering that women had the vote now, which I was pretty sure they did, even in Yorkshire.

Fairly recently, he'd helped us out on a case by doing some research in Yorkshire and, as a 'reciprocal', I had helped him solve a problem in London which turned out to be personal rather than professional, though it still counted when it came to balancing the books. As far as I knew, we didn't owe him any 'person hours', as Veronica would have put it, so perhaps he was opening a new line of credit. More to the point, though, how was he connected to Benji Nicholson, a case file I had only opened that morning?

'Ossie Oesterlein is working the same case I am?' I asked Lorna, and almost immediately bit my tongue. I ought to have remembered never to show any sign of weakness in front of her.

'What case would that be? The one you were just about to send the client a bill for because you'd concluded that a missing person enquiry involved someone who was missing?'

I determined not to give her the satisfaction.

'That'd be the one. So what did Ossie want?' I asked innocently.

'I told you, he wants help tracing Benji Nicholson and...' she looked down at something she'd written on a Post-it note which she'd then stuck to the back of her wrist, '...something called Oradea Films.'

'Did he say why?'

'No.'

'Did he say who his client was?'

'No, of course not.'

Now, I know that in the movies a good private eye will happily get beaten up or spend a night in jail rather than tell the bullying policeman who his client is, thus upholding the Code of Client Confidentiality. When talking amongst themselves or bragging about their expenses, however, private eyes are far less diplomatic and treat the Code more as guidelines than Holy Writ.

'Did you mention that I was interested in that name too?'

'I may have,' she admitted sheepishly, and I knew I had her.

'And that would be when Ossie Oesterlein clammed up and asked to speak to me personally. Am I right, or am I right?'

Lorna's eyes flicked on to full-beam hatred.

'He said he "Didn't want to worry a lass about it" and, yes, he wants to talk to you. That man is a pig *and* a dinosaur.'

'Jurassic Pork in other words?' I offered, trying to lighten the mood, but with Lorna you might as well try teaching a newt to tap-dance.

'He's in his office, waiting for a call. I'll leave you two to some male bonding, or whatever it is you get up to together.'

She sneered at me, then flounced out of the office.

At least I'd got a sneer.

For her that was progress.

*   *   *

'Double-Hoh Enquiries, Oesterlein speaking.'

Ossie answered the phone as he always did. I wondered if he had an answerphone message for when the office was closed over Christmas which started 'Ho-Ho-Ho Enquiries' but then he probably didn't take holidays, they would be for soft southern wimps like me.

'Hi, Ossie, it's Roy Angel from Rudgard & Blugden. You wanted a word?'

'Aye, I do indeed, but I wasn't going to share this business with the Girl Guides you've got working for you down there.'

'Actually, Ossie,' I said loudly so that the Thompson Twins could hear if they were listening, 'I work for them. It was always an all-female agency and they gave me a job just so they could show they didn't discriminate. That, plus the fact I'm sleeping with the owner.'

'Be that as it may, I've no intention of discussing this with one of them posh lasses.'

'Sounds intriguing,' I said. So did the fact that Ossie thought of Laura and Lorna as 'posh'. Perhaps even Veronica? No, surely not. 'Your problem is my problem. How can I help?'

From the office kitchen I heard a female voice shout 'Hah!' and it didn't sound posh at all.

'Well, I only rang really to see if your lot knew owt about television companies and if you'd heard of one in particular. An outfit called Oradea Films?'

There was a grunt down the line as if he was putting his feet up on the desk, making himself comfortable. I had a mental picture of him like that, as if from a classic *film noir*, sitting in his office in the dark, the only light coming from the fizzing neon sign hung vertically outside his window. Admittedly, in an office above a pub in Huddersfield, the sign would probably say Tetley's, but some of the bulbs could have fused to give it more character.

'As it happens, I heard of them only yesterday, but only in passing. I don't know anything about them except that a big German bank here in the City has an interest in them.'

'Have you come across the name Benji Nicholson?'

'Yes. That was the name put in the frame by my client.'

'What's he done?'

'I've no idea,' I said honestly. 'All I had to do was stake out his mother's funeral, see if he turned up.'

'And he didn't show?'

'No, not a sniff of him.'

'His own mother's funeral? The bastard.'

'No, I think she really was his mother, but he wasn't there to see her off. I met his sister though, and she says his name is Ian.'

'Ian?'

'Ian Nicholson, not Benji Nicholson.'

'Well *my* client calls him Benji.'

'So did mine, actually. What exactly is your brief?'

Ossie sighed into the phone. In the background I was sure I could hear music; something with a really thumping bass line.

'To see if I can find him. Seems he went missing about a month ago.'

'That's the story I got,' I agreed, 'but all my client wanted was for me to check out this funeral today.'

'His own mother...' Ossie said quietly to himself, forgetting that I could hear him.

'I know,' I sympathised, 'hard to credit, isn't it?'

'Do you fancy joining forces on this one, Angel?'

'What? You mean do a reciprocal?'

'No, I mean we get together and work as a team. Have a serious brainstorming session.'

'You can't say that any more, Ossie.'

'Say what?'

'"Brainstorming". It's not politically correct. Having a stroke is a sort of brain storm. You might offend somebody.'

'Fuck me, I wouldn't want to do that, would I? What can I say instead?'

'I think the current expression is having "a thought shower".'

'Bloody 'ell, that sounds like something mucky off one of those porno websites.'

'Or we could pull the pins on a few thought-grenades,' I offered.

'Are you taking the piss, Angel?'

'No, honest, I'm not. That's what they call "management-speak" down here.'

'Up here, it's called asking for a good hiding.'

'And quite right too,' I said, but I couldn't resist adding: 'So, are you going to open the kimono?'

'Am I going to fucking *what*?'

'Open the kimono. It means show me what you've got – lay out your proposal.'

'Proposal's this: you're looking for Benji Nicholson and so am I.'

'Well, I'm not sure I am, Ossie. I haven't checked back with my clients. They might be happy to let you have the field to yourself.'

'Why would I want a field to meself?'

'No, that's not management-speak, it just means they might leave it to you to find him.'

'I thought you said your client was a big German bank?'

'I might have implied that,' I said cautiously.

'Then they've got plenty of money. So's my client.'

'Who's your client?'

'A chap called Giancarlo Artesi.'

'An Italian?'

'Nah. He's from Holmfirth.'

'I've heard of it. It's up there in Yorkshire, isn't it?'

'Last time I looked it was. Anyway, point is, if your client has hired you to find this Benji character and my client is happy having me on the case, what say we team up, find the bugger in half the time and both of us get paid?'

'Is that ethical?'

'Where does it say it isn't?'

'I don't know.'

'Then it probably is.'

'Did you ever consider becoming a tax lawyer, Ossie?'

'Couldn't do the maths,' he laughed. 'So what say we pool our efforts and find this bugger Benji?'

'If you like,' I said, not really seeing a downside. 'I'll need to check if my client wants to pursue the matter.'

'Can you get a green light tonight?'

I checked my watch. It was just after 5.30, so Terry Patterson might still be at his desk.

'I can try. Why the rush?'

'Well, I thought you could get up to Manchester tomorrow afternoon. There's a morning flight from London Stansted and I could meet you at the airport.'

'Ossie, why do I have to go to Manchester?'

'That's where this Benji Nicholson lives.'

'It is? I didn't know.'

'This partnership's a bit lopsided before we start if you ask me.'

'Well, if that's your attitude why don't you go to Manchester and see if he's there. You've got an address?'

'Yes, 'course I have, I'm a professional.'

'Then go and check it out. I don't see why you need me.'

There was a silence on the line. Well, it would have been a silence if it hadn't been for Ossie's heavy breathing and the distant hum of what sounded like a jukebox running on empty.

'I thought you could come along as moral support,' he said weakly.

'Are you saying you don't want to go to Manchester on your own?'

'No, nowt like that. I've been to Manchester before; I didn't take me coat off 'cos I wasn't stopping.'

I ignored the standard Yorkshire joke about Manchester, or indeed anywhere outside of Yorkshire.

'So why do you want me to come along and hold your hand tomorrow?'

'So that somebody else doesn't,' he said sharply.

'What are you on about, Ossie? Or should I ask what are you on?'

'It's my client, he's insisting on meeting me at Nicholson's place. He's got a set of keys, you see.'

'That's this Artesi guy? One of the famous Holmfirth Artesi boys?'

'Aye. Him and this Benji bloke, they were, like, an item.'

'What on earth do you mean, Ossie?' I played dumb to wind him up.

'You know, the two of them were...they lived together.'

'You mean as a couple?'

'Exactly.'

'You mean two men living together like man and wife?'

I wondered how far I could push this.

'Worse than that – they were actually *married*. Been through one of these civil ceremony things, or so this Artesi says. It's like a wedding, but for gays.'

'They allow them in Yorkshire?'

'Apparently.'

'So not all the stories are true,' I said trying not to laugh.

'What stories?'

'Nothing, it's best to ignore them. Anyway, what am I supposed to do?'

'Just come along and help me check the place out, see if Nicholson left any clues to where he might have disappeared to.'

'Why can't you do that?'

'Look, Angel, I'm just not comfortable going through somebody's things when I know they're...bent as a nine-bob note; especially if their...partner...is standing right behind me.'

'I understand, Ossie,' I said soothingly.

'You do?'

'Yes, I understand that you're bleeding paranoid. This is why you didn't want to talk to any of the women here, isn't it? You've got a bad attack of the homophobes.'

'I've got nothing against them,' he blustered, 'just I don't feel comfortable in their company. There's no law says I have to, is there?'

'Not yet, but I believe there's a White Paper pending.'

'Stop taking the piss, will you? Are you coming up here or not?'

'What, fly up to God's own country? I'd have to check my passport and vaccinations were up to date.'

'Manchester's not in Yorkshire,' he said fiercely.

'I'll have to check in with my client,' I said, 'but if I do come, I won't take my coat off. I won't be stopping.'

CHAPTER FIVE

To my surprise, Terry Patterson went for it. I didn't exactly tell
him that there was another private detective on the case; I just
made a verbal report on the phone, telling him that Benji
Nicholson had not turned out for his mother's funeral, his
name was actually Ian, not Benji, and he lived in Manchester.

'Manchester?' Patterson had said, genuinely surprised.

'So I'm told. Didn't you know?' I had asked.

'No I didn't.'

'But I thought he worked for you.'

'We might have invested in his company, but we don't
employ him.'

'Well, do you want me to follow it up? I could fly there and
back in a day, and to hell with global warming.'

'Yes, you could, couldn't you? I'll get you a ticket.'

'You don't have to, we have a travel agent on tap who
does...'

'No, it's no problem,' he had said. 'Would you go from
Heathrow?'

'I was thinking of Stansted actually.'

'Not a problem. We have an arrangement with an airline.'

'Let me guess,' I had said, 'German bank – it's gotta be Lufthansa, right?'

'Air Berlin, actually. Give me your email address.'

And about ten minutes later, I was printing off an electronic ticket for a round-trip with Air Berlin to Manchester, the price of which was about one-third of the first-class rail fare. I would have to remember to plant a tree or something to balance my carbon footprint.

Ossie was delighted when I rang him back, and when I told him my flight times he promised faithfully to be at Manchester Airport to meet me and be my chauffeur for the day; which was good, as I didn't have a clue where I was going.

He hung up before I got a chance to ask about the thumping rhythms coming down the line from his office.

Veronica, no doubt tipped off by Lorna that I was up to something, was also supportive and, I suspect, secretly impressed. I'd only been on the case half a day and the client was impressed enough to pay me to go to Manchester. I couched it in such a way that she understood it wasn't going to cost the firm anything (much) and I would be assisting our northern associate, which meant he would be in debit and we would be in credit when it came to 'reciprocals'. I think the clincher was that I would be out of the office for an entire day, in Manchester, which was almost as good as being out of the country.

Which only left Amy to convince. By the time I had sorted everything and kept everybody happy, and then got stuck in a jam on the M25, it was well after 8 p.m. when I arrived home, sneaking in to The Old Rosemary Branch as quietly as I could.

Amy was stretched out on one of the sofas, snoozing gently, the only light in the room coming from the television on mute, showing what looked like a documentary on South African penguins. She had fallen asleep with the remote control in one hand and the baby alarm in the other.

It seemed a shame to wake her, not to mention potentially lethal, to ask if she'd cooked anything, but as I hadn't eaten properly all day, I was starving so I crept into the kitchen and began to trawl the cupboards and the fridge. I'd been there about fifteen seconds when she said:

'Try the oven. You'd probably get there eventually, but I can't stand the noise of your stomach rumbling.'

'Sorry if I woke you,' I said, wondering, for the millionth time, how she could get so close without me hearing her.

'I wasn't asleep; just recharging my batteries.'

It seemed safe enough to kiss her.

'Had a good day?'

'Actually, pretty good.' Her eyes brightened. 'The baby's been as good as gold, which is to say asleep most of the day, and your mother's been really good too, which is to say she's kept out of my way.'

There was an earthenware dish in the oven, still hot, and Amy threw me the oven gloves.

'It's chilli. With your mother out from under my feet, I got the urge to cook.'

'She's gone out?' I asked, remembering my recruitment of Jane Bond to our cause.

'Called a minicab to take her into Cambridge just before lunch; said she had to buy some new clothes for her big night out on the town with Mrs Bond.'

'How much did you lend her?'

'Twenty quid for the cab fare, then I loaned her one of my credit cards and told her the PIN number so she didn't have to forge my signature, though I've got a sneaking suspicion she can do that already.'

'That was a dangerous thing to do,' I said reaching for a plate.

'It's one with a small credit limit and I can cancel it in the morning if I have to.'

'That may already be too late. My mother may just keep on going.'

'Well then, that'd be a result too. Actually, she offered to return it when she got back, but I told her to hang on to it for tonight.'

'It was probably max-ed out if she'd been shopping.'

'She didn't go mad, I saw what she bought. If she would only stop dressing down, like some ageing hippy, she's got quite good taste.'

'But she *is* an ageing hippy.'

'You wouldn't have thought so if you'd seen her tonight, she scrubbed up really well.'

'Not her tart-with-a-heart look?'

'As long as she doesn't stand under a street lamp she'll be OK.'

'So she and Jane are out on the town?'

'Big time, from the spring in her step; probably dancing around their handbags in some club by now.'

'That's an image that will stay with me,' I muttered, spooning chilli from the casserole dish. 'Have you eaten?'

'I had something less spicy,' she said, gently pushing up her breasts with her hands. 'Got to think of the milk supply and the night-time feeds; speaking of which, I'm going to turn in and get some kip before I'm rudely awakened – again.'

'You sure you're quite happy with this routine?' I tasted the chilli and tried not to let my eyes water as the heat hit me.

'It comes with the territory. You volunteering to take over?'

'Not really,' I said quietly to preserve my vocal chords, wondering desperately if we had any beer chilling in the fridge.

'Well then, let me handle that side of things. You just concentrate on going to work and not getting fired, because you might end up the main breadwinner.'

'I might?' I croaked.

'If I decide not to go back to work, or we decide to have another baby.'

She saw the look on my face, and it wasn't all down to the chilli.

'And on that bombshell she went to bed!' she said with a broad grin. 'Don't lock the doors. Your mother will be late and she said not to wait up.'

'I won't, I've got an early start tomorrow,' I said. 'This case I'm working on involves me having to go to Manchester and I bet R & B won't pay danger money either.'

'Chill out, Manchester's not that scary any more. You'll be fine as long as you don't talk to anyone about football, or music, or super-casinos. And don't get into a debate about whether or not the bars on Canal Street should employ bouncers to test you on your gayness before they let you in. In fact, it's probably better if you don't speak to anyone at all while you're there.'

'Fair enough,' I conceded. 'Can I ask you one thing, though?'

'What?'

'Just how many credit cards do you have?'

'More than you,' she said, with a killer smile.

* * *

It only took me less than forty minutes to get to Stansted Airport the next morning. Then it took me almost two hours to get checked in, go through security, walk the several miles to the Air Berlin departure gate and grab myself an aisle seat on a jet which, from the tarmac, looked smaller than some stretch limos I'd seen, but probably wasn't.

The flight was jam-packed, which sort of surprised me as there wasn't a football match on up there, but the cabin crew were polite and efficient, and once we were airborne I got a cup of coffee and a blueberry muffin (though I had asked for neither) with just about enough time to consume them before the captain announced we were on our final approach to Manchester Airport. I wondered if the present airport was the site of the old Ringway airfield where Churchill had established the Parachute Regiment in 1940, having seen what German paratroopers had done in Norway, Belgium and Holland, but thought it best, when travelling Air Berlin, not to mention the war.

There was the usual unseemly scramble to get off the plane once it had landed, which always seemed worse the shorter the flight – something I had never been able to understand. We seemed to have landed, as far away from the terminal buildings as it was possible to get and still be west of the Pennines, and so we all climbed dutifully on to one of those concertina buses which you see at airports but nowhere else because they're probably not safe enough to mix with regular traffic. Even before we had moved off I realised why there had been such a rush to get off the plane. The first clue was hearing an electronic version of Mozart's 'Turkish March', followed by the *Mission Impossible* theme, then several versions of Oasis songs, as just about everybody on the bus switched their mobile phones on. Within two minutes – and I saw it spread like a stain – they were all receiving or making phone calls, except me. It was almost a form of mass hysteria; they had been isolated in a pressurised cabin for almost an hour without being able to talk to or text anybody and now it was absolutely crucial that they communicate the facts that the plane had landed on time, the weather in Manchester was warm but overcast, they were on a bus and they would ring back once they got out of the terminal.

I could remember the days when passengers used to run to the terminal buildings so they could get inside to light up a cigarette. Nowadays they rush, push and shove just to get a signal. I watched them bemused and they stared at me because I was the odd one out: I didn't have a phone, because I'd returned Laura's and I'd left mine in the glove compartment of Armstrong, safely parked in the short term car park back at Stansted.

Still, I didn't need electronic gadgets, not when I was being met by a personal chauffeur, guide and fellow professional. We private detectives are a streetwise lot and we don't need gadgets. Anyway, they probably still had phone boxes up north.

Ossie Oesterlein was indeed there to meet me. It was difficult to miss him. He was the sort of big man who always thought he dressed really snappily, which is nowhere near the same as fashionable, and in Ossie's case 'snappily' would only equate with 'fashionable' if he had access to a time machine or he lived in a world without mirrors.

When I had first met him, down in London, he had walked off a train at King's Cross wearing a dark blue double-breasted suit in the widest pinstripe I had ever seen, a broad-brimmed black fedora hat and a green spotted cravat. If he'd had an ivory tipped walking stick, he could have been an extra in a Harry Potter movie.

This would be the first time I had seen him in his natural element (although as a Yorkshireman in Manchester he would argue with that) and I wasn't quite sure what to expect. He didn't disappoint.

Probably just to prove he wasn't frightened of Manchester's reputation for wet weather, he had dressed like Sidney Greenstreet in *Casablanca* in a white linen suit, but with a panama hat rather than a fez. I half expected him to be wearing spats as well, but he'd settled for plain brown Oxford brogues which were big enough to double as snow shoes when winter came. He still had a thing for cravats, this time a bright red one with a pattern of large white spots. Maybe he bought them wholesale or had never learnt to tie a proper tie-knot. More probably it was the girth of his neck which made him uncomfortable with even the largest size of shirt collar.

'Angel, me man! They let you in without a visa then, did they?' he boomed as soon as he saw me, causing several innocent travellers in the Arrivals area to grab their children and hold them closer.

For a split second I contemplated holding my arms out for a welcoming hug, but I knew he would probably react badly to that, or, if he did give me the hug, he would crush several of my ribs.

We shook hands instead; he, like he was using an old-fashioned water pump; me, concentrating on keeping my shoulder in its socket.

'Didn't even ask to see my passport,' I said with a smile.

'You were lucky, they stamped mine when I came across the border on the M62,' he replied with a wink.

'You still having border disputes with Lancashire up here?'

'A few minor scuffles during the cricket season, nowt to write home about. You managed to get house leave then?'

I wasn't sure whether he meant 'house leave' from Veronica and the office or from Amy and the baby.

'Obviously. I'm here, aren't I? But I've only got a 24-hour pass. I've got be safely back in the south before sunset. Until then, I'm in your capable hands and when we've done our business, you can show me some of the fleshpots of Manchester.'

'I wouldn't touch the fleshpots of Manchester with a Teflon bargepole,' said Ossie, dropping his voice ever so slightly. 'Now, if you were visiting me in Huddersfield, I could do you a proper night on the town.'

'Some other time, I really have to catch the 6.30 flight back to Stansted or I'll be in big trouble.'

'You shouldn't let yourself be bossed around by them lasses in your office,' he said starting to walk to the exit doors.

'It's not the ones in the office I'm frightened of,' I said under my breath.

'Any road, let's get the car and get this job done and dusted, and we'll probably have time for a couple of pies and several pints before I bring you back here.'

'Aren't you driving back to Huddersfield, though?'

'Oh yes, but once I'm on the M62 it's mostly downhill.'

That made me feel so much better.

I wasn't sure what sort of car Ossie would drive and I would never have guessed it would be a ten-year-old Ford Fiesta. I wasn't really surprised by the spotless paintwork and the pristine interior, or the fact that the steering wheel had a woolly white cover and that there was an air freshener in the shape of a fir tree hanging from the rear-view mirror. What amazed me was the fact that Ossie could squash his bulk into the driver's seat and managed to close the door and turn the steering wheel without causing himself an injury.

'It's me mother's car,' he explained, starting the engine. 'Mine's a bit conspicuous for professional work. Nobody'll notice us in this.'

Oh yes they would, I thought to myself, and they'd probably think we were recruiting for the circus.

'Your mother doesn't mind you driving her car to foreign places, then?'

'You mean like Manchester? No, she doesn't mind, she's relying on it getting nicked so she can claim a new one on the insurance.'

'Aren't mothers just the best?'

As I said it, he gave me a sideways glance to see if I was showing the slightest disrespect. I thought it best to change the subject.

'So, you'd better fill me in on this Artesi bloke – and tell me where the hell we're actually going, because this is bandit country to me. The last time I was up here they were calling it "Gunchester".'

'Some still do,' said Ossie, nodding agreement. 'But I don't think it's hardly fair anymore. Nottingham's far worse for gun crime, everybody knows that. Some people I use – just occasionally, like – for heavy jobs, you know, like security at nightclubs or bodyguarding...'

'*You* contract out security work?'

'Of course I do,' he said as we turned out of the airport and followed the signs for Manchester, 'the hours are crap and I need me beauty sleep. Anyway, I usually use just one firm, it's a family firm; well it's not really a firm, just a family who can all handle themselves. Me mum calls them the Cudworth Posse, because they're all from Cudworth, see? *Anyway*, point is, they reckon they could all get tooled up within two hours of arriving in Nottingham just by visiting certain clubs and asking certain people. And it wouldn't be half as dear as you'd expect.'

'What does your mother think of that?'

'Oh bugger, she'd have a fit if she knew. Mind you, I've never taken them up on their offer. Guns are trouble, pure and simple. If it can't be solved with a good slap, we haven't done our job properly.'

'I'm sure that's solid advice,' I said, not following it at all. 'But you're not intending to slap this Artesi fellow are you?'

'Not if he behaves himself,' said Ossie automatically, but then had the decency to blush at his own prejudices.

'And not before he's shown us around Benji Nicholson's flat, where no doubt we will find lots of clues to something or other.'

'It's not a flat,' said Ossie.

'House, bungalow, whatever. If they were partners, doesn't this Artesi live there too?'

'No, I meant it's not a house we're going to. When the two of them are a couple, so to speak, they live at Artesi's house in Holmfirth.'

'That's your side of the border, in Yorkshire, right?' I said just to tease him.

'Aye, of course it is. But this Benji guy kept his place on in

Manchester and used it when he was working on his scripts
and things. Thought of it as his "creative space" or something
similarly poncy.'

'And that's where we're going?'

'Yup. Artesi has a key and wants to be there when we look
around.'

'That's understandable. You'll have to tell me what to do.
I've never searched a house for clues before.'

Well I hadn't; not legally.

Ossie flashed me a look which was part distrust, part
apprehension.

'It won't take long. It's not a house, you see, it's a
houseboat.'

'A boat?' I said without thinking. 'Oh dear, I don't have a
good track record with boats.'

Not that long ago I'd had a ringside seat as one had blown
up in a quiet little cove in Dorset. Before that I was involved
in a car chase (admittedly a short one) on the deck of a
Russian freighter...

'You didn't need to bring your sea legs with you, this boat
ain't going anywhere. It's a longboat, one of them barge things
that used to go on the canals, and it's parked up in Castlefield
Basin.'

'Should I have heard of that?'

'Probably not.'

'Me being a soft southern bastard? Do Leeds fans still call
Chelsea supporters "hairdressers" by the way?'

'How did you know me mum was a Leeds fan?'

'Lucky guess,' I said, but in fact he'd mentioned that his
mother had a season ticket to Leeds United when I'd met him
in London.

'Urban regeneration,' he said, getting back to the subject. 'It's where the old Bridgewater Canal met the Rochdale Canal and the whole area's been gentrified. It's like an inner city marina, except the only boats it attracts are them old canal barges which have been turned into houseboats, and the only people who can afford to live on them are folk who don't have to work for a living.'

'Like writers?'

'Exactly.'

As Ossie drove I made a note of place names we passed; a useful thing to do if you ever have to retrace your steps. When I saw signs for Alexandra Park and Moss Side, I knew we were approaching serious Manchester. On the right-hand side of the road, we cruised by a string of tatty shops which still tried to advertise their wares with colourful signage, but no one was kidding anyone that they'd all seen better days. It was a nice ethnic mix though: a Jamaican deli called 'Jerky', Mubbarek Travel Agents, Cohen's The Chemist and a fast food joint called 'Beltin' Butties'. Apart from that last one, I could have been back in Hackney in a previous life.

Somewhere in the suburbs of Manchester, though I didn't know where, was the headquarters of the national tagging service, the place where they track and try and keep tabs on the 10,000 villains, suspected villains or absconders who are now electronically tagged in the UK. For all I knew, their operational nerve centre could be behind one of those shop fronts. It's not the sort of thing they put on tourist maps.

'So this Giancarlo Artesi bloke comes to see me and says his friend's gone walkabout,' Ossie was saying.

'If they've gone through a civil partnership, especially in

Yorkshire, I think they're probably more than just good
friends, Ossie.'

'Be that as it may, this Artesi bloke hasn't seen Benji
Nicholson for a month and said he'd pay whatever it took to
find him. And that could mean substantial sums.'

'Well-off is he?'

'His family certainly is. They own a string of Italian
restaurants from Wakefield up to Middlesbrough, started by
his grandfather, who was over here as a prisoner-of-war and
he never went home. Any road, this Giancarlo has some stake
in the firm and is obviously not short of a bob or two, but
doesn't have to, like, wash the dishes or anything, so he's got
time on his hands.'

'Sort of self-unemployed? I used to be like that.'

'He calls himself Director of Marketing for the Artesi
restaurants but it's probably not a proper job. Says he met this
Benji Nicholson in their York restaurant about three years ago
and it was love at first sight. Do you know owt about this
chap Benji?'

'Very little. I'm winging this one, picking up scraps along
the way. My client, this German bank, is funding a TV show
which is being done by something called Oradea Films and
Benji was the scriptwriter. Now he's gone walkabout the
filming schedule is all to cock and that means someone is
losing money.'

'Artesi mentioned that. What's "Oradea" when it's at
home? Is it German?'

'I don't know. It could be; whatever they're making is
supposed to be for German television.'

'Who's in it?'

'No idea. Probably nobody we've ever heard of.'

'What's it about?'

'I don't know, didn't you ask Artesi?'

'No, didn't think to. I hope it's a murder mystery. I like a good murder story.'

We came into the city proper down the Oxford Road, passing the BBC studios and then the G-Mex Centre, crossed Deansgate in the shadow of fifty-storey Beetham Tower which contained the Hilton Hotel. There seemed to be cranes looming everywhere and a fine mist of cement dust in the air.

'This is Liverpool Road,' said Ossie. 'The Castlefield Basin is down here. We're not far from Granadaland, the television studios, where you can go on the *Coronation Street* tour if you want.'

'I'll pass on that one, if you don't mind. I'd rather spend the day in there.'

I pointed to the large building we were passing labelled Museum of Science and Industry.

'Each to his own,' said Ossie, despairing of me. 'That's supposed to be a good place though.'

He was pointing to a corner pub on my side of the road called The Ox.

'It's one of them "gastropubs" offering fancy pub grub. It's in all the guide books for its award-winning chargrilled Bury black pudding. Do you have such a thing down in London?'

'Gastropubs, yes, though most are overpriced and underwhelming. Black pudding: that's not so common these days. It was a bit of a fad a couple of years ago, but you have to call it *boudin noir* down south.'

'Yer big girl's blouses,' he said with pity in his voice as he pulled the Fiesta into the kerb and slowed to a crawl. The road seemed to stretch on forever.

'Is this it? I don't see any water.'

'No, the canal basin's down the road a bit. Artesi said he'd meet me along here somewhere at The Vicus Remains, which is a bloody funny name for a pub if you ask me. He said it was just down from The Ox.'

'Stop the car,' I said. 'We're there.'

'Where? You're not going soft on me are you?' growled Ossie, but he stopped the car anyway. We were parked opposite a gap in the buildings, an open space with green grass, park benches, a couple of large visitor information signs and, about twenty yards away, a random collection of blocks of stone. If we had been driving at more than 20 mph, or blinking, we'd have missed it.

'The Vicus Remains is not the name of a pub, though it could be I suppose,' I told Ossie as I climbed out of the Fiesta. 'Artesi must have meant the remains of the *vicus*, it's the name for a small Roman settlement. Those stones over there must be what's left of Roman Manchester.'

'Romans? There were Romans in Manchester, like we had Vikings in York?'

We walked over to one of the display boards, which confirmed what I had told him.

'There you are,' I read, 'the Castlefield *vicus* or small township, established during the rule of Agricola.'

'Who was he? The Emperor or summat?'

'He was Governor of Britain late on in the first century AD. Oh and by the way, the Romans were in York before the Vikings. They called it *Eboracum*.'

'Bugger me, where do you get all this stuff?'

'I don't know,' I said. 'Sometimes I scare myself.'

Any further reflections on Romano-Mancunian heritage were interrupted by three short blasts on a car horn. We turned and saw that a blue open-topped Porsche Boxster had pulled up immediately behind Ossie's mum's Fiesta. The driver had black curly hair and wore aviator sunglasses. He was waving at us.

'That nice man's waving at us, Ossie,' I said just to show that my detective skills were still finely honed.

'That's him,' Ossie said quietly. 'The flash bastard. Just stay close to me, say nowt and follow my lead.'

I wasn't sure whether Ossie wanted me to stay close in order to present a united front or for his personal protection, but if push came to shove, I was going to stay closer to Artesi than I was Ossie. He had far more cool.

'Mr Artesi, this is an associate of mine, Roy Angel, he's been looking into things at the London end for us.'

So now I knew where I stood in the pecking order. Giancarlo still shook hands with me, showing he was not averse to meeting the lower orders.

'Thank you so much for joining us today,' he said politely. 'You have no idea how worried I am about Benji.'

I guessed he was about thirty, clean-shaven and square-jawed. Slightly taller than me, certainly fitter than me, he was dressed in black jeans which looked cheap but weren't, a tailored blue blazer which looked expensive and probably was, and an open-necked white shirt. Wherever he turned up dressed like that and in that car, every female under fifty who could still manage high heels would be over him like a rash, let alone the gay guys. Hell's teeth, *I* thought he was attractive.

'I'm afraid we have no concrete leads on Mr Nicholson's

whereabouts,' Ossie told him, 'and we were rather hoping his houseboat might give us a clue as to where he's gone.'

'I understand that perfectly,' said Artesi. 'I'll take you there right now, but the boat was just an office to Benji. It was where he liked to write, which was something he had to do alone. It was his bolt-hole, not his home. That was with me, back in Holmfirth, where we were very happy together.'

'So you can think of no reason why he might want to leave your relationship?' I asked and winced as Ossie loudly sucked in air over his teeth, so I added: 'If you don't mind me asking.'

'I don't mind in the slightest. Benji and I were a loving couple, dedicated to each other.' I could *hear* Ossie squirming at my side without having to look at him. 'Neither of us were promiscuous, though God knows there's plenty of temptation in this city. It was easier to live together in Yorkshire than fight temptation.'

He said it with a knowing smile and I grinned too. Ossie still squirmed.

'Benji used to live here and write things which he tried to sell to Granada TV down the road, but he never had any luck. After we got together, he kept it on and used to come for a few days at a time, using it just as an office. When he was here, he used to phone me every night and email me what he'd written every day.'

'And he was working on something over here when he disappeared?' said Ossie, re-establishing his authority now we'd moved out of delicate 'relationship' territory.

'Yes he was,' said Giancarlo with a shake in his voice. 'He planned on being here for no more than a week.'

'How did he get here?' Ossie asked, showing that at least one of us knew how to ask proper detective-type questions.

'By train. And then taxi from the station of course. He didn't drive, he never learnt. That's why he was always good at keeping in touch: he was always wanting a lift somewhere.'

Giancarlo allowed himself a brief smile.

'Was he in touch the week he came over here, when he…er…disappeared?' Ossie stumbled.

'He rang me that first night to say he'd got here safely, but I haven't heard from him since. No calls, no emails.'

'And that was about a month ago?'

'Exactly. A month ago today.'

'And that's not like Benji?' I chipped in.

'Not at all, it's completely out of character. I gave it a couple of days and drove over here, thinking maybe he was sulking because his writing wasn't going well, but there was no sign of him. I searched the houseboat and, believe me, there was no clue as to where he had gone.'

'Let us have a go, Mr Artesi,' said Ossie standing tall and puffing out his chest. 'We're professionals.'

Which only reminded me that we weren't.

'Did you report him missing to the police?' I asked.

'After three days I did, not that it did much good. The local coppers back in Holmfirth were about as much use as a chocolate teapot. Once I told them Benji and I were in a civil partnership – when they'd stopped sniggering that is – I think they put it down as a "domestic", which means, in effect, that they make a note of it and then do nothing. "He's over eighteen, sir," they said to me, "he's footloose and fancy-free." Can you believe it? One of them actually said that to me. And they all asked me if I knew how many people went missing each year in Britain.'

'200,000,' I said automatically, and when I saw them both looking at me I shrugged my shoulders. 'I Googled it.'

'Yes, that's what they told me. They also told me to try the Missing Persons Helpline, which I did, along with pestering all of our friends and people I knew Benji had worked with, plus the people he was writing his script for. They just shouted at me saying they bloody well wanted to know where he was too.'

'That would be this Oradea Films company?' Ossie said to show he was paying attention.

'That's right. Benji had been given ten days to do some rewrites and they were screaming for them. They probably still are, because they must be way behind schedule by now.'

'This film – TV show – that Benji is working on for Oradea,' I started, avoiding Ossie's eye, 'what sort of a show is it?'

'An international crime drama, a thriller,' said Artesi. 'It centres on a group of detectives working for Europol.'

'You mean Interpol,' said Ossie.

'No, Eur-o-pol,' he said carefully, so even Ossie and I could follow. 'Interpol is the international police organisation based at Lyon in France. Europol is the European equivalent of the FBI and coordinates actual policing. It's based in The Hague, in the Netherlands, though it conducts its business in English. At least that's what Benji told me. I'd have thought you would have heard of it, you being detectives.'

'Ah,' said Ossie, quick as a whip, 'but we're private sector. Shall we go see this boat of Benji's now?'

'Sure, I'll lead, you follow. It's down this road and hang a left into Potato Wharf. We can park by Giant's Basin and walk to the mooring. I only suggested we meet here because it was easier to find.'

Giancarlo's face suddenly slumped with sadness and he looked out over the few stony outcrops which were the remains of the *vicus*.

'Benji used to come here a lot when he was staying on the boat. He'd bring sandwiches and eat them here. He was into all that Roman stuff and I always had to record *Time Team* for him.'

I noticed that he had slipped into the past tense when talking about Benji.

'I really like your Porsche,' I said to lighten the mood. 'Can I ride with you?'

CHAPTER SIX

It wasn't a long ride in Artesi's Boxster, but it was worth it just to see the look on Ossie's face as we roared off throatily down the Liverpool Road. As the Porsche was a convertible, I was able to turn and wave imperiously to Ossie following on in his mum's Fiesta. Secretly I think he wanted a ride too, but didn't dare ask.

We passed a large, flash sushi restaurant and the Castlefield Hotel on our left, with the Museum of Science and Industry looming in Victorian splendour on our right. Then we turned left into Potato Wharf and, apart from an incongruously modern brick YMCA building, we could have time-slipped into the nineteenth century.

The Castlefield Basin wasn't anything like the marina harbour I would have expected if I'd given the subject any serious thought. It was a crossword-grid pattern of canals, wharves and walkways over dark, dank, unmoving water on which ducks, geese and swans floated in a half-hearted fashion as if they had thought of taking off and flying somewhere better but just couldn't be bothered.

Surrounding the basin were warehouses converted into offices and too many railway bridges to count, their brick pillars rising like a forest, their ironwork toppings rusting quietly away. It was remarkably quiet and empty of people, though thousands had once worked here, loading and unloading the stuff which Manchester took in as raw material and then spat out as finished goods in the heyday of industry and empire.

Although I didn't know him, I could see why Benji Nicholson would have liked this as a place in which to write. He could be here with the ghosts of nineteenth-century bargemen who looked up from their longboats to see steam trains pass overhead, yet within two minutes' walk he could be standing on the remains of a wall built by Roman legionary engineers and then go for a quick sushi lunch before a visit to The Rover's Return on the set of *Coronation Street*. And all this was within strolling distance of the centre of a major university city with a world-class football team. Two, if you counted United. Just how many stimuli did a scriptwriter need?

Giancarlo Artesi parked the Boxster on a square of waste ground near a sign telling us we were looking at the Giant's Basin. It did look a bit like a giant concrete sink with the plug missing, though whatever water was supposed to flow into and down there wasn't moving very fast due to a logjam of empty plastic bottles and other general rubbish, some of which, judging by the smell, was starting to ferment.

Ossie pulled in behind us and Artesi led the way down the old towpath.

I still couldn't see any people or any recent signs of any habitation. Potato Wharf seemed to be the place where 50-foot metal-hulled barges came to die.

These were wrecks, junk or scrap, or whatever the technical term was; not houseboats.

Giancarlo must have read my mind.

'This is, like, the rough end of canal town, the posh bit of the basin is round here.'

We followed him as the towpath curved under an arch where several canals, about 25 feet wide seemed to converge. Barge traffic had probably once been controlled by lock gates or similar, but any superstructure had long gone. Now, there were just channels of dark, unmoving water which came from nowhere and went nowhere. But, once under the arch, it began to feel more like a marina or a harbour. There was order here, and signs of human habitation.

Given the size of the place, there were very few houseboats and there was plenty of space between them. I suppose the proper term was 'narrowboats' and most had been lovingly restored with ornate paint jobs and lots of plants in pots on their decks. Naturally they mostly had cute names like *Tinkertoo, Rosie & Jim* and *The Black Pearl*. Some had TV aerials, one obviously had a wood-burning stove because it had a pile of small logs neatly stacked on the stern and one had two empty pint milk bottles in a small metal crate on the towpath, but I couldn't know if they were expecting a delivery or recycling.

All the narrowboats had runs of curtained windows down the length of the cabin and all had their curtains securely drawn. Considering that pedestrians on the towpath were no more than about three feet away as you slept in your bunk, they quite rightly valued their privacy. This didn't mean Ossie or I could resist trying to look inside one, without success. I did notice that they all displayed British Waterways standard canal and river licences in their windows. I wondered, briefly, if they got involved in incredibly slow, low-speed chases with Police narrowboats with flashing lights and sirens in pursuit if their licences expired.

'I went on a canal holiday once when I was a kid,' Ossie said, paused on the edge of the towpath staring down into the blue-black inky water. 'Me mother must have said "Don't you dare fall in that water" a hundred times a day. Drove her mad with worry it did, the thought of me going overboard.'

'There's dysentery in every ripple,' I said.

'Is that true?'

'Probably not, it was just something Noel Coward once said.'

'Who's he then?'

'He was a real charmer who did drama. Bit of a clever bastard.'

'Never heard of him,' said Ossie.

'Bet your mum has.'

'Probably, she loves them old band leaders. What's funny about that?'

'Nothing,' I said, straightening my face, 'it's just I've never heard him called that before. So, your mother liked messing about in boats, then?'

'No, just canal boats. Barges were the only thing that floated that didn't make her seasick. They were nice and slow and gentle, see? And safe for the most part, but she was worried sick I'd fall in between the boat and the bank, 'cos then you'd get stuck under the keel and never come up. At least, that's what she always thought. You could fall off the front or the stern or the starboard side, but if you went over the port side you got keelered, she used to say.'

'She probably meant "keelhauled",' I said.

'How do you know stuff like that?'

'I've seen more pirate movies than she has, though I've no idea what keel-hauling actually involved.'

We were passing a rather twee houseboat named *The Barbara Bray*, which had been lovingly restored. Her paintwork was multi-coloured and fresh, and there were hanging baskets of flowers dangling from angled brackets fixed along the length of the cabin. It could have been photographed for the lid of a box of chocolates or National Trust fudge, had it not been for the TV aerial and mini satellite dish on the roof of the cabin. Both were discreetly masked by small tubs of flowering plants so that a casual onlooker would have had to look twice to spot them, and an innocent passer-by would certainly not have noticed the two small security cameras hidden in the hanging baskets which were vectored in to cover the pathway and the wheelhouse, just where anyone could step on deck.

But I hardly qualified as an innocent passer-by, so I did spot them, mainly because they were the sort of domestic security equipment which Rudgard & Blugden regularly sold to worried householders at a vast mark-up. It was a highly profitable part of the business and, with there only being one CCTV camera for every twelve people in Britain, there was obviously still room for the market to grow. I don't know what all those cameras did for the crime figures but they certainly helped our balance sheet.

'It's the next boat,' Giancarlo was telling us as the towpath curved around to the left and under a modern brick bridge.

It seemed to be the only barge in this part of the basin. The nearest neighbour was *The Barbara Bray* we had just passed and beyond was a dark rectangle of still water with the odd floating duck or swan the only signs of life.

Artesi stopped, blocking the towpath, while he was still thirty feet or more from the boat, his head bowed as if in prayer, his hands in his jacket pockets.

'Has he stepped in duck shit or summat?' hissed Ossie. 'Because God knows I have, the stuff's everywhere and it's a bugger to get off.'

Giancarlo turned to face us, holding out a set of three keys on a brass ring in his right hand. In his left he clutched a pack of cigarettes and a stick lighter. His bottom lip quivered as he spoke.

'You go ahead, I can't face it. I'll be out here if you need me, otherwise turn the place upside down. I don't mind if it helps to find Benji.'

I took the keys from him.

'We'll be respectful,' I told him and strode on with Ossie at my shoulder.

The longboat was just the same pattern as the others we had seen, though there were no flowers on this one and the paintwork was smart but not cutesy-cutesy. Apart from some highly polished brass fittings, it looked quite drab, with the only splash of colour being its cabin-mounted name board, painted in bright red.

'Who the bloody hell is Felix Dacia?' growled Ossie, stumbling over the rope which anchored the stern of the houseboat to the towpath.

'Was, not is,' I told him, 'and it was a place, not a person.'

I wondered if Benji Nicholson had named the houseboat himself, or whether he'd bought it because the name *Felix*

Dacia appealed, as Artesi had already told us he was into ancient history and all things Roman.

'Go on then, smart arse,' Ossie was saying, 'I can see you're dying to tell me.'

Of course, I couldn't resist.

'Dacia was a country around the Carpathians in central Europe which bordered the Roman Empire until the Emperor Trajan—' Ossie's face was like stone, 'as in Trajan's column in Rome, decided to invade and conquer it in 105 AD or thereabouts.'

Ossie remained impassive and determined to be unimpressed. I could almost hear the sound of tumbleweed drifting through his brain.

'It was a very rich country and the Romans called it Dacia Felix, not Felix Dacia, and it actually meant "wealthy Dacia" rather than "happy Dacia", which it's sometimes translated as.'

'An easy enough mistake to make,' said Ossie with a sneer. 'Does it mean owt significant?'

'I don't know; probably not.'

'So that little history lesson's two minutes of my life I'll never get back?'

'Hey, Ossie, every day is a school day.'

'I never liked school, couldn't wait to leave. The bullying was a nightmare.'

'*You* were bullied at school?'

'Nah, I was the top bully, but I kept getting reported to the teachers, and they told me mum and she gave me hell,' he said wistfully.

'It's what mothers do,' I agreed.

'Any road, this isn't getting the job done. We'd best get

aboard and start looking for clues as to where yon fella's
boyfriend has gone.'

'You're right,' I enthused. 'Those poop-decks won't swab
themselves.'

Ossie shook his giant bald head, almost dislodging his
panama hat.

'You realise that if we were in public, I'd probably have to
say I didn't know you?'

'I know,' I said with a smile, stepping lightly on to the *Felix
Dacia* so I could whistle a two-note salute on an imaginary
hornpipe to pipe Ossie aboard.

'Daft as a brush,' Ossie muttered under his breath.

'You search below,' I said handing him the keys Artesi had
given me. 'I'll look around on deck.'

Ossie looked up and down the flat fifty-foot deck.

'That shouldn't take you long. Why do I have to do the
dirty work?'

'Because you're the professional, I'm just a gifted amateur.'

He perked up at that.

'Well, you're not wrong there,' he said smugly.

The truth was, I really didn't fancy going down into the cabin
of the *Felix Dacia* with Ossie. I doubted there was room down
there for Ossie, let alone the two of us, and the sound of us
blundering about among his partner's private things would only
upset Giancarlo, who was strolling up and down on the towpath
pulling seriously on a cigarette. I gave him a wave and he nodded
back to me, but made no move to offer me a cigarette. I would
have been sorely tempted if he had; might even have accepted.
After all, the setting was tranquil and the weather was warm and
sunny, despite Manchester's reputation. Plus, Amy and the No
Smoking zone around the baby were two hundred miles away,

but it wouldn't look good in front of Ossie's client if I stretched out on the cabin roof for a fag break this early in the case.

So I tried to look busy and slowly strolled the length of the starboard side on the six inches of deck between the cabin and the edge of the barge, examining the decking for clues. I didn't find any, but I did spot a thick rope-end tied off to a brass cleat halfway along before I tripped over it and went headfirst into the inky water.

Down that starboard side, the side away from prying eyes wandering by on the towpath, the cabin's curtains were open so I could look down and in for a practical lesson in how to search a house, or at least a houseboat. Mostly I saw Ossie's broad back and shoulders, filling all available space, but his shiny bald head taught me one bit of private detective etiquette: you always show respect and take your hat off when disturbing a complete stranger's private property.

There didn't seem to be much to search. Most of the cabin space was taken up with a single bunk bed which doubled as the seating area, but over Ossie's shoulder I could make out a small fridge and two gas burner rings. There were a few books scattered about, but no sign of any paper, typewriter or computer, which was surely odd if this was supposed to be a writer's hideaway.

I reached the prow of the barge, stepped over the forward mooring rope and strode down the port side of the deck, stepping off the barge and onto the towpath before I tripped over another thick rope tied to a cleat, going over the side midway, matching the one on the other side.

'Mr Artesi!' I called out and Giancarlo turned to acknowledge me, flicking his cigarette into the canal. 'Did Benji have a laptop?'

'Of course he did,' he answered without hesitation. 'It's at home.'

'But did he work on one when he was here, on the *Felix Dacia*? And did he call the boat that, and if so why?'

Artesi held up the fingers of his right hand as he ticked off his answers.

'Yes he always brought his laptop with him. When I came over to look for him when he didn't answer his phone for three days, it was in there on his bunk where he used to sit with it on his knee. It was open but the battery must have gone flat, so I packed it up and took it back to Holmfirth with me.'

'Didn't the police ask about it?'

'The police didn't ask about anything really. Once they realised we were gay, it was just a "domestic" as far as they were concerned.'

'I'm sorry about that.'

'Don't be. I need your help, not your sympathy,' he said calmly. 'As for the *Felix*, yes, Benji did name it. He said once it meant "Happy Land" or something in Latin, and it just seemed to amuse him. Is that important?'

'I shouldn't think so,' I said, as I honestly couldn't think why it should be.

Behind me I heard the double doors to the cabin open and Ossie's heavy tread on the deck, then the slap of his shoes as he jumped on to the towpath.

'Clean as a whistle,' he announced. 'Can't see anything in there which might help us. No papers, no phone, nothing. Was the boat locked up when you came over to look for him?'

'Yes it was, but I had my set of keys,' said Artesi, his expression fading as whatever slim hope he'd had started to ebb away. 'I was just telling your Mr Angel, I took Benji's laptop home with me, but apart from that I didn't touch anything and nobody's been here since. The police weren't interested.'

'It all seems a bit...spartan,' said Ossie. 'I mean, there's no telly, no radio, no sound system in there.'

'Benji only came here to work,' said Artesi, 'for the peace and quiet.'

'It's certainly peaceful,' Ossie agreed. 'Haven't seen a soul since we got here, which is a pity really, because nosey neighbours are a godsend in our line of work.'

'That's exactly why he liked the place. If you didn't know the basin was here, you'd never know it was here, if you see what I mean.'

'It takes all sorts, I suppose.' Ossie rubbed his chin with his right hand while his left burrowed deep into the capacious pocket of his suit jacket. 'I reckon he ate out a lot, didn't he?'

'As a matter of fact he did. He hated cooking; that's why he jumped into bed with someone who owns a chain of Italian restaurants.' Ossie winced at that, but I didn't think Artesi had said it to embarrass him. 'When he was over here, he used to eat out every meal. Breakfast at the Castlefield Hotel, then lunch and dinner at The Ox or Dimitri's Taverna up the road, or that African place on the corner. Jowata's or something like that.'

'An *African* restaurant?' Ossie asked, wide-eyed.

'Please don't make any cracks about the size of the portions,' I pleaded.

Artesi shrugged his shoulders.

'Why not? Benji always did. Why did you ask about him eating out?'

'There's no food on the boat barring a couple of packets of

peanuts and the pots and pans in the galley area are spotless, almost like they'd never been used. He liked a drink, though. The fridge is stuffed with bottles of lager.' He pulled his left hand out of his jacket pocket and held out an empty bottle. 'I found this one on the floor, rolled into a corner.'

The label on the bottle said that it had once contained Ursus beer, which was one I'd never heard of.

'That's Benji's favourite brand all right,' said Artesi and then paused, remembering something. 'But it's not like him to leave empty bottles rolling around the floor, he was very fastidious. Come to think of it, when I came over looking for him, the cabin stank of beer, like it had soaked into the carpet. You know that smell?'

'Like a pub when the doors are opened first thing in the morning and the sunlight pours in, picking out the dust motes dancing in the air.'

I realised they were both looking at me and frowning.

'Sorry,' I said hastily. 'You reminded me of something Malcolm Lowry once wrote.'

'Malcolm who?' asked Ossie.

'He was a friend of Noel Coward,' I said, which left Ossie confused and Artesi wondering why he had hired a couple of clowns like us.

Ossie cleared his throat loudly.

'I was thinking that it might be worth our while going round some of his regular eating places, ask a few questions. After all, it is lunchtime and they'll all be open.'

'If you think it will do any good, by all means do so.'

'A photograph of Benji which we could show around might jog a few memories,' I said, just to prove I could be useful.

'Yes, Mr Oesterlein mentioned that earlier in the week,' said

Artesi, reaching for his wallet. 'Benji was due for a new passport and he had some head-and-shoulders shots done quite recently. They're only him messing about in one of those photo-booths but they're a good likeness.'

I got my first sight of Benji Nicholson from a 4x5 centimetre mugshot, standing there next to the opaque waters of that canal basin. It told me as much as any passport photograph could, which wasn't much. The face which stared back was a young one, much younger than I had expected. It was a round face with a serious expression, the eyes were blue and the complexion slightly washed-out, as is always the case with a flash photograph against the white background of those photo-booths. He wore a black turtle-neck shirt and had dark brown hair cut short, but spiked with gel at the front. The pictures had come in the standard block of four identical shots and had been cut into two strips of two.

Artesi's hand shook slightly as he handed over the strips and as I passed one strip to Ossie, who was still clutching the empty beer bottle, he said softly:

'Make sure I get them back.'

'Of course.'

'Do you want to hang on to the keys if you're staying around here? I was thinking of heading home unless there's anything I can usefully do here.'

I was about to tell him to go, then I remembered he was Ossie's client, and held my tongue.

'You get on back to Yorkshire,' said Ossie, like he was offering him safe conduct through a war zone. 'Me and Angel'll do some asking around with these pictures, see if we can jog anybody's memories, then we might have another look at the boat, but we won't make a mess and I promise we'll lock up when we go. I can drop the keys in to your place tomorrow.'

'Hang on to them,' said Artesi. 'I'll pick them up at the end of the week from your office when I get your report.'

It was a reminder that Giancarlo was not only a worried client looking for his lost partner, but also a businessman and a Yorkshireman who had remembered he was paying Ossie's wages.

'Aye, right you are then,' said Ossie. 'You leave everything to us. We'll find Benji for you.'

In retrospect, I do wish he hadn't said that.

Artesi said goodbye and walked away down the towpath. Ossie and I walked in the opposite direction to a flight of concrete steps Eisenstein would have appreciated which led up to the Castlefield Hotel and the Liverpool Road.

As we climbed up to road level, I asked Ossie about the report Artesi was expecting.

'It's going to be a lean one,' he said philosophically. 'I reckon there would be more fat on a butcher's pencil.'

'So you've got nothing.'

'Less than that probably.'

'Don't give up, somebody in one of these restaurants may remember him.'

'I shouldn't think so,' said Ossie. 'It's been a month now and I suspect that if he came here to work, he'd keep himself to himself.'

'But you still think it worth trawling the places Artesi mentioned?'

'Oh aye. I'm bloody hungry and it must be dinnertime by now.'

Ossie's 'dinnertime' was what we soft southern hairdressers call lunchtime, and indeed there were diners lurking in the restaurant and bar of the Castlefield, but Ossie didn't fancy the à la carte menu. We had time for just one beer while he showed the barman the photos of Benji Nicholson. The barman didn't recognise him and when prompted that he came in there for breakfast sometimes, he shrugged and suggested we came back at 6 a.m. to ask the breakfast shift, but we'd better bring a Polish phrasebook with us. Ossie glared at him, emptied his glass and demanded a receipt.

We walked up the street we had driven down in convoy with Artesi, passing The Ox gastropub.

'That was one of his regular haunts,' I pointed out.

'I know, but I was saving that one,' said Ossie, patting his belly with the flat of his hand. 'Let's do the others first – work up a bit of an appetite.'

We found the Jowata African restaurant at the top of the road as it turned into the long drag that was Deansgate, just after the Spanish Language and Cultural Centre, but it didn't seem to be open. Ossie perused the menu in the window and made a note of the phone number 'for future reference', then we spotted Dimitri's Taverna down a narrow alley. It had tables and umbrellas outside, but the customers were all inside. I suspected that alfresco dining would come into its own when the smoking ban arrived.

There was a small bar set aside from the restaurant, busy with young black guys in smart suits and ties and casually dressed middle-aged men speaking in thick Greek accents. They all seemed to know each other and the banter between them seemed to be exclusively about the misfortunes of

Manchester City Football Club, but, remembering Amy's advice, I refrained from joining in.

Ossie got straight down to business, chatting up the barman after I had ordered (it having been made clear that it was my round) two bottles of Dos Equis, as if dark Mexican beer in a Greek taverna in Manchester was the natural choice. The barman was pleasant enough, but didn't recognise Benji Nicholson from his passport photograph. Ossie drank half his beer in one go, then held his glass up to the light, sniffed it, nodded in appreciation and drained it. Then he asked for a receipt.

We walked back to The Ox. By now I was warming to the idea of dinner or lunch or anything solid, as I had a feeling Ossie was only just getting started.

I let him go through the door of The Ox first, and suddenly he was at the bar with a menu in his hands, licking his lips. I had no idea he could move that fast. He ordered two pints of Hyde's Anvil bitter without looking up, but long before they were pulled he had finished speed-reading the menu and was offering it to me.

'The mixed grill with the Bury black pudding. That'll get the job done, I reckon,' he said and actually smacked his lips together in anticipation.

I scoured the menu for a vegetarian alternative, just to annoy him, but if there was one I couldn't spot it and, so that Ossie wouldn't think me a wimp, I opted for the devilled kidneys on toasted brioche.

'I wasn't going to have a starter,' Ossie said, threatening to sulk.

'That'll do me,' I explained, 'I'll be having—' I almost said 'dinner' '—a big meal when I get home tonight.'

'So will I,' said Ossie, looking confused.

'Let's grab that table over there,' I distracted him.

'You mean the one next to those two off *Coronation Street*? No, don't look.'

But of course I did. You have to when someone says that, don't you?

'Those two women? Are they actors?'

'Yes, of course they're actresses,' he whispered, 'but they probably want to be left in peace. Pretend we haven't seen them.'

'I have no idea who you're talking about,' I said honestly.

'That's the ticket.'

With the teenage waiter who staggered to our table with Ossie's lunch, we struck lucky. Ossie was far too interested in trying to identify the various meats piled on his plate to pay him any attention, so showing off my professionalism I placed the pictures of Benji on the table and asked if he looked familiar.

'Oh yeah, that's Benji Nicholson,' said the lad, 'the scriptwriter. He comes in from time to time.'

'You know him?'

'I knew who he was, but it wasn't like we were picking out curtains together or anything. He used to give me a few tips.'

That got Ossie's attention.

'Tips on what?'

'Scriptwriting. That's what I want to do, for a living, like. I'm doing Media Studies at uni and I only work in here to pay off my student loan. We get lots of TV people in from Granada.'

Ossie's voice dropped to a whisper and he jerked a finger at the two women on the next table.

'You mean like them, from *Coronation Street*?'

'Christ, no,' said the waiter, shaking his head. 'I mean *important* people like producers and script editors.'

'Did you recognise him when he came in?' I asked.

'Not his face, but I spotted his name when he paid by credit card once and I'd read a bit about him in *Broadcast*, which is, like, the trade paper for people in telly. There was an article on the *Europol* film he was working on. Sounds cool, it's just a pity they're not filming round here.'

'Where are they filming?' He seemed to know far more than me, though that was probably not surprising.

'Over in Sheffield, but I think they must have wrapped by now. I haven't seen Benji for weeks.'

'How many weeks?' said Ossie sharply with a scowl. I couldn't understand why he was being so curt with our waiter. I was finding him a mine of information.

'Three or four, something like that.'

'Do you know where he lives?' Ossie pressed sharply as if something was really bothering him.

'No, and I didn't ask. He's gay, I'm not; not that he seemed interested in me. Why are you interested in him?'

'We're doing a risk assessment for the company financing his film,' I said quickly to cut off Ossie.

Oh, right,' said the waiter, losing interest. 'Enjoy your meal.'

'Hang on a minute,' growled Ossie, grabbing him by the wrist, then pointing at his charnel-house of a plate and jabbing his finger. 'I can see rump steak; I can see a lamb chop. There's a kidney and some bacon. I can see me mushrooms and me tomatoes, but I'm buggered if I can spot any hint of black pudding.'

*   *   *

Ossie got his black pudding on a separate plate with the apologies of the management, then he spent longer perusing the bill and working out the minimum tip he could get away with than he had eating. Once he'd demanded a receipt, we were free to leave and wandered back down the road towards the canal basin.

'That waiter was quite helpful,' I said.

'Was he?' Ossie seemed unimpressed.

'Well, I didn't know they were filming Benji's script in Sheffield until he said.'

'So what?'

'So, maybe the film crew know where he is? They must have missed him.'

'Not likely, is it? I mean the writer is usually the last person they want on the film set unless they're making changes and need some pink pages.'

'You seem to know an awful lot about making a film.'

'I've done quite a bit of work for Yorkshire TV in my time; most of it involved hanging round the studios keeping an eye out for who was fiddling the tea money, but I picked up one or two things.'

'A man of many talents,' I complimented him as we started down the steps to the canal basin and the towpath.

'Often underestimated, occasionally underrated, always underpaid.'

As we neared the *Felix Dacia* again, this time from the prow end, I suggested I took a look around inside, just so I could tell my client I had done so. Ossie said he didn't think it could hurt and a fresh pair of eyes might spot something he'd missed, though his voice didn't carry much conviction.

I took Artesi's keys from him and dropped into the cabin,

leaving Ossie to stomp up and down on deck.

He had been right about it being fairly spartan down there, right about the tiny galley area being basically unused, and right about the fridge being stuffed with Ursus beer and nothing else. As far as I could see he hadn't missed anything significant, but that could have been because the significant things weren't there to miss.

Benji's laptop was missing, but Artesi had told us he'd taken that. What about a mobile phone though? Or clothes, toothbrush, shaving kit, that sort of stuff? If he'd been meaning to stay overnight, surely he would have brought a bag with him? It was possible that Artesi had taken that away too, on the assumption that Benji wasn't coming back. Would he have mentioned it? Should we have asked?

There was a loud crash above my head and I thought for a second the barge was coming under shellfire.

'Fuck!'

Ossie was lying flat along the starboard deck, which was little more than a six-inch shelf, most of him pressed up against the cabin windows, blocking out the sunlight.

'Hey, don't fall overboard,' I yelled up, 'remember what your mother used to say.'

'I'm all right, but me hat's gone for a swim. God damn it, who left that bloody rope there?'

I watched him get to his knees and shuffle back along the deck about a yard. He had tripped over the rope tied to the cleat halfway along the hull, as I almost had.

'What the sodding hell is this tied to?' said Ossie, tugging at the rope with both hands.

I climbed out of the cabin and stepped round the deck to see what he was doing.

'Isn't it a mooring rope?' I said, smiling at Ossie's panama hat floating about six feet away on the dark water.

'Don't be daft, we're tied up fore and aft to the towpath. You tie boats up at the front end and the back end, not in the middle. Any road, there's nothing to tie it up to here.'

He was right of course, the rope didn't go anywhere except over the side and into the water. Even pulling on it quite violently Ossie only managed to produce about eighteen inches of slack.

'Well it seems to be attached to something. Is it an anchor?'

'An anchor? Don't be soft. The water can't be more than five or six feet deep, and I doubt if they're expecting a tsunami here.'

'There's another one in the same place on the port side,' I told him.

'*Port side*, eh? So we know all the nautical terms now do we?' Ossie said sarcastically, straining on the rope. 'Thought you said you didn't like boats.'

'I don't dislike them as such, it's just they haven't been very lucky for me lately.'

And my losing streak was set to continue.

'Well something's moving,' Ossie said showing me that he at last had some play in the rope. 'Still doesn't want to come up though. God knows what's on the end of it.'

I peered over the side to see if I could somehow magically see through six feet of opaque water.

'Ossie,' I said gently. 'Are there fish in this canal?'

'Shouldn't think so,' he grunted, changing his grip on the rope.

'Then I think we need to call the cops,' I said.

And then, with great presence of mind, I hopped over the cabin and on to the towpath before being spectacularly sick.

* * *

About the time I should have been boarding my return flight on Air Berlin, I got through to Amy.

'Hi, honey, just ringing to say I'm going to be late.'

'How late?'

'Er...sometime tomorrow late, I've missed my return flight.'

'Why am I not surprised? What's going on?'

'I'm rather tied up helping the police with their enquiries.'

'Oh Christ, not you as well?'

CHAPTER SEVEN

Ossie had left his mobile phone in his mum's Fiesta but offered to jog down the towpath to get it. There was no way I was going to be left alone near the *Felix Dacia*, so I volunteered to run to the Castlefield Hotel, which was much nearer, where I got a very startled receptionist to phone the police and tell them there was a body in the canal. She was far calmer than I was and asked if she could help as she'd done a course in mouth-to-mouth resuscitation 'down the local swimming baths'. I told her thanks for the offer, but it was probably too late for that, about a month too late.

The police arrived in force and very quickly, with two squad cars pulling up outside the Castlefield. One of the uniforms rushed by me and into the hotel, emerging about thirty seconds later with the receptionist who pointed a finger at me. In turn, I told the policeman it was down there in the water where my friend was standing guard.

'You mean that guy who looks like a white Buddha?' asked the copper.

'That's the one.'

Ossie had sat himself down cross-legged on the roof of the cabin of the *Felix Dacia*. In his white suit and with his bald head glistening in the afternoon sun, I could see the resemblance.

By the time the heavy mob arrived, the Scene of Crime Officers with their white paper suits, rolls of CRIME SCENE tape and huge screens on telescopic legs, Ossie and I had explained our presence on the barge and what we had seen floating just under its keel. But then, hot on the heels of the SOCOs came two CID detectives, so we had to go through our story all over again.

Ossie gave them Giancarlo Artesi's mobile number – so much for client confidentiality – but the lead CID man, a detective sergeant who looked young enough to be still paying off his student loan, preferred his home address, and so Ossie told him where he lived in Holmfirth.

They left us alone for a while then, as they tried to figure out how to remove the body, or what was left of a body, from under the hull of the *Felix Dacia*. I didn't like to enquire too closely. All I had seen was an arm – an arm not attached to anything – and that was quite enough for me. We sat on the towpath, now cordoned off at both ends, well away from the edge of the canal, and watched the police operation get into gear.

'If they have to get divers in,' Ossie said, 'd'you reckon one of 'em will swim out and get me hat?'

His Panama was still floating, now about twenty feet off the barge.

'Don't push it,' I said.

After an hour or more, one of the uniforms asked if we'd like to wait in the Castlefield Hotel until the senior investigating officer got there. We looked at each other and

Ossie said that at least we'd get a cup of tea there, so we followed the policeman down the path and up the steps and into the hotel. A group of a dozen or so onlookers had gathered at the top of the steps, most of them staff from the hotel. They shuffled aside to let us through and concentrated on their shoes, unsure as to whether we were heroes or suspects.

In the hotel lobby, sitting with the uniformed constable, we ordered a pot of tea and watched as more police cars arrived outside, and then two Land Rovers from which men in overalls unloaded wetsuits and shiny metal aqualungs. Ossie made a move to get to his feet, but I put a hand on his arm and pulled him back.

'Leave it. You can always get another hat.'

Eventually, the senior investigating officer, a Detective Chief Inspector Armitage, came to see us and bought us another pot of tea and some Eccles cakes, and was charm and politeness personified. In fact, Ossie was quite taken with her, and not just because she bought him cake.

DCI Armitage, who answered Ossie's first question by saying her name was Heather but he could call her 'Chief Inspector', told us that she had liaised with West Yorkshire CID and they had sent a car to collect Giancarlo Artesi and bring him to Manchester.

'That won't be popular,' said Ossie.

'Mr Artesi is not under arrest, he's merely assisting us in the identification.'

'I didn't mean him,' Ossie explained. 'I meant it wouldn't be popular with the boys from the Huddersfield cop shop having to come over to Manchester, not unless they're getting overtime.'

'Let me worry about that, Mr Oesterlein,' she said coolly. 'Now if the two of you would just like to tell me how you came to be here today and find what you found, then I'll get you processed and you can most likely be on your way.'

'What exactly did we find, Chief Inspector?' I asked politely.

'You managed to disturb a body, or what's left of one, that had been tied – no, not tied – *slung* from ropes under the keel of the narrowboat.'

'Keelhauled! I knew it!' Ossie burst out.

'Ignore him,' I told her, 'he's been talking about pirates since we got here. Do you have any idea whose body it is?'

'At the moment, no, but all indications are that it could be the boat's owner, the man you were looking for...'

She pretended to forget the name, so I obliged.

'Benji Nicholson.'

'That's the one. Now, why exactly were you looking for him?'

So we told our story once again, leaving nothing out and, as far as I could recall, telling nothing but the whole truth. By the time we'd finished, the teapot had been replenished and emptied again and Ossie had seen off the plate of Eccles cakes.

DCI Armitage then asked if we could prove who we were and if anyone could vouch for us professionally. Ossie offered her a business card, which didn't cut the mustard as anyone can run off cards on their computer these day, so he showed his driving licence and gave the name and number of a police chief inspector in Huddersfield who would vouch for him.

I upstaged Ossie by producing my passport and telling him that I had brought it with me in case they didn't let me into 'the north'. I didn't mention the fact that you have to present a passport even for internal UK flights when you buy e-tickets over the Internet, though I suspect from the smile on her face DCI Artmitage did know that. As to who could vouch for me, I had no option but to give her Rudgard & Blugden's number and just hope that Veronica didn't answer the phone and throw a wobbler when she heard I was helping the police with a murder enquiry.

Because it had to be murder. Even in the most depressing parts of Manchester, people didn't keelhaul themselves.

DCI Armitage stepped outside to use her mobile on the patio of the hotel which overlooked the canal basin. Police vehicles were still arriving and there were four or five uniforms on crowd control as guests checked in and out of the hotel and I saw one or two bristling confrontations with middle-aged men in suits with cameras around their neck. Ossie pointed out that this close to Granadaland we should expect the paparazzi to be on 24/7 alert, though I suspected they were ambulance-chasing freelancers hoping to sell a shot to the *Evening News*.

When she'd finished her calls and then given orders to about forty assorted uniforms, SOCOs and plain-clothes officers, DCI Armitage came back inside and I thought I saw a slight spring in her step.

'Well, that's you two checked out,' she announced. 'There's a police car outside which will take you to headquarters where you can make official witness statements. You may have a solicitor present if you wish. Then we'll have to take fingerprints from you both, as you've already told me you've been on board that houseboat. We'll need them for elimination purposes only. Then you'll be free to go with our thanks for your cooperation. Is there anything you need to do; anyone you need to tell where you are?'

Ossie said: 'As long as we can get a lift back here so I can pick up me car. It's round the other side of the basin on Potato Wharf. I gave one of your lads the registration mark.'

'Of course we'll do that, with pleasure,' she said. 'And what about you, Mr Angel? Is there anyone you should call?'

I looked at my watch.

'I suppose I should try the airport, as I'm not going to make my six o'clock flight am I?'

'I shouldn't think so. If you're stranded, I'm sure we can find accommodation for you.'

'Not necessary, love,' said Ossie totally oblivious to the killer look she gave him for calling her 'love'. 'He can come home with me.'

'To Yorkshire?' she said dryly.

'Absolutely,' he said, positively bristling with pride.

'Then the least I can do is get someone to change your flight, Mr Angel. Do you have your ticket on you?'

'Yes I do, but please don't go to any trouble,' I said.

'It's all part of the service,' she said with a smile and produced her mobile from her shoulder bag. 'Shall we step over to the desk?'

I did as I was told, not understanding why she wanted to move away from Ossie, but seeing no reason not to, and put my Air Berlin e-ticket down on the reception desk while she speed-dialled a number.

She gave her name and rank and asked to speak to 'Victim Support' and then someone called Doris. When she made contact, she told 'Doris' to get on to Air Berlin, quoting the reference number she read off my ticket, and tell them to re-book me on the first available flight back to London tomorrow. Then she covered the mouthpiece of her phone and said:

'Will that be soon enough?'

'After a night in Yorkshire?'

'I feel your pain,' she said quietly with a big grin.

A few hours ago, I had found body parts in a canal, but I'd probably get over that; and then a police officer had taken to smiling at me in a very familiar way. Now I was scared.

She finished giving instructions, said 'Thanks, Doris' and closed her phone but remained leaning against the desk and she was still *smiling* at me.

'When I rang your office, you know, to check you out...'

Oh God, what had they said?

'They told me, among other things, that you were married to Amy May, the fashion designer.'

I wondered which particular blabbermouth I had to thank for that.

'Guilty as charged,' I said nervously.

'I just *love* her tops and that last range of bootlegs she did,' said the senior investigating officer, all warmth and goofy smiles.

'You wouldn't like to ring her, tell her I'll be late?' I pleaded, and saw her expression change even as I spoke. 'Oh well, never mind, I suppose I'd better do it.'

'What do you mean me *as well*?'

'When you left this morning, didn't you notice that your mother hadn't come home?'

'Well, I noticed she didn't get up and make me boiled eggs

with Marmite soldiers, but then she hasn't done that since I was eight. Come to think of it, she's *never* done that. So I probably didn't think to check the maximum security granny annexe this morning.'

'Don't call it a granny annexe,' Amy said patiently, 'it's an attic bedroom.'

'You call it the Anne Frank wing!' I countered.

'I'm allowed to be rude, she's my mother-in-law. Aren't you the slightest bit interested to know where she is?'

'From what you've said, I'm guessing she spent the night wearing a paper suit and woke up in a police cell in downtown Cambridge.'

'Spot on. It seems your idea of a girls' night out got a bit out of hand.'

'My idea? Is Mrs Bond all right?'

'Nice of you to ask. Yes, she's fine, apart from a Gothic hangover – well, that's how she described it. It seems she was in the Ladies' when it all kicked off.'

'When what kicked off? No, don't give me details, just tell me in which pubs and clubs I can't show my face now.'

'I'll draw up a list when I've a spare hour or two,' said Amy with a sigh. 'All you need to know is that Jane and your mother's big night out somehow got intertwined with a big hen party of girls from Girton or Newnham or one of the colleges. Anyhoo, your mother tried to lecture the girls on the dangers of marriage, monogamy and men in general. One thing led to another, voices were raised, drinks were spilt, bottles thrown; you know how it goes.'

'Don't these places have bouncers?'

'Your mother put two in hospital.'

'She always did fight dirty,' I said.

'And stupidly, because she did it right in front of their security cameras.'

'Sounds like an open and shut case.'

'That's exactly what the magistrate said this morning.'

'You didn't go to the court, did you?'

'No, but Jane Bond did.'

At least that was something. A personal appearance by Amy would jump my mother's case into a different league of press coverage.

'The magistrates are waiting for some sort of social responsibility report before they sentence her,' Amy said.

'She pleaded guilty?'

'Oh yes, thought it was quite a hoot, the whole thing. Mind you, I suspect she was still pissed. She's been bragging about getting an ASBO ever since she got home.'

'At last she gets letters after her name! Where is she now?'

'She's gone for a walk across the fields to clear her head so she can think straight, or at least that's what she said.'

'She may be gone some time. Apart from that, is everything OK at home?'

'Yeah, we're fine; bonding nicely between naps, feeds and nappy changes. How's your day been?'

'Oh, you know, the usual...'

Detective Chief Inspector Heather Armitage thanked us politely for our cooperation and let us go about six-thirty, providing a police car and two uniformed constables to escort us back to Ossie's mum's Fiesta. The two uniforms didn't say much, but made it clear that their orders included hanging around until they were sure we were on our way and didn't try returning to the crime scene.

Not that I had any desire to do so. There was an ambulance and more police cars parked at the Potato Wharf end of the basin and two female officers were guarding the towpath. We could not see the *Felix Dacia* from there, but the sight of two white-overalled SOCOs unloading a black body bag from the ambulance was enough to curb my enthusiasm for any more sightseeing.

Ossie wasn't keen either, but then he was getting hungry. Once in the car, the first thing he did, even before starting the engine, was take his mobile out of the glove compartment and check his messages. He said 'Oh-oh' at one of them and pressed dial. It seemed to be answered immediately.

'Hello Mam,' he said into the phone which was tiny and seemed to have completely disappeared into his paw. 'Just got your messages. Sorry, but I've been a bit tied up this afternoon. Yes, with my associate from London. I'm still with him. As a matter of fact, he's missed his flight home so I was wondering if he could sleep over.'

If I hadn't gone into shock at the very idea of a sleepover at Ossie's mum's place – he lived with his mum? – I would have screamed in protest, but Ossie left me no room to stage a dignified retreat.

'No, don't you worry about that, we'll get our tea on the way home and mebbe we'll see you for a bite of supper later on. Aye, the usual. We'll see you at the office then. Love and kisses.'

He snapped the phone shut and casually threw it back into the glove compartment, then he started the car.

'Honest to God that wasn't necessary,' I said with a deep sincerity which Ossie totally misunderstood.

'Don't be daft; what else were you going to do? Catch a train?'

'I believe they still run north to south and it's not even dark yet.'

'I suppose you could have wasted good money on a hotel.'

'It wouldn't have been my money,' I argued, 'and then I could have flown back tomorrow.'

'I'll get you back here to the airport tomorrow no problem. Meantime, we can discuss tactics.'

'Tactics?'

'On how we handle the case. We have two clients to satisfy, so we'd better get our stories straight.'

'I'm not sure I have a client any more. I was hired to find Benji Nicholson and if that's him under the barge, or what's left of him, then that's "JD" – Job Done as far as I'm concerned,' I said, using one of Ossie's favourite phrases. 'And you may not have a client at all if Giancarlo Artesi continues to help Greater Manchester police with their enquiries.'

'Aw come on, you can't believe a sweetie like Artesi snuffed his boyfriend, can you?'

'He was probably the last person to see Benji alive; he was very reluctant to come on board the houseboat; and most murder victims are killed by somebody they know well. It doesn't matter what I think, it's how all that adds up to the cops.'

Ossie released the handbrake and reversed the car into a turn, carefully missing the police car which had delivered us.

'Let's let them sort it out then and see how the land lies tomorrow and find out if there's any bits and pieces we can pick up. There's a lot of mileage in being associated with a murder case, you know. It could be good for business.'

'What makes you think the cops will throw us any scraps?'

'You seemed to be well in with that female DCI.'

'We share the same taste in designers,' I said.

Ossie frowned at me, jammed the car into first gear and we pulled away from the Castlefield Basin.

'Anyway, nowt more we can do here, so we might as well chill out and have a night on the town. I reckon we deserve it.'

'Would the town in question be Huddersfield by any chance?'

'You're not wrong there,' said Ossie.

We turned up the Liverpool Road and drove by the Castlefield Hotel and the police vehicles parked there, and then past The Ox, and then Ossie was cutting through the early evening traffic and we were heading for the Ring Road and the unknown.

Or at least Yorkshire.

Ossie decided to take me by the scenic route through Oldham, then over the moors on the A62, and it was a light enough evening to show off the spectacular view. Perhaps it was always this light in the evenings this far north.

I asked Ossie if Artesi had told him anything about Benji's TV project, which the waiter in The Ox had referred to as *Europol*, and he said that other than what Giancarlo had told us that morning about the difference between Interpol and Europol, the subject hadn't come up.

'So you've no idea what this TV programme's about, then?'

'Have you?'

'Not a clue. I wonder how they're coping without a scriptwriter.'

'Very well, I should think. They've probably not missed him yet, but maybe we should have a word with the line producer if we can find out where they're shooting.'

'The waiter in The Ox said Sheffield.'

'Then I might have a few ideas.'

'Well don't keep them to yourself,' I said with a sneaking suspicion I might regret that.

There was a loud burbling noise from the Fiesta's glove compartment...

'That's a message for me. Get it will you?'

I located Ossie's mobile in amongst numerous petrol receipts, menus from Chinese takeaways and at least two 'Disabled' stickers and pressed the most obvious buttons. Miraculously, a text message appeared on the screen.

'It says: Hv tkn yr scoots to office luv mum,' I read.

'Fair enough,' said Ossie, sounding very satisfied.

'Does that make any sense?'

'Perfectly. Me mum's taken me scoots to the office.'

'Scoots?'

'Scoot boots.'

'And you need this particular footwear in your office because...?'

'You can't half talk funny when you want to,' he chortled, having become visibly more relaxed now that we had crossed the Yorkshire border. 'The "office" is what we call The Kayes Arms, because I have my office on the top floor. I rent it from the brewery.'

How could I have forgotten that Ossie's office was above a pub? It was the thing that had first endeared me to him.

'Oh, I see. So you need special footwear to enter this pub and your mother has arranged that?'

Ossie smiled a really big and very unnerving smile.

'You'll see, Angel, you'll see.'

* * *

What struck me most coming down off the high moors and into Huddersfield was the number of street lights. There seemed to be millions of them stretching in all directions. It was the one thing I had noticed after moving out of London to the Cambridgeshire countryside: when it got dark, it really got *dark*. But up here it seemed that they said 'to hell with the electricity bill' and lit up not only every main road but every village street and probably a few farm tracks and goat paths as well.

Ossie told me that we would grab a 'quick bite' in a place called Marsden and that I was in for a rare treat. He said it in such a way that I suspect he had done this before to unsuspecting, soft southerners far from home.

I could smell the fish and chip shop before I saw it, but suddenly, round a bend in a road bordered by unforgiving dry stone walls, was the car park fronting the neon-lit frying emporium signed: Willy Elliff's Fish Bar.

'You stay where you are,' said Ossie having parked and turned off the ignition. 'I told you it was my treat.'

He got out and left me to stare at the sodium orange glow which I guessed was Huddersfield and count the number of cars which zipped by, although a fair number pulled in to the car park. Willy Elliff obviously had a reputation for something, and when Ossie returned after less than ten minutes, I discovered what for.

'Better open the windows,' Ossie said handing me a paper parcel. 'If me mum smells cod 'n' chips, she doesn't half get the munchies.'

I wound my window down and began to open the parcel on my knees, which were already getting uncomfortably warm. Under about five layers of greaseproof was a piece of fried cod no bigger than a rugby ball, enough chips to feed a village primary school and a small polystyrene cup with a plastic lid and a wooden fork.

'I didn't get you the Monster Cod,' said Ossie blithely, 'as I didn't want to overface you.'

'That was thoughtful of you,' I murmured and began to eat, putting all thoughts of what I had seen that afternoon behind me.

'These are bloody good,' I admitted.

'The secret is he uses beef dripping, not sunflower oil or whatever it is they use down south. You won't find fish and chips like this south of Doncaster nowadays. Try the mushy peas.'

I levered off the lid of the cup and dipped the wooden fork into the green slurry.

'Delicious,' I said, and I meant it, though Ossie seemed not to believe me.

'It's not guacamole, you know.'

'I know what marrowfat peas are,' I said, 'and you can still get them in London wherever you get jellied eels, but they're not usually cooked for this long, and I do like the way you put vinegar and sugar on them.'

'My, my, quite the connoisseur, aren't we?'

'I have put quite a range of unusual things in my mouth over the years,' I admitted and then, just to wind him up: 'A glass of cold Semillion Chardonnay would go down very nicely with this.'

'I can do you better than that,' said Ossie with complete confidence. 'They serve Tetley's bitter at the office.'

I had fantasised about what Ossie's office would look like ever since I had heard about him, mostly using American *noir* films of the Forties as a frame of reference. He was, after all, the first proper private detective I had met: the lone white knight pounding the mean cobbled streets of dark, satanic northern mill towns. In my mind's eye I had envisaged him sitting behind a desk with his feet up, bottle of bourbon and a tooth glass within easy reach in the top drawer, hat pushed back on his head. The whole scene would be lit by a desk lamp with a green shade and intermittent flashes of neon light coming in through the venetian blinds from a fizzing sign which said 'Hotel' hanging from the outside of the building. He would, of course, have a snappy line in dialogue when the young blonde with a missing little sister came to hire him. But that was in my imagination. In reality, his opening chat-up line would probably be: 'Have you tried the mushy peas at Willy Elliff's Fish Bar, love?'

Ossie parked the car near the George Hotel and the station. I made a note of both of them in case I needed a bed or an escape route later that night, then he guided me, as I'd requested, to a 24/7 convenience store where I was able to buy a toothbrush and some disposable razors and a fresh pair of socks, even though they were official Huddersfield Town football socks.

The Kayes Arms, Ossie's 'office', turned out to be a large Victorian building which had probably once been the cornerstone of a large mill complex, but the other buildings were long gone and the site had been redeveloped into shops and offices. In turn, they had gone through an economic decline and were now mostly charity shops, greetings card shops or jobcentres.

The pub was lit up and open for business and, according to the sign showing a happy fox-hunting gentleman savouring a pint, it did indeed sell Tetley's beer. Other signs advertised pool tables, live music, hot food, 'basket meals', Sky TV and that there was a function room available.

Ossie led the way in through a side door rather than the main entrance. It was an unlocked door which opened immediately onto an uncarpeted staircase and we clumped up it. On the first floor was a set of brown swing doors with the words 'Function Room' stencilled on them in faded gold paint. Ossie kept on clumping upwards, and on the second floor there were similar doors except with a modern plastic sign saying 'Toilets'.

'One more flight,' wheezed Ossie. 'Can't complain; it keeps me fit does this.'

The stairs were narrower here and would certainly be a hazard for the paramedics if they had to carry Ossie down to street level if he had a heart attack or a stroke while at work, which from the sound of his breathing seemed a distinct possibility.

The second floor had two office doors, both with deadlocks and Yale locks, and they both had plastic signs with black lettering. The door on the right said: Oesterlein Investigations; the one on the left said: Bartholomew & King, Master Tailors.

Ossie jerked his thumb at the sign.

'He's not really Jewish and there aren't really two of them,' he said as if I'd asked a question. 'It's a Russian guy called Bartosz Konius; thought he'd do better if he changed his name to Barty King. A lot of foreigners do that. Then later on he thought it would be good for business if he put the "and" in between so it sounded like a double act. He's a lovable old git and he makes all my suits.'

'I suspected you didn't buy that one off the peg,' I said, and

Ossie took it as a compliment and shot the cuffs of his jacket before unlocking his door and clicking a light switch.

His office was a disappointment, with not a trace of the ghost of Philip Marlowe or Sam Spade. The walls were white and the furniture had come flat-packed. There was a filing cabinet in one corner, a computer on the desk and one wilting potted palm in a pot near the solitary window. The compost holding the palm was peppered with cigarette butts.

'Ah, good girl,' Ossie was saying.

'Excuse me?'

'Me mum's been, and left me boots.'

He moved around the desk and sat down on a swivel chair which creaked ominously as he reached down for something on the floor, then he placed a pair of very large, wing-tip, pointed-toe python skin cowboy boots on the desk so I could admire them in all their glory.

'Me scoot boots,' he said proudly.

As if on cue, there came a loud electronic roar from somewhere beneath our feet, the sort of burping sound which always comes from very powerful amplification equipment being set up by people who don't know what they are doing and have left the volume controls turned up to 11. The rumble of feedback seemed to make the floor vibrate and the window shake in its frame, but was gradually replaced by the muffled sound of voices and applause.

And then the music started.

Dear God, the music.

Ossie had kicked off his shoes and was pulling on his boots.

'Welcome to Line Dance Heaven,' he said with a huge grin, but I knew I was really in hell.

*   *   *

I had never seen so much fringe in one place before and felt sure there should be a Health & Safety regulation about it.

The function room of the Kayes Arms was positively heaving with Yorkshire cowboys and cowgirls, the men wearing fringed shirts, *bolo* ties and, as Ossie told me, authentic Santa Fe Cattleman straw cowboy hats. Most of the women wore fringed cowgirl skirts and fringed jackets and big-brimmed hats, many of them cherry red or white, often matching their white or pink cowgirl boots. Everybody seemed to have a wide leather belt with a big oval Jack Daniels buckle.

Above all, they all had boots and they knew how to stomp them as they marched and wheeled in time to the twanging guitars and the gentle thump of the bass line. I imagined this would be the result if Dolly Parton had been given a free hand to choreograph a Nuremburg rally.

Yet this was by no means a white supremacist meeting. Among the dancers, which were roughly fifty/fifty male and female, and of all ages from fifteen to seventy by the look of them, there were Caribbean, Indian, Pakistani and Chinese faces. In fact, the only person in the room not wearing a cowboy hat apart from me was a Sikh with, incongruously, a Confederate 'stars and bars' badge clipped to his turban.

Even Ossie, when he pushed his way through the crowd with two foaming pints of beer, was wearing a hat.

'Here, get this down you, you look as if you need it.'

I did.

'Nice hat,' I said, when I surfaced from the pint glass.

'It's me mother's spare, it's a Minnetonka.'

'A *what*?' I had to ask.

'It's a hat what folds up so she can carry it in her handbag.'

'Lucky she had it; you don't look under-dressed now.'

'I shall miss me panama, though,' he said ruefully.

'Claim it on expenses,' I suggested and he cheered up immediately.

In fact he cheered up a bit too much.

'Do you fancy a dance then?'

I gulped some more beer down.

'With you?'

'Not with me, you daft apeth, just in the line. C'mon, it's easy.'

'I'm not really a dancer,' I said, anxious not to offend him.

'Fair enough; but I'll warn you now, my mother doesn't take no for an answer.'

'Mothers never do,' I shouted to be heard over a song which sounded to be about losing your heart on the Love Trail or something. 'That's their job.'

In my mostly misspent youth I had heard some pretty loud rock bands, and then I actually played in some raucous jazz bands who could demonstrate, without amplification, why the walls of Jericho needed shoring up, but the disc jockey orchestrating this particular hoedown seemed louder than any of them. Perhaps it was because I wasn't used to the music, with its persistent yet somehow tinny one-two, one-two beat and the whining guitar or fiddle solos that went nowhere. Or perhaps it was the mawkish lyrics to the songs, which I found impossible to tune out of my head; or the claustrophobia of being in a strange room with a hundred or more total strangers all dressed as faux cowboys and stamping their feet roughly in time; or maybe I just hadn't had enough to drink.

Yes, that must have been it. I squinted through the marching, turning lines of dancers and flying strands of fringe and located the door which led down to the main bar of the pub. Taking my life in my hands I cut across the dancing traffic and made it before I had to endure the end of a song about yet another lonesome cowboy who was too far down the *lurve-less* trail to turn back.

Downstairs in the saloon bar, I stood at the bar and ordered two pints, amazingly getting change from a £5 note and noting that there were some advantages to living up north. Above my head the floor of the function room thudded and creaked as if a Roman legion were up there, breaking in a new delivery of hobnail boots, though none of the regular drinkers at the bar seemed to notice or worry about the specks of dust and flecks of plaster floating down through the smoky atmosphere and landing in their beer. Perhaps they were just grateful they couldn't hear the song lyrics clearly down here.

I picked up the beers and set off back upstairs. Ossie was waiting for me at the top outside the function room and linking arms with him was a woman with long blonde hair, wearing a beige suede fringed jacket and three-quarter skirt, a red Stetson and red boots patterned with white roses. This being Yorkshire, they just had to be white roses. They wouldn't wear boots with a red rose on around here, not even to muck out after the rodeo.

'This is Angel, Mum,' Ossie said above a song which seemed to be saying that a weekend was two long nights of love, and most of the line dancers sounded as if they agreed from the way they joined in the chorus.

'He's certainly my angel, if he brings me a drink,' said Ossie's mother in a broad Yorkshire accent.

'I wasn't sure what...' I started but she flashed me a smile and held out a fringed sleeve to take one of the pints of bitter from me. Ossie took the other.

They clinked glasses and toasted me, then Mrs Oesterlein said:

'Didn't you get yourself a drink, luv?'

'It's down on the bar,' I said, flustered. 'Didn't think I could carry three.'

'Well, nip and get it, Angel, you've got some dancing to do and there's that much body heat in there, you'll be sweating cobs. I know I am.'

'I don't really dance,' I said weakly.

'Have you got a belt on?' she asked, and not knowing if this was some Yorkshire code or not, I took the question at face value.

'Yes.'

'Have you got thumbs?'

'Just the two,' I said, showing her by giving her a double thumbs up sign.

'Can you stick them in your belt?'

'I suppose so.'

'Then you can dance. Go get your pint and come and get in the swing of things. Ossie's friends, the Cudworth Posse, they're all here and they want to meet you.'

'Who? Why do they want to meet me?'

'Because I told 'em they had to. Anyway, they could be the solution to all your problems.'

I hadn't really been aware, apart from a missed Air Berlin flight, that I had many problems until I had fetched up at the Kayes Arms, but I was pretty sure I had now.

CHAPTER EIGHT

'She got you *line-dancing*?' Amy said again, once she'd stopped laughing hysterically.

'Sure as shootin' she did. You don't argue with a woman like that.'

More laughter. I could hear her gasping for breath.

'Did you have to wear a cowboy hat?'

'No, they didn't have a spare, so I was excused the hat – and the scoots.'

'Scoots?' she spluttered down the line.

'Scoot boots; that's what we lonesome cowpokes here in the Wild West – or at least the Wild West Riding – call our dancing boots. Actually, they were quite an eye-opener. I've never seen so many endangered species utilised as footwear in one place at the same time.'

'Did anyone take any pictures? Do they have a website?' she giggled.

'I certainly hope not. There were some cowboys there who are definitely outlaws and probably wouldn't have liked their pictures taken.'

'It sounds real classy. You never take me anywhere that interesting. Anyway, where are you now?'

'I'm at Ossie's house.'

'Don't you mean ranch?'

More giggles.

'Ha, ha. Actually it is out in the country and you could run a few hundred steers out here should the whim take you. In fact, I think Mrs Oesterlein is cooking one for breakfast.'

'He lives with his mother?'

I lowered my voice.

'Just as well he does, as I reckon she's the brains of the outfit.'

'There's a whole outfit?'

'We call it a posse,' I said before she could. 'And they might turn out to be useful.'

'Are you ever coming home from the range?'

'Ossie's driving me to Manchester this afternoon, so I'll get my flight back, albeit a day late. You holding up?'

'I'm fine. It's kinda peaceful without you.'

'How are the children?'

'The baby's fine; your mother is sulking up in the attic and hasn't shown her face yet this morning. She did ask if I could recommend her a solicitor, though.'

'She's not thinking of pleading Not Guilty is she?'

'I've a feeling it's about something else. Said she wanted some advice on a point of law.'

'Try and find her an honest one.'

'Is there any other sort?'

Now it was my turn to laugh hysterically.

'I'll ask Jane Bond if she knows what's going on,' Amy said casually, 'when she comes round this afternoon to help me interview prospective nannies.'

'You're hiring a nanny?'

'I'm thinking about it.'

'Without me there?'

'But of course. Better hurry on home, pardner.'

Ossie and his mother – 'You call me Cathy, love' – lived in a ranch-style bungalow called, no word of a lie, *Ponderosa*, about six miles outside Huddersfield at a place called Emley Moor which was famous for having one of the tallest TV transmitter masts in Europe. It certainly looked big from the Oesterleins' kitchen window as we gathered for breakfast and I couldn't resist asking what would happen if it fell over. Ossie just shrugged his shoulders and said the last time one had fallen over it had missed them.

Of course, I'd seen the aircraft warning lights flashing from the mast a long way off the night before as we had driven back from the Kayes Arms, but my beer-fuddled brain hadn't taken in just how big the thing was up close, nor how close I'd be sleeping to it.

The Gunfight at the Line Dance Corral, as I thought of it, had ended just after eleven so that most of those good old cowpokes and cowpokesses had time to buy fish and chips before catching their last buses home, which I'm pretty sure was a scene missing from *Red River* or any other classic western come to that.

But in truth it hadn't been that much of an ordeal, mainly due to frequent trips to the bar. Ossie had warned me to be careful, as the beer was stronger up north. I knew it wasn't, it was just they drank more and when in Rome...

At least the alcohol nullified some of the cringeworthy lyrics. I didn't so much mind the tunes, or the fact that they were essentially all the same, but the lyrics were something else. By the time I reached the pint of no return, I was thoroughly sick of hearing how 'dancing up and down the line' would be 'a love trail' to 'my kind of all-woman'.

And Cathy Oesterlein had been gentle with me, showing me the steps and telling me when to clap my hands (not easy with your thumbs in your belt) or stamp, or do a toe and heel to the side. At one point, she pulled my head uncomfortably close to her fringed bosom so she could make herself heard, to tell me that she also did Appalachian dancing in her spare time and that had steps called things like *Bucks*, *Indians*, *Windmills* and *Drink, Puppy, Drinks* but I wasn't sure I believed her.

The biggest bonus of the night, though, was meeting the Cudworth Posse and realising that Ossie had brought me there for a reason, and not just cultural enlightenment. While we had been helping Greater Manchester police with their enquiries, Ossie had asked to phone home. As we weren't suspects in what was still officially a 'suspicious death' until an autopsy pronounced it a murder, the cops saw no reason why he shouldn't tell his mum that he was going to be late.

They're considerate that way up north.

I don't know how Ossie had briefed his mother, or how much she knew of the case already, but he had obviously mentioned that he was interested in a television company filming in Sheffield and so she rounded up the Cudworth Posse.

Cathy introduced me to them as Dave, David and Colin, though it was hard to tell them apart in full Line Dance regalia. She then confused me further by saying they were all called Smith, but they were cousins, not brothers; and that they were called the Cudworth Posse because they all lived somewhere called Cudworth, which I'd sort of worked out even though I had no idea where it was.

The really interesting thing about Dave, David and Colin Smith was that, for day jobs, they worked as electricians in the family firm of, confusingly, Smith & Nephew. More to the point, they had been working in Sheffield for about three weeks on a job rewiring some student flats for the university there. Not that they usually worked as far away as Sheffield, they assured me, but these days they had to be prepared to travel to compete with the growing number of Polish electricians who charged lower prices, kept appointments, always cleaned up after themselves and didn't see the point of tea breaks. I made the right growling noises and showed them my sympathy face, sharing their pain at having to put up with such unfair and unreasonable competition.

The flats they had been working on were on the edge of the Netherthorpe district of Sheffield. 'Around Broad Lane, tha' knows,' Dave had said with a very obvious wink-and-a-nudge; although it might have been David or even Colin.

I pretended to know what he meant by nodding wisely but it didn't fool Cathy Oesterlein.

'It's what they call a red light district,' she said. 'Though why they think you should know that is beyond me. I bet their mothers don't know *they* know such things.'

From the look on his face, Ossie was quite surprised that his mother knew such things, but fortunately the conversation did not dwell on that point.

It turned out that, from wherever it was they had been working, the Cudworth Posse had seen a mobile catering truck turn off Broad Lane and into the Netherthorpe area every morning around eleven o'clock. When this happened three days running, one of them (possibly David) went to find it, thinking it might be a fish and chip van. It turned out to be the lunch wagon for a film crew and, though the Cudworth Posse did try and sneak a free lunch, they were told politely to piss off.

They were not overly disappointed. After all, they had their own 'snap', as they called it, along with several thermos flasks of tea, so they weren't going to beg for a plate of some foreign muck like the lasagne or moussaka the lunch truck was serving up. And it wasn't as if there were any famous film stars they could get to sign autographs.

'Didn't recognise anyone of 'em,' said the one I was pretty sure was Colin. 'Not one face off the telly. In fact, most of 'em seemed to be foreigners, though the woman doing most of the acting was a bit of a belter. She could have got a right trousering given half a chance.'

'David Smith!' snapped Ossie's mum, 'Don't show yourself up, you mucky little bugger.'

'But she really was a fair bit of stuff, Mrs O,' he said defensively. 'Tall and blonde and dead pretty; held herself like a queen.'

'As long as she was the one doing the holding. Anyway, I thought you said she was foreign?'

She said it as it if being 'foreign' and 'fair bit of stuff' were mutually exclusive; but there again, 'foreign' to her probably started at Doncaster.

'She was. I think all of them were. We couldn't understand a word they said.'

'What exactly were they filming?' I asked, loudly enough to be heard over the stomping coming from the function room.

Standing in the stairwell leading up from the saloon bar of

the Kayes Arms was hardly the best place for a case briefing, if that was what we were doing, but at least out here the coordinated thumping of cowboy boots helped drown out the lyrics to 'Dancin' Down The Love Trail' or whatever it was the disc jockey was playing.

'Looked like some sort of cops-and-robbers thing to me,' said Dave. 'Lots of running in and out of the old houses and the derelict foundries.'

'Foundries?' I asked, not sure I'd heard him right.

'Sheffield – City of Steel,' said Ossie dramatically as if he was narrating a documentary. ''Course it's all gone bollocks now. The steelworks have gone the same way the coal mines have round here.'

'Language,' warned his mother.

'It was called *Unit*,' said the one who was definitely called Colin, 'probably about some special tactical unit or special forces; summat like that.'

'How did you know what it was called?'

'That's what it said on all the arrows.'

'Arrows?'

'There were, like, road signs with "Unit" on them tied to the street lamps and the regular traffic signs all around the area. That's how we found the lunch truck.'

'That just means "Film Unit" and they are put up by the location managers to help direct the crew into where they're going to be filming that day.'

'So it might not be the right film crew?' said Ossie carefully, not wanting to suggest his mother had got it wrong.

'What're the odds on two films being shot with foreign actors in Sheffield at the same time?' I said. 'And we know it's about Euro cops.'

'Oh, there were plenty of cops around. Real ones, from Sheffield,' David confirmed enthusiastically. 'And some from Leeds and even some of our local ones from Barnsley. We recognised them.'

'You did?'

'Oh aye, it was them told us to piss off.'

I got the guest bedroom at the *Ponderosa*, which came with *en suite* bathroom, although there was only a shower in there, as Ossie had said apologetically, and if I wanted a bath in the morning, I could have one just as soon as his mother had gone to work. As it turned out, I had enough trouble washing my face in the sink and thought for a moment that they had pulled a practical joke on me, as I just wasn't able to stop the soap from bubbling up like crazy foam. Then I remembered, through my hangover, that the water up in Yorkshire was soft (just about the only thing that was) as opposed to the harder water of Cambridge and East Anglia. It did seem to improve the tea I was offered at breakfast, though, which is just as well as there was no coffee on offer.

I had rung Amy from the Oesterleins' lounge, which had French windows offering a spectacular view south over the countryside, and then joined them at the breakfast bar in the kitchen. Ossie was dressed in jeans, white T-shirt and brown leather jacket, with more than a passing resemblance to Tony Soprano, if Tony Soprano ever read the *Yorkshire Post* over his bacon, eggs and fried bread.

'Everything all right at home?' Ossie asked without looking up from his newspaper.

'Seems so. I've got another day's house leave.'

'Did you reverse the charges?'

'I...er...'

'Don't listen to him, Angel; he's just playing silly buggers. He claims all the phone calls on his business anyway; I know because I do his books for him. He just likes people to think he's tight – his father was just the same. Fried breakfast do you?'

Mrs Oesterlein didn't appear to be giving me much choice in the matter as she busied herself over the cooker. She was wearing a frilly pink and white apron over a blue jacket and skirt suit, black stockings and black shoes with low chunky heels. The long blonde hair of the line dance had been a wig worn over a short curly perm of black hair. Either that or she had a personal hairdresser living above the garage. She had swapped the Annie Oakley look for the middle-aged businesswoman with just a hint of nostalgia for Mrs Thatcher in her prime image. I was willing to bet she wore a string of pearls under the apron.

'Please don't go to any trouble on my account,' I said, even though she was already draping slices of bacon into a pan. 'I've imposed on you enough.'

'Did you hear that, Ossie?' she asked over her shoulder. 'That's what you call *manners*. Let's hope some of Angel's politeness rubs off of you. It's honestly no trouble, love, one egg or two?'

'Just the one, thank you,' I said politely and caught Ossie scowling at me behind his mother's back. 'But only if I'm not making you late for work or anything.'

'Don't worry about me, I'm on flexi-time,' she said, 'but I'll need my car today, so you'll have to take that beast of yours. I'm amazed you can get it in the garage, what with all your radio equipment. Has he told you about his hobby, Angel? He's a ham radio geek. Takes after his father that way too. He used to lock himself in the garden shed for hours on end then he'd come in and tell me what the weather was like in Goa or some such place I'd never heard of. Why he couldn't just tune in to the BBC and find out what the forecast was for Bridlington on a bank holiday, I just don't know. That would have been some use.'

Ossie raised his eyebrows to the ceiling, then went back to studying the *Yorkshire Post*.

'Now sit yourself down, Angel, and mind out because your plate's hot,' ordered Mrs Oesterlein, so I did as I was told, joining Ossie at the breakfast bar as she put a plate covered in thick slices of bacon and fried tomatoes, with a fried egg sitting atop half a slice of fried bread.

'You're spoiling me, Mrs Oesterlein. I don't get this at home.'

'I should think your wife has enough on her hands, what with a baby and her being a top-notch designer.' She was certainly well briefed. 'Has she ever thought of designing for the older woman?'

I looked up innocently and waited until I'd stopped chewing bacon before I said:

'And how would that benefit you?'

It took her about five seconds, then she smiled broadly and flicked at Ossie's newspaper with the back of her hand.

'He's good, Ossie, you could listen and learn from Angel.'

Ossie merely grunted and hid behind the racing section.

She began to untie her apron.

'But wouldn't the famous Amy May have any fashion tips for me?'

'Depends what image you want to project,' I answered, dipping a forkful of fried bread into the yolk of my egg. 'Is it for work?'

'Oh yes, it helps in my job if you can scare the shit out of people at first sight. Saves time in the long run.'

'Then Amy would say,' I paused with my fork in the air as if getting psychic instructions, 'that what you're wearing comes across as very professional, but you should remember your accessories. I think she'd suggest a single string of fat pearls, for instance. They don't have to be real, just big and shiny.'

I had guessed right. As the apron came off and she smoothed down the suit jacket, there, round her throat, was a necklace of imitation pearls. Probably without meaning to, her fingers fluttered to the necklace and she smiled.

'Then Amy would say you can never have too many accessories,' I added.

'That is *so* true.'

'So she would suggest gloves. Brown leather or suede, if only to carry them.'

She spread the backs of her hands in front of her and examined them.

'Yes,' she said to herself. 'That would work.'

'And Amy's rule of life is that to impress, always wear the highest heels you can suffer in silence.'

It was as if a light bulb had come on just above her head.

'She's dead right, especially as I work mostly with men. I'm just going to change my shoes and then I'll be off. You boys have a nice day in Sheffield and I hope to see you again soon, Angel. Do give my best to your lovely wife; she's so clever.'

As she swept out of the kitchen, she scooped up a faded, soft leather briefcase from one of the chairs. I hadn't noticed it before but now I saw it bore a worryingly familiar embossed crest.

'You don't work for Customs & Excise, Mrs Oesterlein, do you?' I asked hesitantly.

'Well, technically, it's all Her Majesty's Revenue and Customs these days, but I still call it the Inland Revenue. I mean, you know where you are with the Inland Revenue, don't you? Have a nice day.'

'You too,' I said meekly.

'So we're going to Sheffield, are we?' I asked Ossie, as he loaded our dirty plates into the dishwasher.

'Thought you might like to tag along, seeing as how your plane isn't 'til six. We can have a snoop round Sheffield and then I can drive you the pretty way to Manchester.'

'There's a pretty way to Manchester?'

'Certainly is, through the Peak District National Park, up by Ladybower Reservoir on the Glossop road.'

That meant almost nothing to me, but it was his home turf after all.

'Are we looking for anything in particular?'

'Clues. That's what we're paid for, isn't it?'

'Are we still being paid, though? Do we still have clients?'

'Well I have,' said Ossie pugnaciously.

'I thought your client was helping Greater Manchester police with their enquiries.'

'They let him go about nine o'clock last night,' he said, and for a second I thought he was going to be smug about it and not tell me how he knew, but he couldn't resist showing off.

'He left a message on my office answerphone.'

'You mean he was trying to phone you at the Kayes Arms while we were one floor down scooting our boots?'

'Well, I always turn me mobile off when I'm dancing,' he said with prickly heat. 'It would be downright rude if...'

'Yeah, yeah, I get the line dance etiquette bit, but what was Artesi's message?'

'Oh yes, well they got him to do a formal identification and when he'd finished throwing up, they gave him the third degree but in the end they reckoned that if he'd done his partner in, the last thing he would have done would be go to the local cops to report him missing and then hire a private detective to find him.'

'Actually, that's *exactly* what I'd do if I murdered my mother,' I said without thinking. 'To divert suspicion.'

Ossie put his giant head on one side and gave me the look they probably reserve in Yorkshire for people who don't follow cricket.

'You mean your partner.'

'What?'

'You mean if you did away with your partner. You said "mother".'

'Did I? I just meant "domestic",' I said quickly. 'So what did Artesi have to say?'

'Keep on digging. He wants to find out what happened to Benji.'

'Do we know what happened to him? I mean, how he died?'

'They'll do an autopsy later on today, but he sure as hell didn't keelhaul himself. He was dead when he went in the water, but the Manchester cops wouldn't let on how. And of course they've no idea *when*, but from what I saw, he'd been in that canal for a couple of weeks at least.'

I tried not to think of what I'd seen in that inky water, especially not after Mrs Oesterlein's fried breakfast.

'The cops, especially your girlfriend DCI Armitage, seemed really keen to know if Giancarlo had been to Sheffield recently.'

'Well, if the film crew has been working in Sheffield, that makes a sort of sense,' I said. 'I ought to check with my client, see if he wants me to carry on. After all, we have *found* Benji Nicholson, just not alive.'

Ossie stroked his chin as if he had an imaginary goatee beard.

'Well, you're stuck up here until this evening, so why not get the day on expenses? As far as your client knows, you're still on the case. I mean, there's been nothing on the news. Anyway,' he waved an arm to indicate the view from the kitchen window, 'it's a cracking day for a drive across the Peaks.'

'I thought your mother had taken the car?'

'She's taken hers, right enough. We'll be going in The Beast.'

When Ossie pulled up the garage door I saw The Beast and immediately thought it was a shark.

'Oh no, the one they call the shark, that was the 1959 model,' Ossie corrected me. 'This is the 1960 version; it's much more subdued, much smaller fins.'

'Do you really intend taking me to the red light district of Sheffield in a Cadillac convertible?'

'Yes.'

'Well how cool is *that*?'

Ossie beamed when he saw I approved, then his face creased.

'Of course, if we're going on to Manchester, we'll have to stop for petrol,' he said thoughtfully, adding: 'Maybe two or three times.'

'I'll stand this fine creature a tankful,' I said rashly. 'As long as I can keep the receipt. Just how big is the tank, though?'

'Supposed to take 25 gallons, but that might be American gallons. I think there's a difference.'

'There is. The US gallon is smaller than the old UK imperial gallon and the American pint is smaller that the British pint, but the American fluid ounce is bigger than the UK fluid ounce.'

'How come you know stuff like that?' he asked, genuinely interested.

'It comes in handy when you're getting drunk in America.'

'You've been to the States?'

'Lots of times.'

'Good job you didn't tell the Cudworth Posse that last night, they'd have talked your ears off. Have you driven one of these before?'

'It's got wheels, hasn't it? I can drive it.'

'Then let's put the top down, put on our sunglasses and hit the road.'

'I didn't bring any sunglasses,' I said. After all, I'd been coming north, why would I need sunglasses?

'There's loads of spare pairs in the glove compartment. Help yourself.'

'Thanks.'

I did some mental maths. A 25 US-gallon tank would be roughly 20 imperial gallons, which meant about 90 litres these days.

'Ossie,' I asked, 'how much is petrol in Yorkshire?'

Ossie insisted on driving as far as the M1 motorway. I don't think he trusted my ability to steer nineteen feet and two tons of vintage Cadillac out of his garage, let alone down the narrow country lanes, without scratching the magnificent chrome bumpers or getting the white-wall radials dirty. It was a genuine 1960 Caddy, and Ossie was quite right about this version being far more conservative than the 1959 version with the outrageous fins at the back – hence the nickname 'the shark'. It was a two-door, left-hand drive (of course) automatic, with an immaculate black paint-job and a dark red interior, the front bench seat divided by a fat armrest. With the top down and stowed away, there was enough room at the rear to play pool on the boot.

Ossie told me he had bought the Cadillac dirt cheap from an American Air Force sergeant stationed 'down your way', by which I presumed he meant one of the USAF bases in Suffolk. It was, he said, a good little runner, only needing a new fuel pump and new brakes, and had a 'genuine' 54,000 miles on the clock.

I just smiled and nodded my approval, despite the fact that I hadn't believed an odometer reading since I was twelve.

He steered us majestically down twisty lanes and through villages called Emley and Flockton and Midgely, giving a running commentary on the pubs we passed with names like Green Dragon, George & Dragon and Black Bull, being particularly proud of the Green Dragon in Emley which he claimed was the first pub ever to serve chicken-and-chips in the basket, back in the late Sixties. To be fair, he also pointed out the Yorkshire Sculpture Park with its collection of Henry Moore sculptures with almost as much enthusiasm, and I also got the full story of Bretton crossroads (which just looked like a crossroads to me) and how it was haunted by the ghost of a young girl who had fallen off the pillion of a motorbike, again in the late Sixties, presumably on her way to try chicken-and-chips in the basket.

And then we were on a slip road leading to the motorway at a place called Woolley Edge, which Ossie (still in full tourist guide mode) told me used to be a big pit, or coal mine as we soft southerners called them. The only pits left now were heritage museums, but in its day Woolley Edge had been famous for its militant trade unionism and one of its shop stewards, a certain Mr Arthur Scargill, had gone on to make quite a name for himself.

I nodded and feigned interest in all the right places and then asked if it was my turn to drive yet.

'You can have a go,' said Ossie pulling over to the side of the slip road. 'But don't go above forty-five or you'll blow something.'

'Forty-five? Surely it can do more than that.'

'Don't push it; this girl is built for comfort, not for speed.'

'But people towing caravans will overtake us. Everybody will laugh at us,' I wailed pathetically.

'No,' said Ossie firmly. 'Everyone will *notice* us.'

And, of course, he was absolutely right. As we progressed regally southwards in the nearside slow lane, top down, sunglasses on, the cold Yorkshire wind whipping through my hair and skimming off Ossie's bald pate, every type of vehicle

which could carry a tax disc – and several that hadn't
bothered with one – zipped by us with ease. We did attract a
few tooting horns and the occasional wave from a passenger,
but mostly we drew admiring glances of curiosity from
women and drooling envy from middle-aged men. We must
have had our picture taken on a hundred mobile phones
before we reached the Sheffield turn-off and the only way we
would have got more attention was if the car had been
resprayed pink.

I let the Cadillac glide serenely to a halt and dropped the
gear lever into 'park' so that Ossie and I could change places.
I realised that we had only used the motorway so that I could
take a turn driving. Probably with justification, Ossie had not
trusted me on the cross-country route, nor was he going to
allow me to drive The Beast through the centre of Sheffield,
especially when I had no idea where I was going.

But first we had to get some petrol.

'Do you know the area those Cudworth boys were talking
about?' I asked Ossie as he negotiated The Beast carefully into
the mid-morning traffic heading for the city centre.

'Oh aye, I know where Netherthorpe is; it's the edge of the
red light district. Not that I know it intimately – if you see
what I mean.'

'Is it a rough area?'

'Put it this way, I wouldn't go there after dark unless I had
the Cudworth Posse to back me up.'

'Are they really such hard cases? I mean, they were real
friendly last night, and they looked quite cute in their scoot
boots and Stetsons and their fringed shirts,' I said more to
tease him than anything else.

'You take the piss out of those boys at your peril, Angel,

and I mean that. Line-dancing is one thing they care about –
Leeds United is the other. I reckon it gives them a sense of
discipline, as well as putting a bit of colour in their lives. Plus,
of course, it's a chance to meet women. You'd be surprised
how many middle-aged women – fit ones, mind you – use the
dancing to go on the pull.'

'No, I wouldn't,' I said.

'But outside the line and the music, there's very little they
care about,' he continued, 'and that's what makes them
dangerous. Look at me, for instance. I'm a big bloke who
looks as if he could handle himself, but I've never got into a
fight in my life. I wouldn't dare; me mother would kill me.
Then you look at Dave and his cousins: they just don't *care*
because they've never had anyone to care for them. Getting
hurt themselves, or getting arrested, or putting somebody else
in hospital – it just never occurs to them. None of them have
got anyone to remind them of the consequences of their
actions.'

'But you've got your mother.'

'Oh yes. That's what mothers do,' he said with conviction.
'Didn't your mother teach you the rules of life and make you
stick to them?'

When I didn't reply he took his eyes off the road to look at
me.

'Are we there yet?' I asked, wide-eyed and enthusiastic.

Ossie pointed out the university student flats which the
Cudworth Posse had been rewiring and said we were now on
Broad Lane coming up on Netherthorpe. As he drove,
occasionally acknowledging the admiring stares and
occasional wolf whistles from pedestrians and other drivers

(especially those driving rented white vans), he tried to keep up the tourist guide banter, but I could tell his heart wasn't really in it. He bemoaned the fact that Steel City had de-industrialised and was in danger of becoming trendy. Cyber cafés were replacing real cafés, where tea was served in white china pint mugs and beef baps were spread with dripping and not butter. Tapas bars were replacing fish and chip shops at a genocidal rate and the younger generation were flocking to clubs rather than pubs, though not 'proper' clubs, like working men's clubs, but clubs with loud music you could only jump to, not dance to, and expensive drinks which came in the bottle and were usually blue. He did point out one surviving pub which stood on its own on Broad Lane, a bit like the Alamo. It was called Fagan's and, he told me, had been named not after the pickpocket mastermind in *Oliver!* but rather Joe Fagan, who had been the landlord there for 38 years.

'Thirty-eight years in Sheffield?' I said before I could stop myself. 'Bloody hell, not even the Great Train Robbers got that.'

Ossie ignored me and concentrated on turning right. We were suddenly away from the main drag of buildings and, seemingly, the population of Sheffield, for there was, almost instantly, a complete lack of human traffic. The streets here were narrower and had at one time been given over to factories or foundries or warehouses. What domestic buildings there were tended to be in rows or terraces of between six and ten two-up two-down red brick houses with slate roofs. Most looked unoccupied, many of them dangerously derelict. On street corners, some had been converted into shops with iron grilles over the windows and metal doors with padlocks. One had a few crates stacked on the pavement and a sign saying 'Asian Vegetables', three out of four had signs saying 'Off-License' spelt wrongly.

'Nice area,' I said.

'I'm not leaving the car unattended round here, that's for sure,' said Ossie. 'That's why I brought you.'

He pulled in to the kerb by a street light and killed the engine. I turned and looked over the boot of the Cadillac, guessing it was something like the view a Navy pilot got when he took off from an aircraft carrier. Apart from half a dozen Asian kids kicking a football against a wall about two hundred yards back, there was no other sign of life on the street.

'Why have we stopped here, Ossie?'

In answer he simply raised a finger towards the street light, where there was a sign tied halfway up the post saying 'Unit' with an arrow pointing down the road.

'I reckon this is a good place to start earning our corn and asking a few questions.'

'Ask who? The streets aren't exactly teeming with witnesses,' I pointed out.

'That's why I'm going shopping,' said Ossie. 'These little shops are open all hours and I've found the people who run them keep their eyes open. They have to, otherwise their stock would disappear. That's why you're staying with the car, so that there are four wheels on it when I get back.'

'What do I do if someone tries to nick the car?'

'They won't nick the car, it's far too distinctive, but round here they might take the wheels off and then offer to sell them back to us.'

'What do I do if they try?'

I glanced up and down the street anxiously trying to spot gangs of marauding wheeljackers, but still the only sign of life came from the kids playing football.

'Toot the horn, I won't be far away and if the worst comes to the worst, there's a baseball bat in the boot. Or should I say "trunk"?'

'A baseball bat? Are you joking me?'

'Certainly not,' he said seriously. 'I told you it was a rough area.'

CHAPTER NINE

Ossie had said that the Cadillac was far too distinctive a car to steal and I might have added that it didn't go fast enough to appeal to the local joyriders. Even so, I felt pretty distinctive sitting in the passenger seat wearing a pair of fake Ray-Bans especially as the sun had gone in and at the best of times, sunglasses and Cadillac convertibles were rare enough sights in Sheffield.

Perhaps this was how private detectives should operate: not skulking in the bushes with telephoto lenses, but loitering very conspicuously in the middle of the street in the hope that someone would rush up and press some information on them.

Which was more or less exactly what happened.

Whilst Ossie was busying himself in the corner shops on the left side of the street, I watched in the Caddy's huge rear-view mirror as a middle-aged Indian or Pakistani man emerged from the shop which bore the sign 'Asian Vegetables'. I watched him study the car carefully then look both ways up and down the street before he started walking towards me.

I got a good look at him in the mirror. He didn't seem angry and he wasn't armed, unless he had a sawn-off under the brown work coat which is worn as a uniform in the retail trade in the north and is still often referred to as a 'smock'.

When you traded in your smock for a collar and tie, you knew you'd made it.

He called out when he got to the Cadillac's rear bumper, and I felt he was still safely out of range, should he make a sudden move to cosh me with a giant Ooli radish or immobilise me by pushing Scotch Bonnet chillies up my nose (something I had once seen done to somebody in a Bengali greengrocer's out in Southall).

'Hey up, there,' he said in the thickest Yorkshire accent I'd heard so far.

I turned in the seat to face him, way in the distance over the boot of The Beast, and returned his greeting politely.

'Good morning,' I said, flashing my teeth and removing my shades. 'I don't suppose you've seen a film crew around here?'

'I thought as much when I saw the car. Nobody else would be daft enough to drive that thing around these streets. How many does it do to the gallon?'

'Hardly any, but it's not my regular ride,' I improvised, 'it's a prop. It's for the film they're making, we're just delivering it. They pay for the petrol.'

'Well, you've missed 'em, I reckon,' he said, thrusting his hands deep into the pockets of his smock. 'Haven't seen them around here for a week or more, they just packed up and buggered off. One day they were cluttering up the street with police cars, next day they'd gone. I told the wife, we've never had so much community policing as we had when them foreigners were making that film.'

'Foreigners?'

'Right enough they were; most of them didn't speak proper English. That's why they went to Krusty's shop on Sibley Street. They didn't spend a Christmas sixpence in my place, even when I stayed open late for their night shoot as they called it. Not a friggin' penny, thank you very much. All the trade went to Krusty 'cos he speaks their lingo.'

'Do you think this Krusty might know where the crew went?'

'If anybody would, 'e would. 'E was quite taken with that leading lady they had. Got her autograph and everything.'

'And where would I find this Mr Krusty?' I asked hoping and praying that the answer did not include circuses and clowns with big feet.

'His right name's Kruszczyński and he owns the Polish deli on Sibley Street. That's down here to the bottom, turn right, and Sibley Street is the second on the left.'

'Thank you very much, kind sir, you've been very helpful. I'd come in and buy some fresh chillies from you, but I don't like leaving the car here.' I waved an arm vaguely over the dashboard. 'You understand?'

'Oh aye, wise precaution,' he said, then he put two fingers in his mouth and whistled loudly.

Down the street, the six or seven boys kicking a football stopped their game and looked towards him as he yelled instructions in Hindi.

'My sons'll look after your car while you come in the shop,' he said, straight-faced.

'Which of them are yours?' I enquired as I climbed out of the Cadillac. It seemed only polite.

'All of them. Couple more and I'll have me own team.'

'I bet people have said that to you before, haven't they?' I said and a faint smile flickered across his face.

'Plenty have and I always tell them that with United and Wednesday playing the rubbish they're playing at the moment, I might end up with the only decent team in Sheffield.'

I had the Cadillac purring and gliding next to the kerb as Ossie emerged from the third shop he'd checked out, munching on a Mars bar.

'They know nowt useful round here,' he announced as he loomed over the sill of the car door.

'Well I've been busy,' I said, 'and what we need is Kruszczyński's Polish deli round on Sibley Street. That is where the film crew hung out, it seems.'

'By heck, you've got into bed with the locals bloody quick,' he conceded, walking round the Cadillac and opening the passenger door. Then he stopped and looked down at the brown paper bag on the seat.

'What's this then?'

'A pound of mixed chillies. Watch out for the little ones. They're called Scotch Bonnets and they're hot little buggers.'

'What am I supposed to do with these?' he asked, picking up the bag and holding it the way you see dog-walkers holding blue carrier bags after an early morning spell of pooper-scooping.

'Give them to your mother to cook with. I thought chilli con carne would be a big hit sitting round the old chuck wagon.'

'She makes that out of a tin.'

'I can give her a recipe.'

'She'd probably listen to you. After all them fashion tips you gave her, you might as well teach her to cook as well.'

He dropped his backside on the bench seat with such force that I was bounced so that my knees hit the steering wheel. Then he settled down with the brown bag on his lap like a prim old lady guarding a handbag as I steered the huge Caddy round the narrow streets carefully avoiding parked cars and vans, which at any moment might have leapt out and scratched the holy paintwork.

Kruscinksi's delicatessen was only a minute away round the corner and I parked right outside, discovering that the Cadillac was actually longer than the shop.

Even before I had turned the engine off, the multi-coloured plastic curtains which guarded the open door had parted and a jovial, round face topped with a shock of white hair and bisected by a large bushy moustache seemed to have floated through almost like a balloon on a string. The disembodied face smiled at us.

'Are you Lea's people?' the face boomed at us.

I looked at Ossie and he looked at me and shrugged his shoulders.

'Might be,' he said to the face, which I didn't think helped much.

'With a car like that, you must be film stars!' said the face, now grinning madly.

'Hardly film stars, but we are here about the film, Mr Kruszczyński,' I said as the face pushed through the curtain, bringing a body with it. 'It is Mr Kruszczyński, isn't it?'

'Yes, yes, I'm Kruszczyński. Did Lea tell you about me?'

'Who the bloody hell is this Lea?' growled Ossie.

Mr Kruszczyński said a rude word in Polish which neither

Ossie nor I needed translating, then flapped his arms enthusiastically.

'Lea Klemm is a world class actress and the star of the film which features this very shop! Come in and I show you.'

'Thank you,' I said in Polish, which put a spring in his step as he turned and bobbed through the curtain, his arm beckoning us to follow.

'What's he talking about?' Ossie asked as we disembarked from the Cadillac.

'I've no idea. What does it say in the script about a Polish delicatessen in the red light district of Sheffield?'

'What script?'

'The film script Benji wrote.'

'I've never even seen a script. Should we have read it?'

'One of us should.'

Mr Kruszczyński turned out to be a mine of information, all of which he was willing and enthusiastic to share, even when I pointed out that whilst we were not directly involved in making the *Europol* film, we did represent (or so I implied) the producers and we were checking that everything was going to schedule.

I didn't really need to lie or bluff Mr Kruszczyński; the fact that we had turned up wearing sunglasses and riding in a Cadillac seemed to convince him we were 'film people'. The only flicker of doubt to flit across his friendly face was when he asked us if Lea Klemm had remembered him – and perhaps sent a message?

'I'm sorry,' I had to admit, 'I've never met Lea Klemm.'

'I have,' he said proudly.

And he had proof. In fact he had a shrine.

I followed him down an aisle of shelving which displayed

Polish delicacies on both sides. I spotted jars of baby beetroot, red cabbage salad, pickled dill cucumbers, Fasola (beans) and flaki, a Polish 'ready meal' of tripe and vegetables on my right, whilst to my left I noticed bags of Krupczatka flour, whole grain rye bread, packets of instant soup (chicken, borsch and cucumber flavours), tins of cod in tomato sauce and smoked sprats. At the end of the aisle was the cash desk and behind that, on a high shelf to prevent self-service, were bottles of regular vodkas (lemon, rowanberry and bison grass), the really strong stuff (even I could translate the Polish for Rectified Spirit) and plum brandy, as well as cherry syrup and blood orange drink.

But Mr Kruszczyński was waving a hand to show I was looking at the wrong objects of desire. I lowered my gaze and saw the display of photographs he had pasted onto the end of his cash register. Some were actual photographs, some had been cut out of magazines, a few looked to have been printed off the Internet. They were all of the same tall, blonde woman and sometimes she had her hair long, sometimes in Brunhilda-style plaits, sometimes piled high in an old-fashioned beehive. In all of them, she was either scantily clad, often in a uniform of some sort, or the clothes she was wearing had been accidentally shredded by a hedge-trimmer; and she was obviously skilled in the art of posing provocatively with convenient props such as motorbikes, rolling pins and even a lamp-post. In other words, any object longer than it was broad.

'That must be Lea Klemm,' I said, proving I really was a detective after all.

'Those are only pictures I can display,' explained Mr Kruszczyński, 'without offending my Muslim customers. But I

have all Lea's films on DVD in my private collection. Those I
don't sell, just watch. I think you need a special licence to sell
them.'

'Porn films, are they?' Ossie said brutally, and I winced in
anticipation of how the smitten Mr K would take that.

Rather well as it turned out.

'You bet! Shit-hot porno. Lea has been top porno queen in
Poland for last ten years, though really she's German now –
but she was born in Stettin when there was Communism.
German father, Polish mother. Speaks several languages and
loves girls as well as boys in equal abandonment and in many
combinations.'

'Bloody hell,' breathed Ossie as Kruszczyński's words
tumbled out.

'I have followed her career since she was very young,' he
said, and almost immediately waved his hands as if scrubbing
out the words he'd just spoken. 'Not that she did kiddie-porn
or things like that. Child porno is disgusting and only for
paedophiles, and those paedophiliacs should be taken out and
shot in back of neck in my opinion. I even volunteer to do it.
No, my lovely Lea became porno star at nineteen and only
made respectable porn; no animals, no golden showers,
nothing like that.'

'Eh? What...the...?'

I glared at Ossie, willing him to be quiet, and noticed that
he was blushing.

'Oh sure, Lea would sometimes dress up as a schoolgirl, or
even a nun in a convent, but you always know it was not a
real schoolgirl or a real nun, it was always Lea. She is
wonderful actress; very supple.'

'You mean "subtle",' Ossie butted in.

lf visited here when they told her I was her Number One
She loved my shop, said it reminded her of home. She
ght a bottle of *Jarzębiak*—' he pointed over his shoulder
the shelf displaying rowanberry vodka, 'with a twenty
nd note and told me not to bother with any change, so I
ve her some plums in chocolate when she left. She said she
ould send me a message to tell me if she liked them.'

'I'm sure she did, Mr Kruszczyński, and I'll be sure to ask
er when I see her.'

That cheered him up, even if it puzzled Ossie.

'You will be seeing her?'

'Just as soon as we catch up with the film crew. What
exactly were they filming round here?'

'To begin with, it was what they called "exteriors" for setting
the scene and was not very exciting because Lea was not
needed for those. Then they filmed the police raiding the houses
and that was more exciting, especially when they rescued all
those girls. But the best was when Lea came to the set and did
her scenes in the back of a police car out there in the street.'

'She didn't…like…get her kit off in the back of a police car,
did she?' asked Ossie, whose jaw had dropped open again.

Mr Kruszczyński looked at him with disdain.

'I told you, Lea is now straight actress. This was not porno,
this was artistic drama and it will make Lea a star here in
England just as she is in Poland, Germany, Romania and
Hungary.'

'These houses they were filming, the ones with all those
girls in need of rescuing,' I said gently to get him back on
track, 'were they here on Sibley Street?'

'My good God, no; they were round the corner in among
the old factories in Dunjohn Street.' Kruszczyński stopped

'He knows what he means,' I said. 'I thi
has followed Lea's career with interest.'

'Oh yes, yes I have. I have scrapbooks a
sites bookmarked on my computer, but noth.
to seeing her here *in my shop*, even though no
actress and doesn't do the porno any more. She
be sad and that my collection of her films w
valuable collector's items, then she signed a big pl.
herself and added three kisses.' He made three larg
the air with a finger. 'I have had it framed and no
in my bedroom. It's very tasteful picture of Lea as sh
in her new film. Even my wife says she looks very sma
uniform.'

'Your wife doesn't mind your little...enthusiasm?'
asked, open-mouthed.

'Not at all,' he smiled. 'She thinks it good I have su
hobby, that way I don't pester her too much and she has m
free time.'

'Your wife's a Yorkshire woman is she?' I said because
couldn't resist.

'Yes she is, how did you know?'

'Shot in the dark. This picture Lea gave you; you said she's
wearing a uniform. What sort of uniform?'

'The new blue German police uniform. Very smart, very
sexy. She told me it was a publicity shot from the film.'

'That's the film she's making at the moment, called
Europol, right?'

'Yes, yes, and some of it filmed right here in Netherthorpe.'

'Will we see your shop in it?' asked Ossie.

'Sadly not in the final film,' he admitted. 'But all the film
people, they came in for snacks and drinks, and of course Lea

himself as if he'd just applied a handbrake to his brain. 'But I knew nothing of them and now they have all gone. Anyway, it was all just a film. It was all in the script. Lea played the detective, you know.'

It was becoming clear to me that we ought to stick to the script, or at least read the damn thing.

'When did they finish filming here?'

'Two weeks ago. It's been very quiet round here since.'

'I'll bet,' I said. 'Once the film crew circus leaves town, all the glamour goes with them. I don't suppose Lea said where she was filming next did she?'

'Birmingham,' he said confidently. 'She had to do some scenes in Birmingham and she asked me if there were any Polish restaurants there. How would I know? I've never been there. Then she said she would be in London, where she was looking forward to going shopping for new clothes.'

'Doesn't look like she spends much on clothes,' said Ossie pointing to the Lea collage on the cash register. 'Those DVDs you were talking about. Where can you buy them?'

'I'd stick to treating your mum to some plums in chocolate if I were you,' I told him.

'I was only thinking of David and the Cudworth boys. They were quite taken with her,' he muttered sulkily. 'They'd have been over her like a rash given half a chance.'

Mr Kruszczyński nodded in agreement.

'It is a constant problem for her. Poor Lea always has men chasing her.'

'Anyone in particular?' Ossie asked, showing me his mind was back on the job.

The Pole hunched his shoulders.

'She travels with a big minder so that no one can get too

close to her, though there was one, perhaps. He came in a big flash car, a Mercedes – German of course – and drove her back to her hotel.'

'Was he one of the film crew?'

Kruszczyński shook his head.

'None of them seemed to know who he was, but Lea certainly did. She was very friendly with him, or maybe she was friendly with his money. She was all over him like you say, like a rash.'

Ossie reached into his jacket for his wallet and took out the passport photographs of Benji which Giancarlo Artesi had given us.

'Was it this bloke?'

Kruszczyński carried on shaking his head.

'No. I've never seen that bloke before. It's definitely not the man in the Mercedes: he was older and wore a suit. He had very short hair. Not bald, like you, but very short. Lea called him "Terry" and she knew him *very* well, if you know what I mean.'

'Or maybe she really is a good actress,' I said. 'It's been nice chatting to you, Mr Kruszczyński. Let me have a half-bottle of that *Cytrynówka*, would you, and then we'll get out of your hair. Oh, and could you do a till receipt for my friend?'

As Kruszczyński scented a cash sale, Ossie leant in to me and dropped his voice to a whisper.

'What's up? I thought we were just starting to get somewhere.'

'We are,' I agreed. 'I think the "Terry" he was talking about is my client.'

'Oh, bugger.'

* * *

We left the shop with our purchases. Me with the bottle of lemon-flavoured vodka in a brown paper bag and Ossie clutching a box of plums in chocolate. His mother was in for a treat: at least four different varieties of chilli, plums and chocolate, which just about covered all known food groups.

Kruszczyński had told us that the *Europol* film crew had been mostly working around the corner in Dunjohn Street so we crawled round there in the Cadillac as Ossie refused point blank to let it out of his sight. He had already put a crick in his neck glancing over his shoulder while we were in the delicatessen.

Dunjohn Street was the most obviously run-down bit of Netherthorpe we had seen to date, a backstreet of terraced houses and boarded up shops. There wasn't a living soul in sight and probably hadn't been anyone actually living here for twenty years.

With no obvious sign of lurking car-jackers, Ossie parked and we patrolled the left side of the street.

'Bit of a ghost town, isn't it?' said Ossie, though I noticed he seemed more interested in the street and the gutter rather than the empty houses.

'Film crews are supposed to leave locations exactly as they found them. Couldn't have been much of a challenge here. What are you looking for?'

'Them.'

He pointed to a scattering of cigarette butts in the road about two feet out from the gutter.

'Bet you anything that's where they placed the camera,' he said bending over to pick up one of the butts.

'And all film cameramen smoke, do they Sherlock?'

'Very few in my experience and never on the job, but the

script girls and the continuity girls smoke like chimneys 'cos they have to wait around so much, and they usually hang out just behind the camera.' He held up a long butt for inspection. 'See? Only women waste so much of a cigarette and all these filter tips have got lipstick on.'

'That means nothing these days. Anyhow, so what?'

'So it means they were probably filming that house over there on the other side of the street. The one with the repaired door.'

He gave me a glare, defying me to question his logic.

'OK, I have to ask. Why the house with the repaired door?'

'Because they would have smashed the original door down for the film. It's a cop show; they always smash a door in.'

'Are you sure you haven't read the script of this thing?'

'Now that would have been too easy, wouldn't it?' he said smugly.

I was beginning to understand what Dr Watson had had to go through, but I trooped after him and let him put his shoulder to the (now I was up close) obviously fake door made mostly of hardboard. It gave easily and allowed us into a dank hallway which reeked of damp wallpaper and urine.

'We should have brought some torches like the ones they have on *CSI*,' I said. 'Then we would have looked like real investigators.'

'I never could understand why the daft buggers didn't just put the light on,' said Ossie, flicking on a wall switch and illuminating unshaded bulbs in the hall and on the stairs.

'Nobody likes a smart arse,' I hissed.

'I'll take the upstairs,' he ordered, 'you do the front room and the kitchen, and try not to touch anything.'

'Best not to leave fingerprints, right?'

'No, I just meant don't touch anything because the place is downright unsanitary. Gawd knows what you could catch in here just by looking at it. This sort of place is a proper breeding ground for germs.'

'What do you mean "this sort of place"? What sort of place?'

I may have sounded a bit dim, but then Dr Watsons are supposed to be slow.

'Well, it's a knocking shop, isn't it? Bound to be.'

The downstairs front room didn't reveal anything, at least not to me. It was empty apart from two broken chairs and a carpet which had fungus growing on the edge nearest the grimy window. The kitchen at the back of the house did show signs of habitation judging by a pile of matter-encrusted saucepans in the sink and on the draining board, not to mention two plastic dustbin bags full of metal foil containers from takeaway meals, giving off a faint whiff of sweet-and-sour.

'Up here,' Ossie shouted down the stairs, 'but watch your step.'

I tiptoed up the stairs thinking he must have meant that the treads were rotten, but when I got to the landing I saw the need for his warning. The worn and dirty red carpet outside the three doors was dotted with cigarette burns and must have had thirty used condoms trodden into the pile.

Ossie was standing in the nearest of three open doorways.

'Bedrooms 1 and 2, but they come unfurnished apart from wall-to-wall mattresses, giving that padded cell feel. Surprisingly clean considering the traffic they must have had and there's still a faint pong of disinfectant. Bathroom's quite clean too and there's no sign of any used needles, which is usually a dead giveaway. You'll have noticed the doors of course.'

'What *exactly* would I have noticed?'

'The fact that they've got bloody great padlocks on the outside, not to keep the punters out, but to keep the girls in.'

'Oh sure,' I lied, 'I noticed *that*.'

I looked down at my feet, careful of where I was treading between the condoms.

'But this is going a bit far for a film set, isn't it?'

'I don't reckon them things are props, Angel, and I'm surely not going to pick one up to find out. They don't look particularly fresh, do they?'

'I really wouldn't know, I haven't read your latest monograph on the bio-degradable properties of lubricated rubber products.'

'No need to talk dirty,' he protested.

'So what went down here, Sherlock?'

'I think the *Europol* crew were using this place for local colour. You know, a bit of realistic background. It was definitely a knocking shop, but it went out of business quite recently. There's no sign of any female clothes, no make up or anything in the bathroom, not even a toilet roll. The place was cleaned out.'

'There's pans and cooking stuff in the kitchen,' I said to prove that I'd detected something.

'That don't count. If the girls were being moved on quick like, they wouldn't stop to pack the saucepans.'

'So somebody did a moonlight flit before the film crew arrived? Is that what you're getting at?'

'I don't know. They left sharpish, that's for sure. The water and electricity are still connected.'

'I noticed that too,' I said quickly.

'But most of this just flummoxes me, as me mother would say and I never could think straight on an empty stomach. Isn't it nearly dinnertime? I know a cracking pub on the road to Manchester.'

He did too: the Snake Pass Inn out on the A57 just past the watery expanse of the Ladybower Reservoir (where the Dambusters did their practice runs) in the Peak District National Park, that patch of staggering natural beauty which shoulders apart steel city Sheffield and mill town Manchester. On the road to come were the High Peaks and Kinder Scout and Snake Pass itself (which I only knew from radio traffic reports warning when it was closed by snow during the winter), but we weren't there for the scenery; we were there for lunch and, to justify it on expenses, a 'case conference'.

Ossie recommended pints of Black Bull bitter and the sausage and mash, which came served with a Yorkshire pudding, and when it arrived I tried to ingratiate myself by saying that this was indeed God's own county.

'Yorkshire certainly is,' Ossie said with grit in his voice, 'but we might be in Derbyshire here.'

Sometimes you just can't win.

'Wherever. We'd better get down to cases, then. What have we got?'

Ossie looked around, but the restaurant was less than a quarter full and all the other diners had wisely steered clear of our table, though I couldn't think why.

'We've got a dead gay scriptwriter who nobody, except his boyfriend, seems to have missed.'

'That's hardly fair,' I argued. 'His *partner* was the first to miss him and my client hired me because the producers, or at least the money-men behind the film, they missed him too.'

'That would be this Terry guy, who turned up on location in Netherthorpe two weeks ago sniffing around Lea the Porn Star?'

'Terry Patterson, he works for a German investment bank in London.'

'And he drives a Mercedes up from London to pick up a well-known German porn star, who seems to be playing the lead.'

'Hang on, what are you saying here? Anyway, I doubt if Lea Klemm is a really well-known porn star. I'd never heard of her.'

'Nay lad, you're missing the point. What I'm saying is that if Benji's bumping off is anything to do with his gayness, then it's probably a "domestic" which puts my client firmly in the frame. If he got dropped because of the script he wrote for this bloody *Europol* nonsense, then that could put *your* client in the frame. See what I'm getting at?'

'You think we should see that script as soon as possible?'

'No. Well, mebbe we should. But what I'm trying to get across is that we need to work together, pool our resources and mind each other's backs. Are you going to eat that sausage?'

'Help yourself,' I said and must have blinked as his fork flashed over my plate.

'But you're probably right, you ought to try and read that script.'

'Why do I have to?'

'Because you can get a copy from your banker client.'

'You could always ask Giancarlo Artesi for one.'

'I doubt that,' he said whilst chewing. 'I mean, if you'd written a script or a book or anything like that, would you show it to the missus?'

'Probably not.'

'Then what makes you think Benji did?'

'He might have, and it's worth the ask. Remember, Artesi said he's taken home Benji's laptop. There's almost certainly a copy of the script in there somewhere.'

'Well, I'll ask him if you call your friendly Greater Manchester police lady and chase up how the autopsy went.'

'Why on earth should she tell me?'

'She might, she seemed quite taken with you.'

'She's more a fan of Amy's clothes than of me.'

'Get the wife to send her some free samples then.'

'Give me some legal advice, Ossie: would that be bribery or corruption?'

'I think it depends on who complains,' he said, seeming to give the matter some serious thought. 'Anyway, you should always keep in touch with friendly coppers.'

'Come off it, she wasn't that friendly.'

'Hey, she didn't bang you up and throw away the keys. That's a result in my book. Besides, she may have collared somebody by now and beaten a confession out of them.'

'Hardly likely. If Benji has been in that canal for up to a month, it won't be a quick investigation.'

'Then your lady cop should be grateful for any help. You should ring her right now. She gave you a card, didn't she? With her mobile number, I bet.'

'You don't miss much, do you?'

'We try not to in Yorkshire. You can use my phone, but dial 141 first to put the block on. She might have your number but

I don't especially want her to have mine.'

'Cheeky git,' I said quietly as I dialled.

I took the Greater Manchester police card out of my wallet and, sure enough, Detective Chief Inspector Heather Armitage had indeed given me a mobile phone number and when I rang it was she who answered, giving her name and rank, which surprised me but then chatting to police officers on familiar terms was not something I did regularly, or even willingly usually.

'Hello, Chief Inspector, this is Roy Angel. We spoke yesterday about Benji Nicholson.'

'Not much of a chat-up line, that,' Ossie hissed across the table in a whisper. What did he want me to say: *Hi, it's me, the guy who finds rotting bodies in your canals for you?*

'I'm so glad you rang, I tried your office in London but they said you didn't know how to use a mobile, so never carried one.' Thanks for the character reference, guys. 'I even left a message for you at the airport at the Air Berlin desk. Are you still in the area?'

'Well, I haven't managed to get home yet, if that's what you mean, and I'm not that far away, just taking in the scenery in the Peak District about 20 miles away. I was fully intending to catch my six o'clock flight. Why are you after me?'

That brought a stage wink of Cyclops proportions from Ossie, who then flexed his fist and arm in the universal 'giving it some' gesture.

'I wasn't really after you; I was trying to find your large Yorkshire associate, Mr Oesterlein.'

'Why, he's sitting right next to me, finishing my lunch.'

Ossie heard that and took it seriously. So seriously he stopped chewing.

'Have you been with him all day?'

'I've been with him since we left Manchester yesterday,' I said, wondering where this was going.

'Then I probably need to speak to you as well. Is there any chance you could come back into central Manchester before you go to the airport?'

'I'm sure that's possible. Whereabouts? Do we report to your headquarters at Old Trafford?'

'Actually I'm based down at the crime scene at the Castlefield Basin this afternoon. How about we meet at the Castlefield Hotel?'

'We could probably be at the Castlefield Hotel,' I said loudly to include Ossie, 'in about...?'

'Tell her two hours,' whispered Ossie. 'That'll give us time for pudding.'

CHAPTER TEN

'You've been arrested *again*?' Amy shouted down the phone.

'Not exactly.'

'What the sodding hell does that mean?'

'It means I'm helping Greater Manchester police with their enquires again and it looks like I might have to stay up here another night.'

'You're not actually having *fun* up there? In the north I mean; you're not actually enjoying yourself are you?'

'Fear not: I can't wait to get home. Although everybody's very nice up here. Really helpful and friendly.'

'There are other people in the room, aren't there?' she said.

'Absolutely.'

'Police?'

'Certainly.'

'Are you in trouble?'

'Comparatively speaking, no.'

Compared to being stretched and split on an autopsy table like Benji Nicholson, I was in clover.

'Did you take a change of underwear?'

'Not a stitch. I'll have to go shopping,' I said, thinking she could relate to that.

'Have you started to smell yet?'

'I've not had any complaints so far.'

Though she had a point, damn her.

'I bet you've been eating chips and deep-fried Mars bars,' she said petulantly and with just a faint hint of envy.

'You're thinking of Scotland, darling. I may be north of Sainsbury's but I'm not in the land of the midnight sun just yet.'

'Are you developing a Yorkshire accent? Because if you are, you can stay up there.'

'Now you're being paranoid, though I must say there's some wonderful countryside up here and the pubs are really cheap...'

'Stop it! Right now! You're scaring me.'

The trick to the successful manipulation of Amy was always knowing how far was too far to go. Given time, I felt sure I would judge that distance correctly.

'So how has your day gone, dear?' I changed the subject.

'Pretty damn good mostly. The baby has been sleeping and not bothering me; your mother, on the other hand, has been stumbling around the kitchen all afternoon looking for the gin, but that doesn't bother me much. What does bother me is that she's not so much hinted at going home. She won't even discuss the subject with me. I need you to have a word with her – or maybe your father would.'

'My father?' It was my turn to shout. 'Are you mad? Do you want to give him another stroke?'

'It was just a thought.'

'Didn't Jane Bond get anything out of her on their girls' night out?'

'Only that there seems to be a boyfriend waiting for her back in Romanhoe; somebody called Lyndon. Has she ever mentioned a Lyndon?'

'Not to me, but surely a pining boyfriend is a prime reason for her to go home, isn't it?'

'Problem is, according to Jane, she seems a bit frightened of him.'

'Frightened? My mother frightened of a Lyndon? Bloody hell.'

My mother frightened of *anything*?

Bloody hell.

The drive up and over Snake Pass in Ossie's Cadillac with the top down was spectacular. Slow, and distinctly chilly, but scenic. As we came down into Glossop, we had to stop for petrol, which I paid for on a credit card and allowed Ossie to claim the VAT receipt on condition he put the roof up on the car and agreed that we could dispense with the sunglasses. From there, we waved goodbye to the stunning countryside, found the M67 and then got on to the M60 motorway, which surrounds Manchester just as the M25 forms a noose around London.

When I managed to get a signal, which wasn't easy, I used Ossie's mobile to ring the office, offering a silent prayer that it would be picked up by Laura or Lorna, rather than Veronica. My luck held in that it wasn't Veronica, and then ran out.

'Angel? Do you still work here?' It was Lorna, who had never liked me.

'I am out in the field, at the sharp end of what is turning out to be one of the biggest cases Rudgard & Blugden have ever handled, so less of your lip, if you don't mind.'

'I'm *so* sorry,' she said sarcastically. 'I'm sure we should be grateful you've bothered to check in with us. This field you're out in, is it in this country?'

'Problems with the management?' Ossie asked and I covered the phone with my hand before I replied, then thought about it and took my hand away.

'No, just one of our work experience trainees still wet behind the ears,' I said, then back into the phone: 'Look, Lorna, I need you to do something for me.'

'*There's* a surprise. Are you sure a mere *trainee* can handle it?'

'I'll speak slowly. I want you to get hold of Terry Patterson at KSAG, that's a German bank in the city, Kredit Schwaben AG. Do you want me to spell it for you?'

'I'll manage somehow.'

'His phone numbers will be on the dedicated case file.'

'Which I bet hasn't been updated recently,' she snapped.

'Oh, give us a break! I've been helping Greater Manchester police with a murder investigation.'

'Is that on the file?'

'Not exactly,' I admitted. 'Not yet anyway, but that's why you have to use tact and diplomacy when you contact Terry Patterson. All I need you to do is fix up a meeting with him for tomorrow.'

'I'm not your bloody social secretary, you know.'

'Trust me, it won't be a social call, but I do need to talk to him as soon as I get back to London.'

'So you're coming back to London? Oh, joy.'

'Just set up the meeting, would you?'

'First thing be all right for you? Nine o'clock?'

'Now you're just being silly. You can get back to me on this number, which you should have somewhere, it's…'

'Ossie Oesterlein's mobile number,' she said smugly.

'Good girl, you should have been a detective,' I said and ended the call before she started swearing.

'You just can't get the staff these days,' I told Ossie as I handed back his phone.

'That's why I don't have any,' he said, 'except the Cudworth Posse, and they're strictly freelance.'

'Can't your mum claim them against tax for you?'

His face brightened.

'It's a thought. I'll ask her tonight.'

We drove into central Manchester and hardly anyone gave us a second glance; perhaps 1960 Cadillacs were ten-a-penny around here, or maybe they thought we were en route to a drive-by shooting and they didn't want to make eye contact. I didn't mind, I was just glad we'd put the top up as it had started to rain – and that made me happy, for no visit to Manchester would have been complete without a shower to moan about.

There were half a dozen police vehicles parked on Liverpool Road near the Castlefield Hotel, and I told Ossie to park up close to them on the assumption that they were unlikely to get parking tickets from wardens and we were safe from the police themselves as we were only there to help them, weren't we?

In the hotel foyer I approached the reception desk and got as far as saying 'Detective Chief Inspector Armitage—' before she raised a hand and pointed a finger towards the door to the bar which was guarded by a uniformed constable.

The PC standing guard told us to have a seat in the lounge area and that the DCI would be with us shortly. As we settled in a pair of leather armchairs, Ossie asked the copper 'Has she got the kettle on in there?' and the constable said no, Detective Chief Inspectors didn't normally make the tea, but if we wanted anything, we could order it from the hotel.

Consequently, we were hiding behind a pot of tea and a pile of toasted teacakes when the door to the bar opened and out came DCI Armitage. She had a uniformed policewoman with her and, between them, a small blonde female who looked about nineteen, dressed in a sombre black trouser suit. She had her blonde hair scraped back away from her face and her mascara had run where she'd been crying.

The three women stopped about ten feet from our chairs and the blonde in black raised her right arm and pointed at me. Didn't say a word; just pointed straight at my face. Then DCI Armitage nodded a signal to the policewoman who put an arm around the blonde's shoulders and all three walked towards the hotel door.

'Friend of yours?' whispered Ossie casually, but I knew he'd been spooked because he'd paused in his eating.

I saw Heather Armitage give a slight nod to the uniformed copper by the bar entrance and he stood up straight and tried not to look at us, but I knew his orders were to give chase if we tried to make a run for it. There was not much scope for that, as we would have had to trample over the three women in the doorway to get out and, in any case, Ossie hadn't finished his tea yet.

'That's Benji's sister,' I whispered.

'Probably here for the formal identification,' Ossie

whispered, holding his teacup in front of his mouth.

'Yes, that must be it,' I breathed.

I saw Phoebe Nicholson shake hands with DCI Armitage and then disappear across the concrete concourse and drop out of sight with the policewoman, presumably to get into one of the cop cars. Then Armitage pulled out her mobile phone and made a brief call before turning and walking slowly back into the foyer.

'Thank you for coming, gentlemen,' she said as she reached us. 'I'm just waiting for one of my colleagues to join us and then we can get started.'

'Started on what?' asked Ossie.

'Clearing up a few loose ends following our interviews yesterday,' she said and flicked us a polite but totally insincere smile. 'And I'd like to take statements from you individually, if that's OK with you.'

'It's not like we're joined at the hip or anything,' I said. 'Will it take long? I'm still trying to catch yesterday's plane back to Stansted.'

She didn't bother looking at her watch.

'It depends on what you can tell us.'

She turned to acknowledge a figure coming into the hotel. He looked just about old enough to drink as long as he remembered to carry his Proof of Age card, and even at his tender age he had probably heard all the jokes and jibes about people with ginger hair. He had a good tailor, though, for there was no way that three-piece suit came off the peg.

'This is Detective Inspector Jebb, who will be joining us. Thanks for coming, Tim. I thought we'd start with Mr Oesterlein. Shall we use the bar?'

'Thought you'd never ask, love.'

DCI Armitage winced. The smart young detective called Timothy Jebb winced. The uniformed copper by the door to the bar fought to suppress a smirk.

I just looked at the floor and pretended I wasn't with Ossie.

Somehow, he managed to keep them entertained for over an hour.

When the door to the bar opened and DCI Armitage, with spots of colour on her cheeks and her hair in need of a comb, signalled that it was my turn, I made a point of looking at my watch.

'I'm not going to make my flight, am I?'

'I'm very sorry, Mr Angel,' she said glaring at Ossie, 'but that took rather longer than I anticipated. Can we not put you on a late train to London?'

'My car is at Stansted Airport,' I said lamely.

'You could always stop over with us again,' Ossie offered. 'It's quiz night down the local pub tonight.'

I turned so that he couldn't see my face and softly pleaded with DCI Armitage: 'Arrest me – please.'

In the end, I settled for a phone call to Amy and they let me book a room in the Castlefield Hotel, where the staff were starting to recognise me, even if they didn't exactly welcome my custom.

Ossie said he would go for a walk while I was having my 'interview', which probably meant he was going back up the road to The Ox to try the rest of the menu. I think he was sulking but trying hard not to show it.

'Everything all right at home?' Heather Armitage had asked as I hung up the reception desk phone. She had stood close enough to me to hear my side of the conversation and, from the way Amy had been shouting, probably hers too.

'Oh, you know, one of those rash promises you make when you get married about how you'll try and get home every three or four days.'

'I'm a police officer, tell me about it. Better still, tell my husband.'

'He's not in the Job then?'

'He's a primary school teacher. Home by four o'clock every afternoon.'

'And all those long summer holidays,' I sympathised.

'Yeah, you've got to feel for him. Shall we get on with it?'

We sat around a circular table in the bar, which was not only closed off to the public, but the actual bar itself had a wire grille pulled down and padlocked so we couldn't help ourselves. It was almost as if they didn't trust us.

DCI Armitage sat opposite with DI Jebb on her left. There was no tape recorder in evidence and neither of them had pens or notebooks, though I bet myself that young Jebb had a Palm Pilot somewhere in the lining of that suit.

'This is an informal interview, Mr Angel. You have not been cautioned because you have not been charged with an offence, nor are you an official suspect in the ongoing investigation here in Castlefield Basin. You are perfectly entitled to have a solicitor present, though I hope that will not prove necessary.'

'Let's keep it friendly,' I said flashing my best teeth. 'Solicitors always bring a party down. Anyway, Ossie – Mr Oesterlein – didn't seem to need the good of one, so why should I?'

She rested her arms on the table and interlinked her fingers. I noticed she wasn't wearing a wedding ring, even though she'd told me she was married. Perhaps they took them off when on duty to make it easier to beat up suspects.

'I take it you recognised the young lady who was here when you arrived?' she said, suddenly all business.

'You mean the one who pointed me out like she was directing the wrath of God? Yes, that's Phoebe Nicholson, Benji Nicholson's sister.'

'So you do know her?'

'Not in the biblical sense. I only met her this week, at her mother's funeral.'

'Did you know the Nicholson family?'

'Not at all. I was at Mrs Nicholson's funeral because I was paid to be there. I was working.'

'Doing what exactly?' This from DI Jebb, in a distinctive Yorkshire accent, speaking for the first time.

'Looking out for Benji Nicholson. He didn't turn up, not even to his mother's funeral. Oi! Such disrespect. Can you credit it? Mind you, as we've discovered, he had a pretty good excuse for not going, him being dead himself.'

'You didn't mention this yesterday,' DCI Armitage scolded me.

'I told you I had been hired to find Benji by the bank that's financing this film he's written. They hadn't heard from him in about a month and thought there was a chance he'd put in an appearance at his mother's funeral. I was just doing the legwork.'

'Ms Nicholson told us there was something of an altercation at the funeral.'

'My phone went off. It wasn't a good time.'

'And then you chose to gatecrash the reception at a local wine bar.'

She said it like she was reading from a charge sheet.

'Hey, come on, fair play. I was invited in after giving some of the guests a lift.'

'You're not exactly inconspicuous for a private detective, are you, Mr Angel?' said DI Jebb smugly.

I thought about the Nicholson funeral, then how Ossie and I had clambered over the *Felix Dacia* in broad daylight, how we'd discovered bits of Benji Nicholson floating in the water and how I'd thrown up on the towpath. And then there had been me and Ossie kerb-crawling around the red light district of Sheffield that morning, in sunglasses and a classic Cadillac convertible.

'Possibly not,' I admitted. 'But can I ask what brings you here today?'

Jebb was surprised by the question.

'I'm here assisting DCI Armitage,' he said formally, as if for the record.

'But this isn't your usual beat, is it? The DCI introduced you as one of her "colleagues"; she didn't say you were one of her officers – her junior officers.'

Heather Armitage didn't allow him to rise to the bait.

'DI Jebb is working with us on secondment from South Yorkshire police on this enquiry.'

'I knew you weren't from around here, pardner,' I drawled, cowboy-style.

'And he'd be interested to know what you and Mr Oesterlein were doing in Netherthorpe this morning.'

'Getting the lie of the land, making a few discreet enquiries,' I said.

'Discreet?' Jebb spluttered. 'In a Cadillac looking like you were going to a Blues Brothers convention?'

'Inconspicuous – that's me.' Then it struck me. 'But our plan worked, didn't it? *You* certainly noticed us. How did you do that? And so fast?'

I made eye contact with Heather Armitage.

'When I rang you at lunchtime, you said you were looking for Ossie, not me. Have you got someone following him?'

'We've got better things to do in South Yorkshire,' growled Jebb.

'But somehow you knew we were in Sheffield this morning. What was it? You got cameras there with ANRS?'

Now I was showing off, which I knew was always a dangerous thing to do in front of policemen, but I'd read about the Automatic Numberplate Recognition System when it had been trialled by the cops in the West Midlands. Basically it worked like a speed camera but was tied in to the DVLA computer so that an image of a car's number plate went in one end and within seconds came back to the Bobby On The Beat with the owner's name and address.

'I don't have to reveal our methods to the likes of you. Let's just say you were observed in the Netherthorpe area and it's an area we have under observation.'

'Why?'

'That's our business. What was your business in Netherthorpe?'

I didn't see any advantage in annoying DI Timothy Jebb more than I had to, especially as I was getting no hint of protection from DCI Armitage. If anything, she seemed to be deferring to him despite being her junior in rank, years and the fact that his fingernails were better manicured.

'Benji Nicholson scripted a film called *Europol* and we heard, that's Ossie Oesterlein and I, that they'd been shooting on location in Sheffield, as indeed they had. We just went for a snoop around to see if they'd left any traces there which might give us a line on Benji and what happened to him.'

'Have you got a copy of the script he wrote?'

'No, I've never seen one.'

'Then how did you know they were filming in Sheffield?'

'A man in a pub told me.'

'Please don't piss us about, Mr Angel,' said Heather Armitage acting as referee.

'It's true.' Why didn't the police ever believe me? Or was it just women? 'A waiter in The Ox, just up the road, turns out to have been a film buff and had actually talked to Benji Nicholson. Didn't your lads pick up on that when they canvassed the area?'

They exchanged embarrassed glances, but I wasn't one to dwell on a moral victory.

'He told us the film was being shot in Sheffield and Ossie – Mr Oesterlein – narrowed it down to the Netherthorpe area and, as I was stuck up here overnight, we thought we'd give it a look.'

'Why?' snapped Jebb.

'No particular reason, just to see if there was anything to be seen. Turns out the film crew was there but moved on about two weeks ago. So, if there was a trail, it's well cold now.'

'Why were you interested in trailing the film crew?' asked Heather Armitage.

'Why are you interested in us being interested?'

'Do you always answer a question with a question?'

'Do you?' I said, playing hard to get.

It got a faint smile from her, but a scowl from Jebb.

'I was hired by the film's financiers to find their missing

scriptwriter. It seemed logical to ask around the film crew, but, like I said, we'd missed them.'

'But hadn't you already found Benji Nicholson?' Jebb said slyly.

'Are you asking me or telling me?'

'Don't start that again!' he snarled.

It was proving far too easy to wind him up.

'I found *something* under that houseboat. Are you telling me it was definitely Benji Nicholson?'

'It seems so, Mr Angel, though after several weeks in the water, identification is difficult,' said DCI Armitage. 'Miss Nicholson, however, proved very helpful and even supplied us with a DNA sample, which should confirm things in two or three weeks.'

'So it's only on *CSI Miami* that they get the results back within the hour?'

'I'm afraid so. The Forensic Science Service is very thorough but, by God, it's slow. However, we are ninety-nine per cent certain that the body in the basin was indeed Benji Nicholson, though of course there will be a formal inquest at which, of course, you might have to appear.'

'Can you tell me how he got to be under that boat?'

'I think I can, but I'm not sure whether I will.'

'Ossie thinks he was keelhauled.'

'I've no idea what that means,' she said, 'and I certainly don't want to read that in a tabloid newspaper tomorrow. If I do, I'm coming looking for you and your comedy double-act partner and, believe me, I can make your life a misery.'

'Join the queue,' I sighed, then tried reasoning with them. 'Look, who am I going to tell? Where's the percentage for me in going to the newspapers? The only person I have to satisfy is my client, who was concerned enough to worry about Benji being missing. Do I tell him Benji was murdered or died as a result of a bizarre canal boat accident? If he wants me to go on digging, you never know, I might turn up something useful.'

'Can't see that happening,' muttered Jebb.

DCI Armitage shot him the evils then took a deep breath.

'Well, this is pure guesswork, and until we get the pathologist's report, totally deniable, but it seems like Benji Nicholson was dead before he went into the water. Somebody put a bullet in the back of his head and then strapped his body to the underside of his boat. It was elaborate and probably done at night, but we think one person could have done it alone.'

'Would have been easier with two,' Jebb growled.

'Seems like a lot of trouble,' I said, not dignifying that with a reply.

'It worked, if the murderer didn't want Benji found for a while,' said the DCI, 'and if you hadn't gone poking about and disturbed him, he could have been there still. You didn't by any chance see a spent cartridge case kicking around on the boat did you?'

'I didn't find anything. The only thing rolling around on the floor was an empty beer bottle, and I only really took notice because I'd never heard of the brand before.'

'What did you do with it?'

I had a sudden premonition of being charged with removing evidence from a crime scene. That beer bottle might have been important: fingerprints, DNA saliva, stuff like that. I had to come clean and be responsible about it.

'Actually, it was Mr Oesterlein who found it. I never touched it.'

'What did he do with it?'

'I think he put it in a litter bin, I don't really remember. Naturally, he had no idea it might be important.'

'Having ideas doesn't seem to be his strong point.'

'Hey, don't diss Ossie,' I told Jebb.

Otherwise I might tell his mother on you, and she's a tax inspector.

Even cocky policemen are frightened of them.

'Come on, Tim, lighten up,' said Heather Armitage.

'I'm sorry, ma'am, but these two comedians could have disrupted the chain of evidence in a murder enquiry...'

'*My* murder enquiry, Tim. I'm the senior investigating officer.'

That put him in his place, so naturally I tried to put the boot in.

'Yes, Tim, you never did explain properly why a Sheffield copper is snooping around a Manchester murder case.'

'I don't have to explain anything to you,' he said firmly.

'I'm afraid he doesn't,' said DCI Armitage. 'In fact, I'm not even sure he has to explain anything to me, but unless he has any further points, I think we're done here.'

'For now,' Jebb added ominously.

I could see through the hotel's glass doors that Ossie was shuffling up and down on the small concrete patio which looked out over the canal basin, looking like the school bully waiting for a victim after the bell has gone.

DCI Armitage and her pet Yorkshire terrier DI Jebb marched straight out to have words with him and I took the opportunity to book a room for the night at reception on a credit card. The hotel was expecting me and the receptionist told me 'the police lady' had said to keep a room on hold for me, which was thoughtful, but there was no indication that Greater Manchester police were going to offer to pick up the tab.

I admitted that I had no luggage and, as I had left the toothbrush and razors I had bought in Huddersfield at Ossie's house, I asked where I might buy a few essentials. The receptionist recommended Kendal's down Deansgate, but didn't know what time it closed and warned me it was quite a walk. I said I wasn't worried about that and only then did I remember I was wearing Huddersfield Town football socks in Manchester.

When I turned away from the desk with my room key I saw that Ossie was alone on the concrete terrace and went to join him.

'Did they give you a hard time just now?'

'Not really,' he said, hands in pockets, 'just some rubbish about picking up a beer bottle on the boat.'

'Can you remember what you did with it?'

'I chucked it in the canal, didn't I? Shouldn't think it would do them any good if they found it; mind you, it's not as if they're not looking. They've been dragging the canal all afternoon.'

'I think they're looking for a gun,' I said and his face jerked up in surprise.

'A shooter?'

'It seems Benji was popped in the head and then strapped to the bottom of the boat.'

'Bloody hell, that's a bit extreme isn't it? Mind you, perfect place to hide a body if you didn't have the means to move it. I mean, if you'd just pushed him overboard, he'd have floated up before this.'

'So whoever did it didn't want the body found for a while,' I said, thinking aloud. 'Or at least that's the assumption they're working on.'

'They told you all this?'

'About the gun, yes. Everything else I'm making up as I go along. What did they ask you?'

'Mostly it was that little git from Sheffield wanting to know what we were looking for in Netherthorpe this morning, though fuck knows how they knew we were there so quick. Mebbe one of them shopkeepers is a registered informant.'

'Could be,' I agreed, 'but I think they might have had the area under surveillance with remote cameras. God knows why, though.'

I leant on the concrete balustrade and looked down along the towpath. There was still POLICE AWARE tape blocking it off and several white-suited SOCOs still working the scene in addition to two guys in overalls and thigh-length waders pulling what looked like a broad garden rake on a chain along the canal bottom around the *Felix Dacia*.

'Ossie,' I said, focusing on the curving path beyond the *Felix*, 'what was the name of the boat beyond Benji's? The brightly coloured one with the flower baskets we walked by when we got here yesterday? It's the next berth round the corner under the bridge.'

'I don't bloody know, *The Barbary Coast* or *The Barbara Steele*; summat like that.'

'*The Barbara Bray*,' I said, remembering.

'What about it?'

'It had security cameras. Little ones, mounted in the flower baskets on the deck.'

'I saw them, but so what? Looked to me like they'd only be

useful for catching somebody trying to nick the flower baskets. They were vectored on the towpath, not on Benji's boat.'

'But they might just have picked up somebody walking along the towpath. It doesn't seem that busy and the cameras would be motion sensitive so if they're wired up to a hard drive, they might still have pictures going back a month. It's worth a shot.'

'Won't the cops have thought of that?'

'They might get round to it but at the moment it looks as if they're concentrating on the *Felix Dacia*.'

'Well they would, wouldn't they, if they think the killer went on board? If he went on board, he left a trace somewhere and that's how they'll get him. If you want to bump somebody off, shoot them when they answer the door. Don't touch anything and never go inside. Every CID man knows that.'

'And now so do I, but do you think you could track down the owner of that boat and see if he was around a month ago, and, if he wasn't, whether his cameras were activated?'

'If Giancarlo still wants me on the case and will cover my expenses, I'll give it a go, but I reckon it's a long shot.'

'If you've got any better ideas, I'll listen,' I said, hoping that I was tacitly implying: *as long as they don't include line-dancing or pub quizzes*. 'Did they ask you anything specific when you got the third degree?'

'Had I seen a copy of this bloody film script seemed to be their main concern; that and just what the hell was I hoping to find in Sheffield this morning. To which I answered "No" and "Don't know", but nothing seemed to please that little shite in the flash suit.'

'What's he doing here? Where's he coming from? I don't

think there's any love lost between DCI Armitage and him.'

'I told you, she only has eyes for you. I reckon you could be in there.'

'You're just jealous,' I said with a slight toss of the head which turned out far more camp than I had intended. 'But she did sort of hint that Jebb only reported to her when he felt like. So what's his agenda?'

'I've never come across him before, but I can ask around Snig Hill. I have a few mates there.'

'Snig Hill?'

'It's the headquarters of South Yorkshire Police, in Sheffield. If there's any dirt on him, I'll get it,' he said confidently. 'And if I can't, me mother will.'

Ossie drove me round into Deansgate so I could catch the shops before they closed, then he headed off back to God's Own Country, leaving me wincing at the thought of the Cadillac's petrol consumption in rush hour traffic and what it was doing for global warming.

I 'passed the plastic' as Amy would say and bought a denim shirt, a three-pack of boxer shorts, some plain non-specific football club socks, yet another toothbrush, a pack of disposable razors, some shaving foam, toothpaste and deodorant. I even treated myself to a canvas shopping bag to put everything in. At first I thought the design on it was a crude sort of Fair Trade logo but once on the street, I saw it was a really crude, almost certainly bootlegged, picture of Oasis in concert. I turned the bag around so that the printed side was against my leg and only the blank half could be seen by passing pedestrians. The last thing I needed now was to be beaten up by members of the extended Gallagher family for infringement of copyright.

I decided to eat at Dimitri's Taverna, which we'd visited the day before, partly because they'd seemed a friendly crew there and partly because eating at The Ox would have brought back memories of what had happened to yesterday's lunch. Eating without Ossie for company might also mean I got some of my five-a-day fruit and vegetable allocation.

The tables were filling up nicely with an early evening trade of office workers, girls on a girls' night out and half a dozen young black guys in very sharp suits celebrating a birthday. I sat at a corner table and ate a passable moussaka and Greek salad washed down with a large glass of Othello red wine.

It was relaxing, but rather odd, not to have Ossie there and it seemed like months since I'd been at home, but Manchester wasn't a place to get maudlin, so I joined the black guys at the bar for a birthday beer or three.

They were drinking *San Miguel* from the bottle, then they switched to *Rolling Rock* and then to *Dos Equis*. In between the banter and dirty jokes I realised that these guys, all from the same office, had an established birthday tradition of never drinking the same beer twice. And why not? I'd heard of far dafter rituals.

I asked Carlton, the one whose birthday it was, if he'd ever drunk a beer called *Ursus* and he said he'd never heard of it. When I said that neither had I, Carlton called the barman over and asked him. He shook his head, but said he had all the imported beers available on the price list issued by his wholesaler and he'd check it out.

Eager to be helpful, he produced a printed catalogue from under the bar and flipped the pages.

'Here we are,' he told Carlton, '*Ursus*, premium lager,

brewed in Romania, wherever the fuck that is.'

'*Romanian* lager?'

'That's what it says here but we don't stock it. There's not much call for it.'

'That doesn't surprise me,' I said, but it had proved the point I made to the cops.

If you want to find something out, ask a man in a pub.

The birthday beer drinkers were still going strong when I sneaked back to the hotel about ten o'clock. From the concrete patio outside the Castlefield, I looked down over the deserted basin, but all was quiet apart from the occasional slap on the water or the tinkling of metal, the sound you always hear around moored boats even when it's flat calm and there's no tide.

A receptionist I hadn't seen before asked if my name was Angel as soon as I got through the door, and when I agreed it might be, she said there was a phone message for me. She handed me a square of paper on which she'd written a mobile number which I vaguely recognised as Ossie's.

I returned his call from my room, lying on the bed with the hotel phone on my chest. When he answered I could only just hear him over a background roar which I eventually identified as the song 'Walking On Sunshine' played too loud through a particularly tinny amplifier.

'You were trying to get me,' I said.

'Angel? Oh, aye. Hang on a sec…' There was a muffled thump which I guessed was him slapping a hand over the phone, but even so I could hear him mutter: 'I don't bloody know. Do I look as if I'd know summat like that? Any road, I've got to talk to Angel. What? Yeah, don't worry, will do.'

Then he was back to me full volume, though I could still hear the music in the background.

'That was me mum; she sends her best.'

'Same to her. I hope she enjoys the chillies. What did you want?'

And then he said something which surprised even me.

'Which first-century Roman Emperor is best known from his nickname which means "little boots"?'

'You're in the pub quiz then?'

'Yes we are and we're stuck.'

'I didn't think you were allowed to phone a friend,' I said snootily.

'I didn't. You rang me.'

'Fair enough. It was Caligula.'

'Cal-ig-ula,' he repeated so it could be written down. 'Told you he'd know. Job done,' he said to someone else.

'Was that it?' I asked.

'Oh, no, that female from your office rang. You know, the one with attitude.'

'Ossie, they've *all* got attitude where you're concerned, but it was probably Lorna.'

'Aye, that was it. She said to tell you that she tried to find your fella Patterson for a meeting tomorrow but she couldn't.'

'What, couldn't get an appointment?'

'No, couldn't find him. Nobody can. It seems that your client has disappeared. He's not been at his desk for the last two days and nobody would give out his home number.'

'Bugger. I'll find him once I get back to London,' I said, hoping I sounded more confident than I felt. 'Was that it?'

'Yeah, that was all, unless you know who this is,' said Ossie then he held the phone away from his head so I got a clear burst of the song being played.

'It's "Walking On Sunshine" by Katrina and the Waves,' I said.

'Top man. You wouldn't know what year it came out?'

'1985, I think.'

'Bloody hell, you're older than you look.'

'Thanks Ossie, it's been educational working with you too.'

'Make sure you lock your hotel room door,' he said.

'What for?'

'That Detective Chief Inspector lady who fancies you; I reckon she'll be prowling the corridors of that hotel looking for you.'

'In your dreams, Ossie, in your dreams.'

Absolutely no senior policewoman, or any other female, tried my door and I slept solidly until an alarm call woke me at seven o'clock. All in all, it was a peaceful, untroubled night.

It was not until after breakfast, while I was in the process of checking out, that somebody began shooting at me.

CHAPTER ELEVEN

'Of course somebody took a shot at you,' Amy said, 'you're in Manchester, that's what they do there. Who did you upset? I told you not to talk about football.'

I knew it had been a mistake to phone home for sympathy.

'I haven't upset anyone up here. They're all really, really friendly, and I haven't talked to anyone about football.'

Amy though, as usual, had sown a seed of doubt in my mind (she was good at that) and I seriously began to worry if anyone had seen me wearing those Huddersfield Town socks.

'This isn't just an elaborate ruse to stay up north for another day, is it? I think you secretly love it up there and don't want to come home. Where the hell are you anyway? It sounds like you're having a party already and it's... Christ, it's not even nine o'clock in the morning! Are you in one of those clubs on Canal Street?'

'I wish,' I said. 'I'm in a phone box outside a Yates's Wine Lodge at Manchester Piccadilly, waiting for a train.'

'A phone box? Do they still exist?'

'They do up here.'

'What's a Yates's Wine Lodge?'

'It's a sort of pub that specialises in offering shelter to innocent victims of drive-by shootings,' I said through gritted teeth.

'Busy, is it?'

'Packed. I'm not kidding, you know, somebody really did take a shot at me this morning.'

'But they missed, right?'

'Yes they did! Thank you for your concern!'

'Calm down, drama queen, calm down. It probably means you're doing something right if you've provoked someone into shooting you.'

'You think?'

'Trust me; I know how good you are at provoking people. God knows, I've felt like shooting you before now; a hundred times. What's that noise?'

'It's the pips. It means I've run out of change.'

'Make that a hundred and one,' she said just before the line went dead.

But I hadn't upset anyone, I really hadn't.

After the phone call from Ossie, I had toyed with the idea of finding a porn film on the hotel's cable TV, not because I particularly wanted to watch one, but I would have liked to see Veronica's face when she went through my itemised expenses claim. In the event, sleep seemed a far more sensible option and in any case, the remote control was so complicated it would probably have defeated me.

I awoke when the phone buzzed me an alarm call at 7 a.m., even though I couldn't remember ordering one. After a shave and a shower, I hit the dining room and grabbed a window seat which looked out on the corner of Liverpool Road and Potato Wharf. A pretty, but scarily quiet young waitress told me to help myself to fruit juice and cereals from the buffet and asked if I wanted tea or coffee and did I want my eggs boiled, fried, poached or scrabbled? I told her scrabbled, because it sounded interesting, but it turned out that was the last thing they were and I suspected they'd been kept stewing longer than the coffee had.

Clutching my Oasis bag of travelling necessities I asked the reception desk for my bill and slid across a credit card, not even pausing to be shocked at the amount they had charged for the phone call to Ossie.

The receptionist this time was a middle-aged man going bald on top, but with extensively cultivated sideboards and ferociously bad breath, though the two things were not necessarily connected. As he handed me back my card, he told me that my minicab was waiting outside.

I told him I hadn't ordered one and, in fact, was just about to ask him to get me one. In fact, it was only whilst trying to chew my scrabbled eggs that I had decided to go out to the airport and camp outside the Air Berlin desk until they put me on the first flight back to Stansted.

The cab company had rung, he told me, whilst I was having breakfast, to make sure I was up, they'd said. There was no rush; their car would be waiting out on Liverpool Road.

Who was I to look a gift-horse in the mouth? I reasoned that it must be a parting gesture from DCI Armitage, anxious to get me out of Manchester and her hair. With a bit of luck, Greater Manchester police might have picked up the tab.

And so it was with a jaunty spring in my heels, my Oasis bag swinging at my side, that I stepped through the front door of the Castlefield and onto the concrete patio. There I paused to take a last (I hoped) look down into the canal basin where the *Felix Dacia* now stood alone and abandoned apart from the fluttering strip of blue Police Aware tape, which still cordoned off the towpath.

It was as I was looking down to my right that I saw, or half-saw, the top of the concrete wall in front of me explode into dust. It wasn't a big explosion – there was no sound for a start – but there was suddenly a two-inch groove where there hadn't been one before, and then there *was* the sound of something smacking against the hotel wall behind my head and I felt the Oasis bag jerked out my hand.

My initial thought was that somebody was throwing stones at me, perhaps in some quaint Mancunian farewell ritual, but my second thought was to shout 'Fuck!', and my third and best thought was to let gravity do what it does best and fall on the floor.

The patio had waist-high walls forming three sides of a square, which instinct told me would offer me some protection. It also had a thick wooden table-and-bench arrangement where people could sit and drink on sunny days, which looked new and little used but also very solid, so it seemed sensible to crawl under that.

I still had no real idea what was going on and the scariest thing was that it was so quiet. There had definitely been projectiles whizzing about my personal space, but I had not heard any shots, only the sound of an engine revving and then disappearing into the distance. So, had someone been sniping at me with a catapult? I realised I was clutching my bag to my chest and saw that there was a hole in the illustrated side big enough for me to poke my little finger through. Although no expert, that certainly looked like a bullet hole to me.

I turned the bag over but couldn't see an exit hole, so I tipped the contents onto the patio floor in front of me. I must have been doing a fair impression of a homeless guy desperately trying to find the can of Special Brew he just knew he had somewhere. Instead I found, nestling in my rolled up pair of Huddersfield Town socks, a small lump of bent metal suspiciously like lead. This was, I deduced, stifling a scream of panic, a spent bullet which had ricocheted off the patio wall somehow and penetrated my bag through the bootlegged illustration of Oasis in concert, obliterating the head of the lead singer.

That was the most amazing thing about the whole experience: Liam Gallagher had taken a bullet for me!

I concentrated on listening hard for any sound from beyond the patio, and when I had convinced myself that there was nothing more incoming, I got out from under the table and stuffed my scattered possessions back into my bag. Hugging it tightly – for this was no longer a carrier bag but a talismanic flak-jacket – and crouched low in a Groucho Marx walk, I scuttled to the hotel door and pushed it with my forehead.

The receptionist barely gave me a first look, let alone a second; he'd probably seen stranger behaviour from guests that early in the morning and was far too busy tapping at his computer keyboard.

'Could you get me another minicab, please?' I asked, straightening up to full height when I was by his desk, but watching the door and the patio out of the corner of one eye.

'Airport is it, sir?'

'No, railway station. Manchester Piccadilly.' I fished a five-pound note out of my wallet and slid it across the desk towards him. 'And use a company you know, if you wouldn't mind.'

He palmed the note like a croupier, without looking away from his computer screen.

'Something wrong with your other cab, was there?'

'The driver was far too aggressive,' I said.

'Well,' he said with a shrug, 'that's Manchester minicabs for you.'

After phoning Amy, I bought a first-class single to London on Virgin for about twice my original Air Berlin fare. No doubt I could have got a supersaver deal or similar if I had waited until after nine-thirty, or pretended to be a student (the state I was in I might have got away with it), or if I'd had the foresight to book three months in advance, making sure there was an 'R' in the month. I had never pretended to understand railway ticket pricing, and was willing to use my flexible friend to get me out of Manchester whatever the cost to whichever poor client we would charge it to.

I flexed the credit card again to buy a large coffee and two miniature bottles of brandy in the buffet car, and I wasn't out of place. A couple of businessmen in suits they looked to have slept in were already quaffing from cans of lager, and a television journalist I vaguely recognised from the BBC was breakfasting on two doubles of Scotch and a small can of ginger ale.

As the coffee burnt my mouth and the brandy took care of any remaining taste buds, I kept my head down and watched the train kiss goodbye to Manchester through the smears on the window, trying not to jump out of my seat every time the door between the carriages slid open with a loud thump. But the brandy did the trick and I calmed down enough to start to plan the rest of my day, now that I was almost certain I was going to have a rest of the day.

The train would get me into Euston just after 11 a.m. unless the timetable lied, which I had been assured it frequently did on this line. With Armstrong stuck out in a field at Stansted, that meant I was reduced to taking the Circle Line round to Notting Hill and then Shepherd's Bush in order to get to the office where a mountain of grief over incomplete Case Reports and outrageous expenses claims would greet me.

Alternatively, I convinced myself, I could catch the Circle Line going the other way to Liverpool Street, charge into the City for a quick meeting with my client (which surely ought to take precedence over boring paperwork), maybe a light lunch which didn't involve chips or black pudding, and then I could slip back to Liverpool Street and catch the Stansted Express, negotiate Armstrong's release from the maximum security car park and be home in time for tea.

That sounded like a plan: boxes ticked, job done.

Except that I remembered talking to Ossie at his pub quiz and the message from Lorna that my client had gone absent-without-leave from his office. I fumed silently about people going walkabout and not being where they should be when you needed them and about how incompetent and inconsiderate they were. If I hadn't been stuck on a train two hundred miles away without a mobile phone, I would have given them a piece of my mind.

It wasn't a hard choice in the end: go to work in the office or go find my client. The missing client won hands down. The office might pay the wages, but the client paid the office, and if I couldn't find my client I was facing one hell of a credit card bill next month.

I hadn't known what to expect of the offices of KSAG, but there again, I hadn't actually been inside many merchant banks before. It wasn't difficult to find; only a minute's walk round onto Bishopsgate from Liverpool Street tube station and there was a brass plaque on the wall with the bank's name in big enough letters even I couldn't miss. But that was about the only part of the bank I was allowed to see.

Once up the steps from the street and through the heavy but fake oak door (probably sheet steel thinly veneered) I found myself in a reception area manned by a uniformed security guard behind a desk which was itself behind a floor-to-ceiling sheet of thick perspex. At what was bound to be the accurate average height, this being a German company and very thorough, a triangle of tiny holes in the perspex formed a crude intercom through which I had to talk my way in, though that didn't seem likely. The only door leading off reception was to a lift and that was secured by an electronic swipe-card mechanism.

The security man eyed me suspiciously even though I was holding the Oasis bag so he couldn't see the bullet hole.

'Can I help you,' he said in a magically amplified voice, then as an afterthought: 'Sir?'

'I'd like to see Terry Patterson in Human Resources, please.'

'Do you have an appointment?' he asked glancing at a large desk diary.

'No, because I was told he wasn't here.'

'But you came anyway?'

Now he was giving me a distinctly shifty look.

'I was told he wasn't here yesterday, when I was out of London...when my secretary rang. I was hoping he might be back at his desk this morning, but I didn't get a chance to ring ahead.'

'Well, I'm afraid Mr Patterson isn't in the bank today.'

'Does he have a secretary?'

'In a paperless office we have no need for secretaries,' he said deadpan, like he had been tutored to say.

'Any assistant, a deputy, an associate?'

'He does have an assistant but she's tied up in a meeting, standing in for him.'

'Any idea when he'll be back?'

'No, sir.'

'Could I leave a message?'

'We only take messages electronically, sir.'

'I don't have a computer on me,' I pointed out, though I probably came across as a street-dweller who lived out of one carrier bag.

'I believe there is a cyber café at Liverpool Street station,' he said, not blinking.

'I suppose a home phone number for Mr Patterson is out of the question?'

'Oh yes, sir, I'm afraid so, sir, totally.'

And for the first time that morning, or probably that year, he smiled and looked perfectly happy in his work.

I was not going to be defeated, though. I was, after all, supposed to be a detective and all detectives have a secret safe house from which they operate, don't they? Or is that spies?

Across the road from KSAG I hopped on a bus which took me round to Hackney and my own personal secret base, 9 Stuart Street, and although I hadn't been there for a while, it was comforting to see nothing had changed.

I heard at least six languages spoken as I walked down the street – seven if you include English – and returned more than two polite greetings and one cheery wave, which for any part of London is pretty good going. It was comforting to know I was still remembered as I had long memories and deep affection for the place. The house at number 9 had been a good friend to me and continued to provide a home for my cat Springsteen, now ageing but still crazy after all these years, thanks to a peppercorn rent from an understanding but easily fooled landlord called Nasseem Nasseem. That wasn't his proper name, but he'd insisted that his family name was too difficult for us to pronounce and had said 'Nasseem Nasseem is good' and it had stuck. I think he used it himself in certain of his many businesses.

When I had met up with Amy and moved into her more-than-comfortable house in Hampstead, I hadn't been able to fully cut the cord on Flat 3 in the Stuart Street house, which had served me so faithfully for so many years, even though Hackney and Hampstead are six miles, two universes and several lifestyles apart. I also realised the value of having a second (authentic) address. These days, you could get credit cards, open a bank account, apply for a second driving licence and lots of other good stuff simply by having a gas bill or a rates demand with an address on it. A kosher address was better than photo-ID and this address was my old friend.

So why the hell didn't my key work in the front door?

Because the antisocial, unthinking, selfish bastards who still lived there had changed the lock on me. How friendly was that?

Undeterred, I rang the doorbell knowing that there would be at least two people at home; one of them human.

Fenella, sometimes known as 'Binky' because of her surname Binkworthy, had lived with her partner Lisabeth in Flat 2, the one below mine, since before I arrived in Hackney. I had no idea what Lisabeth did for a living these days, but it almost certainly involved selling New Age crystals to help fellow vegans with their digestive problems. However, I knew that Fenella worked from home in a job which enabled her to maximise her natural talents of a very posh southern home counties middle-class accent and a degree of naivety akin to a tyrannosaurus rex trying to do a Rubik's cube. She did phone sex; though I wasn't totally convinced she knew that was what it was called. And it seems she did it wearing faded tracksuit bottoms, a white cable-knit fisherman's pullover which came down to her knees it had been machine-washed so many times, and what could only charitably be described as Burberry bedsocks.

'Angel! Long time no see! Huggsies!' she gushed as she opened the door and flung her arms around me.

'You've changed the lock, Binky. You trying to keep me out or Springsteen in?'

She untangled herself, leaving me with the scent of aloe vera moisturiser in my nostrils, and waved me inside.

'It was the new people in Flat 1, Sally and Barry, who wanted the locks changed; they said it helped reduce their insurance premiums and Nasseem saw the logic of that. Anyway, Springsteen's too old to pick locks these days.'

'How is the old boy?'

'Oh, you know. He doesn't go out much – hardly ever in fact – and he has trouble with the stairs and is a very messy eater. He's also started to smell a bit.'

'Well, so much for Nasseem, but how's Springsteen?'

It took her a good ten seconds to get it, then she smiled and punched me playfully in the chest. A few years ago it would have taken her an hour to work that one out, but her role as Springsteen's carer/home-help/jailer had sharpened up her reflexes.

'Ha, ha, very funny. To what do we owe the honour of your visit?'

'I'm in need of safe, familiar surroundings. You see, I've been working up north.'

'Oh, you poor thing,' she said, and she wasn't kidding.

'So this is just a quick pit-stop to grab a few things out of the flat and say hello, of course, and make a few phone calls.'

We were in the hallway at the foot of the stairs and I instinctively turned to the communal wall-mounted phone outside the door to Flat 1, the ground floor flat previously occupied by the polite and reclusive Mr Goodson, whom I had almost totally forgotten about.

'Where's the phone gone, Binky?'

'Oh, that was another improvement suggested by Sally and Barry. They said why have a landline when everyone has mobile phones or Internet connections?'

'That was thoughtful of them.'

I always subscribed to the maxim that it is possible to hate people on first sight, and that way you can save valuable time. I was working up to dislike Sally and Barry even earlier than that.

'Don't you have a mobile? I would have thought they were essential in your job.'

'A lot of people take that rather blinkered view,' I snarled.

'And how is Veronica?'

I had forgotten that Fenella had always been impressed with Veronica Blugden. It wasn't a crush or anything – Lisabeth certainly wouldn't have allowed that – it was the image of the strong businesswoman running her own firm which appealed and maybe the added bonus of Veronica being my boss.

'Oh, much the same. Doesn't get out much, has trouble with the stairs, makes a mess when she's eating and, I'm sorry to say, is starting to smell a bit.'

That bought me another, harder, punch to the chest. Her reaction times really were improving.

'Don't be such a Blue Meanie! I bet as an employee you make Veronica's life hell. I couldn't possibly imagine what it would be like to have you under me.'

'No, you probably couldn't,' I said straight-faced, mentally ticking off the seconds, but this time she didn't react.

'And you should think about poor Springsteen seriously for once. He really is quite old for a cat, you know, and the vet says you have to face the facts of life.'

'You used the local vet?'

I had set up an account with the nearest vet so that Fenella could go there in cases of emergency, even though I'd had to pay a premium as the vet had treated Springsteen in the past and put him in the 'Dangerous Animals' bracket to cover the medical insurance on the surgery's staff.

'Yes, they're ever so nice there. They were treating this sweet little...'

'Did he go quietly?'

The last time I'd taken him had involved flesh wounds. Not his.

'Quiet as a lamb, the vet didn't need to wear the gauntlets.'

'My God, the old boy must be in a bad way. I'd better say hello.'

Fenella started up the stairs and I followed resisting the urge to tell her that yes, her bum did look big in those tracksuit trousers.

'Don't you think it a bit unfair to keep renting Flat 3 when you're hardly ever here?' she said over her shoulder. 'Are you staring at my bottom?'

'No – and no, I wasn't.'

'But it seems a bit wasteful just to keep it on for a cat.'

'Do you want him to move in with you and Lisabeth?'

'I wasn't suggesting *that*,' she said quickly, 'and don't you dare tell her I did. I just thought that now you live out in the countryside, with all those green fields and forests...surely, he'd love that.'

'No he wouldn't, he'd hate it. He's a city cat through and through and, anyway, at his time of life he'd probably get mugged by voles or bullied by owls.'

She stopped in her tracks and being two steps below her I almost made contact with the part of her I wasn't staring at.

'I was *forgetting!*' she squealed. 'You've got a baby in the house now, so you can't have a cat because they leap into the baby's cot and lie across their faces and smother them. Or at least that's what my granny used to say.'

'She was a wise woman. Yes, *that's* the reason Springsteen can't come out to us.'

'And how is the lovely baby, not to mention the lovely mother?'

'Both doing extremely well last time I looked,' I said

honestly, 'and I really need to get home to them, so can I borrow your phone?'

'As long as you give them both my love,' she said sunnily.

'Actually, I wanted to ring the office.'

'Then give Veronica my love.'

'Will do. Oh, and I also need to get in touch with Salome. Remember her, from Flat 4?'

'Of course I remember the lovely Salome Asmoyah, who could forget *her*?'

'You wouldn't happen to have a number for her, would you?'

'Of course. She and Frank live in a lovely house in Basingstoke now.'

'That figures. Can you jot the number down for me?'

'Sure. Step into my parlour.'

We had reached the door to Flat 2 and I let Fenella lead the way just in case Lisabeth was at home. Their tiny living room had once been so bedecked with soft toys and printed fabrics, on the walls as well as any surface you could possibly sit on, that it had resembled the aftermath of an explosion in a Laura Ashley shop. But now it had been minimalised to provide a functional workspace to accommodate Fenella working from home.

There was a large, fake leather armchair up against a long metal-framed table on which sat an open laptop computer showing an email inbox, a webcam and six mobile phones in their charger sockets, each with an open shorthand notebook and a different coloured felt-tip pen next to it.

'You wanted to use a phone?' she said. 'Help yourself to one.'

In fact, she picked one out for me; one that had a number

which 'didn't get used much except at weekends'. I didn't like to ask, and she deliberately stood between me and the desk so I couldn't see what she'd written on the notepad obviously belonging to the phone she handed over.

'It's fully charged,' she said, defying me to ask for sordid details.

I thanked her and she picked up a pen from the desk and wrote a number starting 01256 on the back on my hand.

'Salome's number,' she said, 'but remember to wash it off before you get home.'

'Good thinking, that girl. Do you give that advice to your regular callers?'

'Knowing the way your mind works, I'm not going to answer that.'

I hefted the phone she had given me.

'Thanks for this. I always said you gave good phone.'

Nobody had changed the lock on Flat 3; Springsteen wouldn't have let them. In his prime he wouldn't have let anyone put a foot inside the place, and I'd always said he was cheaper than insurance and as daunting as those criss-cross laser beam alarms – he could certainly come out of the blue from more different angles.

But I had to concede he was no longer in his prime, so it was just as well there wasn't much in the flat to attract a burglar. I had left a futon sofa which turned into a bed for humans in an emergency, a couple of chairs and a small midi hi-fi system with all the jazz CDs I liked but Amy didn't. The kitchen was stuffed with tins of tuna and Canadian salmon in case Fenella forgot to buy cat food, and the small fridge I still kept running contained a tray of ice cubes, a bottle of vodka and a couple of Tetra pack litres of orange juice still within their 'best before' dates. The bedroom was completely bare apart from the carpet and a large sports bag which contained a clean pair of jeans, three multi-packs of boxers and socks still in their M&S packaging. Stuffed into the side pockets of the bag were a couple of books, one of which opened to reveal (after page 34) a cut-away depression big enough to take a spare driving licence, two credit cards and £500 in folded £20 notes. I checked my stash and left it where it was.

Springsteen had remained completely motionless, curled up on the futon as I had entered, although I saw a single flicker of green eye in among the long black fur, which was his way of signalling that he was well aware of my presence. Even when I was up close and standing over him, not a hair rippled nor a whisker twitched. I reached out to tickle him playfully behind the ear, but jerked my fingers back as a front paw came out of the mass of fur and the claws missed my flesh by half an inch.

'Hah! Too slow, old boy,' I shouted in triumph although I knew from bitter experience that such victories were rare and tended to be short-lived.

His claws had stuck into the fabric of the futon, which meant he had to raise himself up to extricate them. He did it in such a way – and cats do this so well – that it looked as if that had been what he had meant to do all along. Then he yawned to show me the pink and black roof of his mouth and to remind me that he still had all his teeth.

I followed him into the kitchen where I opened a tin of salmon for him and checked that Fenella had laid in supplies of cat litter and filter pads for the air-vents in his deluxe and very private Kitty Loo. I had instructed Fenella only to line the tray with copies of the *Daily Mail* as Springsteen liked a bit of

right-wing posturing for his morning read. I don't think
Fenella ever actually believed that, but I wasn't complaining.
From the state of the place she'd obviously been cleaning it
regularly, though I hadn't asked her to, nor offered to pay her.
Bless.

While Springsteen was eating, I sat on the futon bed and
dialled the number written on my hand, innocently assuming
that, now Salome was a respectable middle-class mum living in
Basingstoke, she would naturally be at home in the afternoon
with her feet up, waiting for *Countdown* to come on the telly.

When the phone was answered it was as if I'd interrupted a
performance of the Chippendales at a Licensed Victuallers'
Ladies' Night.

'Salome? It's Roy.'

'Angel? Good grief, you're a rave from the grave,' she
giggled. 'Keep it down girls.'

'What's going on Salome? Is this a bad time?'

'No, we're having a great time here! How the devil are you?
Pop round and join in.'

From the background noise there was a party in full swing
with lots of high-pitched female laughter and clinking of
glassware. I checked my watch and concluded that lunchtimes
in Basingstoke sounded fun.

'I'm afraid I'm nowhere near Basingstoke, or I would.'

'Of course, I'd forgotten you're a daddy now. I suppose
you're at home changing nappies and hanging up mobiles.'

'Not exactly, I'm at work – well I'm working – in London;
in fact I'm at Stuart Street at the old house. Fenella gave me
your number because I need your help.'

'What? I can't hear you. Just a minute: Ladies! Shut the
fuck up will you! There, that's better. They really are a noisy

bunch when they get outside a bottle of Chardonnay.'

'Exactly what's going on there, Salome?'

'It's our monthly book club. We all park our kids at the local nursery and discuss high literature over a glass of wine.'

'So what was the book this month?'

'Some chick lit shit, I can't remember. Anyway, what can I do for you? Just name it. You know I could never resist a musician.'

There was a loud murmured 'Oooh!' in the background and more than one cry of 'Hey, get her!'

'I take it Frank doesn't go to this book club of yours,' I said.

'Oh no, darling, my husband's at work earning disgusting amounts of money and he never reads anything but the share prices in the *Financial Times*. So you can be sure that there's only us girls here every third Thursday of the month.' There was a big, drunken cheer at that. 'Carefully discussing modern literature, of course; you'd be quite safe.'

'It's in my diary already, Sal, but now I need a favour.'

'I don't do phone sex,' she said, her giggles drowned out by more catcalls in the background. 'You need your little girlfriend Fenella for that.'

'Actually, I'm using her phone – well, one of them.'

'Hope you used a wet-wipe on it.'

'Don't be a bitch, you bitch. Now listen: Terry Patterson. Ring a bell?'

''Course it does. Knew him way back when in the City. He's working for some Kraut investment bank these days. Met him at a party a couple of weeks ago. He's lost weight, which is good, but his hair is going too, which isn't, which explains a lot really.'

'Did you mention me to him at this party?'

'I think I did. Yes, I did. We were reminiscing about the good old days when I shared a house in Hackney with a reprobate trumpet player who drove around in a de-licensed cab. He thought it quite funny that you were now a private detective.'

'So funny he hired me.'

'Well, slap my thighs and call me Samantha! The sad git was serious!'

'What do you mean "serious"?' I asked, adding: 'Samantha.'

'He was moaning about being in the doghouse with his girlfriend. This was the girlfriend he was thinking of leaving his wife for, mind you, so at that point I sort of switched off the sympathy button.'

'So he was looking for someone to do divorce work?'

'No, I don't think so. It was something to do with his new girlfriend that was giving him grief. I wasn't really listening, but I did give him your name.'

'Do you know where he lives? I need to get in touch with him.'

'I've got a vague memory of him saying he had a place down in Little Portugal, but I honestly don't know where.'

I knew that Little Portugal was the area down around South Lambeth Road and Vauxhall, south of the river, but it didn't help.

'I don't suppose you've got a mobile number or anything, have you? His office won't give out his home address and it's really, really important that I speak to him.'

'Sorry, my old lover, but I can't help you there. In any case, he's most likely shacked up with his girlfriend up west.'

'What do you mean up west?'

'She's staying at the Mount Royal near Marble Arch, or so he said. If I know men, he's in there bumping uglies with her and living off room service. I mean, how many middle-aged balding men get a chance like that?'

'A chance like what?'

'To bonk the brains out of a real live porn star.'

'Lea Klemm,' I said.

'Why am I not surprised you knew her?' said Salome, jumping, as women always do, to conclusions.

CHAPTER TWELVE

Marble Arch was only ten or twelve minutes on the Central Line from Liverpool Street this time of day. I could get there, meet the hottest porn film star this side of the River Oder, get back to Liverpool Street to catch the Stansted Express, pick up Armstrong and be home in time for dinner, if not tea.

I could do that.

I said goodbye to Springsteen, but he didn't reply. On the stairs, I knocked on Fenella's door and shouted that I was borrowing her phone for a few minutes more, then legged it down the street before she could say 'Just a sec...'

Around the corner I caught a number 253 bus, adding the ticket to my growing wad of receipts, and once I had a seat I phoned the office. I was prepared to keep my voice down and look suitably self-conscious, but at least four elderly black women sitting around me with shopping bags on their knees were carrying on conversations on phones, one of them a very flash hands-free ear-piece arrangement, so I just blended in. I tried to remember the last time I had heard people actually talk to each other face-to-face on a bus and decided it must have been on that school trip where we'd managed to smuggle a crate of brown ale onto the back seat, but perhaps my memory was playing tricks.

'Lorna? It's Angel.'

'Angel who?'

'Ha, ha, very droll. The Angel that you spoke to yesterday, except I'm not in the frozen north any more.'

'I didn't speak to anyone called Angel yesterday.'

'Don't mess me about, kiddo, I need you to do something... Oops, it's Laura, isn't it? Look, I'm sorry about your phone – and about your mother. Where's Lorna?'

'She's busy on the other job for you. So whose phone have you borrowed now? It's not yours.'

'No, actually it's a friend's phone...how did you know it wasn't mine?'

'Because the number isn't recognised on our caller recognition.'

'We have caller recognition? Can you read the number of this phone?'

'Yes of course.'

'Could you tell me what it is? No, never mind, just ring Ossie Oesterlein and give him the number. He was checking something out for me.'

'Isn't everybody?'

'It's a very complicated case, Laura, so just do that, would you? Oh, and tell him there may be no signal for the next half-hour as I'll be on the Underground.'

'You're in London?'

'Yes.'

'London, *England?*'

'Sarcasm really doesn't become you, Laura dear. In fact I might tell your mother that the next time she rings me.'

'Don't you mess with my mother.'

'Wouldn't dream of it, especially not as I want you to do something for me.'

'Do you know, I just thought you might. I mean, why should I be exempt? The entire agency seems to be running around on your behalf, not to mention our Huddersfield associate, why shouldn't I join the Angel private workforce?'

'Cheers my dear, I knew you wouldn't mind,' I said cheerfully ignoring her complaints, which is surely a golden rule in the book of personnel management skills if there is such a thing. 'Be a sweetie and see what you can find on Oradea Films. My bet is they'll have an office in Soho if they've got one anywhere.'

'That's O-r-a-d-e-a? Like the Romanian one?'

'What?' I said, loudly enough for the women on the bus to turn and stare.

'Oradea, it's a place in Romania,' Laura said, delighted to be able to show off. 'In Transylvania I think, or maybe it's in the western end near the Hungarian border. I think there's a university there.'

'And what beer do they drink?'

'Now who's being sarcastic? I was only trying to help. There really is a town called Oradea in Romania, you know.'

'Hey, I believe you and I bet they drink Ursus beer there. See, I know stuff too.'

Usually a couple of days, sometimes months, after everyone else.

For example, it wasn't until I was on the tube, halfway

between Chancery Lane and Holborn that I wondered what Laura had meant when she said that Lorna was busy on 'the other' job for me. What other job?

My phone, or rather Fenella's phone, started ringing as I was climbing the stairs out of Marble Arch tube station. The downloaded ringtone was Sting singing 'Roxanne', which was embarrassing enough but would be even worse if it turned out to be one of Fenella's clients demanding to speak with a Roxanne. Fortunately it was Ossie.

'Hey up, Angel, how're you doing?'

'I've had better days, Ossie,' I said, talking as I walked around the corner into Old Quebec Street which was famous for having one of the oldest, yet least infamous gay pubs in the West End.

'You home in the bosom of your family yet?'

'Not exactly.'

'Oh, bloody hell, you're not still in Manchester with that female DCI sniffing after you, are you?'

'Fear not, me old mate, I'm safely back in the soft south. Manchester was a bit too rough for me.'

'I told you, you should have come to our pub quiz.'

'It might have been safer,' I admitted, 'if not as much fun. Still, you got any news for me?'

'I popped over to see Artesi this morning. He's still gutted as you can imagine, but the cops seem to be leaving him alone. I asked him about a script for this *Europol* film but he said he's never seen one. He showed me Benji's laptop and there doesn't seem to be anything on there.'

'Have the police asked for access to it?'

'No they haven't, and that struck me as odd too.'

'It might be in there and Artesi just couldn't get at it.'

'Don't think so. Giancarlo seemed to know what he was doing. He and Benji shared the same passwords, would you believe? Must be a gay thing.'

'Perhaps they just didn't believe in keeping secrets from each other,' I ventured.

'Well, that doesn't sound like a married couple to me,' Ossie snorted.

'You have a point,' I admitted. 'So there was definitely no script on his computer?'

'Not for a film. There was all the stuff he'd written but he'd never sold to anybody. He did a thing called *Tunnel Cops* about English police and French police patrolling the Channel Tunnel. Didn't look half bad to me, what I saw of it.'

'But no script? Or anything of interest?'

'No script, but I didn't say there was nowt interesting; far from it. I got into his email account and that was an eye-opener, I can tell you.'

'Then tell me, Ossie, tell me.'

'Well you'll never guess who was emailing him every day, sometimes twice, for about two weeks before he disappeared and just about every other day since.'

'No, I probably wouldn't,' I admitted.

'The luscious Lea Klemm, would you credit it? And some of those messages were a bit near the knuckle, I don't mind telling you. She definitely had the hots for young Benji. Giancarlo found them quite upsetting.'

'He didn't know she was emailing him?'

'No he didn't, or says he didn't, and I believe him. If he did, it would give him a bloody good motive for offing Benji, though, wouldn't it?'

'Especially if he knew Benji's passwords and could get into his computer at any time.'

'Now that's another funny thing. He says he would never read Benji's emails, just as Benji would never open his letters. It would have been a breach of privacy, he called it. Mind you, just because he said he never *would* isn't the same as saying he never *did*, is it?'

'Maybe they trusted each other,' I said.

'But that's not like a married couple either, is it?'

There was no arguing with him on that one.

'Did he reply to any of the emails from Lea?'

'Doesn't look like it.'

'Well then, Giancarlo's probably got nothing to worry about.'

I realised that was a crass thing to say as soon as it popped out. Artesi had a dead partner to mourn.

'I'm not so sure,' said Ossie and I could hear him leering. 'I've checked out Lea Klemm on the Internet and, by God, she'd turn anyone away from the dark side. You ought to check her out.'

'I don't have a computer about my person just at the moment,' I told him. 'Anyway, I don't have time, as I'm on my way to meet Lea Klemm.'

'In the flesh?'

'Well, in her hotel room at least. It might turn out to be the same thing, you never know your luck.'

'That's the trouble. I do know my luck and nowt like that would ever come my way. You enjoy yerself and let me have a blow-by-blow account, if you'll pardon my French, of how you get on.'

'Ossie, I lost count of the number of double entendres in

between Chancery Lane and Holborn that I wondered what Laura had meant when she said that Lorna was busy on 'the other' job for me. What other job?

My phone, or rather Fenella's phone, started ringing as I was climbing the stairs out of Marble Arch tube station. The downloaded ringtone was Sting singing 'Roxanne', which was embarrassing enough but would be even worse if it turned out to be one of Fenella's clients demanding to speak with a Roxanne. Fortunately it was Ossie.

'Hey up, Angel, how're you doing?'

'I've had better days, Ossie,' I said, talking as I walked around the corner into Old Quebec Street which was famous for having one of the oldest, yet least infamous gay pubs in the West End.

'You home in the bosom of your family yet?'

'Not exactly.'

'Oh, bloody hell, you're not still in Manchester with that female DCI sniffing after you, are you?'

'Fear not, me old mate, I'm safely back in the soft south. Manchester was a bit too rough for me.'

'I told you, you should have come to our pub quiz.'

'It might have been safer,' I admitted, 'if not as much fun. Still, you got any news for me?'

'I popped over to see Artesi this morning. He's still gutted as you can imagine, but the cops seem to be leaving him alone. I asked him about a script for this *Europol* film but he said he's never seen one. He showed me Benji's laptop and there doesn't seem to be anything on there.'

'Have the police asked for access to it?'

'No they haven't, and that struck me as odd too.'

'It might be in there and Artesi just couldn't get at it.'

'Don't think so. Giancarlo seemed to know what he was doing. He and Benji shared the same passwords, would you believe? Must be a gay thing.'

'Perhaps they just didn't believe in keeping secrets from each other,' I ventured.

'Well, that doesn't sound like a married couple to me,' Ossie snorted.

'You have a point,' I admitted. 'So there was definitely no script on his computer?'

'Not for a film. There was all the stuff he'd written but he never sold to anybody. He did a thing called *Tunnel* Co about English police and French police patrolling the Chan Tunnel. Didn't look half bad to me, what I saw of it.'

'But no script? Or anything of interest?'

'No script, but I didn't say there was nowt interesting from it. I got into his email account and that was an opener, I can tell you.'

'Then tell me, Ossie, tell me.'

'Well you'll never guess who was emailing him ever sometimes twice, for about two weeks before he disap and just about every other day since.'

'No, I probably wouldn't,' I admitted.

'The luscious Lea Klemm, would you credit it? And those messages were a bit near the knuckle, I do telling you. She definitely had the hots for your Giancarlo found them quite upsetting.'

'He didn't know she was emailing him?'

'No he didn't, or says he didn't, and I believe him it would give him a bloody good motive for of though, wouldn't it?'

that, but I will let you know if I get any hard and fast results. Did you get anywhere tracing the owner of that boat, *The Barbara Bray*, by the way?'

'Not yet, but I'm on it. I turned up something from my chums down at Snig Hill, though.'

It took me a second or two to remember that was the police HQ in Sheffield.

'Oh yeah; our friend DI Timothy Jebb.'

'Who according to my sources isn't exactly a friend of the other plods there. He seems to be a bit of a fast-tracker and a specialist, been drafted in there to help with a specific job.'

'Doing what?'

'I've no idea, but it's called Operation Pentameter.'

'What's that all about then?'

'Search me, but my sources tell me we'll hear all about it any day now. It's summat to do with people-trafficking from Eastern Europe; you know, places like Poland and Hungary...'

'And Romania,' I added, almost to myself.

My normal tactic would have been to drive up to the front door of the hotel, park on the double yellow lines, get out of Armstrong, walk up to the desk jangling my keys and announce to all and sundry that Miss Klemm's taxi had arrived. But of course Armstrong was stuck in a maximum security field out at Stansted and, in any case, the Mount Royal is a weird hotel in that the entrance lobby is one floor up from the street and access is by escalator. So I went straight into Plan B and bought a dozen red roses in the hotel gift shop near the door, plus a small card in an envelope. Then I ran a hand through my hair, zipped up my jacket and rode the escalator up to the massive lobby, taking cover behind a family of Americans struggling with too much luggage and too few hands.

In the far distance of the lobby some poor sod was tinkling at a grand piano, trying to compete heroically with a hundred tourists sitting around low tables taking afternoon tea and paying absolutely no attention to the music. It was an old-fashioned tea dance without the dancing and my heart went out to the pianist.

The long reception desk was staffed entirely by pretty young French women, a fact I filed away for future reference (in case I ever had to recommend a hotel to a party of non-English speakers from the Champagne region, or similar), and none of them looked particularly surprised when I planted myself in front of them and announced that I had flowers for a Miss Klemm who was supposed to be a resident.

'Leave them with the concierge please,' said the nearest one, pointing with her pen to the porters' desk.

'Got to get a signature, darling,' I said, talking fast. 'Got to have proof of delivery, see? There's a card with the flowers, personal like. Got to show they was delivered. More than my job's worth, you know, got to tick the box. Can't you ring her room, see if she's in?'

The receptionist sighed and tapped her keyboard, then picked up a house phone and pressed buttons, but making sure I couldn't see a room number on either her computer screen or the phone. Not that I was interested and to show that, I concentrated on the receptionist standing next to her filing some bills and pretending not to notice the dazzling smile I was giving her.

The two women edged closer to each other, then the one doing the bills spoke in soft rapid French, with just a hint of a Breton accent, to the one on the phone.

'She'll need more vases in 667 if she gets any more fucking flowers', and the other one nodded in agreement before speaking very politely into the phone:

'Madame Klemm, there is a delivery for you at reception which requires a signature. Could you possibly come down?'

She waited a beat then put a hand over the mouthpiece.

'What name is it this time?' she asked me, not attempting to keep the boredom out of her voice.

'Terry Patterson,' I said confidently.

She said "Terree Patterce" into the phone, listened and then said 'Straight away, madame.'

Her colleague was still shuffling bills and checking figures on a calculator, but she had definitely pricked up her ears.

'You may go up to the sixth floor,' I was told. 'Room 667.'

'667? The Neighbour of the Beast, eh?' I said, but I don't think either of them got it.

As I walked across the football pitch-sized lobby towards the lifts I could feel their eyes boring into the back of my neck and I was sure I heard them sniggering in Breton-accented French.

I had forgotten what a big hotel the Mount Royal was, and how long and claustrophobic the corridors on the bedroom floors were. Stanley Kubrick would have had a ball filming there.

If there was a Room 666, I didn't see it. The hotel had probably 'lost' that number (just as they sometimes ignore a 'thirteenth floor' so as not to upset superstitious residents) in order to deter any fanatical devil worshippers looking for a weekend break in the city.

Oddly enough, in the lift going up to the sixth floor, there was an advert in one of the wall panels for something called 'Guest Invest'. Apparently, for a paltry quarter of a million quid, I could actually *buy* a hotel room in London these days and I could stay in it rent-free for 52 nights in the year and share in the income generated from lettings over the other 313 nights. It seemed a strange thing to advertise in a hotel, but then I saw myself in the mirror and realised I was taking roses to the bedroom of the queen of Polish porn and admitted to myself that some people – especially those with suspicious minds – might think that a tad strange also.

Room 667 was the first one facing me as the lift doors opened. I checked myself once more in the mirror and took three steps across the corridor and knocked, smiling politely (not leering at all) up at the glass spyhole in the door.

As soon as the door swung open I realised that I had either made a terrible mistake or the Sex Siren of Stettin had put on six stones in weight, gone totally bald and become a man.

'I'm terribly sorry,' I said, holding the roses like a peace offering. 'I was looking for a Miss Lea Klemm.'

The short fat bald guy looked at me and said nothing; just breathed at me. I had long enough to take in the fact that he'd eaten something pickled recently and some of it had gone down the front of his chocolate and stone wide-striped Joe Brown hoody.

Then a female voice from behind him said:

'That's not my Terence.'

Short fat bald guy raised his right eyebrow at me.

'No, I'm not Terry Patterson,' I said, aiming over his shoulder, 'I just work for him. If that's Lea Klemm, I've brought you flowers.'

'You'd better let him in, Tor,' said the voice, then added

something in a language which might have been Polish but I couldn't swear to it.

I had conditioned myself to expect her to sound something like a cross between Zsa Zsa Gabor and the woman who does the voice-overs for the Cadbury Easter Bunny. What I actually heard was high-pitched and squeaky with, though I thought my ears were deceiving me, a distinct Liverpool twang.

Even if I was way off-target when it came to my expectations of what a porn star sounded like, I was spot on when it came to what they might look like. I forced myself to remember that she was an actress and it was all an act, but I had to give her top marks for staying in character.

I squeezed by Tor, careful not to step on his remarkably small feet in their small but expensive K-Swiss trainers, and into the room. I was taller than he was, although only a third as wide, but he didn't seem bothered by the fact. I wondered if he was the minder the Polish deli owner Kruszczyński had mentioned when he described her visit to Sheffield. She was likely to be wasting her money, for as soon as I saw her I realised that Lea Klemm could take care of herself.

I recognised her immediately from the collage of pictures Kruszczyński had stuck to his cash register, even though she was wearing clothes today. She was sitting on the edge of the double bed, balancing a teacup and saucer daintily in her right hand. If it had been a film set, her next line of dialogue could have been 'More tea, vicar?' but it probably wouldn't have been that sort of movie.

She was wearing a light blue sheath of a satin dress with a single chrysanthemum design in black on the left hip. The left side was slit from ankle to thigh and had fallen away to reveal a long length of dark tan hold-up stocking with a filigree top

and a half-inch of white flesh above it. The dress formed a
two-inch collar around her neck, but then cut away in a
perfect heart shape to reveal a pair of formidable bosoms
fighting for stretch room. Her hair was bottle-blonde and had
been straightened until it could scream no more; her make-up
said she was always ready for her close up.

I wished I still had Laura's phone with the built in camera.
I could have asked Tor to take a picture of us sitting together
on that bed and had it on display in a delicatessen in Sheffield
within minutes.

'Where's Terry?' she said, looking up at me through cold
blue eyes which were obviously from the 'Strict Mistress' part
of her portfolio, but somehow just didn't gel with the Scouse
accent as her question came out as 'Wares Turree?'

'I was sort of hoping you could tell me. I've brought you
these, by the way.'

As I held out the bunch of roses, she leant forward until low
enough to place her cup on the floor, giving me a deliberate
eyeful of her heart-framed cleavage.

When she had straightened up, she stood up, maintaining
eye contact all the time. She took the roses from me and
casually tossed them over her shoulder on to the bed.

I hadn't actually noticed her feet for some reason, so I didn't
know if she was wearing heels or not, but she was certainly a
good six inches taller than me now that she had uncoiled.
Purists might have said that her nose was just a little bit too
long and sharp, and her cheekbones a fraction too high for her
to be a classic beauty, but hey, nobody's perfect.

'Did you say you worked for Terry?'

'Yes I did. He hired me a few days ago to find Benji
Nicholson.'

Her face softened and genuinely so. She wasn't that good an actress.

'So, you must be the Angel. Terry told me he was getting you to help us. He said you were the best, a top-notch investigator, whatever that means.'

'I'm not sure myself.'

'Terry spoke highly of you and told me that he knew you many years ago when he was a security chief.'

'Well that's certainly true, but...'

She held the tips of three fingers up to my mouth to stop me speaking. Her fingers smelt faintly of coconut.

'My darling Terry said you were the best and would get quick results. He even gave me your address in Hackney in case I had to go and see you, though I am not sure where Hackney is. He said I could always find you there because you were always under the covers and your office would never divulge your location.'

What the hell was Patterson doing? Perhaps he hadn't realised that I no longer lived in Hackney, which was fair enough, but why give Lea Klemm a domestic address at all?

'Did he give you an office number for me?'

'No, no phone number, just Angel Investigations, 9 Stuart Street, Hackney. See? I have a good memory.'

She was holding out her hand towards me and it seemed churlish not to fondle it.

'Roy Angel, pleased to meet you. I have heard all about you.'

'You have seen my films?' She might not have been a good actress, but she certainly was an actress all right. 'Or visited my website?'

'Your website?'

'It's www.countesslea.com but make sure that you spell Lea as L-E-A and do not spell it "Leah" with an "h", for that is another site completely; one for a New York dominatrix, or so she claims.'

'I'm sorry, I didn't know you had a website.'

'It's very popular, it attracts ten thousand spanks a day.'

I stopped myself from laughing just in time.

'I think you mean "hits",' I said.

'I do, but on porno sites we call them spanks.'

'I never knew that.'

But I've always said that as long as you learn something new, no day is wasted.

'Then how do you know of me?'

'You have a very big fan in Sheffield.'

Her eyes widened.

'My little Polish grocer! Oh yes, he's a sweetie, a big fan. Come, sit down and tell me how you know him.'

She sat down on the edge of the bed again, batting the bunch of roses out of the way with her arm and then patted the bedspread next to her. So I sat down as instructed.

'We were looking for your film crew actually,' I started, wondering why the heating had to be always on so high in hotel rooms.

'We?'

'Myself and a...northern associate...someone who does legwork for me up north.'

She flashed a smile which I think was her attempt at 'coy', then crossed her right leg over her left, taking full advantage of the slit in her dress so I was treated to a full length of stockinged leg. And she was wearing heels, black leather, pointed-toe, strappy ones; the sort all the young *fashionistas* back in the Nineties had and called them "FMs"; their 'Fuck Me Shoes'.

'In my business, "legwork" is something quite different,' she said, trying to lower her voice a notch to theatrical husky. It was a valiant attempt, but she wasn't *that* good.

'I must say, your English is excellent,' I said and I meant it. The suggestive double entendre is the most difficult thing to do in a foreign language, especially if you have a Scouse accent.

'My first boyfriend and my first director, he was an English seaman, a bosun on an oil tanker from Liverpool. He jumped ship in Stettin in order to make porno films.'

'That's an unusual career path,' I observed, biting my lip.

'He knew nothing about film-making, but he was a quick learner. I knew no English, but I was a quick learner too. I realised pretty damn quick that he had run out of ideas and it was time for me to move on in my career. But that's enough about me,' she patted my leg and I almost reciprocated until I remembered that Tor was still in the room, about five feet away, staring at us.

'Tell me how you found Benji.'

'I never said I had, did I?'

'But my Terry, he hired you to find Benji for me, did he not?'

'Well, technically, Terry Patterson was the one who contracted me and so I am supposed to report to him, but I'm told he has not been at his office for a couple of days. I understand the two of you were close, so I thought you might know where he is.'

'Close? We are soon to be engaged to be married!' she said proudly.

'Really?' I said, startled. 'He didn't mention that.'

'I think my Terry is shy,' she said, and now she was definitely trying to sound like Zsa Zsa Gabor and allowed herself to gently fall backwards across the bed so that she was supported by her elbows. 'But he said he would help me find Benji, even though it was a little embarrassing for him.'

'Why would that be embarrassing?' I asked trying to find a neutral part of the bed to concentrate on. I couldn't decide whether it was the statuesque reclining Lea or the rigidly immobile and staring Tor which was unnerving me most.

She looked away from me, up into space. It was probably one of her better acting moods.

'When I first met Terry, it was in Hungary, in Budapest, which is an important city in the porno industry; many productions are filmed there. Terry was on a business trip and became – what is the word? – smitten with me. He said he was madly in love with me and pleaded with me to come to England and marry him. He said he made plenty of money and had a good job, and I would not have to go on making the porno videos.'

She glanced at me to make sure I was following her story.

'This was back in the days of video, before DVDs and uploads and downloads and websites, you understand?'

I nodded to show that I had kept abreast of modern technology.

'But I could not do it,' she sighed.

'Because of your career...?' I asked carefully.

Her mouth popped open and her eyes widened in stage surprise. I suspected it was one of her signature acting expressions.

'Oh no,' she said, trying to up a gear into pure innocence.

'I could not do it because I was already married to Ioan.'

She pronounced it 'Eye-on' and I automatically assumed she was talking about somebody called Ian.

'Ian was the sailor from Liverpool who directed your films?'

'No, his name was Robby and that was earlier, in Poland. Robby got into trouble with the police there and tried to offer them bribes. It was a very sad experience. Robby attempted to bribe the only two honest policemen in Poland and he said at his trial that he did not know such policemen existed, for they had not in Liverpool.'

'At least he kept his Scouser sense of humour,' I admitted. 'What happened to him?'

'Half a year in jail and then he was deported,' she said airily, 'but by that time I had moved to Hungary and met Ioan. He was very young but had a flair for porno and one eye always on the future and things like digital cameras and websites. He also had a rare talent in porno, some would say the rarest talent.'

My mind boggled, but I managed to keep quiet.

'He could write stories and scripts: give the actors words, good words which made sense, not just grunts and moans. Scriptwriting – that was Ioan's great talent.'

'Just like Benji's,' I said, careful not to use the past tense.

Now she really did show her mettle as an actress, for she was totally convincing in the role of 'woman looking at complete idiot'.

'Ioan *is* Benji,' she said slowly. 'Since he came back to England, he has been known as Benji Nicholson, but he was Ioan Nicousci when I married him.'

'You...married...Benji Nicholson?'

'Yes, that's right.' She sat up and patted my knees with both hands as if rewarding a pet who had finally understood a command. 'And technically, we are still married, so you can see how that could be embarrassing.'

I felt like shaking my head to clear it, though I seemed to be the only one in the room who was confused. Tor just stood there, squat and impassive, and Lea was looking into my face with an expression of pure innocence.

'But I thought Benji was gay,' I said, not quite sure how she'd take it.

She laughed.

'We all *knew* he was gay! All Budapest knew he was gay in those days. Only Ioan wasn't sure. He thought of himself as simply bisexual.'

'But you still married him?'

'Why not? We were younger, of course, and carefree, but we loved each other and we were both lonely strangers in a foreign country. It seemed perfectly natural to us.'

'You know that Benji...Ioan...has a legal partner, another man, in this country?'

'Oh yes, he told me he had a gay husband now and that he loves him very much. I am very happy for him and I wish them a long and happy life together.'

'Then I think I've got some bad news for you, Miss Klemm,' I said.

I suppose I could have done the 'good news/bad news' routine on the basis that at least now she wouldn't need to get a divorce, but I didn't want to be cruel; she hadn't done me any harm other than causing my blood pressure to rise.

'I'm afraid that, if the man you call Ioan is the man I think of as Benji Nicholson, then he's dead. I'm so sorry.'

She snapped to her feet like a gymnast doing a formal 'present' before a move, leaving the bed, and me, rocking in her slipstream.

'He cannot be dead! He was not ill!'

She had her hands in her hair and was looking around the room wildly, as if Ioan/Benji was really here with us, somehow blended with the wallpaper.

'No, no, no, nooooooo...' she wailed, and I really couldn't tell if 'Distraught Widow' was one of the characters in her repertoire or the grief was genuine.

'He was so young,' she said suddenly, spinning around to face me, her hands at the side of her head grasping fistfuls of hair. 'How can he be dead?'

'He didn't die naturally,' I said softly and sincerely, proving I could act as well, 'he was killed. The police in Manchester found his body earlier this week.'

Now I was watching her face closely to see if the actress really was acting. Would she go with outraged innocence ('Who could have done such a thing?') or despair ('Why would anyone kill my beloved Ioan?')? Would she demand gruesome details? Would she want to know if he suffered? Would she ask if an arrest had been made, or go straight into preparing an alibi for herself?

She threw me by pointing a finger down at my chest and saying:

'You are not police, though?'

'Me? No, I'm just a private investigator, working for Terry Patterson. I told you.'

She seemed satisfied with that and turned to look at Tor. His face was impassive, hers was businesslike, as she spoke to him in what I guessed was Hungarian.

Tor reached down behind the back cushion of the room's only armchair and pulled out a clear plastic zip-lock freezer bag and handed it to Lea. As I was still sitting on the bed, I saw it pass at eye-level as she took it with a shaking hand. It contained a white powdery substance, a red plastic drinking straw cut down to about three inches and a credit card size piece of plastic which I recognised, bizarrely, as a Sainsbury's Nectar card.

'I need to do a line,' said Lea Klemm striding towards the en suite bathroom. 'You're welcome to join me.'

I held my hands up, palms out.

'Thanks, but no thanks,' I said.

At least I knew she wasn't acting.

She closed the bathroom door, leaving Tor and I together, eyeing each other uneasily. I got the feeling that to shrug my shoulders in a laddish way and say 'Women, eh? What are you gonna do?' probably wouldn't work. He didn't seem at all inclined to be friendly and hadn't struck me as a natural conversationalist. I wasn't scared of him, as he had not been in the slightest way aggressive towards me, I just couldn't think of anything to say to him. No doubt Amy would come up with a dozen possible gambits when I got to tell her about the time I was trapped in a hotel room with a Hungarian minder who was wider than he was tall and a Polish porn star who was snorting cocaine off a toilet seat.

Perhaps I would edit the Amy version.

'Lea is not addict you know.'

For a moment, I didn't realise that it was Tor who had spoken, even though I knew it wasn't me, so it had to be him.

'She only takes drugs to keep her figure,' he added.

'I don't think hard drugs are recommended for slimming, even by the Provisional Wing of Weight Watchers,' I said.

'Her body is important to her work,' said Tor impassively.

'I can see that.'

'It does not mean she is bad person.'

'Of course not.'

That seemed to end that particular conversation, but as I had discovered that Tor could talk, I wanted to encourage him.

'Do you usually travel with Lea?'

'No.'

'Did you know Benji? I'm sorry, I mean Ioan.'

'No.'

'Your English is very good,' I said in desperation.

'Fucking should be. I was brought up in Lewisham.'

I tried to keep the surprise off my face and out of my voice.

'But you speak Hungarian, don't you?'

'Never said I *was* Hungarian.'

And that seemed to be as far as Tor's soul was going to be bared, but they say that nature abhors a vacuum and so that was the moment my telephone rang with the chorus from 'Roxanne'. I was quite grateful for the interruption until I heard a husky male voice say:

'Is that Roxanne?'

'No it isn't!' I snapped. Then I realised I didn't have the right to deprive Fenella of her customers. 'She's tied up right now,' I said before I could bite my tongue.

'That sounds very interesting,' said the voice, now even huskier.

'She can't possibly come to the phone right now. Could you please ring back later?'

'How much later?'

'How about tomorrow?' I tried.

'Oh, I can't wait *that* long. I might have to phone Samantha instead.'

'Why don't you do that?' I suggested. 'I'm sure Roxanne wouldn't mind. She and Samantha are the *very* best of friends.'

'They are?'

My mystery caller sounded positively bouncy at that.

'Of course they are,' I reassured him. 'Who do you think tied her up?'

I ended the call and switched off the mobile faster than I had ever done before.

The sound of the ringtone brought Lea from the bathroom, wiping her teeth with the forefinger of her right hand. Perhaps I should have waited and let her answer it. She sniffed loudly, but whether that was a delayed reaction to the news about Benji, or to the coke she'd snorted, I couldn't tell.

'That wasn't Terry was it?' she asked me.

'No, wrong number,' I said, deciding it was best not to elaborate.

'Does Terry know that Benji is dead?'

'I don't think so. I haven't been able to contact him; that's why I came to see you. Can I ask when you last saw him?'

'At the weekend. He took me to dinner at The Ivy. Do you know it?'

'I only know it's too expensive for the likes of me.'

'Terry loves spending money on me,' she said, almost dreamily. 'He pays for this room for me and much else besides.'

Why was I not surprised?

'And he visited you here?' I asked.

'Yes of course,' she said, 'whenever I am in London.'

'You didn't go to his house?'

'No, never. Terry said it was only a flat and this place was better because it had room service. After we were married, we would go to live in the country. Some place he called the Home Counties. Do you know it?'

'Yes, it's wonderful there,' I said airily. 'But you do *know* where Terry lives?'

'Of course: 16 Lulworth Mews, Vauxhall. See, I told you I have a good memory for addresses.'

'But you've never been there?'

'No.'

She had dropped the woman-dealing-with-simpleton act, but I think that was the coke kicking in rather than anything I'd said.

'Did you think of going round there to see if he was home?'

'Why? If he was there he would answer his mobile.'

She sat down on the bed next to me; heavily this time, not playing for effect.

'Did you try a landline number?'

She flicked a wrist in front of her face.

'Landline? Pah! Who has landlines these days? Terry always used mobile phones. Perhaps he is away on business.'

'I didn't get that impression from his office. Aren't you worried about him?'

She turned her face towards mine, trying to express interest but I could see she was fading out. I wanted to shake her but didn't think it a good idea. She might get hysterical and short, squat, but probably loyal Tor might get aggressive and then I would get hysterical.

'Terry Patterson hires me to find Benji Nicholson,' I said slowly, 'which I do, only Benji turns up dead – murdered – and the police are naturally somewhat interested. Now I find that Terry, my client, has a fiancée who is also suddenly a widow, and Terry has disappeared, not to mention the fact that this Benji is not really Benji at all but someone called Ioan Nicholson, who's Hungarian.'

'Nicousci, not Nicholson,' she said soothingly, placing her finger against my lips to stop me talking. 'His name was Ioan Nicousci when I married him in Budapest, but he was born in England where he took the name Benji Nicholson.'

'So. that's what you meant when you said you were two lonely foreigners together, when you were in Budapest?'

'Exactly. I was a foreigner there and so was Ioan, and we met because he could speak Hungarian and I could not.'

'So he had Hungarian parents?' I shot a look at Tor as I spoke.

'Oh no,' she said, tapping my lips with her finger again as if scolding me for being slow on the uptake. 'Ioan's family was Romanian, not Hungarian, but they came from Bihor province near the border, where they are all bilingual in Romanian and Hungarian.'

I was beginning to feel out of my depth in among people who spoke more languages than I did and seemed familiar with countries and cities I had only ever seen on maps or read about in *Dracula*.

'But Ioan was English?'

'Oh yes, he was born in London. His parents left Romania to get away from the dictator Ceauçescu and his Securitate police and changed their name to Nicholson. But when he was a man and it was safe to go back, Ioan always went by his family name whenever he went back to Oradea.'

'Oradea?'

'It is the capital of Bihor province and the Nicousci family still have business interests there.'

'Oradea – as in the name of the production company?'

Lea Klemm simply shrugged her silky shoulders as if she'd never heard of the company making the film she was starring in.

'Do you know what sort of business the Nicousci family was in?' I tried.

'Import and export,' she said. 'Is it important?'

'I don't know,' I said honestly, 'but if it isn't, it leaves your fiancé Terry with the best motive for wanting Benji Nicholson, or Ioan Nicousci, out of the way.'

'I don't understand,' she said, though I didn't believe her.

'Terry wanted to marry you, but you're already married to Benji. Oldest motive in the book.'

'*Too* old,' she pouted, going into playful kitten mode. 'Nobody worries about things like that these days.'

'You might be surprised how many do,' I said, 'and I admit it's a long shot, but that's the way it might appear.'

'I see that,' she agreed, 'and you must find Terry for me. Now, go now. I have told you his address.'

'But you said he wasn't answering his phone.'

'So find out why he isn't. You are the detective, aren't you? Do some detecting!'

CHAPTER THIRTEEN

I knew I wasn't going to make it back home in time for tea and decided I had better bite the bullet and phone Amy, so I fumbled with Fenella's phone and managed to get it turned on as I stood on the down escalator taking me from the lobby of the Mount Royal and out on to Bryanston Street, almost opposite the police station.

I checked I had a signal and was about to tap in the number when I realised I still had Salome's number written on the back of my hand, so I rang that instead. It wasn't that I was avoiding talking to Amy; I just needed more rehearsal time.

Anyway, thinking of Amy had given me an idea.

When Salome answered, I could hear music in the background – an upbeat salsa arrangement I couldn't quite identify – along with a hum of voices and the occasional high-pitched laugh.

'It's Angel again,' I said.

'Wow! Twice in one afternoon! You been taking those little blue man pills again?' she said loudly for the benefit of her crowd of friends.

'I see the book group is still in progress, Salome dear. I hope you're not leading them astray.'

'Come off it, Angel, it's Thursday.'

'It is?'

'Yes, it is and Thursday night is the new Friday night, when everybody parties. Why have your hangovers on your own time at the weekend when you can have them on the firm's time on Friday?'

'I didn't know you'd gone back to work, Sal.'

'Well I haven't, but looking after a husband and bringing up two kids is a job and a half, so I get Thursdays off.'

I heard a group cheer in the background at that.

'Good for you, Sal, you go for it, but just let me ask you one thing I forgot earlier.'

'Make it quick, lover boy, my Chardonnay's getting warm.'

'It's about Terry Patterson again.'

'Oh God, what now? I don't hear from you for ages and then you just want to talk about that sad loser.'

'Why do you call him that? You didn't before.'

'I hadn't had a bottle of Chardonnay when you rang before,' she said primly. 'Anyway, he is a loser. He was Pluto-ed at Prior, Keen, Baldwin before they got taken over and there have been rumours that the forensic accountants might be taking an interest in him.'

Surprisingly, I understood most of that, even though she was starting to slur her words. Being 'Pluto-ed' in City-speak meant being downgraded, just as the planet Pluto had been downgraded to a minor star or a firework or something or other. Forensic accountants were the hunting dogs a company turned loose if they suspected an employee was skimming the till or living out of the shop. If Patterson really was paying for a porn star's West End hotel, then I could see why suspicions might be raised.

'How do you know all this Salome? I thought you were out of that world.'

'Hey, just because I've got kids and we live in Basingstoke, it doesn't mean we've dropped off the edge.'

'Didn't you tell me that Terry had a wife he was thinking of leaving?'

'Yes, he has. Bit of a surly cow called Sally. I thought at first she had a problem with me being black, then I realised she had a problem with any woman who was more successful than she was.'

'Not to mention more intelligent and far more attractive,' I said on cue.

'I didn't say that,' Salome protested.

'No, but you'd have been really pissed off if I hadn't. Listen, Sal, thanks for that. Got to go.'

She started to say something else but I really did have to go.

I had seen a figure emerge from the ramp which led down into the hotel's underground car park, riding a motorbike which looked like a Suzuki with a 750 cc engine. I couldn't see the rider's face because of the black visor on his helmet, but from his overall shape and the Joe Brown hoody he was wearing, I was pretty sure it was Tor.

He eased the bike into the street and accelerated towards the Edgware Road, passing within a few feet of me but giving no indication that he had noticed me.

I was tempted to flag down a cab and shout 'Follow that bike!', as most cabbies love things like that, but I knew that the only way to successfully follow a motorbike in London traffic was on another bike.

In any case, I had a feeling I knew where he was going.

I did jump into a cab, though not before calling in at one of the Lebanese-run 7/11 shops on the Edgware Road (not known as 'Little Beirut' for nothing) and buying a spicy sausage and harissa baguette and a copy of the *Evening Standard*. I covered the sandwich with the newspaper while I flagged down a black cab – some cabbies are a bit iffy about picnics on the back seat – and asked the driver to take me to Victoria. The rush hour was starting to form up and I didn't want to spook him by demanding to be taken south of the river to Vauxhall until it was too late for him to refuse. (Not that a kosher cabby would have refused, but he would have bitched about it, spoiling my lunch.)

Halfway down Park Lane Fenella's bloody phone went off again and, sure enough, it was a man looking to share some very expensive airtime minutes with Roxanne, though from the excitement in his voice that might have been seconds rather than minutes. I told him she was out and when he demanded to know where she was, I told him she'd just popped down the STD clinic for her prescription. He hung up before I did.

I used the call as a pretence to tap on the sliding screen behind the driver's head and told him there had been a change of plan and could he go on past Victoria and over Vauxhall Bridge as I was looking for Lulworth Mews?

He thought for almost a minute, negotiating the traffic on automatic pilot, in the way that professional cabbies do when they're given an off-the-beaten-track address. You can almost hear the gears in their brains working.

'Isn't that Stockwell way down Clapham Road? Or is it up nearer Vauxhall and the Fentiman Road end?' he asked, but I think he was just testing me to see if I was testing him.

'Dunno, mate. I've never been there before. I was just told Lulworth Mews, down in something called Little Portugal, does that help?' I said politely. It pays to be polite to black cab drivers.

'Oh, right; I know the one you mean, now.'

'Top man,' I said as he closed the glass screen and I went back to eating my sandwich under cover of my newspaper.

Of course I knew of Little Portugal, but I didn't know it that well.

There are reckoned to be about 27,000 Portuguese living in the borough of Lambeth but you hardly ever notice them until the Portugal national football team does well, which admittedly is more often than England. The area known as Little Portugal is generally taken to be within the 'V' formed by South Lambeth Road and Clapham Road, with Vauxhall to the north and Stockwell to the south. Thousands of cricket fans will have passed through it on the way to the Kennington Oval without stopping off to buy *bacalhau*, the salted fish which seems to be the national dish, or pausing to sip a *Sagres* beer in a bar, or showing off by going into a café and asking for a *galao* rather than a latte. There are plenty of music stores as well, most of them selling traditional, melancholic 'fado' compilations, although both the soft rockers Wray Gunn and the Gothic metal band Moonspell do good business down in South Lambeth.

I had been there on shopping expeditions for the odd delicacy, mostly for my father, who had a flat not far from Westminster Cathedral off the Vauxhall Bridge Road – which reminded me that I was supposed to call in and see how his recovery was going, but that would have to wait. He might be recovering from a stroke but he was living with a Page Three model over thirty years his junior, so I felt he could survive a few more days without a visit from me.

Amy, on the other hand, was another matter.

There was no way I was going to get home in time for tea now, so I thought it best to get my alibi in first. So as my cab started across Vauxhall Bridge, I phoned home.

I wasn't exactly expecting a warm and loving reception, and was bracing myself to take a bit of flak over the fact that I'd been absent without leave for three days, but as usual, Amy surprised me.

'Oh, it's you. Just who the fuck is this Lyndon Baines?'

'I have no idea; should I have?'

'I told you it was your mother's latest boyfriend; at least, I think it was you I told. It might have been a complete stranger. Remind me: what do you look like?'

'I'm the white-haired, slightly twitchy one with the humped back from having to carry all the troubles of the world around.'

'Oh, right, now I can place you.'

'Look, I'm sorry, but I really am on my way home, it's just going to take longer than I thought,' I soothed.

'Where are you?'

'Vauxhall.'

'Then it would take longer, wouldn't it? Last time I looked, Cambridge was north of the river Thames.'

'Point taken. I have just one more thing to do and then I'm on my way, promise. Everything OK back at the ranch?'

'Absolutely peachy,' she exhaled. Amy was the only person

I knew who could breathe sarcastically. 'Apart from your mother throwing a right hissy fit when I brought up the subject of her odious boyfriend.'

'Why is he odious?'

'Because your mother's terrified of him!'

Now, that wouldn't automatically condemn a bloke in my book and my father might even put him on his Christmas card list, but I thought it best to go with the flow.

'What exactly is the problem?'

'The problem is she's not going to go home while this Lyndon Baines creep is hanging around. She's going to stay here with us. For ever!'

'Yeah, I get that bit and I appreciate the gravity of the situation. What I meant was what is *her* problem with this Lyndon Baines?'

'From what she's said, which isn't much, he's a bit of a control freak who likes messing with her head. Jane Bond reckons it's more serious and thinks he's a stone-cold bully who likes hurting women. She's pretty sure he's hit your mother more than once.'

'That's incredible,' I said slowly.

'It happens, you know.'

'I know it does, it's just the idea of my mother as the *victim* that's incredible.'

'That's harsh,' said Amy sternly.

'Don't tell me you hadn't thought that. I just can't imagine my mother backing off from a row, that's all.'

'I think this is more than a row, I think she's deeply scared of this guy and if she does go back to Romanhoe, there could be violence. We don't want her to get a CRASBO.'

'A *what*?' I almost burst out laughing.

'She's got herself an ASBO, and if she breaks that it becomes a Criminal Anti-Social Behaviour Order – a CRASBO. If we send her back home, and she snaps and reaches for the knife drawer, of course, it could be more serious.'

'So what do we do?'

'We have to do something about this Lyndon Baines. He seems to have moved into her house and she daren't throw him out. She's genuinely frightened of him; says he told her he'd been in the SAS.'

'Men who brag about being in the SAS are almost certainly the ones who never were,' I said to reassure her.

'That's good to know. I told your mother you'd go over there and have a word with him, soon as you get back. OK?'

Lulworth Mews turned out to be off Fentiman Road, just down from the Oval tube station, and I got my cab driver to drop me at the end rather than have to go in there and mess about doing a U-turn. As I paid him off, I surveyed the amount of cash I had left in my wallet and realised I had more receipts in there than notes, so I resolved to call at an ATM or hole-in-the-wall before I went much further, as I still had to get back to Stansted somehow and pick up Armstrong.

All I had to do was find my client and ask him what the hell was going on, then I could go home with a clear conscience. I'd found a body, met a porn star, visited a red-light district, helped the police with their enquiries, been shot at and forced to line-dance. Good God, I'd even had to go up north. Surely I deserved a few weeks' holiday or at least compassionate leave.

It wasn't going to happen.

I wasn't surprised that my cab driver had had to think carefully about Lulworth Mews. It was utterly missable; a

'Everyone else is out working for you. I'm thinking of changing the name to Angel Incorporated.'

'Great idea, Veronica, and I'm sure we can find a place for you somewhere in the organisation. In the meantime, you're the boss so I'm giving you the heads-up that my current investigation has got deadly serious.'

'How serious is "serious"? Have you been caught fiddling your expenses?'

'Not yet, but it's worse than that.'

'You haven't lost your client?' she demanded, outraged.

'In a manner of speaking,' I said, wincing as I did so. 'I know exactly where he is, it's just that he's dead.'

'Another one? You've found another body?' she shouted, and I just hoped that she didn't have the windows of the office open. 'Are you moonlighting for the Grim Reaper or something?'

'It's starting to feel like that,' I admitted.

'Where was this one?'

'At home, in Lambeth.' I made her take a note of the address. 'And I'm afraid he wasn't alone. I think whoever did him did his wife as well.'

'Why?' she asked, not able to hide the shock in her voice.

'I don't know, boss, I really don't know. In fact I've got very little idea of what's going on.'

That wasn't strictly true. I think my problem was I had too many ideas (none of them good) about what was going down.

Veronica finally did the mental maths.

'Hang on, are you saying you've found *three* bodies?'

'And you thought I was skiving off and enjoying myself, didn't you?'

'That's sick, Angel.'

grey and soulless cul-de-sac of small box-like houses probably built while there was still rubble on the ground after Luftwaffe bombers, and later 'doodlebug' flying bombs, had aimed for Chelsea Bridge or Battersea Power Station and fallen short. One or two of the houses had made an effort with window boxes, but that was about it. Three of the houses had estate agent 'For Sale' signs outside, but apart from that, the only way to tell the houses apart was by looking for the numbers. It didn't seem the right sort of area for a City high-flyer to live; maybe Terry Patterson's downsizing had been really serious.

The mews was completely deserted; a few chocolate bar wrappers and the ubiquitous McDonald's carton lying in the gutter dust the only signs of human habitation.

I found number 16 easily enough and I didn't have to worry about pressing the doorbell, for the door was open. Only a half-inch or so, and anyone walking by might have missed the fact, even the milkman if they still had such things in Lambeth.

What was odd was that the postman could not possibly have. In fact he hadn't, because a wedge of what was obviously junk mail was still just protruding from the letter-box where it hadn't gone all the way through. Why had the door not opened more when he pushed the mail in?

For some reason I wasn't totally sure of, I made a fist of my right hand and pushed at the door with my knuckles rather than my fingers but it yielded no more than two inches and then gently squeezed itself back again. I was beginning to get a very bad feeling about this, as they say in the best movies, although they can't show you the very bad smells you start to imagine you can smell.

I still had my *Evening Standard*, so I rolled it tightly into a rod and gently poked the logjam of junk mail blocking the letterbox until it fell inside the house, then I used the paper to hold the flap open and bent down to peer in, hoping that if anyone did see me from the street, they would think me too blatantly stupid a burglar to worry about.

What was it Ossie had said about the best way to get away with murdering somebody was to shoot them as they answered the door and never to step inside the house yourself?

Somebody must have overheard him, because I reckon that was exactly what had happened to Terry Patterson.

And, from the way she was lying just a little further down the hallway, his poor wife as well.

I left Lulworth Mews at a brisk pace, holding the *Standard* up in front of me just in case I had the misfortune to be caught by a CCTV camera. Britain is supposed to have one fifth of all the security cameras in the world, but thankfully less than half of them work properly.

I headed towards Vauxhall Station and the river, mingling with the thickening stream of commuters and shoppers heading homewards. Which is what I should have done.

There was nothing more I could usefully do on this case, as I was at least three murders out of my depth and now I didn't even have a client any more. I suppose I could have gone back to see Lea Klemm to tell her that she'd lost a fiancé as well as a husband, which made her sound really careless and would only have been cruel. Maybe it would be better to go home and see how things looked in the morning.

For a microsecond I thought about just heading out of town and forgetting everything, prepared to plead total ignorance if I should ever be asked about Terry Patterson. Then remembered how many people I had told that I was working for him: Benji's sister Phoebe at the funeral, Ossie, Giancarlo Artesi, the cops in Manchester, Salome and goodness knew who else, plus I'd even called at his office and his office would have taken calls from Rudgard & Blugden.

That didn't seem an option and I guessed that, somewhere in the Private Eye's Code of Conduct, probably in the small print I hadn't bothered to read yet, was a clause which said something to the effect that, should your client happen to get murdered, it might be a good idea to tell the police.

So that was the choice facing me as I looked over the river from Vauxhall Bridge: stay in London and try and persuade the forces of law and order that turning up three dead bodies in a week was par for the course for a private detective of my calibre, or getting myself home to the peace and quiet of the countryside where it seemed my mother was expecting me to go and beat seven bells out of her psychotic, ex-SAS boyfriend.

Some choice.

It brought to mind the first rule of feng shui: never put the rock too close to the hard place.

I compromised with myself and decided to ring the office before I did anything drastic like phone the police. It was only fair that Veronica knew what was going on and it might help me if, when the police contacted her, as they would, she didn't say 'Never heard of him'. That never went down well with the police in my experience.

I didn't actually expect her to answer the phone and I told her so.

'I'm the only one left in the office,' she said sulkily.

'Sorry. It's been a rough week and it's not over yet.'

'Fricking hell, you're not planning on finding any more stiffs are you?' she exploded.

'Calm down, dear, calm down, I was thinking of something else, something on the domestic front.'

'Is that what Lorna's working on?'

'I've no idea what Lorna's working on,' I said. 'Which one's Lorna?'

'Have you been drinking?'

'It's only a matter of time,' I admitted. 'What's Lorna doing?'

'She's checking something out for Amy, isn't she?' she said primly.

'My Amy? I'm sorry, boss, that's news to me. I've got my own problems – like how to report a dead married couple in Lambeth without finding myself down the Old Bailey?'

'How should I know?' said Veronica with just a trace of hysteria. 'We've never had anything to do with a murder before.'

'*Murders*, boss. Plural.'

'Thank you for reminding me. What do you expect me to do?'

'I don't know. You're the boss, Boss.'

I heard her take a deep breath in through the nose and let it out slowly through the mouth, just as she'd been told to do by the panic attack counsellors.

'I'm going to talk to our solicitor,' she said eventually.

'We have a solicitor?'

She ignored me.

'I'm pretty sure the advice will be to phone the police.'

'And how much are we paying for advice like that?'

'Just shut the frick up, will you? Let me see what the lawyer says and I'll get back to you. Will you be on this number? I don't recognise it.'

'It's a borrowed mobile. It's been quite useful. I think I might get one.'

I heard her groan.

'Don't mention mobiles to Laura, she still hasn't forgiven you,' she said, 'and by the way, she's left you a message about something she was looking into for you. I tell you, you've got us all running around after you, haven't you?'

I tried to remember which one was Laura and then what I'd asked her to do for me.

'Oh yeah, she was looking up a film company for me. Oradea Films.'

'Hang on,' said Veronica, 'I've got her notes here, up on the screen. You see, some people believe in keeping a work log so that we can all *share* information. That's probably a new concept for you.'

'Not new, Veronica, just difficult.'

'I should say. Anyway, I hope this makes more sense to you than it does to me, but according to Laura, Oradea Films doesn't actually exist. It has no listing, no offices, no telephone numbers, nothing.'

'But that doesn't make sense,' I said.

'So little does where you're concerned,' she said. 'But fortunately for you Laura is a conscientious operative and she's turned up something called Oradea Imports, which seems to be based in Southwark, though the list of directors sounds all foreign.'

'Laura got a list of directors? Top girl!'

'She's even put a note on the file that she thought you'd be

interested in this because you'd been asking about Romania.
Oradea Imports deals in food and drink from Romania and
the directors are – if I can pronounce them right – Gheorge
Nicousci, Lara Marie Nicousci, P. Nicousci and I. Nicousci.
Am I saying those properly?'

'I think so.'

'So those names do mean something to you, then? Clever
little Laura.'

'Hate to be a damp squib, Von, but I found one of them
dead in Manchester and I'm pretty sure I went to the funeral
of another one. Nicousci is the Romanian family name of
Benji Nicholson. He was called Ioan, so that's the I. Nicousci
and his sister Phoebe will be the P. Nicousci. Lara Marie is
almost certainly the mother, whose funeral I went to. I think
she was known as Clara Maria over here.'

'And this Gheorge – or is it George? – Nicousci?'

'I don't know. Could be Benji's dad. Not come across him,
no wait; somebody told me he died a few years back.'

'And the other one?'

'What other one?'

'The other one of the directors: Tor Szatmari. That's sounds
Romanian too, doesn't it?'

'No, it's Hungarian,' I said.

'How do you know stuff like that?'

'I've met him.'

'So these people, they all mean something?'

'Yes, but I don't know what.'

'Well, Laura certainly thought they must be important,' she
said sniffily.

'Why do you say that?'

'Because she went down to investigate this Oradea Imports.'

'Went where – and when?'

'About an hour ago to the registered address of Oradea Imports...' she paused, probably to read off the computer screen '...at numbers 1–3 The Arches, Redcross Way, Southwark. Do you know it?'

'No, but I know a convenient wine bar.'

I told Veronica to try and raise Laura on her mobile, but she adopted a rather superior tone and informed me that Laura's mobile was in for repair – as if that was my fault. I said I didn't know you could repair them, I thought you just dropped them into rubbish bins as you walked by, like they did in *The Matrix*.

Veronica told me to grow up, though I think only because she didn't know what *The Matrix* was, and asked why I was worried about Laura going down to Southwark as she had actually been a professional investigator longer than I had.

I didn't want to spook her by suggesting Laura might be out of her league and possibly in danger, so I planted the idea in her mind that until she talked to the firm's lawyers, we ought to call a halt to the investigation. She went along with that and I told her I would swing round to Southwark myself to try and head Laura off at the pass. Veronica asked if it was clever for me to leave the scene of a crime we were about to report to the police, and I said that sounded more than reasonable to me.

I was lucky to spot a taxi with its light on heading towards Vauxhall Bridge, though the driver's face fell when I told him I wanted to stay south of the river. He asked if I preferred to go via the Albert Embankment or through Kennington and the Elephant and Castle. I asked for the quickest route that

took in a hole-in-the-wall cash dispenser. He growled a bit at
that, but I was in the cab with the door shut, so he accepted
the situation and he delivered me to the Marshalsea Road end
of Redcross Way complete with a £200 cash withdrawal in my
wallet, from which I gave him a £10 tip, though it didn't seem
to cheer him up and he thanked me with a sour expression on
his face. Mind you, that might have been because Fenella's
bloody phone had rung twice whilst I was his passenger, the
callers asking to speak to 'Roxanne'. I had shouted 'Fuck off,
you perv!' at both of them and I think the cabby didn't
approve of my telephone manner.

Redcross Way was deserted, as I expected it be at this time
of day. The local primary school had long since sent its kids
home for the day, and even the cleaners had been and gone.
There was no reason for the street to be busy; it wasn't a main
thoroughfare to anywhere and there were no businesses down
there apart from The Boot and Flogger, which I knew would
be closing soon as there was no evening trade.

All I had was the address Laura had unearthed and she
might easily be there by now, snooping around and making a
nuisance of herself. I wasn't sure how Benji Nicholson or
Terry Patterson (or his wife) had been a nuisance, or to whom,
but somebody had been peeved enough to kill them –
probably the same person who took a shot at me two hundred
miles away in Manchester that morning. Had it really been
less than twelve hours ago?

Logic told me that something called 'The Arches' would be
beyond The Boot and Flogger at the other end of Redcross
Way where it was crossed by Southwark Street and by the
railway lines going into London Bridge station or across the
river and into Cannon Street. Where there were railway lines

and viaducts, there were arches, and it had been common practice since Victorian times to brick up one end of an archway and put doors on the other, creating workshops, lock-up stores or shops. Down near Waterloo I knew several wine bars which had prospered underneath the arches there.

And thinking of wine bars led automatically to me calling in at The Boot and Flogger, as somebody there might know something useful. After all, some of the staff, like Irene, had been there forever and if she was on duty she might even be pleased to see me for the second time that week, as I would now qualify for prodigal customer status.

Irene was not only on duty, but she was standing in the entrance of The Boot, and she was expecting me.

'Thank Gawd you're here, Mr Angel.'

'Hello, Irene,' I said politely, taken aback as I always was by being addressed as 'Mr'.

'We were just closing up – I almost had me coat on 'cos I've got some left-over smoked salmon for me husband's dinner – but I couldn't leave her, not in the state she was in. I was all for calling an ambulance, but your friend said no and asked to use the phone. She said you were on the way and you'd know what to do. Bloody Romanians! My old mother, Gawd rest her, told me never to trust Gypsies, but I used to think she was just being racist, like you had to if you were brought up in Poplar like she was.'

'Irene, my love, you lost me shortly after you said you were putting your coat on. Now calm down, relax and tell me what's been happening.'

'If you won't listen to a word of mine, then you'd better come in and see for yourself.'

It was strange being in The Boot when it was empty –

empty of cooking smells, empty of the clanking of cutlery and the chinking of glasses. Even that day's sawdust had been swept up. No doubt a fresh sprinkling, like dew, would appear in the morning. It was probably just a deception of the low-level lighting and the smoke-blackened interior, but the place actually looked smaller when it was empty than when packed with diners and drinkers.

That was surprise number one. Number two was when a female figure in a trench coat rushed out of the gloom and embraced me in a rib-creaking hug. I could tell from the texture of the body parts pressed up against me and the smell of the hair on the head buried in my chest that it was definitely female, but it was only when she pulled back to take a breath that I was sure it was Laura.

'I am *so* glad to see you, Angel,' she said.

'That's a first,' I said, in no particular hurry to let go of her.

'Hey, you two, we don't do rooms here, you know,' said Irene loudly.

Laura put her fingertips on my shoulders and gently levered herself away.

'I knew you'd come here,' Laura said breathily.

'You must have read my case notes on the Nicholson funeral,' I said, though I wasn't terribly sure I had actually written any up yet.

'No, I realised this was the only bar on the street, so you were bound to turn up sooner or later. This lady let us in and let me use the phone, and Veronica told me to stay put as you were on your way. She said she'd ring you to tell you what happened.'

I frowned at that and dug out Fenella's phone.

'Oops, I must have turned it off.' I had, after the last call for

'Roxanne'. 'Sorry about that, you'll have to bring me up to speed.'

'Then you'd better come and meet Zsofia.'

'Sophia – as in Sophia Loren?'

'Who? Never mind. It's Zsofia with a 'Z', she wrote it on a serviette for me. She's Hungarian.'

'Don't tell me you speak Hungarian.'

'No, I don't. It's a really, really difficult language to learn.'

'So how did you meet this Zsofia with a Zed?'

'I found her lying in the street outside.'

Given my history of some extended lunches at The Boot, I thought of saying *We've all been there*, but the expression on Laura's face told me not to mess about.

Irene pushed by me to lock and bolt the door to the street.

'You can go on through,' she said, 'and sit in one of the booths, but don't be long because I've got to get meself home.'

'The bar's shut?' I asked, and felt rather than saw Laura giving me the evils.

'Just asking,' I said. 'So how did you find this Zsofia, then?'

In hushed tones, Laura rapidly sketched her adventures in Redcross Way over the past hour or so.

She had found Oradea Imports where I suspected they were, operating from three converted archways just across Southwark Street down near the river where Redcross Way gave way to Bankside and a pedestrian walk which led round to the Globe Theatre and the Millennium Bridge – the one that had wobbled so much it had been closed for repairs almost as soon as it had opened.

Laura had noted activity at one of the Oradea lock-ups, with a motorbike and a white Transit van labelled 'Oradea Imports' parked out front. She had, of course, made a note of their numbers in her Girl Guide diary or Filofax or whatever, the point being that she wouldn't have had to write anything down, she could have taken a photograph, if only her mobile phone had been working.

I let her have that one without comment. She would forgive me some day. Not soon, but some day.

She couldn't understand why an area of London so close to Shakespeare's Globe, the Tate Modern, a mainline railway station and Southwark Cathedral would be so deserted this early of an evening (which simply confirmed her in my mind as a West One Warrior who was never happy out of sight of a Starbucks), but fortunately there was a building site across the road and Laura had hidden herself behind a palette load of bricks, so she could observe but not be observed. Clever girl, I thought.

She had only just managed to conceal herself, she said, when the doors of one of the archway units had opened and two men had appeared. They had checked the coast was clear in an obviously furtive manner and then proceeded to shepherd more than a dozen young women from the lock-up and into the back of the Transit van.

'They were being led like prisoners,' Laura said, 'or those women you see in the films of the concentration camps, who know they're walking to their deaths but can't do anything about it. It was that bad; it was that sad, Angel, it really was. They didn't have proper clothes – it was as if they'd been dressed at Oxfam. Some were wearing nothing but slips or long T-shirts. They didn't have shoes, Angel. They didn't have shoes, for Christ's sake!'

I put an arm around her. So did Irene.

'What happened?'

'The two men, they pushed and shoved the girls to make them get in that van. And you could see it was a van, it wasn't a little bus or anything. There were no seats, so they had to sit on the floor.'

'These two men, what were they like?'

'One was tall and quite young. He seemed to be the driver of the van. The other one, who was giving the orders, was short and squat, almost box-shaped, a bit like Spongebob Squarepants.'

'I have no idea who Spongebob Squarepants is,' I said, 'but you're describing a man called Tor, though I wouldn't try to pronounce his surname. But where does this Zsofia come into things?'

'OK, so there were about twelve girls shuffling out of that Arches place – it must be a prison – and they were all bunched up. The driver guy, he was holding the back doors of the van open and fat old Spongebob was right at the back of the group. They must have rehearsed it because the girls all stayed together and then Zsofia, who was right in the middle of the group, sort of hidden by them, well she dropped to her knees and crawled *under* the parked van, I could see her from across the street but those two bastards were so close, they couldn't. Luckily they were also too stupid to count them all out and count them back in again.'

She paused, flushed and breathless.

'So what happened then?'

'The younger one said something to the fat one, but I couldn't hear properly. It wasn't English, I do know that. Then he shut the doors, got in the van and drove off as the fat bastard went back inside the warehouse. When the van pulled away I saw that there was a girl face down in the road where the van had been. I thought she was dead…but she was just terrified. She couldn't move so I had to pick her up and carry her out of there. Fortunately Irene here saw us and let us come in here.'

'I thought they were pissed,' said Irene, then she blushed. 'Sorry, but I did.'

'Thanks, Irene,' I said, 'you're an absolute star.'

Laura grabbed a fistful of my shirt front.

'What's this all about Angel?'

'I'm still not sure,' I said without a word of a lie.

'Then what do we do now?'

'Are you *sure* the bar's shut, Irene?' I asked, more in hope than expectation.

CHAPTER FOURTEEN

Actually, Irene had already reopened the bar, out of the goodness of her heart, but only to provide a large schooner of port for Zsofia who had her hands clasped around it as if it gave off heat and she had frostbite. Irene made no effort to extend the out-of-hours hospitality of The Boot to anyone else, but even I had to admit that Zsofia was the most deserving case.

She looked awful; but then anyone would who had lain face down in a Southwark gutter and allowed a few tons of Transit van to drive over them. Or, at least, anyone who had done that voluntarily without the aid of drugs or excessive alcohol consumption.

Irene had put her in one of The Boot's enclosed booths, their small wood-and-glass eating rooms where you wouldn't be surprised to find Charlie Dickens and Wilkie Collins fighting over the last Barnsley chop.

She sat at the far end of the table, her back to the wall, watching the doorway with an expressionless face and eyes which seemed dead to the world, or at least this world. Her hair needed washing – about three weeks ago – and her face was deathly white with not a trace of make-up apart from a thick smear of bright red lipstick which looked as if it had been applied not just in haste but in hatred. I had once read somewhere that it was an established Gestapo technique to keep female prisoners in conditions of utter squalor for weeks on end and then to break them by offering them a stub of lipstick.

She was wearing a sleeveless light blue woollen dress which revealed a tattoo of a swallow in flight on the right side of her neck. The dress and her arms were stained dark with dirt, and as soon as I put my head into the booth I could smell the body odours mingled with petrol exhaust fumes shimmering off her.

Laura put her arm out to block my progress into the booth and said very loudly and slowly: 'This is my friend. He's come to help.'

There was no sign Zsofia had understood. She remained immobile, hands wrapped around her glass, her fingernails short and black with dirt, staring at us with those blank eyes.

'He's not friend,' she said eventually, 'he's man.'

We didn't get much more out of Zsofia, not because she was dumb or because there was a man in the dining booth (though I kept my distance), it was simply the language barrier which defeated us. She could talk quite animatedly and angrily when she wanted to, but it was in a torrent of Hungarian which none of us could understand, not even Laura who was a bit of a boffin at languages and whom I knew spoke Russian.

'English? Can you speak English?' Laura pleaded with her.

Zsofia glared at her, and for the first time there was light in her eyes as she spat the words:

'Dick! Cock! Spread! Suck! Down!'

'Oh my good Lord,' muttered Irene behind me somewhere. 'You poor child.'

Laura looked at me, lost.

'Try and ask her how long she's been in Britain,' I told her, thinking it best not to push myself forward.

Laura took out a pocket diary from her trench coat and opened it at a page which gave the complete calendar for a year. She held this out in front of Zsofia, pointed at it, then at her.

'When did you come here? To England,' she said slowly and loudly, as the British always do when talking to foreigners.

I watched Zsofia's eyes focus on the page with a difficulty which suggested a history of drug abuse, but she got there in the end and recognised the calendar for what it was.

Speaking in a rapid, guttural growl she tried to tell us something. When we didn't respond, she jabbed a finger at the calendar page, where each month was laid out as a small boxed table.

'*Január,*' she said, which even I could understand.

'January?' asked Laura, shocked. 'You've been here since January?'

Zsofia rattled something off and shook her head violently, then grabbed the diary and made a show of turning the page over, but going backwards, jabbing her finger to make sure we got the direction.

'January *last year?*' Laura said ever so quietly. 'Fucking hell – oops! Sorry about that.'

'Don't worry, I think Zsofia's heard worse judging by the English vocabulary she's picked up in the last eighteen months.'

'Where in God's name has the poor girl been all that time?' Irene said aloud, but not as if she expected an answer. 'You don't imagine she's been under the Arches down the road all this time?'

'There were about a dozen girls in there,' Laura offered. 'Surely somebody would have noticed if they'd been there over a year.'

'I wouldn't bet on that, but we won't know until we can find somebody to translate for us. I think they may have come from Sheffield, but it's only a guess at the moment.'

'They were living in Sheffield?'

'In a brothel,' I said, 'and I don't think it was a voluntary lifestyle choice.'

'You mean she's a sex slave – she's been people-trafficked?'

'That's exactly what I mean.'

'But who'd do such a thing?'

'It's an import/export company, isn't it? Well, they export girls from Eastern Europe and import them as sex workers to the UK.'

'The bastards,' said Irene, with feeling.

'Are you sure about this, Angel?'

I reached into my jacket for my wallet, but slowed down my movements when I saw Zsofia flinch. I produced the passport photographs of Benji Nicholson, placed them on the table and gently pushed them towards the suspicious girl. She looked at them for about five seconds, then spat on them.

'That's not nice, dear,' Irene chided her gently. 'I'll get a cloth.'

'Ossie started to tell me something about this,' I admitted. 'I should have paid more attention. It was something to do with a policeman I ran into in Manchester and an Operation

Pentameter, he thought it had something to do with bringing in girls from places like Hungary and Poland and Romania.'

'Old Maria always used to have a string of girls working for her,' said Irene.

She had magically produced a sponge and was wiping down the table and carefully dabbing Zsofia's spittle off the picture of Benji Nicholson.

'Who's Maria?' Laura asked her.

Irene held up the photograph.

'Ian's mum.'

'Benji's Romanian name was Ioan,' I said, 'and his mother was Clara Maria Nicholson when she lived round here, but she'll be the Lara Marie Nicousci you found as a director of Oradea Imports.'

'Nicousci!'

We all looked at Zsofia who was pointing at the photograph and working herself up to some serious projectile vomiting.

'They were the Nicholsons round here,' Irene said calmly, 'and they always had a string of foreign girls hanging about the house, you know, as home helps, au pair girls, nannies, that sort of thing. At least, that's what Maria called them, but if you ask me they was little more than skivvies. Mind you, I'm talking of a few years back, when Maria's husband George was alive. He used to say they were all students from the university he taught at back home, but nobody gave that any credit.'

'Sounds like a family business,' I said.

'And you knew the family?' Laura asked Irene, her mouth falling open.

'Oh yes, I was telling Mr Angel here all about them the

other day, when we had the funeral meats for Maria.'

Now Laura was eyeing me with the same suspicion Zsofia was.

'You really should pay more attention to what people tell you, Angel,' she scolded me. 'The staff in pubs and bars are as good as trained observers. In our line of work they're an invaluable source of information. You should listen to them more.'

'That sounds like good advice, I'll try and remember it,' I said humbly. 'You wouldn't happen to have Ossie Oesterlein's number in that smart little diary of yours, would you?'

'As a matter of fact I do,' she said sniffly. 'Irene, is it all right to use the phone again? We'll pay.'

'No need,' I said producing Fenella's mobile. 'I've come equipped.'

When Ossie answered his phone it was grumpily and he sounded half asleep. I suspected I had disturbed him having an early evening nap in front of the television, gathering his strength for a hard night out on the tiles, or down the snooker hall, or at the wrestling, or, if his mother was involved, something with an air of danger about it such as ballroom dancing (with Ossie that would be dangerous).

I told him it was me and he perked up almost immediately.

'What was she like?'

'Who?'

'Don't play daft with me, Angel, you know very well who I mean – Lea Klemm. What's she like in the flesh?'

'Well, there was plenty of it on display and it gets her an ANB rating.'

Ossie didn't have to query that 'ANB' stood for 'All

Natural Bosom', meaning no implants, which showed he was
getting out more than I thought.

'So what did you get up to? And don't spare any of the filth
and smut.'

'Can't do, Ossie, I'm a bit up against it right now. We had
tea together and she took two spoonfuls, if that's any help.'

That was true enough, except that Ossie probably thought
I meant sugar.

'I expected a bit more than that,' he said, 'or can you not
talk now?'

'Got it in one, Os. Listen, what you were saying about
Operation Pentameter earlier. Run that by me again.'

'Told you everything I know, mate. You must have had your
mind on other things.'

'It's been happening a lot lately,' I admitted. 'Just remind
me.'

'All I know is that Detective Inspector Jebb, the odious little
geek, is fronting up something called Operation Pentameter, at
least in Sheffield, which is taking up a lot of police manpower
without being generous on the old overtime.'

'That's a recipe for disaster,' I said.

'You're not wrong there, that's why none of my mates on
the job are keen to get too involved. Some of the old lags I talk
to reckon it's just a bit of public relations.'

'How do they figure that?'

'It was like the Cudworth Posse boys said, there was cops
from all areas down in Sheffield when they were there.'

'They said that?'

I really must start listening to people in pubs.

'Oh aye, they recognised a few from Barnsley Division.
They reckon it was all a jolly, the rozzers turning out to be

extras in that film Benji was making, what was it? *Europol.*
That way they get to swan around the red-light district all day
and pretend they're Steven Segal.'

'I thought you said it was about people-trafficking.'

'Inasmuch as all the girls that work in the brothels and the
massage parlours are from Eastern Europe these days, aren't
they? I think it'll all be in Benji's script if we ever find one.'

'I don't think there ever was a script, Ossie,' I said.

'But the bloke that hired you, didn't you say he wanted to
find Benji because the script needed amending or something
like that?'

'That's what he said, but it was a blind. He had another
motive for wanting Benji found. I'm not sure there ever was
going to be a film.'

'So what was the luscious Lea Klemm doing wandering
around Sheffield in her undies?'

'Steady on there, you're imagining things.'

'You mean she doesn't wear any?'

'You might speculate on that, I couldn't possibly confirm
one way or the other. I just think Lea and the whole *Europol*
film was some sort of front for something else.'

'What did she say about the film?'

'I didn't actually get around to asking her about that,' I said
lamely, aware of Laura glaring at me again. 'Something came
up.'

'I bet it did, you lucky bleeder. But there was a film crew in
Sheffield. The Cudworth Posse saw them and so did that
Polish greengrocer chap. Oh, and by the way, me mum says
thanks for them chilli pods, though she's not sure what to do
with them.'

'I'm sure she'll think of something, and you're right, there was a film crew and a film star in Sheffield. Even if the cops were acting as unpaid extras, somebody had to foot the bills.'

'That'd be that company Oradea Films, surely? I mean, film crews just don't grow on trees.'

'Actually, with digital cameras, I suspect it's dead easy to put together a film crew, but somebody has to pick up the bill.'

'That'd be Oradea Films, surely?'

'Except they don't exist,' I repeated. 'We've had one of our best operatives trying to find a trace of them, but not a sausage.'

I smiled at Laura to make sure she'd overheard herself being appreciated.

'So where's the money coming from? I doubt that actresses like Lea Klemm work for peanuts.'

I resisted the temptation to comment on any of that. It was not the time; it was not the place; it was just too easy.

'I've got a nasty feeling that my client's bank may have been forking out for a film that doesn't actually exist.'

Hadn't Salome said something about them calling in the forensic accountants on Terry Patterson? If only somebody would invent some sort of hand-held tool which made marks on the back of all those receipts I was carrying in my wallet, then perhaps I could invent some sort of system of runic symbols by which I could take notes for future reference.

'Are you going to tell your client about this?' Ossie demanded.

'Not without the help of a medium.'

'You're joking me! Two murders in one week, that's bloody awesome!'

'Calm yourself, you great Yorkshire pudding. I've got a

nasty feeling I shall be helping police with their enquiries any minute, so I just want you to remember that my alibi is that I was line-dancing with you and your mum should anyone ask in an official capacity. On second thoughts, just say I was in Huddersfield with you and your mum.'

I did have some standards left.

'And if you can get word to the odious DI Jebb, tell him that it might just be worth him checking out Oradea Imports rather than Oradea Films. Give him the R & B number and say that Laura will have all the details.'

Laura furrowed her brow and mouthed 'I will?' in my direction.

'Regard it as Job Almost Done,' said Ossie. 'Oh, and I've got another box to tick for you.'

'You have?'

'You asked about tracking down the owner of *The Barbara Bray*.'

'I did?'

'The canal boat near Benji's; the one you said had security cameras on covering the towpath.'

'Oh yeah, it's all coming back to me now,' I confessed.

'So anyway, I tracked the owner through the Inland Waterways Agency, who give out the driving licences for those things or whatever they call them. It's a bloke called Dexter, lives near Banbury but goes to Manchester to relax on his narrowboat. Can you believe that? Anyway, you were right about his cameras being motion-sensitive.'

'You've spoken to him?'

'On the phone, like. I'm not trekking down to Banbury this time of night. It's somewhere down south innit?'

'Near Oxford,' I said, willing him to get on with it.

'Yes, well, he did talk quite posh this Mr Dexter, but he turned out to be quite a nice chap. His system records everything, when its triggered that is, onto a DVD, but he says there's so little activity down that canal basin that he can get a couple of months' worth of camera shots on one disk. When the disk's full, he wipes it.'

'I don't suppose he noticed any activity about a month ago, did he?'

'Matter of fact he did – wasn't very exciting though. He really did sound a bit pissed off that nobody's ever tried to burgle his boat and he's well miffed that the cops haven't been to interview him as a vital witness – not that he was on his boat at the time in question, that's why he had the security system on.'

'So what did his cameras pick up?'

'Just one thing out of the ordinary in the right time frame. It was late at night, about eleven o'clock according to the recording and somebody walked along the towpath towards Benji's boat.'

'That's it? That's hardly Hold-The-Front-Page stuff, is it?'

'Not of itself, and the way his cameras are sighted, he only got their legs – no faces – and of course it was dark.'

'Brilliant, that sounds a fat lot of use.'

'Hang on a minute, I haven't told you the best bit,' he moaned.

'It gets better?'

'Hold yer horses. The cameras picked up somebody wearing leathers and pushing a motorbike. Now that makes you think, doesn't it?'

'It does?'

'Who the bloody hell *pushes* a motorbike down a canal

towpath late at night? A path which only leads to one thing: Benji's boat. There's no way off that path onto the street, unless they ride it up the steps by the hotel, in which case they'd make a noise. No, this was somebody going down the towpath specifically to the *Felix Dacia*, there's no other explanation. And an hour later the cameras picked up that same pair of legs, pushing a bike going back the other way.'

'I think that might be actually clever of you, Ossie my man. It also explains something else.'

'It does?'

'It's a bit difficult to carry a dead body away on a motorbike.'

'So they tied it to the bottom of the boat.'

'Exactly. I think you're on to something. I reckon our hit man could ride a motorbike.'

And thinking back to first thing that morning in Manchester, the engine I had heard just after someone had taken a pot-shot at me: that had been a motorbike.

Probably quite similar to the one Lea Klemm's minder Tor had ridden out of the Mount Royal car park.

I told Irene that if she rang for a minicab, with a firm she knew she could trust, I would pay if it could take her, Laura and Zsofia out of here, drop Irene off wherever she lived and then take the girls back to the office in Shepherd's Bush Green. Laura asked what did I think she was supposed to do with Zsofia? Irene asked if I thought she was out of her bleeding mind if she was going to leave me locked in an unguarded wine bar.

I calmed them down by telling Laura that Veronica was waiting for her at the office and would know what to do. I didn't know whether she would be or not, but Shepherd's Bush was a safe distance away and Laura didn't have a phone so couldn't check, and then I promised Irene that as soon as the minicab turned up she could lock up and I would be on the outside.

It was only after the cab had arrived and we were out on the steps of The Boot, and Irene was locking the door and Zsofia was standing shivering with an overcoat (one of the many in the lost property room of The Boot) around her shoulders, nervously looking up and down the deserted street, that Laura asked me what I was going to do.

'I've no idea,' I said truthfully, 'I'm making this up as I go along.'

It was getting dark and Redcross Way was totally deserted, as was Southwark Street when I crossed it. The minicab that had picked up Irene, Laura and Zsofia could have been the last vehicle in town, except I knew it wasn't. There was still that omnipresent background hum of traffic noise in the undefined distance which is not so much the heartbeat of London, more the sound of its high blood pressure.

The Arches were where they said they were, under the railway arches right at the end of Redcross Way, where it starts to curve around into Bankside and the river. There were three distinct properties with solid, double wooden doors made to fit the arches, each with a modern security lock and burglar alarms way above head height. I bet myself they were not connected to the local police station; just there to make a noise if anyone broke in – or perhaps tried to break out.

There was no official sign up anywhere saying that the Arches housed Oradea Imports, but there was a Continental-style metal mailbox screwed to the brickwork around the farthest door, so that the postman had somewhere to put their junk mail. Presumably he also delivered council tax, power and water bills, which meant there would be a paper trail for Laura to follow in the morning. I would leave it to her; she was much better at that sort of thing than I was.

I was going to do what I did best: blunder in where others feared to tread.

Around the door frame of the far lock-up, which I guessed was No 1 The Arches, I could detect a faint penumbra of light coming from inside and could hear a muffled, monotone background hum which seemed vaguely familiar.

The droning noise, interrupted by the occasional bump, was one of those household sounds you know you know, but just didn't expect in a strange environment. It took me a full minute before I realised it was the sound of a vacuum cleaner.

I wasn't surprised; it had been that sort of day.

At that point, I suppose I could have taken a step back from the door, raised my right foot and kicked it in, making for a dramatic entrance. Instead, I glanced up Redcross Way to my right and then to my left down towards Bankside and saw no one who would be impressed by such flamboyance. In fact, I saw no one at all and with the street lights now on and my view framed by a railway arch, The Boot and Flogger looked less like a friendly hostelry and more like the set of a Jack the Ripper movie.

With no one to impress, I went for the more subtle approach and simply tested that the door wasn't locked, then pushed it slowly open.

It took me a minute to absorb the scene which greeted me. There was a lot to absorb.

The lock-up was built under the arch of a viaduct, so the ceiling was domed like a medieval chapel, with a modern lighting rail containing multiple spotlights hanging from the centre. The walls were Victorian brick with the soot and grime cleaned off but otherwise unadorned, and the floor was covered with a cold brown linoleum which had been worn through to grey flagstones in several places, as well as being stained with oil and imprinted with tyre tracks.

There was a motorbike, a Suzuki, on its stand, to the left of the door, with a crash helmet resting on the seat, otherwise the front half of the lock-up was empty. Halfway in, or so I estimated, were stacks of cardboard boxes reaching almost to the ceiling in places. Some were obviously boxes of wine or some other booze from the printing on their sides, others were anonymous, and several had been damaged and repaired with vast amounts of brown plastic tape. The boxes had obviously formed a wall, cutting off the rear portion of the lock-up. That half had been used as an emergency crash pad, judging by the mattresses on the floor or stacked up against the back wall, the filthy blankets thrown over some of the boxes and the amount of food wrappers and cartons which covered the floor like fallen leaves. In the far right corner there was a sink mounted on the wall and on the floor, two galvanised metal buckets. I could smell from where I was what they had been used for.

And there was Tor, busy pushing the hose of a vacuum cleaner over a mattress, though I wasn't sure whether he was removing forensic evidence or giving it a token clean for a new occupant. Either way, he hadn't heard me enter the lock-up.

How many girls had Laura seen troop out of there? How long had they been there? Zsofia had indicated she had been in the life for over a year, but that lock-up in Southwark was surely only a temporary staging area. But even an hour in this dank, windowless brick prison would be more than enough to account for the dead look in Zsofia's eyes.

Tor still had not noticed me and was concentrating on his cleaning, his back to me.

I scooped the crash helmet off the seat of the Suzuki, ran across the lino floor and smashed it round the back of his head.

When someone loses consciousness, the paramedics or the nurse always insist on knowing how long they've been out for. I don't know why it matters, but it's probably something to do with the risk of brain damage and I just assumed it must be important. Therefore, I sat on a box of Romanian red wine and looked at my watch while I waited for Tor to come round. It took him two minutes and thirty-four seconds. I hoped that was long enough to be serious.

'Moonlighting as a cleaner, Tor? Does Lea Klemm know you have a second job?'

Even though I had unplugged the vacuum cleaner, I spoke loudly and realised that my voice was echoing off the brick walls. The urge to shout at him might have been righteous anger but was more probably just nerves. When I had hit him, all I was thinking about was Zsofia and the look on Laura's face as she had described those girls being herded into the Transit van. It had not occurred to me, until now, that when he came round he might stand up and beat the crap out of me. On paper, I was taller, slimmer and younger, and I was not going to allow myself to be intimidated by this squat little toad who looked like Uncle Fester from the Addams family and probably got his jollies by beating up shell-shocked and terrified young girls.

I decided to keep my distance though, as I didn't fancy a bear hug from those ham shanks of arms of his.

Slowly and deliberately he levered himself onto his knees and then used both hands to carefully examine every inch of his bald head whilst gently rotating his neck, as if he was checking to see if I had loosened his brain.

'How much does Lea Klemm actually know, Tor?'

''Bout as much as you, smart arse,' he said calmly, wincing slightly as his fingers explored a sore spot.

'You should always wear one of these,' I said, hefting the crash helmet which I'd decided to keep hold of, 'they can save lives.'

'Go fuck yourself.'

'Your English really is good, for somebody from – where was it – Lewisham?'

He took his right hand from his head and held up the middle finger at me.

'Sit on this and swivel.'

'Now, now, Mr Szatmari – is that how you pronounce it? I don't really care, I'm sure the Crown Prosecution Service will get it right for your day in court. Could be more than one day, thinking about it.'

'What have I done?'

'Only followed orders, probably; but you would say that, wouldn't you? You had plenty of time to get from the Mount Royal down to Little Portugal on your bike and off Terry Patterson before I got there. Why did you have to kill his wife, though? Did she see you? Recognise you?'

I knew, of course, that the Pattersons had been dead long

before that afternoon, but I wanted to see his reaction.

He shook his head slowly in puzzlement.

'I've not killed anyone and you can't prove I have.'

He probably hadn't and he was right that I couldn't prove anything, but he hadn't shown any shock or surprise at the news that Terry and his wife were dead. I tried to remember whether he had reacted when I'd told Lea Klemm that Benji had been killed, but my only recollection from the hotel room that afternoon was that he had remained as emotional as an Easter Island statue.

'Of course, Lea probably had the best motive,' I said, 'if she found out that she'd killed a past husband in order to land a new one, only to find the new one was already married. I can see that working in front of a jury.'

Tor snorted something in Hungarian at me and turned his head slowly, flexing his neck muscles.

'Lea's a stupid tart,' he said.

'That's odd; I got the impression you were quite fond of her.'

'She was a "Babe" once, but now she's a "Mature" with a drug habit, and very soon she'll be a "Granny" and nobody will be interested.'

Although I was no expert, I knew that female porno stars went from being called 'Babes' to 'Matures' at the age of about twenty-five, although in California (thanks to the climate and cosmetic surgery) this could be extended to forty with a catch-all category of 'dirty housewives'. After 'Mature' though, the only category open for career progression was 'Granny'. The world of porn movies can be ruthless in more ways than one.

'So, this business—' I waved the crash helmet towards the

filthy mattresses and the crude sanitation facilities, 'bringing in girls from the East, is that Lea diversifying her business interests? Building up a pension fund, perhaps?'

I had no real idea how he would react to that, but I didn't expect him to burst out laughing, then get from his knees to his feet, casually brushing the dirt off the knees of his trousers.

I stood up as he did, keeping sufficient distance between us so that I could get in a good swing with the crash helmet if he put his head down and charged me. Just the thought of that made me realise he could be difficult to stop as, given his shape and weight, it would be like tackling a wild boar, and so I glanced around for more weaponry. There was an open wine box within my reach, with the necks of several bottles sticking out. The box had a gothic 'D' logo printed on the side along with the words: Dracula Pinot Noir 2004 – Produce of Transylvania. I had no idea whether 2004 had been a vintage year or not, but the bottles might serve as effective hand grenades. People are usually very wary when they see bottles thrown at them; or at least in some of the pubs I used to frequent.

I took a step nearer the box. Tor didn't seem to notice and was still chuckling to himself. His overconfidence was a tad unnerving. Perhaps he had a gun in his pocket and I kicked myself for not even thinking to search him. I really ought to pay more attention to little details like that.

He straightened himself up, glanced at his watch, then put his hands in the pockets of his hoody, but didn't produce a gun.

'Lea Klemm never knew about the girls. Well, she did, but only because she auditioned them for us?'

'Auditioned?' I gasped.

'Recruited, then. There are lots of lovely young girls in Hungary and Romania looking for a career in porno and Lea showed them the good life for a while.'

'Got them hooked on drugs, you mean.'

'And the sex. Most of them get to like it and soon can't live without it.'

'I...doubt...that.'

I had almost said that Zsofia might have a different view on that, but then I realised that he didn't know Zsofia had escaped the transportation that evening and had no idea that an eye-witness was on the loose and telling her side of the story, just as soon as we found a translator.

'Oh, but it's true,' he said, and he was actually smiling in a way that made the temptation to smash the crash helmet into his face almost irresistible. 'Lea helped get them into the life – a life where they could earn more in an hour than their mothers had got paid in a week. After all, we helped make them film stars.'

'But this isn't Hollywood,' I pointed out, through gritted teeth.

'The girls – they got greedy,'

'*They* got greedy?'

'Sure they did. For where they were they were rich; but no, they dreamt of coming to London or Paris, where suddenly they would be not so rich. All we did was help them.'

'Help them?'

'We helped them get into England.'

'Disguised as cases of Transylvanian Merlot, I suppose?'

'In the same truck,' he admitted cheerfully. 'There are many trucks on the road these days and very few customs checks, thanks to the glorious European Union.'

'Hang on – if we're in the EU, what's to stop the girls just coming here and getting honest jobs? Freedom of movement, economic migration, all that stuff?'

He shrugged his ridiculously wide shoulders.

'Polish girls do now. There are lots of beautiful Polish girls working in hotels and pubs. They no longer need our help. Same with many Hungarian girls, but in Romanian girls we had a good supply.'

Somewhere in my brain a penny dropped.

'Because Romania is not yet a full member of the EU. That's why, isn't it?'

'Not until January next year, when they join along with Bulgaria, though the firm has no trading links with Bulgaria.'

'You make it sound like an established business.'

'It's been going for over ten years,' he said casually, not looking at me, but pretending to look down his left trouser leg, though I could tell he was sneaking a look at his watch again.

'So you bring the girls over here and put them to work in brothels?'

That got no more than a casual shrug out of him.

'They call them knocking shops in the north, and they are still popular up there, but we also supply massage parlours and escort agencies. Occasionally someone making porno wants some girls, but British porn films have very little market share these days.'

'My heart bleeds for you,' I said, but I think sarcasm was lost on him. 'How long do you keep the girls in the lap of luxury, then?'

'Two years,' said Tor, businesslike. 'That's what their families are told back home in Romania. After that, they can send money home, apply for asylum seeker status, get a job in the service industries or agriculture...'

'You mean cleaners or strawberry pickers.'

'Yeah, that sort of thing. Shit, some of them go into business for themselves. You been down King's Cross of an evening recently? It's like the European Parliament down there.'

'That must be terrible for a Lewisham lad like yourself, watching all those immigrants come over here and take all our sex jobs.'

He looked almost hurt at that jibe.

'Hey, you'd be surprised how many end up marrying their clients and living in the suburbs, having a couple of kids and a double garage.'

Actually that did not surprise me. After the boom in 'mail order brides' from Thailand and the Philippines in the Nineties, the main drivers of the marriage market were now Russia and the Ukraine, in the populations of which women grossly outnumbered men. There was even a website where you could meet them online, called, deliciously (and genuinely) KGB Spouse dot com.

'You make it sound like you're doing some sort of social service,' I said.

He took his hands out of his pockets, linked his fingers in front of his chest and flexed them until his knuckles cracked. He managed to get another look at his watch as he did so.

'It's just a business,' he said.

'A well-established family business, wouldn't you say?'

'You could say that,' he admitted calmly. 'It's certainly been going for a good few years now, but nothing lasts forever.'

'People getting murdered does tend to cramp even the most flexible business plan.'

'Nothing to do with me, mate. I never killed anybody; you've got nothing on me.'

'You could not be in more shit if you went and stood in those buckets in the corner!' I yelled at him. I was losing it, I knew, but it seemed worth it. 'You should have double-checked the number of girls you loaded into the back of that van tonight.'

For the first time since I'd hit him with his crash helmet, his expression changed and there was – wonderfully – fear in his face.

'I've got one of your workhorses now, Tor, and I've got her stashed away in a safe house. I reckon she'll brush up really well for when she goes to court to testify against you. I think they'll start with people-trafficking – what's the legal term? "Trade in human beings", isn't it? Then they'll go on to organised prostitution, extortion, living off immoral earnings – that one's always been popular down the Old Bailey.'

'The girl won't talk, she has too much to lose.'

'I wouldn't bet on that, my slimy friend. This one's called Zsofia and she doesn't strike me as having anything left to lose. She's talking already.'

If Laura had got her to Veronica safely, she probably was, even though it would be in Hungarian and no one could understand her, but I didn't let that fact spoil my moment of triumph over Tor.

The only problem was that he was suddenly looking a lot more relaxed. And he was *listening*. But not to me.

Then I heard the sound of a motorbike engine as well, suddenly loud and very close to the door of the lock-up. And then the door of the lock-up began to open inwards.

'That'll be the boss,' said Tor. 'You'd better take it up with her.'

CHAPTER FIFTEEN

The wheel of a motorbike came through the doorway first, then the handlebars and then, pushing it, a small, obviously female, form dressed in black biking leathers and boots, the face hidden behind the black visor of a crash helmet which looked like something an Imperial Stormtrooper would wear in a *Star Wars* epic. The black visor turned first towards Tor so that I could see him reflected in its shine, then the helmet swivelled in my direction and I caught a reflection of myself.

The biker pushed the machine, another Suzuki, into the lock-up and manoeuvred it until it stood next to Tor's bike, then kicked down the stand and pulled the bike on to it.

As there were now two of them and only one of me, I took a couple of instinctive steps backwards, the only way I could go, into the area which Tor had been cleaning, in among the dirty mattresses and the overflowing slop buckets, hoping vaguely that the smell would deter them from coming any closer.

The leather-clad biker put both gauntlet-covered hands up and lifted off the black helmet. Then she shook her head and the short blonde pony tail whipped back and forth across her shoulders. I had only ever seen her three times, all within the last week, and each time she had been wearing black.

'I knew you were going to be trouble the first time I saw you,' said Phoebe Nicholson.

'That's funny, because I didn't know for sure that you were such an evil bitch until you took a shot at me this morning,' I said.

'You couldn't have seen me, you were too busy hiding under a table.'

Her sharp little face remained impassive. If she ever smiled she would be very pretty, and I still couldn't get over how young she looked. Even in her best going-out clothes and with a good make-up job, she'd still get asked for ID in a lot of bars.

'I didn't see you, I heard the bike. Just out of interest, where were you? Down on that towpath near your brother's boat?'

'No, I was in the street outside the hotel,' she said, sounding quite bored with my question, 'standing behind a parked police car as a matter of fact. There was no one around and if I had compensated for the silencer correctly, I would not have missed you.'

'I just assumed you'd gone back to London,' I said, trying to watch both her and Tor at the same time.

'So did the Manchester police. They never asked me how I'd got to Manchester in the first place; they just assumed it was by train so they kindly gave me a lift to the station. Soon as they'd dropped me off and waved goodbye, I took a taxi to one of our franchise businesses and collected the bike.'

'I've seen some of your franchises in Sheffield,' I snarled, then said: 'You rang the hotel later to see if I was checked in, didn't you?'

'Yes and I even ordered the alarm call which woke you up. The only police around were down by the canal.'

'It was still risky,' I said, trying to keep my voice calm.

'Perhaps I was a touch hot-headed, but you were a threat and had to be eliminated, especially after I saw you with that policeman.'

'You mean Jebb, don't you, the one with DCI Armitage.'

'The policewoman is nothing. Jebb is the troublesome one.'

'So why not shoot him?'

She pulled off her gauntlets slowly by the fingers, almost like a stripper, and laid them on the Suzuki's petrol tank.

'It is not good business to shoot policemen,' she said calmly.

'But it's OK to shoot your brother and feed his body to the fishes?'

If I was looking for a dramatic reaction, I was going to wait in vain.

'Ioan was betraying the family business. He had to be stopped.'

'But you didn't want your mother to know, did you?' I said with sudden inspiration. 'That's why you slung him underneath the *Felix Dacia*. Your mother never knew because she died before we found him.'

'She was ill anyway. Why make her last days more unpleasant?'

'How thoughtful of you, and there was me thinking you were the Ice Queen when you're really a softy at heart.'

She slowly unzipped her leather biker's jacket, looking down at her chest as she did so and all the time talking in rapid Hungarian, or it may have been Romanian. I wasn't sure and I wasn't going to get a translation, but from the gist of it I didn't think it would be anything to my advantage.

Tor answered in equally rapid and unintelligible speech. In fact they began to argue and I suspected they were arguing about where they would dump my body.

The only thing I was sure of was that they were between me and the only door out of the lock-up and that suddenly they were glaring and gesticulating at one another and not looking at me.

It was time to fight dirty. Really dirty.

I let the crash helmet I was still holding drop to the floor, bouncing it on my shoe to cushion the noise, and reached down for the handle of the nearest toilet bucket whilst taking a deep breath and carefully averting my eyes from the contents.

As a weapon it was ungainly and non-aerodynamic, but it had weight and even as I swung it through a half-turn like a hammer-thrower and then let go I had total confidence that it would be more effective than a hand grenade. It sailed past Tor at head height, some of the liquid sloshing out and splashing him, before bucket and contents slammed into Phoebe Nicholson's chest, making her shout out in surprise, then in pain, then in disgust and when somebody does that in Romanian, you certainly get a lot of guttural vowels for your money.

Phoebe fell backwards against her motorbike, knocking it off its stand and then it toppled, domino-like, into Tor's bike standing next to it, both machines clattering to the ground. Tor lurched towards her, scrabbling at his eyes with both hands like a hamster cleaning its face fur at high speed, but whether it was to help her or to rescue his bike, I didn't know or care.

As soon as the slop bucket had flown from my hand, I was

diving for the open case of wine I'd spotted earlier as a potential weapon supply. I grabbed a bottle of Dracula Red, or whatever it was called, by the neck as I charged by the box, hefted it above my head and then smashed it downwards, aiming for the back of Tor's skull. He really should have learnt not to turn his back on me by now. All my best attacking moves came from behind.

In fact, I missed his bald skull completely and the bottle pounded down onto his right shoulder sending shock waves juddering up my arm, but judging by his yelping, the impact had hurt him far more and he dropped like a lift down onto his knees.

Amazingly, the bottle of wine was still intact and still in my grip and because I couldn't resist – and because she deserved it, but mostly because I couldn't resist – I swung it at Phoebe Nicholson just as she was trying to struggle to her feet, slipping on the unspeakable wetness which now covered the floor and wrestling to be free of the pig-pile of motorbikes she was lying on.

The arc of the bottle took her on the right cheek bone and spun her so she fell face down over the rear wheel of her bike. She didn't scream, but I heard a satisfyingly loud click as her upper and lower teeth smashed together.

I threw the bottle at the wall just to hear it smash, then I was ripping the door open and I was out into the night and running for the river.

I didn't have a plan. Amy always said that I hadn't had a plan since I'd made the move into long trousers, which I thought was a bit harsh. But I just knew that Veronica was going to berate me for not doing a proper risk assessment on the potential dangers of blundering into what was basically a brick prison with one door, which was being used as a warehouse by a gang of people-traffickers with a proven track record in murder.

I didn't head for the river for any reason other than instinct. The alternative, down Redcross Way, was a dead straight, totally deserted street offering no witnesses and few places to hide. Round the corner and on to Bankside offered the possibility of more people being around (and the best place to hide in London is among a crowd of Londoners), as well as various bridges which would take me to the north side of the Thames where, at this time of night, I had far more options when it came to taxis, tubes and buses.

I was speeding on adrenalin and was under the approach to Southwark Bridge when Fenella's bloody phone started playing 'Roxanne' again. I had forgotten to switch it off after ringing Ossie from The Boot.

I answered the call as I ran. It didn't take long.

'Is Rox…?'

'Fuck off!'

While I had the phone in my hand I thought of calling the office to see if Laura and Zsofia had got there safely, or Amy to see if I still had a home to go to, or even the police, just to keep in touch. But then I heard a shout and turned to see the unmistakably squat and square outline of Tor coming through the Southwark Bridge underpass, his arms out in front of him, his hands flailing at the air, anxious to meet around my neck. I assumed the things he was shouting in a language I didn't understand were less than complimentary. I didn't need a translator to realise he was seriously pissed at me, but I couldn't stop myself giggling nervously because his lumbering run made me think of him as one of the grotesque, not terribly frightening monsters from the Scooby Doo cartoons.

I had, however, no intention of letting him get close enough so I could taunt him about how he might have got away with it if it hadn't been for those pesky private detectives.

I had a good fifty yards on him and as I took to my heels I was confident I could outrun him along Bankside and lose him among the tourists around the Globe Theatre.

Except I had forgotten that, at getting on for 9 p.m., there were not many tourists to be found hanging around the Globe, or any other bit of this part of the south bank of the Thames. Perhaps they should have built a few more pubs instead of theatres and galleries. Culture's all very well, but not in isolation. I bet that when Will Shakespeare was auditioning for *King Lear* four hundred years ago, he had to drag most of his actors out of the nearby pubs and bear pits.

If Tor caught me, I guessed I would soon find out what it was like to be in a bear pit. The south bank looked deserted and dark – not even an annoying jogger to be seen – whereas the other side of the river seemed to be humming with light and buzzing with life. I decided to get myself over the safe side as soon as possible.

The Millennium Bridge got a bad press when it opened because it wobbled too much when pedestrians walked over it for the first time. As one of the first pedestrians just happened to be the Queen, the bridge was immediately shut down until it was made more secure. Now, a decent risk assessment on behalf of Her Majesty might have flagged that up, but God knows what it would have said about her running across it in the dark with a mad Hungarian in hot pursuit.

As I ran up the zigzag access ramp to the bridge, I saw Tor

down to my left. He wasn't gaining, but he didn't seem to be tiring either; in fact from the angle I was at, he gave the impression of one of those fat Russian wooden dolls, except one that was lifesize and on wheels.

I knew that all the textbooks, personal trainers, and even the Neanderthal PE teachers I'd had at school would have warned of the dangers of attempting a 300-metre sprint without previous conditioning and a thorough warm-up, but there again, they didn't have Tor chasing them.

I started my run determined not to look back. By the time I got to the safety of the north bank, I reasoned, Tor would have given up or collapsed with a heart attack. There was no logical way somebody that shape and weight, not to mention age, should be able to catch somebody like me, especially as I was turbo-boosted by pure fear. It did occur to me that running wide-eyed and in an obvious panic like that, honest citizens out for an evening stroll would naturally assume I was a mugger legging it with a recent haul and the more public-spirited among them might even try and bring me down in a rugby tackle. Alternatively, given that I would look as if I was running away from the Globe, they might just think I was a theatre critic escaping from a particularly gruelling performance of *Titus Andronicus* and leave it at that.

Not that there were many pedestrians on the bridge. In fact, I had it virtually to myself, apart from a few tourists at the halfway point keen to try out the twilight function on their phone cameras to get a blurry shot of a lit-up Tower Bridge in the distance to the east.

I wasn't thinking of the tourist panorama, all I knew was that the river was about thirty feet below me as the tide was in, the end of the bridge was another hundred metres away, and the blood booming in my head like a bass amp turned all the way up to 11 was ready to burst my eardrums. My brain kept up a 'Don't look back, don't look back' mantra, my chest burnt and the soles of my feet hurt every time they pounded the walkway. I knew I was in no condition for this sort of thing but I was gambling on the fact that the shorter, fatter, older Tor was even more unfit.

And then I felt the bridge starting to gently slope downwards and I could make out the dome of St Paul's ahead of me – it had always been there, I just hadn't registered it before – and, closer, the dark outline of what I knew was the City of London School, which on a normal summer afternoon always gave off the comforting scent of marijuana smoke.

I slowed my run, but didn't stop as I could hear the sound of an old-fashioned steam pump cranking up and thought for a second that it meant the bridge would start to swing up into the air. I even remembered that the technical term for such a bridge was a *bascule*, from the French for see-saw, and then I realised that the Millennium Bridge was a fixed structure and didn't raise its arms like Tower Bridge to let tall ships through, and in any case the wheezing hydraulic hiss I could hear was me gasping for breath.

I reached the end of the bridge and the pedestrian exit on the left, which led down to the path running along the riverbank towards Blackfriars railway bridge and, just beyond it, Blackfriars road bridge. I collapsed against the railings there and for the first time looked back towards the south bank.

Tor was not right behind me, as he would have been if this had been a Zombie film or a slasher movie. He was no more than a third of the way across the bridge and, thanks to the under-span lighting, I could see him quite clearly. He was leaning on the rail, much the same as I was, and I just assumed he was retching and struggling for breath just like I was. In fact he was using a mobile phone and, even though I *knew* I wasn't thinking straight, I half-expected the phone in my pocket to start burbling that sodding Sting song again.

But Tor wasn't ringing me.

He was calling for back-up.

I heard the motorbike's engine revving wildly even at that distance across the river before my eyes registered the flickering stab of its headlight illuminating the hoardings outside the Globe Theatre.

It could only be Phoebe Nicousci or whatever her name was this week. She would be just as annoyed with me as Tor and she probably had a gun. Maybe I should have searched her. Maybe I wasn't really cut out for this line of work.

I saw the headlight beam zigzag its way up the access ramp to the bridge and realised she intended to ride across.

I started to run again.

If I hadn't been so spooked I might have stayed near the bridge and watched her progress. Hell, given half a chance it was the sort of thing I would have enjoyed doing: the wind in your hair, the spectacular views, the chance to cross the Thames at speed on your own personal motorway with no oncoming traffic and only a few ditzy tourists with cameras to get in your way. I could set a crossing time and challenge other bikers on the Internet to beat it; there would certainly be plenty of riders up for the challenge. Of course, the police might have something to say about it. I knew Amy would.

I kept to the riverbank, running west. To my right, Upper

Thames Street would soon disappear into that black hole of traffic known as the Blackfriars underpass, a notorious rat run where travellers on foot were not so much discouraged as declared legitimate targets.

The riverbank path was dark and deserted, lit only by globe lights set into the concrete balustrade which probably gave out the same wattage as the Victorian gas lamps they had replaced. To my left was the dark, dank river where, bizarrely, a long pleasure cruiser with half its lights off was motoring serenely upriver parallel to me, though it showed no sign of pulling into to the bank and offering me a lift. To my right was manicured shrubbery interspersed with park benches, the sole purpose of which seemed to be as useful collection points for empty McDonald's milkshake cups.

Blackfriars railway bridge loomed ahead of me. There was a train on it, waiting for clearance to proceed, heading south back across the river. I could see the passengers sitting on board reading their newspapers or lost in their iPod cocoons, totally oblivious to the fact that thirty feet below (and slightly behind) them, I was waving frantically at them trying to tell them to get help.

It was under the railway bridge that I did what I had tried not to do on the Millennium Bridge – I looked back.

The bike had stopped almost midway across the bridge, its headlight beam a finger of light against the night sky. It would have made a great picture for an album cover.

She must have caught up with Tor, who would have seen which way I had exited the bridge. She seemed oblivious to the passers-by who had turned their camera phones away from Tower Bridge and towards the novel attraction of a psychotic Romanian woman smelling slightly of the sewer coming at them like a bat out of hell. Maybe that was the album cover I was thinking of.

When she gunned the engine, I saw the tourists dive for the side rails but they kept their camera phones going as the bike set off, their electronic flashes pricking the night like silent gunfire. Just the sort of gunfire I might experience if Phoebe caught up with me.

I started running again, into the gloom under the railway bridge where above me all those commuters were sitting safe and snug on their train. And then I was out from under and to my left was a rippling expanse of black water with, in the distance, just a glimpse of an illuminated quadrant of the London Eye.

I knew that above me and to my right, just across the road, but far enough away to be on another planet, theatre-goers would be celebrating the end of Act I of something or other in the bar of The Mermaid on Puddle Dock. Down here in the real world, I was running out of places to run to and I was sure I could hear a motorbike behind me.

Almost immediately I was under the shadow of Blackfriars road bridge, but here, to my right, there were no bushes or park benches, for the whole area had been cordoned off with railings and ten-foot high sheets of metal fencing. It was probably something to do with Health & Safety regulations, though nobody had been thinking about my health or safety.

To my left was the underbelly of the bridge which looked as if it had been made out of a giant rusty Meccano set, and over the concrete parapet the Thames swirled dark and uninviting between the bank and the first supporting pillar. But not as much Thames as between the bank and the pillars holding up the railway bridge; the actual structure of the road bridge, its guts and muscles, were a lot closer to the bank.

So close, in fact, that a really desperate person might be tempted to stand on the concrete balustrade right under the middle of the bridge on the spot where a Victorian gas light had obviously been removed because the bridge's girders came *so low* at that point that a gas flame might have damaged the cast iron. Which just goes to prove that even the Victorians had Health & Safety nerds dogging their attempts at Imperial bombast. One of them had probably asked if anyone had done a risk assessment on invading Afghanistan, or if they hadn't, they should have.

There was no one around to forbid it and, more importantly, no one around to talk me out of it, so I climbed on to the concrete balustrade and slowly straightened up, very conscious of the fact that below me the lapping waters of old Father Thames looked very dark, very cold and very wet.

With my arms above my head at full stretch I could touch the thick cold girders that ran as cross-supports out to the first pillar sitting on its own island of concrete a few metres from the embankment. It was a positive maze of criss-cross girders up there, but there seemed to be plenty of room to get in among them and once there I would be well hidden even if anyone thought to look up.

If only I could haul myself up there without falling into the water with a girlish scream, no doubt breaking my back on some concrete block just under the surface (or, knowing my luck, an abandoned supermarket trolley) and then drowning, my body being washed up at Greenwich in about a week's time.

But now I could definitely hear a motorbike coming and, as I glanced nervously to my left I saw, framed by the railway bridge, a single headlight weave its way down from the Millennium Bridge and on to the pathway.

I thought about trying to work out how long it would take a motorbike going at around 40 mph to cover the 400 yards or so from there to here. Then I thought *Sod it* and jumped.

I was upside down, my legs and arms tightly wrapped around a girder, hanging there like some giant sloth, when the bike shot by on the pathway in a blur of light and noise and oily exhaust fumes.

I allowed myself to exhale, but didn't relax my grip – any of my grips. I was hanging on to that girder with every muscle I could flex and some I didn't know I had.

What I did know was the Phoebe Nicousci wouldn't think twice about riding her bike up onto the pavement of Victoria Embankment which started just beyond the Blackfriars underpass; but, once there, she would start to run into pedestrians, cyclists, joggers and even, if she was really unlucky, a police car, as that part of the riverbank was beginning to look like Hong Kong harbour these days – though the food was nowhere near as good.

There had been a time when the *Tattershall Castle*, round towards Westminster, had been the only place where you could get drunk and seasick simultaneously whilst being on the Thames but still tied up to the bank. Now, it seemed that every hulk that could still float was tied to a pier between Blackfriars and Waterloo Bridge and had a bar or a restaurant or nightclub on board. The Thames barge previously known as *The Wilfred* now claimed to be *El Barco Latino* by virtue of the fact that somebody had put a Homebase barbecue set on deck along with plastic garden chairs and tables. A sign said it offered salsa dancing, but there seemed room on deck to either eat or dance, not both. The crew of these floating pubs, or 'waiters' as they were known for tax reasons, would run down the covered boarding walkways to try and entice unsuspecting tourists aboard with offers of free drinks or discounts for groups, but they might as well have worn eye-patches and had parrots on their shoulders for all the trade they press-ganged.

Sure enough, I heard the bike making a return sweep and saw it and its anonymous rider, upside down, pass me by no more than fifteen feet away. In a few seconds, the bike was disappearing from my view (admittedly a rather strange angle) under the railway bridge. Then I heard it slow, and then rev up again, and eventually the roar of its engine became a distant popping echo.

Even though my arms and knees were aching, and my fingers had locked like clamps around the lip of the girder I was clinging to, I waited until I had counted to a hundred as slowly as I could in my head before I made a move to unpeel myself. Once I got myself the right way up and had allowed the blood to drain back into the bits of my body where it was happiest, I worked out that I could inch my way along one of the central girders until I would be over the concrete balustrade. By dangling at arms length I could get my toes on the top of the balustrade and with a giant, if not literal, leap of faith I let go of the beam and pushed off with my feet, dropping to the pathway with an ankle-jarring thump. But at least I was on the river path and not in the river itself.

So was Tor.

He was standing under the railway bridge just as I was standing under the road bridge, and it was unmistakably him; I could tell from the outline shape even though I couldn't see his face in the dark. I think he was more surprised than I was, given that I must have appeared to drop out of nowhere like Spiderman.

But then he surprised me by turning slowly around until his back was to me and then setting off in a slow shambling jog. When I realised he was running *away* from me, I shouted 'Oi!' at the top of my voice and set off in weary pursuit, thinking that all this exercise was going to be the death of me.

It wasn't much of a chase. As soon as he cleared the bridge, he stumbled to a halt and collapsed on to the nearest park bench nestling in the carefully planted shrubbery.

I juddered to a halt, my leaden legs almost collapsing under me as Tor's seemed to have given way under him, but I was still careful not to get too close.

He sat with his head lolling over the back of the bench, his knees wide apart, his hands resting on his thighs, palms upwards. His breathing sounded like gas escaping from a punctured balloon.

He wheezed something at me, which at first I thought was him cursing in Hungarian, but then he said it again and I realised it was:

'Help. Help me.'

I risked putting my face a bit closer.

'What's the matter, Tor?' I said, trying to control my breathing after all that exertion. At least I didn't look as bad as he did. 'You having a heart attack or something?'

'Yes, I think I am,' he gasped.

I wasn't sure what someone having a heart attack looked like, or what an innocent bystander such as myself should do in order to help; always assuming that I wanted to help. A quick turn of the head to check that there was no one else on the pathway and I realised I was on my own. There was no help in sight, which also meant no witnesses.

I stepped up closer and punched him in the stomach as hard as I could.

He groaned, but otherwise hardly moved.

'You're not kidding me, are you, Tor?' I said right in his face, which I examined carefully to see if his lips had turned blue even though I couldn't honestly remember if that was heart attacks or hypothermia.

I didn't need to feel his forehead for a temperature – he was sweating as much as I was after all our exertions – and I didn't need to take his pulse as I had just seen his eyeballs move.

'Phone...in pocket...' he was saying, '...ring...ambulance.'

'That's a bit rich, isn't it, Tor, me old mate? You've spent the last half hour trying to kill me. Why should I give a monkey's what happens to you? I don't think you're a very nice man, Tor. You had all those girls locked up in Southwark. Why was that?'

I had to put my head close to his head to hear him.

'We were...moving them...out of the way...it was only temporary.'

'Where are they now?' I pressed.

'On their way to Brighton,' he winced as a wave of pain washed over him. 'To a massage parlour called Southern Lights off St James Street. Christ, this hurts... Ring...ambulance... Get help.'

I reached into the pocket of his hoody and pulled out his phone. The cover slid up to reveal the illuminated buttons. It was rather cool.

'Before I ring anyone, Tor – and I have to say, you really don't look well at all – tell me where Phoebe is.'

'Ruxandra,' he said, or something like it.

'What?'

'Ruxandra Nicousci, that's her real name...her Romanian name.'

'That's fascinating, Tor, but you're wasting good ambulance-calling time. I don't know what the target response rate is for this time of night. Could be ten, fifteen minutes...who's to know?'

'She's a Romanian...'

'Yes I know she is, Tor, but I'm not going to dial 999 until you tell me where she is.'

He was panting, wide-mouthed now, trying to jerk his massive shoulders away from the bench but his body just didn't seem to be working.

'Come on, Tor, what did she ever do for you? She left you here, didn't she?' I said.

'Romanian gangsters...they don't like to leave loose ends...'

'What are you talking about?'

'The girl who got away... For Christ's sake, make the call.'

'Zsofia?'

He nodded. It seemed painful.

'She's gone to get her back... Get her...property back...'

'Gone where?' I said deliberately, hoping he could tell I was prepared to hit him again.

'Your...place...'

'My place?'

'Office...in Hackney.'

'Hackney? Why Hackney? How...?'

Then something clicked. Lea Klemm had said that afternoon that Terry Patterson had mentioned me and knew me from my time in Hackney. She'd even quoted the Stuart

Street address as if it was where I ran my detective business from. Tor had been in the room with us.

'You gave her my address, you bastard, didn't you?'

He said nothing. He probably couldn't say anything, just pleaded with his eyes.

I looked up and down the embankment path to check we were still alone and unobserved.

'Tell you what, Tor, let's ask Zsofia if she thinks I should call an ambulance.'

I pressed some buttons randomly, holding the phone near his face so he could see then held the phone to my ear.

'Hello Zsofia? Got a little moral dilemma for you. Your friend Tor, the one who was your – what shall we call it – jailer? How about slave boss? You like that better? Fine. Well, Tor thinks he's having a heart attack, and I think he might be right. Should we do the decent thing and call an ambulance for him?'

I kept the phone to my ear for a couple of beats, nodding and saying 'Uh-hu, uh-hu' into the dead connection, and finally 'OK, thanks'.

'Zsofia says no,' I said to Tor, then threw his phone over my shoulder and into the river.

I was running again by the time it made a splash.

CHAPTER SIXTEEN

I turned back on myself, running once again under both Blackfriars bridges and then up the ramp until I emerged on to Victoria Embankment opposite the illuminated OXO building across the river. There were people here and traffic, lots of traffic, which was both comforting and terrifying because this stretch of road was the most unforgiving in central London. If they ever held a Grand Prix in London, this would be the prime spot for the TV cameras. Some days they wouldn't even have to bother with Formula 1 cars, all they would have to do was line up the chauffeur-driven Mercedes, the taxis and all those coaches full of day-trippers, form them up on a grid and fire a starting gun. There would be no need for practice laps, as the drivers did the run that way every evening Monday to Friday.

The only problem was that I had to cross the westbound carriageway and the barrier in the middle of the road in order to get over to the eastbound carriageway, and there was no way I was going to do that if I thought about it too much. So I ran through the traffic, vaulted the middle crash barrier with an agility that surprised even me, and somehow ended up on the right side of the road near the Inner Temple Gardens with the sound of angry car horns and squealing tyres still ringing in my ears.

I put my hands on my knees and bent over until I got my breath back. That would allow any taxi driver who had seen my kamikaze run from the riverbank to get clear, as none of them would have stopped to pick up such an obvious maniac.

When I had almost stopped shaking, I raised my arm and a black cab pulled up almost immediately. I had the money out of my wallet ready to wave in the driver's face as he lowered the passenger side window.

'Fifty quid if you can get me to Hackney in ten minutes, mate,' I said.

'Hackney? This time of night?' He looked at the notes I was holding out. 'I'll give it a go.'

He didn't do it in ten minutes, but it was close enough, so I gave him the fifty and he gave me a receipt without me having to ask for one.

On the way, round about the Bank of England, I'd got enough breath back to pull out Fenella's phone and try ringing the office. The phone was making a bleeping noise, which my cab driver, very helpfully, told me meant that my battery was low. Bloody Fenella, I fumed, why couldn't she keep her sex chat lines fully charged?

I tried anyway and the number rang and Veronica answered then was almost immediately cut off. I swore ferociously at the handset and that seemed to work, for it played that all-too-familiar 'Roxanne' tune and, miraculously, it was Veronica.

'Angel? Were you just trying to ring me?'

'Yes I was, you clever girl, but my phone seemed to die on me.'

I hope she could tell from my voice that I was genuinely pleased to hear hers. She should treasure the moment; it was a first.

'You don't seem to have much luck with phones, do you?' she said with a large hint of disapproval.

'That reminds me,' I said casually, not wishing to spook her if anything had gone wrong, 'has Laura got back there yet?'

'Yes she has and she's got a girl with her who...' her voice dropped to a whisper '...looks absolutely awful and won't speak a word. Has she escaped from a psychiatric hospital or something? Laura says she's Hungarian but I think she's in shock.'

'She's Hungarian *and* in shock,' I said. 'She's been used as a sex slave, but not in a good way.'

'There's a good way?' she boomed, bringing the volume back.

'Not really. Now listen, I want you to do something for me.'

'Before or after you come and explain to the nice police officers about what you found down in Vauxhall a few hours ago?'

'I want you to have the police come to me,' I said.

That was a first as well.

'I'm listening,' she said like she was enjoying the moment.

'Send them to number 9 Stuart Street, Hackney. Tell them there's been a break-in and an assault is in progress. Tell them it's all in connection with an ongoing investigation called Operation Pentameter and the liaison officer is a

Detective Inspector Timothy Jebb of South Yorkshire police in Sheffield. And tell them to hurry.'

'Should I tell them about all the bodies you've found?'

Now she was just being sarcastic.

'You might mention them in passing.'

'And what will you be doing?'

'Me? I'm speeding to Hackney as we speak, to meet them.'

Before anything serious happened.

I asked my cabby to drop me at the end of Stuart Street then walked the length of it on the opposite side from number 9, staying out of the street lights as much as I could. The aromas of at least five different ethnic types of cooking wafted over my taste buds, reminding me that all that exercise had generated quite an appetite, and the muffled sound of a Punjabi lounge CD told me that Mr and Mrs Singh at number 24 were hosting one of their famous candlelit suppers, which were known throughout Hackney for excellent food and rubbish music.

A cat crossed the street just in front of me and disappeared through a cat flap into number 23. That would be where nice Mr Tomlin probably still lived, though I wasn't sure he'd forgiven me yet for the way Springsteen had despoiled and impregnated his prize female moggy on more than one occasion. I had, of course, remonstrated with Springsteen about his lack of morals, but he'd just laughed at me. And anyone who says that humans are the only animals who can laugh doesn't know cats.

I got to the end of the street without seeing a motorbike or being shot at, and as I had passed it, I had scrutinised number 9 carefully. Everything seemed in order as far as I could tell, though there was not much to see. Only two of the flats had windows overlooking the street: Flat 1 on the ground floor next to the front door, now occupied by – what had Fenella told me? – a couple called Barry and Sally, who sounded as if they might wear matching cardigans; and Flat 4, the one above mine, occupied by Inverness Doogie and his soul mate (or 'cell mate' as he called her) Miranda. Doogie was a chef in some fancy restaurant in the West End and the pair kept odd hours, so it was not unusual for their window to be in darkness, though there was a light on in Flat 1. Flat 2 – Lisabeth and Fenella – and my Flat 3 both had unenviable views over an unattractive handkerchief-sized backyard; an unwashed handkerchief at that, but then Hackney wasn't exactly known for its panoramic views.

There was no sign of a police car or an Armed Response Unit or a helicopter gunship yet and, though I strained my ears, I could not detect any wailing sirens in the distance. I was going to have something to say about the Metropolitan Police's response times – there was never a target to be met when you wanted one to be.

I crossed the street and started down 'my' side until I got to number 9. Everything looked kosher and it occurred to me that I might be safer hiding inside the house than hanging about, exposed, on the street. As I no longer had a key which worked, I would have to ring the bell and it was only when I was close enough, finger poised, and about to do it, that I noticed the damage.

It was as if someone with a very sharp apple-corer had taken two scoops of wood out of the door where the lock was supposed to connect with the frame, leaving the tongue of the lock with nothing to cling to. I thought of how many times I had read the phrase 'shot the lock off' whereas, in practical terms, what you do is shoot the wood off the lock.

If you had a gun, that is.

It appeared somebody did.

The sensible thing would have been to walk away.

The really sensible thing would have been to run away, but I'd done enough running that night and, in any case, there were innocent people in the house. There might also be a bonkers nut-job psycho-killer in there as well, so I stepped to my left keeping most of my body behind a nice solid wall and pushed the door open very gently with my fingertips.

She had mentioned that she had used a silencer that morning in Manchester (only that morning?) and I was working on the assumption that she had used one when she had shot her way through the door, otherwise someone would have heard the noise. Even in Hackney, gunshots on a residential street usually get noticed, especially since the area got gentrified and people started to grow flowers instead of skunk in their window boxes.

I didn't hear any gunshots, not even very, very quiet ones, so I poked my head around the door frame. The hallway was empty, the light was on and I could see the empty staircase up to the empty landing outside my flat.

Even so, I went in cautiously. The door to Flat 1 seemed intact and if I held my breath, I thought I could hear a TV playing inside. I decided that Barry and Sally could look after themselves. I was keen to check on Fenella, though. If Lisabeth was home there was no problem. Lisabeth formed a pretty effective line of defence, one a Panzer Army would think twice about going round let alone attacking. But if Lisabeth was out and Fenella was home alone, she was just daft enough to invite Phoebe Nicousci in and make her a cup of tea.

I crept up the stairs like a husband coming home late from the pub; a skill (or 'competency', as Veronica would call it) I had acquired at an early age.

I was almost at her door when my nose hairs began to tingle and I got a faint whiff of an aroma which definitely shouldn't have been present on the stairs. I had experienced some bizarre experimental cooking at the hands of Lisabeth and Fenella over the years, but nothing which smelt like the aftermath of a firework display on a wet autumn night before. Cordite; that was it, as found in gunpowder. And just to confirm that my nose was not misleading me, there on the fourth step down from the landing, just beyond the door to Flat 2, was a single spent cartridge case.

I bent over to pick it up but willed my hand to freeze about two inches above it. I had seen enough TV cop shows to know that you only picked up cartridge cases by poking a pencil into them and I didn't have a pencil. There again, there was absolutely no reason on earth why I should pick it up; I wouldn't know what to do with it if I did.

I would leave that for the cops – if they ever got here.

It was as I was straightening up and my eye-line came level with the floor of the landing and the bottom step of the next flight of stairs leading up to Flat 4 that I noticed the blood on the wall.

There wasn't much – it was not like somebody had slit a vein or anything – perhaps five or six large drops in a diagonal line down the wall about a foot off the floor and something else which looked like black hair was smeared there too.

'Fucking cat attacked me,' said a voice from somewhere above me.

I didn't look up at the voice. My eyes went instead to the blood trail and followed it down the wall until I focused on the length of black fur which lay inert next to the skirting board.

'You've shot Springsteen, you sick bitch.'

'Cute name; nasty cat,' said Phoebe Nicousci as she stepped down the upper staircase and into the light.

She must have hidden up near Doogie and Miranda's flat as soon as she'd heard me opening the front door. From the cordite smell in the air, she could only have had her run-in with Springsteen moments before. If I'd got there thirty seconds earlier instead of wandering up and down the street...

'Leave the animal alone.'

Somehow I was suddenly at his side, kneeling over him, my hand stroking fur matted wet with warm blood. In fact his whole body was warm and it was moving, ever so slightly.

'I said leave the animal alone. Where's my property?'

Phoebe Nicousci was standing at the top of the main stairs, holding a pistol. I knew it was an automatic because I'd already seen one of the ejected cartridge cases (if you don't want to leave a forensic footprint, use a revolver and take your cartridge cases home with you) and I knew that long black cylinder extension on the barrel must be the silencer. I was close enough to her so that when she extended her arm she was able to push the black cold eye of the suppressor into my cheek.

'I won't ask again,' she said, turning the gun slightly so the weapon screwed into the skin and ground it against my cheekbone.

I could see why she was doing that. Almost the entire right side of her face was blossoming into a red, blue, black and yellow bruise from where I'd hit her with that bottle of Dracula Shiraz, or whatever it was, less than two hours ago in Southwark. If that wasn't enough to remind her why she didn't like me, her biker's leathers still gave off a faint whiff of old toilet. Despite riding through the evening air across the Millennium Bridge, some of the contents of the slop bucket I had thrown at her still clung to her.

'Yes you will,' I said with far more confidence than I felt. 'You could have shot me as I came through the door, a bit like you shot Terry Patterson when he came to his door. Why did you kill his wife, by the way?'

'She appeared out of nowhere and saw me. It was an unfortunate complication.'

'Like your brother?'

Through the cold of the gunmetal I felt her hand tremble.

'I don't have to answer your questions, you have to answer mine,' she said through gritted teeth, teeth which I hoped still hurt.

I could have told her that it was traditional for the villain, when holding the hero at gunpoint in the final scene, to segue into a monologue about how brilliant they were, conveniently listing all their crimes along the way, this whole exercise usually taking just enough time for the hero to work out how to overpower the villain and/or escape with one bound. Yet I had a terrible suspicion that she wouldn't be amused by such ramblings and, realistically, my negotiating options seemed limited unless the cops decided to finally put in an appearance.

'Where's the girl?' she said.

'She's not here,' I said, trying honesty as a last resort.

'I don't believe you.'

She pressed the gun even harder into my cheek and I felt my eyes watering.

I thought about leaping over the banister and jumping down into the hallway, but that would only give her time to get a clear shot at my back and, in any case, with my luck I'd probably break a leg. I even considered trying to make a grab for the gun, or at least knock it to one side and then get in close and grapple with her, but I didn't rate my chances of getting my hands up to the gun before the bullet left the barrel. I needed a distraction, so I tried honesty again. When I'd tried it with women in the past it had worked. They hadn't believed me, but it had distracted them.

'She really isn't here. This is my flat here,' I moved my head slightly to indicate the door to Flat 3 behind me, 'take a look. The key's in my pocket.'

'If she's not in there, I *will* shoot you.'

Now there was female logic for you.

'But I've told you she's not in there!' I said in desperation, hearing my voice crack.

'What about the other flats? Should I look in there? How about the one downstairs? There are people in there.'

'They live here. Zsofia's not in there. Why do want her back so badly? Haven't you got enough girls locked away in your sordid little business premises?'

She didn't say anything; not a word and her face remained impassive. It was the scariest thing she could have done.

'You don't want her back, do you?' I said. 'You're going to kill her.'

'Zsofia always was troublesome. Now she's a loose end which needs to be tied up.'

'Were they all loose ends?'

I didn't have to explain what I meant.

'Only the girl and you,' she said dead-faced, not even allowing herself an evil grin. 'Ioan and that fool Patterson were conspiring to destroy my business and I could not allow that.'

'How? I don't understand.'

'You never did, you just blundered into things that were none of your business. Now where's that girl?'

'The family business means a lot to you, doesn't it?'

I tried to control the desperation I knew was in my voice. Where the bloody hell were the police when you needed them? If you read some newspapers, you'd think that trigger-happy squads from the Armed Response Unit were constantly cruising areas like Hackney in unmarked cars just waiting for a chance like this. Mind you, just then I would have settled for one of the new breed of Community Support Officers wandering in off the street to investigate an unpaid library fine. I needed a distraction badly.

'My family's honour means everything to me,' said the mad woman with the gun.

'Honour? Where's the honour in people-trafficking and pimping prostitutes?'

'Do not dare to lecture me!' At last there was a flash of emotion and I immediately regretted provoking it as she jabbed the gun into my cheek. 'It was a question of loyalty. I could not allow such a betrayal to go unpunished.'

What on earth was the woman talking about? At least she was talking and not shooting. It still wasn't the big distraction

I needed. I could really have done with good old Springsteen producing one of his really loud 'Feed me!' shouts at that moment. I had seen people drop glasses at parties when he'd done that in the past.

For once, I wasn't able to rely on him to make a nuisance of himself. When cats are threatened, they will scream and hiss, but when they're hurt and in pain they go into silent running mode on the principle that you should never let an enemy know you are injured.

But Springsteen wasn't out of it completely. He might not have been up to shouting at his assailant but he was moving, ever so slowly, as cats do when they are in a hunting crouch, keeping low against the skirting board. He was also leaving a trail of droplets of blood as he moved.

I tried to keep eye contact with Phoebe. I didn't want her to follow my glance downwards and notice him.

'So Benji wanted out of the family business, did he?' I said for the sake of something to say which would keep her focused on my face.

'His name was Ioan, only his English boyfriends called him Benji.'

'Whatever he was called, he wanted out, but you just dragged him right back in, didn't you?'

She shook her head slowly as if not believing what she was hearing.

'You really don't know anything, do you?'

'Almost certainly less than you think I do, but I do know that Zsofia is safe and probably talking to the police right now.'

'She won't talk, she knows she's an illegal immigrant. She'll be deported immediately.'

'I wouldn't bank on that,' I said and meant it; the Home Office could screw up the case for years. 'Anyway, Hungary is part of the European Union now, so she can come and go as she pleases.'

'Zsofia is not Hungarian; she is part of the Hungarian-speaking minority in Bihor in Romania. She cannot go back there and she is not free to do anything, she belongs to me.'

'I don't think she sees it that way,' I said, trying to put some sympathy into my voice.

'Again, you don't understand, you stupid man, I *own* her.'

I stared at her knowing what she was going to say next but not wanting to believe it.

'I *bought* her nearly two years ago in Oradea.'

'You *bought* her? Who the fuck *from*? Was there a sale on?'

'From her parents. They were well paid. They have other children and could not feed them all. Some parts of Romania are very poor. They would not take her back, we have a contract and it would be dishonourable. Now tell me where my property is or I will shoot you.'

I motioned to the door of Flat 3 with my head. The pressure of the silenced gun barrel came with me.

'She's in there, hiding,' I said.

I tried to think of an answer if she asked who had helped Zsofia, with no money and no English, get from the Oradea Imports lock-up in Southwark to inside my flat in Hackney, but then crazy women who like to carry guns rarely think things through.

'Open it.'

'Open it yourself,' I said, 'you crazy bitch.'

'Oh, I will,' she said and allowed herself a wince of a smile, which meant her jaw still hurt. Good.

She took a step backwards and adopted a two-handed grip on her gun as if she was on a pistol shooting range. I was so relieved to have it out of my face, it didn't occur to me that it might be still pointed at me, but it wasn't. She was taking aim at the Yale lock on the flat's door and I had to lean back against the banister to let the bullets fly past me at chest height.

She snapped off two quick shots – *phut, phut* – but I didn't see where they hit because I was turning away with my arms up around my face to deflect flying splinters of cheap wood. I was going to have almost as much trouble explaining the bullet holes in the doors to Nasseem Nasseem as I had when he discovered the cat flap I'd installed.

But I didn't have time to worry about that, I had other things on my mind. Fortunately, so did Phoebe Nicousci.

Though my eyes and nostrils stung with the gun-smoke which hung like a tiny cloud on the landing, I was aware that she had dropped her pistol-range stance and was waving the gun down in front of her, around her knees as if trying to bat something off her leather trousers.

As she had stepped back to take aim at the door lock, she had become entangled with Springsteen who was trying to commando-crawl unnoticed from the field of battle. Perhaps Phoebe had trodden on him. Either way, there was a black paw scrabbling at her calves and, as I knew to my cost, leather trousers were no defence against Springsteen's claws.

She yelped and staggered back another half-step almost as if she was trying not to tread on him, even though she had shot him on sight a few minutes ago. She wouldn't shoot now as she might shoot her own foot off. Instead, she was trying to jab him loose with the silencer and, as long as her gun was doing that, it wasn't pointing at me.

She was so intent on poking at Springsteen, she didn't realise how close she was standing to the top of the stairs.

I did.

'Leave my cat alone,' I shouted as I punched her in the chest with both fists.

She screamed as she crashed down the stairs head first; Springsteen didn't.

There was a sickening click when she came to rest in the hallway about a yard from the door of Flat 1, and her neck was at such an angle there was no way she was going to get up again.

Springsteen had come to rest on the third step down and, as I got to him, he was trying to curl himself into a ball. He wasn't moving much and there was a lot of blood on his fur.

I scrambled down and sat on the step next to him, offering to scratch behind his ears. He attempted to bite me as he always did, just for old times' sake. I don't think his heart was in it.

I slipped off my jacket and gently wrapped him in it then stood up with him in my arms. He weighed next to nothing.

In the hallway below, the door to Flat 1 opened and a couple I'd never seen before stood there taking in the scene before them. I couldn't tell which horrified them more: a young woman with her head twisted at an unnatural and obviously fatal angle, lying at their feet, or me, holding a black and bloody bundle half way up the stairs. It was a hell of a way to meet Barry and Sally.

Fair play to Sally, she didn't scream, though Barry looked as if he was going to throw up when what was before his eyes registered in his brain.

'Did you push her down those stairs?' Sally accused me.

'No,' I said holding up Springsteen's body. 'He did.'

'Oh my God, should I call an ambulance?'

'Screw the ambulance, get a vet.'

'So who exactly are you helping with their enquiries now?' asked Amy in a voice which took no prisoners.

'The Metropolitan Police this time,' I said meekly, 'also a Special Task Force running something called Operation Pentameter in conjunction with Europol.'

'You mean Interpol.'

'Whatever you say, dear. The good news is that I should be finished by lunchtime.'

'Where are you?' she asked wearily.

'Bishopsgate. It's a high-security police station these days with bulletproof glass and bombproof doors in case of terrorist attacks, so I couldn't be safer, and it's ever so convenient for Liverpool Street. Soon as I've finished here, I'll jump on a train back to Stansted, pick up Armstrong and be home before you know it.'

'That's assuming I let you in the door. I think I might actually have forgotten what you look like – and without the use of alcohol, too.'

'How's the baby?'

'Not missing you at all, but do try and make it back here for the christening.'

'The *christening*?'

'A week on Sunday. Do try not to be under arrest or swanning around up north with your new chums. It would be so nice if you could make it.'

'What do you mean a *christening*?'

'Well, not the religious part, obviously. I mean they'd have to reconsecrate any church you used, wouldn't they?'

'Harsh, but fair,' I agreed.

'So I thought we'd have a sort of combined house-warming and wetting of the baby's head. A sort of naming ceremony in front of a few witnesses.'

'You mean a party?' I said, cheering up immediately.

'I knew you'd spoil it,' she said primly, 'so I've just invited a few close friends. All you have to do is turn up on the right day. Oh, and invite your father. And stay sober enough to pick up a few people from Cambridge station. And help set up the bar and the sound system in the marquee I've hired.'

'Marquee?'

'It might rain,' she said, then mumbled something I couldn't hear properly.

'What was that?'

'I said that afterwards you can take your mother back home to Romanhoe. I mean there won't be anything to keep her with us, will there? She will have discharged all her grandmotherly duties.'

'So this christening, it's all in aid of getting rid of my mother?'

'It's a catalyst. It will provide a focus by which she will be able to make important life choices.'

'It's to get rid of her, isn't it?'

'In a word: yes. With you home that'll make three babies in the house and that's like the best margaritas: one leaves you wanting and three is too many. I can just about cope with two.'

'But I thought you said she couldn't go home because of

some guy called Lyndon something-or-other,' I said just to prove I had been paying attention that week.

'Lyndon Baines, and he really does sound like a 24-carat shit,' Amy said with a touch of relish. 'Miss Horwood has checked him out and he really does have form of the nastiest kind...'

'Hang on a minute. Who checked him out?'

'Miss Horwood. I was very impressed with her and the results she got in twenty-four hours.'

'Amy, who is this Miss Horwood?'

'Lorna Horwood. She works with you in the same office.'

'Oh *that* Lorna.'

'Yes, the one you probably get to make the tea. She's a good operative and I predict she'll go far. In fact, as the major shareholder in the firm I can almost guarantee it. *She* managed to go out to Romanhoe, snoop around and get back without getting arrested.'

'I haven't been arrested, I keep telling you, I'm just helping them out.'

'They must be desperate. Anyway, you said you'd go and have a word with this creep Baines.'

'I did?'

'If you didn't, you're going to. I heard a message he'd left on your mother's mobile. No wonder she went for the gin bottle, he sounds a complete thug and really scary. You've got to get rid of him. He's living in her house, you know. I think he could be violent after listening to that message.'

'What was the message you accidentally overheard?' I said but she didn't notice the sarcasm.

'It was a threat pure and simple. He said: *Get yourself back here right now, Bethany. Don't forget I own you. You're mine.* Can you believe that people talk like that in the twenty-first century?'

'I'm afraid I can. Don't worry, I'll sort it.'

The uniformed sergeant placed another mug of tea in front of me and asked if everything was all right 'back at the ranch'. I told him everything would be fine once my wife calmed down, and in the meantime I asked if I could stay here in Bishopsgate nick as I felt safer, and the beds in the cells were really quite comfortable when the cell doors were left open. He muttered something about this not being a hotel, but would I like him to send out for lunch from Dirty Dick's, the Young's pub just down the road? Detective Inspector Jebb was on his way down from Yorkshire to see me and had told them to look after me, so they could recharge the cost of lunch to South Yorkshire. He couldn't let me have a beer with it, he said apologetically, but he could recommend the steak and ale pie.

They had eventually arrived at Stuart Street: three cars answering three different 999 calls from Veronica, from Barry and Sally and, when she'd stopped saying *Oh my God, Oh my God!*, one from Fenella.

Fenella and Lisabeth had been at home the whole time but only emerged from their flat when they heard Sally screaming at the sight of the bloody bundle of fur I was holding. (The dead woman on the hall carpet had not impressed her half as much.)

Lisabeth, it seems, had had her iPod on as she usually did when Fenella was working her phone lines and, as Fenella pointed out, it had been a busy night with a lot of Roxanne's regular customers having to be rerouted to Samantha or the very strict Miss Primrose, about whom I didn't like to ask.

They had a million questions of course, but they could see I was in no mood to answer them. The fact that they obviously knew me seemed to reassure Sally, and the fact that I was ordering them around actually impressed Barry. But I had always been able to rely on the Flat 2 girls in a crisis. I told everybody to ring the police (the more calls logged the better it would look), then instructed Fenella to call the local vet whose number I knew she had on speed-dial, and who actually did do out-of-surgery house calls, albeit at extortionate rates. Then I told Barry to throw a blanket or a coat or something over Phoebe Nicousci's body so we didn't have to look at her and he disappeared back into Flat 1, glad of something to do, even if a minute later I heard Sally say loudly: 'Not our fucking duvet, you moron!'

I told Lisabeth to hide all Fenella's telephones, and make sure they were switched off, before the cops arrived. It took a few seconds before it clicked with her, then she grasped my arm in a rare display of physical affection, at least towards me.

'Good thinking, Angel. I'm so sorry about Springsteen. What happened?'

'She shot him and she was going to shoot me. He went for her, and she tripped and fell down the stairs.'

Lisabeth's grip tightened, cutting off the circulation to my elbow.

'She *shot* a cat? What sort of twisted bitch does such a thing?' She looked down to Phoebe's inert body. 'She got what she deserved.'

Now, Lisabeth had never approved of Springsteen being in the house in the first place, and he'd often had to dodge a carefully aimed desert boot should he ever wander into range, but you shouldn't judge people on first impressions. I was learning that if you scratch the skin of even the most fearsome overweight butch lesbian, you find a good old British cat-lover not far under the surface, and you really don't want to get on the wrong side of one of them.

The first pair of policemen to arrive just stood in the doorway taking in the scene, not sure who to talk to or who to arrest. They were further confused when a dark-haired young woman wearing a white coat and carrying a leather Gladstone bag pushed into the back of them.

'Let me through, I was told there was an emergency,' she said in an East European accent.

'That's Hannah, the on-call vet,' Fenella whispered in my ear. 'She's Polish and rather dishy, don't you think?'

I could have made some comment about her response times being almost as good as those of the police, but I just didn't feel up to it.

More police arrived and we were all ushered into Flat 1, so the stairs could be marked off with blue and white Crime Scene tape. I carry a roll of the same stuff marked 'Police Aware' in the boot of Armstrong and it had often come in useful in the past.

Barry and Sally rallied around as best they could to make tea for everyone as policemen and women came and went, along with a platoon of SOCOs in their white suits with their cameras and brushes and plastic evidence bags, just like I had seen crawling over Benji Nicholson's boat up in Manchester.

Eventually, a plain clothes detective who said he was the senior investigating officer told us that a doctor had been and pronounced death, and the body was about to be moved. He

offered Lisabeth and Fenella and Barry and Sally a night in a
hotel if they didn't fancy staying in the house for what was left
of the night, but it was OK if they wanted to, though he
couldn't spare a uniformed officer to stay with them. He also
asked if anyone knew the whereabouts of the occupants of
Flat 4, and Fenella told him that Doogie and Miranda were on
a cooking holiday in southern Italy for the week. No one said
anything about my plans for the night; I was booked into an
interview room at the nearest nick, which turned out to be
Bishopsgate.

They treated me well enough, all things considered, even
after it became clear that they were dealing with a suspicious
death in Hackney, a double murder down in Southwark and a
month-old murder in Manchester, all impinging somehow on
a major investigation called Operation Pentameter, about
which the boys in the Met seemed to know less than I did.

The first interview conducted by a detective chief inspector
who looked younger than me was pretty much one-way
traffic: me telling my story, him making a few notes and only
querying me on certain dates and times. Then he received a
fax from Manchester, read it, and asked me if I could account
for my movements between certain dates a month ago. I told
him I had no idea what I was doing a month ago, but I
certainly wasn't keelhauling anyone in Manchester. Later that
night another fax came in and seemed to be a preliminary
report on the death of Mr and Mrs Patterson down in
Vauxhall. The DCI asked me if I could account for my
movements on Tuesday night and I said I could, as I had a
hundred witnesses who saw me line-dancing in a pub in
Huddersfield, and would I admit to an alibi like that if it
wasn't true? He agreed with me on that one.

Messages, phone calls and more faxes continued to arrive at Bishopsgate. I was asked if I knew a Miss Sheridan, because she'd turned up at Hammersmith police station with a young woman she claimed had been forced into prostitution, but who only spoke Hungarian, so that couldn't be corroborated. I told my increasingly harassed DCI that she was in fact Romanian, but from a part of Transylvania where they spoke Hungarian.

At the mention of Transylvania, the young DCI obviously thought I was pulling his chain and muttered that the case could not possibly get any more complex.

Still later, he told me that there was indeed a DCI Heather Armitage with Greater Manchester police and indeed a DI Timothy Jebb with South Yorkshire, and asked if there were any other police forces involved he ought to know about.

And then a uniformed constable brought in another phone message to tell him that Sussex police had just raided a massage parlour in Brighton and arrested a vanload of young females who appeared to be illegal immigrants and captive sex workers.

The DCI asked if there was anything else I'd like to add at this point and I helpfully suggested that he might check with his colleagues in Brighton as to what was written on the side of the van they had pulled. Most likely, it would say Oradea Imports on the side. Oh, and he might like to check with the ambulance service and the hospitals to see if they'd picked up a heavy-set guy with a heart condition in the Blackfriars Bridge area that night, name of Tor Szatmari, which I even offered to spell for him.

Wearily, he wondered if this Tor character was from Transylvania as well and I said no, Lewisham, but he didn't look as if he believed me. At this point, my interviewer asked if I wanted a cigarette break, and when I told him I didn't smoke any more, he asked if I minded if he did.

When he came back in, he was clutching yet another message slip. Now, it appeared there was a Ms Veronica Blugden on the phone offering to send over a Mr Berlins, who apparently was her firm's solicitor, should I be in need of legal advice.

I shook my head at the suggestion.

'No thanks,' I said. 'Let's keep things simple.'

CHAPTER SEVENTEEN

I got about six hours sleep before the sergeant woke me up with a mug of tea and a bacon roll, told me DI Jebb was on his way down from Sheffield to interview me, and allowed me to ring Amy.

When I enquired as to what had happened to the DCI who had interviewed me for a large chunk of the night, the sergeant said he had gone home to lie down in a darkened room and all he knew was that 'Mr Jebb' was taking it from here. He allowed me a few more phone calls, as it didn't seem as if I was under arrest and no one had said anything about charging me.

I rang Fenella on a number she'd lodged with the Scene of Crime team (hopefully not one of her working lines) and persuaded her to check with the vet to see what the situation was, then I rang the office and spoke to Veronica.

I told her that, in view of the hours of overtime I had worked, time away from home and general stress, I would be taking some time off in lieu.

'In lieu of what?' she'd said.

I also asked to speak to Lorna.

'You mean Laura,' she challenged.

'No, Lorna Horwood,' I insisted, showing off that I knew her surname.

'But you never talk to Lorna.'

'Tell her I've spent the night in a police cell, that'll cheer her up.'

When she transferred the call and Lorna picked up, she was instantly suspicious.

'What do you want?'

'To congratulate you. Amy tells me you did a really good job for her, asked me to pass on our thanks.'

'Oh...that's nice. It was nothing really.'

'Never say that to a paying client,' I scolded her.

'But Amy May is the Chairman of our Board.'

We had a Board?

'Look, Lorna, she might be the biggest shareholder, but she won't want any favours. You make sure Veronica sends her a fully itemised bill for your services and don't forget the out-of-pocket expenses. I can always help you out with a few receipts if you need them.'

'Oh, I don't think...'

'Trust me, Amy will think badly of the firm if it tries to allow her a freebie on this one. She'll expect to pay a full commercial rate for a full professional service.'

'Well, if you say so...'

'No, don't say I said so, make her think it was your idea. Now, tell me what you found out about this guy Lyndon Baines.'

'I'm typing up my report at the moment. I haven't emailed it to Amy May yet,' she whined.

'Just give me the gist. Amy thinks my mother is scared of this man.'

'With bloody good reason,' said Lorna with sudden enthusiasm, showing I had pulled the right trigger. 'I'm still waiting to hear from the Criminal Records Bureau, but everyone I talked to thinks he's done time inside, probably for assault. His technique seems to be to target middle-aged widows or sad divorcees and... Oh, sorry, no offence.'

'None taken.'

'Anyway, he targets them and plays the absolute gentleman until he gets into their pants...'

'Hold it! Now I'm offended, and just a little bit queasy.'

'Sorry, but once he moves in with them, he just won't leave and he starts to intimidate the women. He's careful not to steal from them; he gets his kicks from controlling them. Mind you, I can see why old bid...the older woman might fall for him, he's got a well hard body.'

'Excuse me?'

'Bodywise he's really fit. Muscles, no fat, buns of steel and a six-pack you could bounce a cricket ball off. The face isn't much to write home about, though, and those tattoos do nothing for me.'

'You've *seen* this guy?'

'From the pub. Some of the locals pointed him out to me.'

'How old is he?'

'About thirty, I'd say, and apparently he's never had a girlfriend his own age, he always goes for older women.'

'Would you say he was a hard man?'

'He looks to keep himself in shape. He's a roofer, you know, a guy who fixes roofs.'

'You learnt all this from people gossiping down the pub in Romanhoe?'

'And in the coffee bar there. People in bars and restaurants are really useful sources of information in our business and, you know, if you ask people the right way they'll usually tell you anything.'

'That sounds like good advice, Lorna, I'll try and remember it.'

When DI Timothy Jebb finally arrived at Bishopsgate, he looked hot, tired and dishevelled. He had a bulging briefcase under one arm and a laptop in a bag hanging from a shoulder strap. He stared hungrily at the plate of steak pie and chips I was devouring with some relish.

'So you're the wise guy who's after my job,' was his opening gambit.

'No way, Inspector. I'm not even after *my* job. All I've been doing since Tuesday is trying to get home.'

'Yeah, that sounds like my job.'

Jebb laughed, but not with his eyes, then plonked the briefcase down on the table I was eating at. The desk sergeant had kindly let me use the interview room I'd spent half the previous night in, and it wasn't too bad if you thought of it as a private dining room.

'That,' said Jebb pointing at the briefcase, 'is the paperwork on just this week's work on Operation Pentameter and you already feature in quite a bit of it. From what I've been hearing, you've generated another filing cabinet's worth since yesterday.'

'There's no need to thank me. Want a chip? I can't eat all these.'

He pulled up a chair with his foot and sat down opposite me.

'Thought you'd never ask.'

So, he was a genuine Yorkshireman and not just based there.

'Knock yourself out,' I said, and he grabbed three chips between two fingers.

'I've been hearing what you've been up to,' he said whilst chewing, 'but I still can't work out how you've managed to cause such chaos in such a short period of time. We've spent the best part of a year planning to bring down the Nicousci clan and you wipe most of them out in a few days.'

'That's hardly fair, I haven't hurt anyone,' I said, all wide-eyed and innocent though I was thinking: *And you can't prove I have.*

'But you must have the evil eye on them. I mean, you turn up at the mother's funeral, you find the dead son under a barge and then the daughter falls down a flight of stairs and breaks her neck right in front of you. You must have put a powerful curse on that family.'

'I understand it's traditional in Transylvania.'

He smiled at that and helped himself to more chips.

'How much do you know about Romania?'

I hadn't been expecting a pop quiz, but if it got him to tell me what was going on, I would play along. I put down my knife and fork and pushed my plate towards him.

'Not a lot,' I said. 'Transylvania, home of Dracula; formed part of the Roman Empire's province of Dacia.' Jebb raised his eyebrows at that to show he was impressed. 'They play rugby there and they've produced good tennis players and Olympic gymnasts, at least under the Communist regime, which was genuinely reckoned to be the worst Communist regime after Albania. On the downside, they gave us the Cheeky Girls, and that's about it. Oh, and they're going to join the EU next year.'

'You know more than most, and probably more than I did a year ago when I got this job.'

'You're with Europol, aren't you?'

'What do you know about Europol?'

'Less than I do about Romania. I know it's not the same as Interpol, because it's spelt differently for a start, and I know that Benji Nicholson was supposed to be writing a film called *Europol* starring the lovely Lea Klemm, only nobody seemed to have a copy of the script.'

'There wasn't one,' said Jebb, 'there never was.'

As he digested the last of the chips, he came to a decision.

'Look, I think you're a pain in the arse, right? I don't give a shit that Heather Armitage over in Manchester has the hots for you, as...'

'She does?'

He ignored me.

'...As far as I'm concerned, you've buggered in where you shouldn't have and created a hell of a lot of paperwork for me. But, having said that, you might just have done us a favour in the long run, especially by pushing that Nicousci bitch down those stairs.'

'I didn't push her,' I said quickly just in case the room was bugged. 'She tripped over my cat and fell.'

Jebb shrugged his shoulders.

'OK, have it your way, the cat pushed her down the stairs. To be honest, I don't really care. Like I say, in the long run, you've probably saved the cost of a lengthy trial and deprived lots of lawyers of fat fees. That would be a result in some people's book.'

'I can relate to that,' I said. 'So what was all this film crap?'

Jebb finished the last chip and instantly looked depressed.

'Still peckish?' I asked him. 'They do a good bacon roll here. Shall I ask the desk sergeant to get you one?'

'Hell's teeth, you've got your feet under the table pretty quickly, haven't you? How did you manage that? Did you threaten to sue them for false arrest or make a complaint under the Health & Safety Act? That's the one that really terrifies the uniforms.'

'Nothing like that, they've just treated me very well, that's all.'

I didn't tell him that the desk sergeant had recognised the name Amy May when I asked to use the phone, and it turned out that his wife was a big fan of her designs. If I ever managed to make it home, I would get her to autograph some of her TALtops, her most successful product by far, and carry them around with me.

With a pair of bacon rolls in front of him, Jebb warmed to his story.

'You're right, the film was crap, or it would have been a crap film if it had ever got made. Truth is, it was a crap idea from the start, but those space cadets over in The Hague thought it would be a giggle.'

'Now you've lost me,' I interrupted him.

Jebb exhaled slowly, but cheered up after another bite of sandwich.

'Right then. You've got to remember that Europol is a very young organisation, founded in 1999, but only going operational in 2004. It has about 500 staff, mostly Dutch, based in The Hague in Holland and it has to liaise with the police forces in twenty-odd countries. Basically what it wants to be is the FBI of Europe, but it doesn't have 27,000 staff and a budget of about $4 billion like the FBI does. It also has a very low public profile, so any public relations gimmick, however daft, is jumped on from a great height.'

'Public relations? You're losing me again,' I said honestly.

'Well, perhaps not public relations, but they are keen on any project with a publicity angle which makes Europol look good. Did you see that film with the gorgeous Welsh bird in it? A caper movie – *Ocean's Twelve*, that was it. They loved that because her character was supposed to be a Europol agent.'

'You don't look remotely like Catherine Zeta-Jones,' I observed.

'Few of us do,' he said philosophically. 'Anyway, when Benji Nicholson turned up with his idea, as soon as he mentioned the word "film" he was guaranteed at least a hearing at Europol. When he said that Lea Klemm was attached to the project, they loved it because all the Dutch guys knew her films. I'd never heard of her.'

'Hold on, you're drifting off again. Step back towards the light and use small words. Are you saying that Benji and Lea were working for Europol?'

'Lea, eh?' his eyes flashed at me. 'So you've heard of her then?'

'I've met her,' I said proudly, 'though I've never seen any of her films.'

'Where did you meet her?' he snapped.

'She's staying at the Mount Royal – that's a hotel near Marble Arch – or at least she was yesterday.'

'Have you told anybody that?'

'Nobody asked. Is it important?'

'I suspect she would have been on Phoebe's hit-list if you hadn't...'

'It wasn't me!'

'Yeah, right, it was the cat.'

'You don't know the cat in question.'

He ignored that and took out a mobile phone. Whoever answered was told to go and check on Lea Klemm, and when Jebb said 'Mount Royal' he looked at me and I nodded and then confirmed that she was there under her own name.

'So there was a film after all...?' I prompted as he folded his phone away.

'It was never going to happen,' Jebb said putting more bacon roll to his mouth, 'but Benji did manage to be in the right place at exactly the right time.

'We'd all been aware for some time that Romania had a problem with organised crime families and that they were in to people-trafficking and enforced prostitution in a big way. The Romanian Ministry of the Interior is already cooperating with us, even though Romania doesn't join the EU until next January, and stopping the "trade in human beings", which is what it's called officially, is a high priority. In fact, there's going to be a conference on it next year in Romania itself.

'So when young Benji turns up at Europol pitching a film about the sex traffic in Romanian girls being transported to England like indentured servants and claimed that he could back up his idea with actual locations and details of how the girls were transported, he was listened to. When he told us his real name was Ioan Nicousci, the ears really pricked up.'

'It was a family business,' I said.

'Absolutely, and it was *his* family, though he claimed he had got out of the business and was determined to stay out.'

'Why?'

'Because he'd fallen in love, believe it or not, and with

another bloke! Married to a porn star one minute, picking out curtains with his boyfriend the next. You did know he was married to Lea Klemm, didn't you?'

'She mentioned it in passing,' I said. 'She didn't seem to hold any ill-feelings towards him.'

'No, I don't think she did and, in any case, Benji was doing it mostly for her. He didn't just want to be an informer, he wanted to script the whole thing as a film, with Lea in the lead role. He would provide addresses of brothels and massage parlours in England on condition that he could film the local police raids and then splice in some additional scenes with Lea, using the locations, but after the event. He was planning on getting some realistic footage without having the cost of sets and extras and all that stuff. He had lots of ideas about getting a grainy, documentary feel and how it could be a prize-winning drama-documentary, and it would get Lea Klemm out of the porn industry and into straight acting.'

'So Europol went into the film business with a Romanian gangster and a Polish porn star?'

'Of course not. We agreed to allow Benji filming rights under police supervision, provided he hired his own crew, but there was no question of backing such a film.'

'And he went along with that?'

'He did when we agreed to provide immunity for Lea on various outstanding charges of procuring and prostitution.'

'You can do that?'

'Not really, but Benji thought we could.'

'That's a bit naughty, isn't it?'

'We wanted the addresses Benji could provide, and he offered us *a lot* of locations we didn't know about. I said he was in the right place at the right time. Operation Pentameter was being planned as the British contribution to the war against the traffickers, though the name doesn't mean anything in particular.'

I nodded wisely as I knew that British police operations were named by running a random word search through a computer.

'Benji's idea was a bit of a godsend. We could target our activities without months of intelligence gathering and get a really cost-effective result and, as it turned out, we were able to use the filming process as a cover. If our boys in blue turn up in a van in a seedy area, everyone runs for the hills. If somebody sets up a film camera, they all come out onto the street and want to be extras. Made our job easier if anything, given that the main point of Pentameter was to free the girls who had been trafficked. The chance to bring down a whole organisational network as well was too good to pass up.'

'But Lea really wanted to be a proper film star, didn't she?' I said. 'And somebody had to pay the bills if Europol wouldn't, so she involved her latest lover, Terry Patterson, who just happened to work for a bank, and banks have money.'

'You're right,' agreed Jebb. 'We had Patterson on our radar because he was all over the lovely Lea like a rash, but I don't think he knew the extent of what was going on. He really thought it was a genuine film career opportunity for her.'

'Do you think he was slush-funding the film out of petty cash or something?'

'Don't know, don't really care. Fraud isn't my problem and banks are big enough to take care of themselves. The only odd thing is how Patterson became a target for young Phoebe. Lea and Benji were thick as thieves on this, well I suppose they *were* thieves really, but it was *their* thing and they went to extraordinary lengths to keep Patterson and that boyfriend of Benji's...'

'Giancarlo Artesi,' I supplied, 'and they were civil partners.'

'Whatever. I'm convinced Artesi and Patterson had no idea what the Nicousci family business really was, they thought it was just a film. I don't even know how Phoebe got to hear of Patterson.'

I had a flashback to my conversation with Phoebe Nicholson at her mother's wake in The Boot and Flogger.

'No, that's a puzzler,' I said, 'and why did she have to kill him?'

'Best guess? She was a nutter. Anyone who threatened or betrayed the family business had to be taught a lesson; that's standard procedure in gangs like these. For them it's not just business, it's family honour.

'You've got to bear in mind she'd been brought up in the business. We reckon her father started importing girls from Eastern Europe as soon as he came over here, pretending they were home helps or nannies or au pair girls, things like that. Once he became a naturalised British citizen, he set up Oradea Imports to bring in cheap wine and foodstuffs, but it was probably never more than a front for the real commodity – sex. When the father, George, died a few years back, the mother took over the business, and Benji and Phoebe would be sent to Hungary and Romania to recruit the girls, but once Benji decided he was gay and had met the love of his life, he wanted out of that life and set his sights on a career in television.'

'I heard he actually had done some scripts before.'

'Oh yes, he fancied himself as a writer, that's for sure. I saw a script he'd done about coppers working both sides of the Channel Tunnel. It wasn't that bad, God knows I've seen worse on the box, but it never got made. *Europol* was to be his breakthrough, and to get it made he was willing to bring down the filthy family business.'

'So Benji was really one of the good guys?'

'Ask some of the girls we got out of those houses in Netherthorpe,' he said grimly.

'Fair point. When did Phoebe get onto him?'

'We may never know, but it was probably after the first Pentameter raids on some of the family's brothels in Leeds and Hull, especially when bloody Lea turned up on site demanding to be filmed. My guess is that she lost it big time with brother Benji and did for him, not realising that he'd already passed us a complete list of addresses. When Lea turned up in Netherthorpe with a film crew, she sent her pet gorilla Tor to act as Lea's minder, but really to keep an eye on where the crew was going next, so they could move their girls around and stay one step ahead of us. Nobody was sure where they were supposed to go next because Benji had disappeared.'

'And your lot didn't really care about that, not now you had Benji's list.'

He had the good grace to look uncomfortable at that.

'There was a failure of communication, I'll admit. Artesi tried to file a missing persons report, but nobody took him seriously at local level.'

'And when Lea couldn't find him, she got Terry Patterson to hire me.'

'We missed a trick there, too. Somebody should have warned him to keep at arm's length from the whole business. He might still be alive.'

Now it was my turn to be uncomfortable.

Detective Inspector Jebb eventually ran out of things to ask me, though not before I had long since run out of things I wanted to tell him, so reluctantly he suggested I go home.

He insisted on escorting me out onto the street, just in case I walked off with one of the station's plastic chairs or a paper clip or something, but just as we were about to leave the building a uniformed constable I hadn't seen before handed him another message slip.

'Our mutual friend Tor Szatmari died in the back of an ambulance last night after collapsing at Blackfriars station, it seems,' Jebb read from the note he was holding. 'You wouldn't know anything about that would you?'

'Not a thing,' I said, holding his gaze.

It was true. I hadn't seen or heard an ambulance last night.

'Just wondered,' said Jebb, 'as that means all the directors of Oradea Imports are now dead, which means we've put them out of business without the expense of a trial. I call that a box well ticked. Job done, in fact.'

'Thanks,' I said.

'What for?'

'You've just given me an idea.'

By the time I had negotiated the release of Armstrong from the car park at Stansted, it was getting dark and I had almost max-ed out my credit card paying the overcharge. It would have been cheaper for me to have bought a second-hand Ford

Escort in Manchester, filled it with petrol and driven to Stansted, leaving it in the long-term car park for them to sort out. I didn't even have the comfort of knowing I could pass my expenses on to my client as I didn't have a client any more.

I thought about calling in at the terminal building to see if they had a florist, but I knew deep down that nothing you could buy at an airport short of a Lear Jet would be enough to distract the wrath of Amy. So I headed home to face the music, not even calling in at The New Rosemary Branch at the end of our lane for a drink, even though I needed one.

But I always used to say that it was better to be lucky than good, and thanked all the stars, gods and pagan idols I could think of when I saw Jane Bond's Aston Martin parked next to Amy's Freelander.

The two of them were sitting with their legs curled under them, at either end of the long sofa in the living room, which had been the lounge bar when the house had been a pub. Jane Bond was sipping from a glass of white wine; Amy was drinking from a bottle of Perrier. On a low table in front of them were various magazines, a Yellow Pages and two baby alarm receivers.

'Honey, I'm home!' I said cheerfully, because I'd always wanted to say that.

'Who the hell are you?' said Amy.

'Don't be like that,' Jane Bond told her reaching out and playfully slapping her knees. 'This is the father of your child.'

'That's what he likes to think,' Amy said through narrowed eyes. 'So the police let you go? How did that happen?'

'The jails are terribly overcrowded these days, you know,' said Jane Bond with a smirk. 'They have to wait for one to come out before a new one can be sent down.'

'I can wait.'

'Then you will wait in vain,' I announced pompously, 'for I have been helping the police with their enquiries into the activities of an international criminal gang.'

'Line-dancers in Huddersfield,' Amy said knowingly to Jane, and she burst into a fit of giggles.

'Have you been telling people about that?'

'Well, I don't get out much lately, not like you, charging about the frozen north having so much fun you didn't come home for a week.'

'It wasn't all fun, there was quite a bit of work involved. So much so that I'm taking next week as holiday.'

As soon as the words were out of my mouth I knew I had made a tactical mistake.

'Excellent!' chirped Amy, all smiles. 'There's so much to do before the christening next Sunday. Jane's offered to help with the planning, but there'll be lots of fetching and carrying to do.'

'Oh yes,' I said, remembering. 'How is the baby by the way?'

'Our baby's well-behaved and asleep, and is not to be disturbed.' She pointed to the two baby alarms on the table. 'The other, bigger one is lying in her bedroom in a drunken stupor after doing serious damage to a bottle of Gordon's this afternoon. We put an alarm in there so we'd hear if she started throwing up.'

'Again,' said Jane Bond quietly.

'She's been drinking solidly since I told her that she really has to go home after the christening, even though Jane offered to drive her over to Romanhoe in her Aston.'

'She's terrified of that scumbag she's involved with,' said

Jane. 'I'm sure he hits her, you know, treats her like a slave.'

'I get the picture.'

'So, you've got just over a week to sort things out,' Amy stated.

'I'll get it sorted,' I promised.

'You'll go over there and see this Lyndon creep?'

'Well, maybe not me personally, I was thinking of subcontracting the job to some specialists I know.'

'What sort of specialists?'

'Relationship counsellors – they come highly recommended.'

Later that night, in bed, I told Amy what had happened at Stuart Street, as it seemed the right thing to do. She was the boss after all and lots of employees have to report to the big boss, even if they don't get to do it whilst snuggling.

'Poor Springsteen. So brave, him trying to save you like that. It's really quite sad. I mean, you've had him longer than you've known me.'

'That's why I thought it would be a good idea to combine with the christening party, especially if all our friends are going to be here…'

'Just a moment. Combine with what?'

'The funeral.'

EPILOGUE

'Have you done a proper risk assessment on that bonfire?'

'I can't believe you just said that, Veronica. Now for God's sake chill out and have another drink, go mingle with people, do some networking. This is supposed to be a party.'

'I still think you're building it too close to that hedge, and if the wind changes, it will fill your nice marquee with smoke. I don't know why you want a bonfire anyway, it's a lovely summer's day.'

'It's not a bonfire,' I said patiently. 'It's a pyre.'

The hardest thing about organising the party had been negotiating the guest list with Amy. She had loads of friends she wanted to invite from the fashion business whom I'd never met, but I didn't mind. I had a few old friends I wanted to invite, and unfortunately Amy had met them.

We invited my father and his girlfriend Kim, and I had to speak severely when laying down some basic ground rules of acceptable behaviour to my mother. Veronica, Lorna and Laura would come from the office, of course, and Lisabeth and

Fenella from Stuart Street, which meant Duncan the Drunken (Probably the Best Car Mechanic in the World) and his wife Doreen had to come from Barking, so they could give them a lift. Amy went 'hem-hem' a few times, but only seriously questioned two names on my list: Werewolf and Gearoid.

'Those aren't names,' she'd complained, 'that's a medical condition.'

'They're brothers and they're Irish. Francis and Gearoid Dromey,' I said, emphasising that it was pronounced 'Garodth', 'and very old friends. Werewolf – Francis – used to be a great guitar player and Gearoid, his brother, actually is a *brother*, a sort of monk. He'd be very upset to miss a christening...and we're going to need godparents aren't we?'

'No godparents,' she said firmly.

'But think of the presents...'

'No godparents, no churches, no religion – and no impromptu jam sessions either.'

'Oh be fair, I haven't even looked at my old trumpet since we moved here. I'm not sure I even know where it is.'

'I hid it under the bed your mother sleeps in with all the empty gin bottles,' she said heartlessly. 'Make sure it stays there.'

'Anything you say, darling.'

'And don't forget you have to get your mother's domestic situation sorted. After the party, she's out of here.'

'I'm working on it,' I said.

On the Sunday, I rang Ossie Oesterlein at home, right around the time his mother was putting the Yorkshire puddings in the oven, and brought him up rapidly up to speed on what had happened in London.

I suggested that he did a report for Giancarlo Artesi based
on what I'd discovered about the Nicousci family business,
but glossing over some of the sex-slavery details. The point to
emphasise was that Benji was getting out of the underworld
and was determined to go straight, although he'd better
choose a different way of saying that, and had been actively
cooperating with the Europol police agency. Ossie might even
mention that he was doing all this so he could be with
Giancarlo and had been determined to keep him safely out of
things. I promised to email Ossie a draft report just as soon as
I got round to writing one, and if he asked he might get Artesi
an apology out of DI Jebb for the way he was ignored when
he tried to report Benji missing.

'Do I let Artesi believe that I found this all out by myself?'
Ossie asked innocently.

Bless.

'He's your client, mate; take the praise and the fee.'

'That's right decent of you, Angel old lad. If there's ever
anything I can do for you, just ask.'

'Well, actually there might be.'

'Do y'know, I somehow thought there might. What's on
your mind?'

'I was just wondering if you and the Cudworth Posse
fancied a day trip to the seaside, down to the East Coast, say,
Essex and Suffolk border area?'

'I just didn't know what to wear,' Fenella was saying, 'so I
tried to cover all contingencies. The white lace shawl has a
sort of christening feel to it, and the little black party frock is,
well, black, and you should wear black for funerals, shouldn't
you?'

'It was good of you to think that through,' I said. 'You did bring him, didn't you?'

'Oh yes. I collected the urn, though it's more of a box really, from the vet's yesterday. He's in the boot of Duncan's car, I'm afraid. Lisabeth wouldn't let me carry him on my knee.'

'You wouldn't have dared when he was alive.'

'That's true,' she said with a smile. I had forgotten how nicely she smiled and how good her legs were in a short frock and black tights.

'I still think it's in bad taste,' growled Lisabeth who had sneaked up on my blind side in total silence.

'What is?'

'Cremating a dead cat in public, and at a christening.'

'It's a naming ceremony, and it's not a cremation. Springsteen's already been cremated by the vet. We're just going to put his ashes on a small funeral pyre so he can have a proper send-off. It's called a pyre cremation. Archaeologists think they were quite common once, especially when a warrior died nobly in battle a long way from home. Rather than drag a body all the way home, they had a quick cremation, put the ashes in an urn, and then ceremonially cremated the urn when they got back.'

She looked at me as if I was mad, but then she usually did.

'Sounds a bit pagan to me.'

'That's exactly the look we're going for.'

My father appeared healthier than he had for weeks, though the sight of Kim McIntosh on his arm probably helped the overall impression. And when he was sure, after about an hour, that my mother wasn't going to attack him with a steak knife, he started to relax.

'Your mother's looking good,' he told me. 'Seems happier in herself.'

'I think she's looking forward to going back to Romanhoe,' said Amy, the baby cradled in her arms for Kim to coo jealously over.

'She is? Jane Bond sort of hinted there was trouble back in her village. Man trouble.'

'Is there any other sort?' said Kim dreamily, still trying to get the baby to grasp her finger.

'That's all history,' I reassured him. 'Everything's sorted itself out and she's packed her bags and Jane is running her back tomorrow.'

'Sounds like you got a result there,' Dad said with a sly wink. 'I bet she was driving Amy mental.'

'Oh I wouldn't say that...' Amy murmured politely. '...but she clearly missed her friends and there wasn't much for her to do here. Roy's been working away—' she turned to give me a quick glare, 'and I've been busy with the new house, and the baby of course.'

'And face it, Dad,' I said, 'she was never very good with kids.'

'You have a point there,' he said.

My mother's domestic problem had been 'sorted' sometime on the Wednesday.

I knew because that evening, I got the call from Ossie.

'Box ticked. Job done,' was all he'd had to say.

'You have a lovely house,' said Laura, picking over a tray of canapés whilst trying to balance a glass of champagne.

'We can see why you don't like coming into the office,' said

Lorna, snatching the one Laura had finally decided upon. 'Well, neither would I if I lived somewhere like this,' she added, misinterpreting Laura's filthy look.

'It's not the office I mind,' I said, 'it's the work.'

'Why? You've just completed a complex case very successfully,' Laura said supportively. 'It wasn't your fault the client got murdered and we won't get paid.'

'No, it's not the particular kind of work I don't like, it's work in general. In any case, you two are much better at the detective business than I am.'

For once I had their complete and undivided attention.

'I am?' they both said together.

'Sure you are.' I pointed a finger at Laura. 'You found that lock-up in Southwark and staked it out without the benefit of back-up or even a mobile phone, and then helped to look after poor Zsofia. I couldn't have done that.'

I turned the finger on Lorna.

'And you went out alone to the Essex marshes to dig the dirt on a very nasty piece of work called Lyndon Baines. That was brave. Oh, and by the way, thanks for emailing that picture of him you took on your phone. It came in very handy.'

'It did?' she said and I do believe she was blushing. 'I'm glad. He sounded a horrible man, a proper bully and I felt so sorry for your mother. Is that your mother over there by the bar?'

'That sounds like her,' I said without turning round.

'She looks happy.'

Stick around, I thought, and you'll probably see her *very* happy.

'She's going home to Romanhoe tomorrow,' I said.

'Not back to that pig?'

'Oh no. Didn't I mention it? Lyndon Baines has had a nasty accident and has broken both his legs. He must have fallen off a roof.'

Several times.

'Gosh, that's lucky,' Lorna said making a toast with her glass.

'Not for Lyndon Baines,' I murmured.

It had better not have been dumb luck, not after the amount of petrol money I'd had to reimburse Ossie for driving the Cudworth Posse down from Yorkshire in his Cadillac.

Then a distinctive, if slightly slurred, voice cut across the general hubbub of voices and chinking cutlery filling the garden.

'Angel! Do I put these behind the feckin' bar or what?'

'There's a man with a beard trying to get in the back door of your house,' said Laura, concerned. 'I think it might be a tramp. He's waving a couple of bottles in the air.'

At least Lorna saw the funny side, but then she'd had more champagne.

'And there seems to be a priest chasing him,' she giggled. 'What can it all mean?'

'It means the Ryanair flight from Dublin to Stansted has landed right on schedule,' I said happily.

Werewolf and Gearoid had brought two bottles (each) of fifteen-year-old whiskey with them 'to wet the baby's head', but when they heard about Springsteen, we decided that the first toast should be his.

A select few of us gathered at the bottom of the garden, each with an empty glass, around the small bonfire of kindling and logs I had constructed: just me, Fenella, Lisabeth, Werewolf and Gearoid.

The small pine box containing Springsteen's ashes was no bigger than the sort which might hold a set of chess pieces, and I placed it firmly in the centre of the pyre.

Gearoid opened one of the bottles of whiskey and splashed a generous amount over the wood.

'An offering to the pagan gods?' I asked him. 'Should a man in your line of work really be doing such a thing?'

'Ah sure, I'm Irish,' he grinned. 'I like to hedge my bets. Anyway, it'll help the fire catch. Who's got a match?'

'I've got a light,' I said, producing my old Fatboy Zippo which I hadn't used since a pregnant Amy had imposed a smoking *fatwah*.

'Let's do it,' said Werewolf holding out his glass.

Gearoid poured us all a generous measure, and I flicked the Zippo into life and touched the kindling. There was a soft *whoof* as the spirit caught and the fire was lit.

Werewolf raised his glass.

'I always said he deserved a Viking funeral,' he said.

'I thought he was bad-tempered and vindictive,' said Lisabeth.

'He did smell a bit as he got older,' said Fenella, her eyes watering as she tried to drink the whiskey.

'I never actually knew him,' said Gearoid.

'Bloody hell you lot,' I said, 'that sounds like *my* funeral ovation. This is Springsteen we're talking about.'

'He was a noble beast,' toasted Gearoid.

'A fine cat,' said Lisabeth.

'A faithful friend,' choked Fenella as she tried to drink.

'He was a randy old sod who ate everything put in front of

him and screwed anything that couldn't run fast enough,' said Werewolf, and then realised we were all looking at him. 'Well that's how I remember him.'

'That's better. So long, old friend.'

I raised my glass to the flames, then drank.

'And that's quite enough of that,' said Gearoid, putting one arm around my shoulders and pouring more whiskey into my glass. He seemed to have lost the top from the whiskey bottle, then I saw where he'd thrown it on the pyre. In a thousand years archaeologists might find it in the ashes and say wisely to each other: 'Ritual.'

'We've got a christening to go to, haven't we?' he said cheerfully.

'Yeah, that's right,' said Werewolf, as if he'd just remembered. 'A cat dies, but a baby is born. Hey, it's the circle of life.'

'My idiot brother is right,' Gearoid said in my ear as he shepherded me back towards the marquee and the milling guests. 'What's gone is gone, you've got new responsibilities now. You've got a lovely wife, a fine house and a beautiful baby.'

'I know,' I said.

'It's certainly a bonny baby,' said Werewolf, straining to see exactly where the free bar was in the marquee whilst also appraising at least a dozen females in the process. 'Have you decided on a name?'

'Of course we have, but you'll have to wait until Amy announces it. I'm sworn to secrecy.'

'I didn't actually get close to the proud mother, didn't want to scare her,' he said casually, 'so I didn't get a good look. Is it a boy or a girl?

'With my luck? Guess.'

'Girl.'

'Spot on. You know me: always outnumbered, always outgunned.'

AUTHOR'S NOTE

I have taken numerous liberties with the real Operation Pentameter, which took place in June 2006 and resulted in 130 arrests and the freeing of more than 80 females from sexual slavery. A second operation, Pentameter 2, took place in October 2007, included the Republic of Ireland, and was coordinated across Europe by both Europol and Interpol.

Angels Unaware appears exactly (almost to the day) twenty years after the first Angel tale. Readers who have kept faith with the whole series may well recognise a few familiar names and faces herein. New readers should forgive such indulgences and ask themselves what on earth they've been doing for the last two decades.

MR, August 2008